SIMIAKIA

PRAISE FOR SIMIAKIA

"Lori Windows brings horses and the special coy dog, Cantar, to life in her writing . . . as the plot develops, the growing self-confidence of the young and displaced Nez Perce character, Alicut George, is revealed. He learns to endurance ride on Folly, and care for an orphan foal named Gambler's Hand. Interspersed throughout are Alicut's flashback dreams about his Nez Perce ancestors as they attempted to escape the US Calvary . . . The strength and endurance of the Appaloosa horse was instrumental in their arduous journey and connects Alicut to his past and his identity. Female characters are dynamic and strong . . . romance is sprinkled throughout and the ending is satisfying. I love reading about horses, especially where animals are not just props, but are characters in the story!"

GAYLE M. SMITH, AWARD-NOMINATED AUTHOR OF *THICKWOOD*

SÍMIAKIA

LORI WINDOWS

SIMIAKIA

Published by
Endless Sky Books
Regina, Saskatchewan, Canada
www.endless-sky-books.com

Print ISBN: 978-1-989398-76-0
Ebook ISBN: 978-1-989398-77-7

Cover design by Shaun Stevens
flintlockcovers.com

CHAPTER 1

CELIA BOLT WAS a strange and lonely child, born in the winter of 1958 to a father who thought children an inconvenience but was willing and more than able to support her in the most lavish of fashions; born of a mother who pictured her as nothing more than a life-sized doll to dress in expensive, frilly costumes and display to friends. But the little girl's gawky body and clumsy motions did not lend themselves well to silk and lace, and it wasn't long before even her mother lost interest in physical contact with young Celia. She was left to her own designs, her mother and father paying as little attention to her as possible, and her needs catered to by hired people, usually different ones every month. When the subject of children and their accomplishments was brought up during social gatherings, Audria Bolt always managed to divert the line of discussion.

Celia compensated for such neglect. She spun a cocoon of fantasies around herself and spent her days huddled inside, harboring her only friends—books. Tales of mystery and adventure, stories about animals and the often fierce beauty of nature, myths and legends surrounding the great people of the past. All of these and more, even some too sophisticated for her young mind, she read, and at night, Celia's restless dreams would carry on where the books left off. Only this time, she would be the hero of her tales. It seemed that with such a vivid imagination and a mind so hungry for knowledge, the girl would accomplish great deeds in school, topping her classes scholastically and, for once, making her parents proud.

"SHE JUST ISN'T TRYING," the school psychologist announced after a week of afternoon sessions with Celia. "She's a bright child, and basically, there is no reason why she can't do the work. Now, I'm not saying she's failing deliberately, but it's almost as if she's doing poorly in order to punish you, as though she has some sort of mental block preventing her from making good grades."

"Punish us! For Christ's sake, what do you mean, 'punish us'? We've given her everything!"

"Now, Roman, don't get so excited. We'll never achieve anything that way." Audria patted her husband's hand comfortingly.

"I'll show her what punishment is, by God. As soon as we get home, that damn TV is coming out of her room." Roman Bolt slammed his fist on the arm of the leather chair, barely missing his wife's consoling hand and with such an air of finality that it appeared as if he believed he had put an end to their problem.

"Roman, dear, Celia asked me to take the television from her bedroom several weeks ago. She said she wanted the extra room on her bookcase."

"And that's another thing, those books of hers," Bolt stormed, not realizing or caring how hopelessly remote he was from his daughter. Dr. Shneider realized, though. "You tell me,

Doctor. Is it normal for an eleven-year-old girl to spend all her spare time reading? Her head is so full of fairy tales she can't face reality."

Dr. Shneider wanted to sigh, but he felt he must retain his professional image as long as possible. Being head psychologist for Crandhill Park Private Elementary School would never be an easy job. With so many parents whose idea of showing affection for their children was to send them to a supervised play camp in Alaska for the summer and whose substitute for love was a six-thousand-dollar scale-model fully automatic playhouse for Christmas, it was a wonder that *any* of the students could adjust normally. "Sometimes, when a child cannot cope or isn't satisfied with her surroundings, she will construct a make-believe existence. An escape hatch, so to speak. Most children will grow out of this when they realize the real world offers more exciting things."

Bolt, half-listening, stole a glance at his chronometer and had to suppress a smile. His anger faded. Surely the brief show of emotion had sufficiently displayed parental concern. Besides, he had a plane to catch in an hour and would soon be soaring his way eastward to a business conference in Geneva. Ah, Geneva! That fabulous playground where last year, at this same time, he had purchased his impressive timepiece. Geneva and its snow-capped mountains jutting towards the sky; Geneva and its lovely women, breasts jutting towards the shadowy ceilings of cozy hotel rooms. Soon he would be far beyond all this worthless talk of fairy tales and escape hatches. But for now, he could just take the whole mess and drop it in Dr. Shneider's lap. "Well, you're the doctor. What do we do, and how much will it cost?"

"I'd suggest acting as if she were not failing, letting her know that it doesn't matter what grades she gets, that you love her anyway. You do love her, don't you?"

"What the hell kind of question is that? Of course, we love

her. She's our daughter, isn't she?" His anger was not a sham now. Roman Bolt was on the defense.

Dr. Shneider stacked some loose papers on his desk, not looking at either of the Bolts. "Mr. Bolt, did you read the paper last night?"

"Paper! What in God's name does that have to do with anything? I thought we were talking about our daughter."

"I was just wondering if you happened to see the article about the man who was arrested in the lobby of the Queen Elizabeth Hotel. It seems he pushed someone out of his twenty-third-story room."

"Please come to the point, sir," came from a thoroughly perplexed and impatient Bolt.

"Investigation revealed that the girl who fell from the window was the gentleman's daughter. It seems as if there was some . . ."

Bolt stormed to his feet and Mrs. Bolt gasped audibly and plucked at her husband's sleeve. "Are you suggesting that I'm going to take my child home and throw her off our roof because she's flunking Geography?

"I'm afraid you've missed my intent entirely, Mr. Bolt. I was merely pointing out, rather graphically, I must admit, that love and relation are not necessarily synonymous."

Audria Bolt always seemed to be able to stay cool in situations where her husband could only fume. Clinging to Roman's arm, she intoned calmly, "Thank you for the illustration, Dr. Shneider, but I don't think we'll be in need of your services anymore." She turned primly around and, tugging her still-sputtering husband after her, left the office.

CELIA BOLT GRADUATED from Crandhill Park that spring. Three private tutors saw to that. And yet, her grades were still disappointingly low, her mind still filled with dreams, and her life depressingly empty. In the best interests of all concerned, her parents sent Celia to a New Haven boarding school in the fall.

Celia Bolt was now a troubled and wild youth. Her cocoon of fantasy had burst, and from its depths emerged a restless butterfly. From an awkward, retiring child, Celia had transformed into a rebel, challenging authority and no longer content to read of others' deeds and adventures, satisfied only to experience these joys herself.

Normal school routine did not hold enough outlets for her unnatural energies. Many nights she would sneak out of the dormitory, unable to sleep, and spend hours conditioning her supple and blossoming body on the gymnastic equipment or saddle a pony from the stable and ride in crazy patterns around the athletic field until she and the pony were both exhausted. She had no friends among the students or staff and wanted none. The other girls would laugh when Celia's name was mentioned but never when Celia was within sight.

The years at New Haven were boring but better than living at home, where Celia couldn't endure the stormy relationship she maintained with her parents. She found enough to keep her body occupied as she flung herself into school activities with the same gusto she once reserved for her books alone. She was the best in the school at sports but was often found sitting out a game for some infraction of the rules. Academically, she was at the head of most of her classes and retained that position not because she wanted to please anyone but simply because she liked feeling superior to the other girls.

When Celia was seventeen, it was inevitable that she would meet Clark or someone just like him. One of Celia's classes had taken a bus trip to town, but Celia didn't remember for what purpose, nor did she think it was of importance. Instead, she slipped away from the group shortly after the bus parked and spent a pleasant afternoon on her own, wandering the streets of New Haven. She knew someone from the school would find her, if not that night, then the following morning, and take her back. It had happened like that before, and even though Miss Cruston had promised to expel her if Celia ever ran away again (how silly to call it "running away;" she wasn't trying to get away from or go anywhere, she just wanted a little excitement and a change of pace), the girl knew expulsion was only a threat that held no punch. Her parents had just spearheaded a campaign to raise the funds for a new Olympic-sized swimming pool for the school. How could they expel her?

"Hey, gypsy! Sleep with anybody last night?"

Celia turned quickly to see who would have been brazen enough to yell something of that nature on a crowded street. She wasn't mad, just curious. What she saw made her smile. "Sure, I did! I do every night!"

The young man, surprised at the response, swung a denim-clad leg over his Harley. "Who with?" he bantered and then gave the bike some gas and kicked it into life. The roar of the souped-up machine as it revved made it impossible for Clark to hear Celia's answer, but he saw her point at the little man propped up against a store window selling pencils.

Clark pulled his Harley over to the curb beside the girl. "Want a ride?" He mouthed the words. He didn't have to ask twice, and no one from the school found Celia that night.

Celia found a new sport to which her body reacted readily. She wasn't sure whether it was Clark she loved or the excitement of the illicit affair, but whichever, it made her feel better than she had ever felt before. The two reaped enjoyment out of finding new places to meet, each one more daring than the last. It was two months after their strange encounter in New Haven that they lay together in the loft of the school barn, sweating and panting from their recent exertion, demanding and almost violent in nature. But already, excitement was mounting in Celia again as thoughts raced through her head.

"Here, right on the school grounds, only a few hundred feet from Miss Cruston, the frigid old lady's bedroom window. I wonder what she does at night? I almost wish they'd catch us. The shock would kill the old bat, like as not. She probably doesn't even know how it's done. But we know, don't we, Clark." Celia rolled over on her tummy and slid an exploratory toe up Clark's thigh, but the response was not what she expected.

"For Christ's sake, Celia. Will ya leave me alone?"

Celia sat up quickly. "What's the matter?" Pain and puzzlement permeated her voice.

"What's the matter? Jesus, you really don't understand, do you? Listen. I'm not coming around anymore. I can't take any more of you, you hear?"

"But Clark, baby, I love you."

"Shit! You don't love me, Celia, and I don't love you. We had a good thing going for a while; we kept each other happy, that's all. But you've turned out to be a fuckin' ball cracker."

Clark started pulling on his jeans, and Celia became desperate. She put a hand on his arm and pleaded. "Please don't leave me. I'll do anything you want, anything you ask."

The boy jerked away angrily and shook a strand of greasy blond hair from his eyes. "All I ask is for you to get your claws out of me. I ain't man enough for you, and I ain't ashamed to admit it." He started down the hayloft ladder, carrying his shirt and shoes. "I'm gone, sweety. I'm off to find me a broad who ain't built like a bottomless well. My suggestion to you is to get intimately acquainted with one of them horses down there."

The rebuke knocked Celia back down into the hay, where she lay, whispering, pleading, tears seeping out of tightly closed eyes. How could he do this? She thought she was making him so happy.

Suddenly, the girl jumped to her feet and flung open the loft window, just in time to see the cause of this grief, the most heartfelt grief she had ever experienced in her short life, disappear into the grove of trees that surrounded the school.

"You bastard!" She stood in the open window, moonlight making shadows on her naked body. "You fucking bastard! I hope you rot! I hope your balls fall off and rot!"

The school officials were thus awakened and found her only moments later, near-delirious and still shouting obscenities into the night air. Two days later, Celia Bolt returned to Waterbury and her family.

CELIA BOLT HAD BECOME A MOST remarkable woman. For even though she had just turned eighteen, she was undoubtedly a woman.

"I'm leaving home, Mother; not that you care, but I want you to know why I'll not be down for breakfast tomorrow."

"Oh, really." Audria Bolt lay her teaspoon beside her coffee. "You know, I really must learn how to drink coffee without sugar. It doesn't do me much good to go without cream in my coffee if I'm going to put twice as much sugar in it."

"Did you hear me?"

"Of course. You said you were going to leave home. Tell me, darling, where do you think you'll go? Out looking for that horrible motorcycle bum?"

"How many times must I explain? I couldn't care less about Clark. He was nothing but a child's rebellion. I'd have forgotten him by now if you didn't bring him up every morning over toast and coffee like morning sickness."

Mrs. Bolt stopped her cup in mid-trip to her mouth. "Morning sickness! Oh my God, Celia. You aren't pregnant, are you?"

"Sometimes I really think you're crazy. You know damn well I'm not pregnant. You have the word of the three physicians you hustled me off to the day I came home, remember?"

Regaining her composure, Audria queried, "Tell me, dear, what are you going to do? When you leave home, I mean." A sip of her sweetened coffee.

"I could get a job. You know, there are a lot of people in this world who work for a living. Not everyone lives like you."

"A job! Who'd hire you? What can you do? You've never had to work a day in your life. All you've seemed to prepare yourself for at school is rolling in the hay with some greasy dropout."

So you're trying to shock me, Celia thought. *I think I'm just as adept at this game.* She smirked. "I've been thinking about going professional; the pay is good."

"Celia! I'll have no more talk of this kind." Mrs. Bolt slammed her cup onto the saucer with such force that a wave of steaming liquid splashed on her hand. "You silly little bitch. Now see what you've made me do."

"That's so typical. So terribly typical of your attitude toward me my whole life. I'm to blame for everything bad that's ever happened to you, from labor pains to that burn on your hand, aren't I? I'd think you'd be glad to see me leave."

Audria grew angry. Her thumb smarted from the burn, and this was no longer a playful banter of words. "I'll not have you speaking to me like this, Celia."

"And just how do you plan to stop me? I'm eighteen years old, and in the eyes of the law, I'm a woman. I can come and go as I please regardless of what you and Daddy say, although Daddy couldn't give a damn what either of us does as long as we don't interfere in his affairs. Incidentally, the pun wasn't intentional, but you must admit, it was rather humorous."

Fighting to gain control of herself and the conversation, Audria said as if to a child, "You have two choices. One, you can begin classes this fall at the excellent French finishing school we have selected for you. You should be thankful that they have accepted you after learning your history."

"Oh, but how could they refuse after you and Father so generously bribed them?"

"I'll ignore that remark since it is, unfortunately, true. Maybe they can succeed in making a lady out of you."

"A lady. You mean a lady like you, Mother? Please, tell me my second choice."

"Or, two, you may leave. But if you leave, Celia, you'll never come back. Do you hear me? We'll forget we ever had a daughter."

"Do you really believe that you have presented me with a problem, that I'm going to retire to my room and weigh the pros and cons of my decision?" Celia threw her napkin to her plate, and the corner of the material permeated the golden yolk of the untouched sunny-side-up egg. "The only thing I'm going to do is retire to my room and pack. As I said before, don't expect me down for breakfast tomorrow. And as for forgetting you ever had a daughter—that shouldn't be too hard. You've been practicing at it since the day I was old enough to send off to school."

Celia did go to her room and pack her bags. Two, to be precise. Not very much to take with her for a girl who had thousands of dollars' worth of clothes stuffed into the walk-in closet of her bedroom and a whole museum's worth of rare keepsakes from her parents' world travels displayed in glass-fronted cases. The only things she regretted leaving behind were her books, rows upon rows of maple bookcase shelves of books, her friends and confidants of childhood. With much deliberation, she selected only a few favorites and placed them at the bottom of the largest suitcase. Then she called a taxi from the pink Princess line installed next to her bed and waited. When the cab arrived, Celia walked out the front door of her parent's home and didn't look back. She never would look back, and, true to her word, her mother did forget that she ever had a daughter.

SHE HAD JUST enough money in her purse to pay the cab driver when he let her off at the airport. Inquiring as to the destination of the very next flight out, Celia paid for a one-way ticket by check, cashed an additional check for $200 at the cashier window, and then, amid puzzled stares from onlookers, tore the remaining checks into as many pieces as possible.

That was the end of her parents' world: the end of the easy life and high living; the end of boarding school and debutant balls; the end of everything they had given her and everything they would have given her. Moreover, it quite possibly could be the end of a normal life, the end of three meals a day and a secure roof over her head. The fact her mother had pointed out was painfully true—Celia had no training in any field and no previous employment record. In order to support herself, she would have to take any job she was lucky enough to be offered. No longer could she afford to display haughty indifference to people around her. The friendship, or at least the acceptance, of others would be necessary for the girl to make it in this big, new world.

A half-hour later, Celia found herself watching the runway turn to grey-blue beneath the rear seat of the plane. That the little jet was flying west was the only thing of which she was certain. Her destination was unsure. She had no way of knowing what her future would bring, no way of knowing that after ten months of traveling from town to town and from one meaningless job to another, she would arrive in a small Idaho city.

"BUT I DON'T UNDERSTAND. Why me?"

"You did know Mr. Bloodstone, didn't you, Miss Bolt?"

"Yes. As a matter of fact, I knew him quite well."

"Then why not you?"

"But he had children, a daughter and a son. I know because he had talked about them a few times."

"Children, I'm afraid, who shunned the old man. He hadn't heard from either one of them for more than twenty years. Never even saw his grandkids."

"Oh, the poor man." Celia sank deep into the leather chair in the office of J. Michael Peadot of Peadot and Ferison, Attorneys at Law. "I never realized he was so alone. No wonder he always seemed so glad to see me," she added almost to herself.

"What was your relationship with Mr. Bloodstone?"

"Friends," she answered emphatically. "Just very good friends. He used to come into the restaurant where I worked part-time. Every Friday night, he'd show up for the fish dinner—all you could eat for $3.99." Celia smiled in remembrance. "He could really pack it in for such a skinny little guy.

"He always sat in my section, and you can't wait on a man every Friday night for months on end without learning a little about him. I found out he owned a small ranch just outside of Lewiston, raised horses. I told him how much I liked horses, used to be quite a rider back at school, but that I hadn't ridden for over a year. He invited me out to the ranch on Sunday, and I took him up on it. It was kind of funny, and I know there were some people who talked about us—" she flashed an accusing look towards the lawyer—"but there was nothing ulterior in his invitation. He never made a pass or anything like that. Always treated me kind of like a daughter, and from what you just told me, I guess I was more of a daughter to him than his real daughter was.

"Anyway, I started going out there regularly, every weekend. I'd help him around the barn, and in exchange, he was teaching me about horses. He always said it was a pleasure to find a lady who didn't mind getting her hands dirty. Two years ago, he gave me a filly for Christmas."

Peadot looked up from the papers he was holding. "Aren't you underrating your horse a little, Miss Bolt? Just a filly?"

Celia laughed a genuine laugh. This man certainly did a thorough investigation. "You're right. A daughter of Chico's Medicine Box isn't exactly just a filly. I was angry at him at first for giving me such an expensive gift, but he got so much pleasure out of helping me train her. When we'd take her to a show, he'd be as nervous as I and twice as proud when Baby won."

She grew somber, remembering last Saturday morning. They were supposed to take Baby Box to an Appaloosa show in Spokane, but Bloodstone backed out at the last minute, complaining of a pain in his chest. The girl went alone, and Baby made a fine showing.

Celia's pleasure was short-lived, however. When she returned to Lewiston on Sunday night, it was to find the old man had died only two hours earlier. "Since Baby is out at the ranch, it hasn't been an inconvenience for me to drive out there every night to feed the stock. I was hoping that whoever took over the place would let me board her there."

"Well, you won't have to worry about that now, will you?"

"I guess not. Where do I sign?"

Peadot slid an official-looking document across the desk to where Celia sat on the edge of the leather chair, fountain pen poised in midair. "On the dotted lines, here and here." He watched Celia's signature take shape, large, carefully rounded letters. "Now that the ranch and property are legally yours, would you be interested in selling? I'm prepared to offer a fine price."

"Sell to you? From what I hear, your law practice is so extensive it's all you can do to keep up with it."

"Oh, I'd have someone else do the real work, keep the place functioning. Bloodstone had some fine stock out there, and if I may say so myself, I have quite a hand with horses. It would be something to keep me occupied during my off days."

Celia was irritated. Shades of her father began clouding her vision. "Those horses were Mr. Bloodstone's life. I don't want to see them become a rich man's plaything. And you don't have to tell me what fine stock they are. I know horses, too, Mr. Peadot. I was taught by an expert."

"Please, Miss Bolt. I didn't mean to upset you."

He was sincere, and Celia felt foolish for snapping at him. "I'm sorry. It's just that so much has happened in the past few days, and I'm exhausted from trying to keep abreast." She folded her copy of the deed and slipped it into her purse. "That ranch has a lot of promise, and, like Mr. Bloodstone said, I'm not afraid of getting dirty. I'm going to take a stab at fulfilling that promise."

"I wish you luck." Mr. Peadot rose and extended his hand. A firm handshake, Celia noted. He probably did have quite a hand with horses. "If you need any help or advice, legal or otherwise, don't hesitate to call."

"Thank you. I'll remember that. I really will."

CHAPTER 2

SPRING 1986

"MORGAN, I don't know how you do it. Anyone who can make good coffee is a wonder in himself. But someone who can make good coffee at 6 a.m. is a miracle!"

"I have a powerful force driving me, honey. I know what you're like when you don't have your morning cup."

Celia laughed and set her half-empty mug on the table beside her bed. "Oh, come on now! I'm not that bad." She stretched, pulling her small breasts almost flat and her smooth skin taut over her ribs.

Morgan turned away from the woman and concentrated on pouring himself a second cup of the dark liquid. He caught her sensuous form in the wardrobe mirror, grew angry at himself, and grumbled. "The hell you ain't." He tried to ignore her, but even after five years, she could still easily excite him with such a simple, uninhibited act. This time, though, he fought against his desires. He was determined not to give in.

"Even if I'm not that bad, I'm not half as good as you treat me."

"That's for sure."

Celia finished her stretch and let her hands fall beside her in slight annoyance. "My, you're snarly this morning. What's the matter?"

"You know damn well what the matter is. Every time we have to go to these meetings, it's the same thing. I can't take that bunch."

"I know, baby, but if we don't endorse them, they won't endorse us, and that could make things a little difficult. Did you ever wonder why Bloodstone never made a real go at this place? I'm willing to bet it's because he refused to join when they invited him. That Saddle Club really holds the cards with most of the Appaloosa breeders in this part of the country."

"Saddle club, shit! Most of those stuffed shirts are too damn high up in the world to keep their butts in their saddles." He walked towards the bed, coffee pot in his hand, and refilled Celia's mug.

"To us, they're stuffed shirts; to the rest of the American Appaloosa Horse Club, they're the Saddle Club of the nation." Looking up at Morgan, she smiled.

The smile had no visible effect. "The Blue Bloods of the spotted-horse society," said Morgan sarcastically.

"You must admit," Celia shrugged and slid all the way under the sheet, "they have a right. The Palouse Valley being the very birthplace of the Appaloosa breed."

"But who developed the breed? Tell me that, will you?"

Celia knew Morgan's next statement by heart, and she chanted along with him, "Indians, by God! And there's not one Indian in the whole club!" She had heard the same argument once a month for the past four years, ever since she and Morgan had elected to join the Palouse Valley Saddle Club. It wasn't a choice as much as a necessary obligation. The club wanted to keep as many of the best and oldest Appaloosa bloodlines within their membership roster as possible, and since Bloodstone Ranch owned and bred many of these same bloodlines, the Club officials approached Celia to become a member. In return, her ranch and stock would be placed on the list of members in good standing, and customers would be sent to her, via the Club, from all parts of the continent—people who were interested in buying, breeding, or having their horses trained. But neither she nor Morgan enjoyed the monthly meetings.

"I'm not going to argue with you. I feel exactly the same as you do. Eighty percent of the members are snobs and bigots. You can stay home if you want."

Morgan switched from offense to defense immediately. "And leave you to face them by yourself? Not on your life. Besides, what would they do if we both didn't show up? No one to spread dirt about. They'd think you finally got morals and kicked me out."

"Come on then." Celia lifted the single white sheet that covered her. "Let's give them something to talk about and prove I didn't."

Morgan Kylies, already heated with anger, felt the quick surge of heat spread downward into his loins as he gazed at Celia's invitation. He wasn't actually giving in; she'd said he didn't have to go. It was all his own decision. Besides, it made no difference if she had tricked him with her gentle persuasion. The love of this woman was worth his pride anytime.

Quickly, he slipped out of his terrycloth bathrobe. He was a large man with bulky muscles on a big frame—the kind of muscles that developed from a lifetime of hard work, not by scientific theories of dynamic tension or isometric exercises. Sun and wind had made his face leathery and stole the handsomeness from it. His hands were scarred and fingers twisted from the hazards of ranch duties, but they were large, capable hands. Hands that could hold a struggling calf for castration or reach inside a tortured mare and shift the position of her unborn foal. Hands that could stroke fires of desire in Celia Bolt with just a caress, as they were doing now.

"Christ, how did I ever live without you?" he whispered. Her fingers were sliding over his hard buttocks, and she shuddered with pleasure as she felt him grow and probe into her waiting warmth.

Climax was simultaneous, their bodies like two finely tuned instruments brought together in the final chord of an orchestration to produce a sound of beauty that stayed in the air long after the actual tone had died. They lay quite still for several minutes, savoring the rapture.

From her position, Celia could see the stage being set for one of the most reliable miracles of nature. The horizon was growing hazy with streaks of yellow and red; the sun was about to rise. She always slept with her feet pointed east so as to watch every morning. It was undoubtedly a holdover from the days when things weren't so easy on the ranch: when the secondhand car sat idly in the shed because she didn't have the $530 the man at the station required before he would fix the transmission; when she had to ride one of the horses ten miles to town to pick up the mail, which was only full of notices, most past due, from other business proprietors who wanted accounts settled; when she had to sell the entire spring crop of horse colts for hundreds instead of training them and letting them mature into animals well worth thousands; when her body ached every night from a day's work not fit for any woman, but she didn't have the money to hire help. In those days, the sight of the morning in bloom was a sign of hope. God had seen fit to grant His children still another day; maybe He would soon grant her some heavenly aid.

And He did. Her heavenly aid came in the form of a man named Morgan Kyles, who knew and loved horses, wasn't a stranger to back-breaking work, and, in a few short weeks, came to know and love Celia. And now, as she watched the sunrise, Morgan's head nestled between her breasts, she told herself that its beauty was the only thing that surpassed the beauty of their love and the life they had on the ranch.

Morgan shifted his weight to his hands. Swiftly he kissed a rosy nipple, then pushed up, so his face hovered above Celia's. "If we're going, babe, we better get ready." His mood noticeably improved by the lovemaking, he whistled the melody of a current country/western hit while gathering together the day's attire.

Celia dragged herself from the lingering warmth of the bed. The sudden cold of the tile floor on the soles of her bare feet was more than enough to shock her into action. She shuddered. "Jeeze, it's cold! Like goddamn December."

Morgan laughed and slapped her bottom playfully as she ran past him toward the bathroom. "Toughen up, little lady."

"I'm as tough as I care to be, thank you. Any tougher, and I'll be frozen solid," she called through the closing door.

"Listen, babe. Do me a favor, and don't wear a skirt today. All right?"

"Oh, Morgan. I'm so sick of work jeans. This is the first excuse I've had to dress up all month."

"You know what's going to happen. Carla Fairfax will bring one of her newest "wonder horses" along, or that son-of-a-bitch Grant Castor will say how his contest stud's knocked another second off of the barrel run. They'll ask you to try them out, and you just can't refuse. Then you'll hike that skirt of yours up around your belly button and climb aboard, and all those horny old goons will drop their jaws and start slobbering over their chins when they get an eyeful of your pretty thighs."

She opened the bathroom door slightly and poked her head through. "You're nasty. You make me sound like a regular little trollop."

"Well, what else could you call it? Living in sin with no-account, fortune-hunting drifter whose . . ." Morgan's jestful accusations were cut short. A damp towel, precisely aimed and projected from the interior of the bathroom, hit him directly in the back of the head.

Not long afterward, three blasts from the pickup marked his growing impatience. Once Morgan decided to set himself to a task, even an unpleasant one, he wanted to get right to it and not waste any time. It was more than an hour's drive to Colfax, the meeting place of the Saddle Club, and if they were to be there on time, they had to leave soon. He reached in through the open cab window and tooted the horn again.

"Just a second," came the annoyed reply from inside the house.

"Second, my foot," he muttered. Knowing Celia well enough to know he had at least ten minutes to wait, he flicked his eyes over the area, making sure they were leaving it in good shape. All gates shut. Tools put in the shed. All outbuildings locked. As he surveyed the property, he could not help but feel a deep sense of pride. Sure, he'd seen bigger ranches, richer and more luxurious ones, but none better, in his opinion.

The house, for instance, was modest but effectively unique. A replica of an early American log cabin, it had been lovingly constructed by rancher Bloodstone thirty years prior. The historical sturdiness of the design, combined with the advantage of modern tools and equipment, had produced a compact, cozy dwelling place requiring little maintenance or upkeep. Three steps cut from a single massive log led up to a front porch that ran the length of the cabin. Supported by many log pillars, the roof of the porch served as the floor of a sundeck. Rising above the house in the back was the chimney—not as precise in dimension as one made of factory-cut bricks but similarly structured by Bloodstone out of self-quarried stone and home-mixed cement.

Unlike many of the ranches in the area, the cabin was surrounded by a bit of color. Evergreen trees flanked the house, and a flower garden, still far from full bloom in the early May weather, graced the rich soil in front of the porch. Rather than hard-packed earth that turned to mud in the rainy times and filled the air with dust during the hot, dry weeks of late summer, the yard was an emerald-green carpet of spring grass. The lawn extended for at least twenty feet from all sides of the cabin, and at its edge was a clearly marked border: a low stone wall. A heavy wooden gate controlled the entrance, and a stone pathway, painstakingly cleared of any stray grass blades shooting up between stones, led to the cabin porch.

Celia loved her little picture-book abode. When the other ranchers chided her for spending valuable time weeding the flower bed or using precious water to keep the grass green in hot weather, she merely told them to mind their own business. Even Morgan learned to disregard the sarcastic inquiries of, "When are you gonna join the Garden Club?"

Despite all the time and effort that contributed to the upkeep of the house, the rest of the ranch, the business end of it, never suffered from neglect. There were two barns on the property, one big one where hay and grain were stored and where the young colts and fillies were kept during training, and another, much smaller, barn that was reserved for foaling mares or convalescing horses. Each barn opened into an adjoining corral, and the whole affair was kept well-laundered and painted in shades of brown.

The corral was empty at the moment Morgan had let the eight young horses that were presently being schooled into the enclosure several hours earlier, but he disliked leaving them in the open when no one was on the premises, so he had returned them to their stalls after a brief exercise period.

The other door of the big barn led to a schooling ring. It was a multi-purpose arena. Here, the yearlings were worked on the long rein, the three-year-olds were ridden for the first time, the broke-to-ride horses were taught leads and the finesse of gaits, contest horses learned to run the cloverleaf barrel race and the weaving in-and-out pole-bending pattern, working stock cut unruly calves from groups of equally tricky cattle, and, as evidenced by the series of makeshift obstacles scattered strategically around the arena, the occasional hunter-type horse with sufficient promise was taught to jump.

Several hundred feet behind the barn area, more removed from the commotion of normal ranch comings and goings, was the breeding area. As a rule, the ranch stallion ran on the one hundred acres of carefully fenced pasture with the small but very selective herd of ranch mares. But when mares were brought to the ranch for servicing, the pride and joy of the Bloodstone Ranch, Conquering Joseph, was brought to the home pasture.

The breeding area was equipped with a doubly secure pen, where the stallion was kept for the first day or so. The mare was allowed the freedom of the one-acre paddock to stand under the shade of the clustering dogwood trees or drink from the spring-fed stream that shimmered through the pasture like an ice-blue ribbon on a green-wrapped birthday present. Within sight and smell of the hungering stallion at all times, the mare was more than ready to accept his services once Joseph was released from the pen.

To assure a good mating, the two horses were given the paddock as a honeymoon suite for the remainder of the mare's stay on the ranch, under careful supervision to protect both horses from possible injury, a fate open-range breeding often allowed. The breeding paddock was also empty now as Joseph was more than occupied this time of year tending to his own mares.

The last clump of outbuildings was located on the opposite side of the cabin from the barns. They sat at the end of the long, spruce-lined drive that led from I-195, the main highway. In keeping with the décor of the rest of the homestead, they were painted a dark chocolate with tan trim. The largest of the three was a garage that usually housed the new pickup truck Morgan was now lounging against. Safely locked inside were the older secondhand Chevy, the tractor, and Celia's latest mechanical acquisition—a snowmobile. On either side of the garage were two smaller sheds. One served as both a small workshop and a tool storehouse, and the other was for non-utility stable equipment such as the seldom-used Victoria left over from Bloodstone's era.

Yes, it was a fine ranch. Well laid out. Well kept up. And even if the profits hadn't yet allowed for anything but necessities, at least there were profits. In another five years? No telling what the operation might yield. The plans he and Celia had were limitless.

Morgan's forehead creased into a quick frown, and he shook his head to relieve it of a cobweb of bad thoughts. After he glanced down at his watch, the frown grew deeper. Once again, he blasted the horn of the pickup, this time sustaining the harsh signal for a full ten seconds.

Very seldom did he think about the fact that his name appeared nowhere on the ranch deed. But there were times.

CHAPTER 3

IN THE GREEN PICKUP, Morgan and Celia drove down the main street of Colfax, making slightly erratic progress. As in most small rural communities, Saturday morning was prime time for the Colfax storekeepers, and the invasion of additional autos and pedestrians on the two-lane thoroughfare made a shambles of the usually trickling traffic flow. Vehicles of all manner were angle-parked along the row of shops in none-too-orderly a fashion. Occasionally, a pickup truck, the bed already half filled with a week's shopping, would be sitting with its tail end a good foot into the traffic lane. Motorists would be forced to slow down and swerve around the obstruction and, at the same time, avoid being hit by an oncoming vehicle from the other direction. After making that successful detour, they would encounter, in the next block, a jeep, tires caked with spring mud, double-parked in the lane while its driver made a quick run to the hardware store to grab a new hammer.

Pedestrians added to the confusion by practicing the breaking of almost all "safety on the streets" rules ever diagrammed. They crossed the streets without the aid of the traffic signals, diagonally from corner to corner and in the middle of the block. They stepped out between parked cars and generally assumed traffic would stop for them or flow around them, and they generally assumed correctly.

Morgan swore softly as he waited for his turn at the four-way stop. In front of him was a two-tone station wagon bearing out-of-state license plates. Its operator obviously had no idea where he was going; he was hunched over a road map spread across the steering wheel. Every few seconds, he would look up and wave his finger to the drivers of the cars stopped at the corners. Five times he had extended this courtesy and had yet to move across the intersection. Forgetting legendary western hospitality, Morgan laid a heavy fist on the horn. The fellow from Illinois jerked his head suddenly as if pinched. He twisted around and stared in the direction from whence came the piercing signal.

Unable to read the expression on the out-of-towner's face, Morgan swore more audibly as the Illini lumbered out of his vehicle. "Oh, Christ," he muttered. "A real Chicago hot-head, I bet. Gonna storm back here and punch my lights out."

Celia smiled. "And he probably knows karate, too."

But the gentleman approaching the truck appeared anything but lethal. He was short and stout and had a shiny bald head to match his shiny, smooth-shaven, round face. Despite the nip in the spring breeze, sweat beads dotted his forehead, and his cheeks were flushed a rosy hue. Dressed in a suit and tie, dress shoes on his feet, he looked painfully out of place amongst the gathering of cowboys and ranchers. He wore an expression of sheer frustration, but his words held a trace of hope. "Sorry to hold you up, fella, but I don't know where the hell I am. Maybe you could help me?" The voice was heavy with a Midwestern twang.

Morgan had a gnawing desire to indicate his Idaho plates, stress the fact they were now in Washington, and plead helplessness, but he forced patience. "Can try. Where you going?"

"Portland. I came down from Spokane on I-95 and was

supposed to catch I-27 here at Colfax. And I'll be damned if I didn't get lost. Can you believe that? I can find my way around Peoria, Chicago, and even New York with my eyes closed, and I get lost in a hick town like this." The portly man gulped slightly guiltily and quickly continued. "I mean, this is a fine little town, real fine. But don't you people believe in street signs?"

Celia leaned over towards the window and addressed the man cheerfully. "Why, that's no problem, just let us pass and fall in behind. We're catching I-27 too."

The frustrated look disappeared. He beamed. "Why, that's real kind of you. You know, I've heard you westerners always help out when a person's in a jam. I'm from Peoria myself. Peoria, Illinois. Ever been to Peoria?"

Morgan checked the time on his wristwatch and replied without a hint of interest. "No. Never been there."

"Well, I'll tell you. Peoria's nothing like this place. People talking and smiling at each other. Why, if I asked for directions in Peoria, they'd either think I was trying to mug them, or they'd try to mug me. But I'd rather . . ."

"I think we'd better be going, don't you?" Morgan glanced over his shoulder and indicated two more cars in the line behind them.

"Oh, sure." The man made no move to return to his station wagon, though. Instead, he reached into his inside pocket and produced a business card. "My name's Denker. I sell appliances. Stoves, 'frigerators, freezers, washer-dryers—you name it, we sell it. Opening a new store in Portland." He extended the card to Morgan. "Ever out our way and need a new whatever, I'm sure I can fix you up."

Morgan hastily grabbed the card and pushed it at Celia. "We'll remember that, Mr. Denker. Better be on our way now, though. Looks like we're holding up traffic." He stabbed a thumb at the line of autos, now almost half a block long.

"Yep, nice friendly little town. Really makes you feel at home."

Fast losing what meager ration of patience he had left, Morgan shifted the truck into gear and inched ahead. "Mr. Denker. If you stand around much longer, they'll expect you to make your home here. Now just follow us. Okay?"

The cheerful, plump man held up a pudgy hand. He jounced back to his Rambler Country Squire as Morgan eased the pickup around him. Celia hung out the window and called sweetly, "Stick close now. We're just going a few miles out of town, but you follow I-27 south to Dodge." Denker flashed an "okay" sign, encircled thumb and forefinger, climbed into the wagon, and pulled the door shut behind him. Both autos crossed the intersection, and traffic resumed its normal pace.

"Now, doesn't that make you feel good, being able to help like that?" Celia said.

"Not especially," replied Morgan sulkily. "With the combined efforts of you and your friend Dunkerk . . ."

"Denker."

"You and Mr. *Denker*," the name was enunciated with emphasis, "we are now exactly twenty-seven minutes late to the meeting." He cut his wheels sharply to avoid the tall, rangy cowboy who suddenly appeared from between a stock truck and a Ranchero. The cowboy, not the least shaken by his narrow escape, smiled a slow smile and waited for Denker to pass before continuing across the street. "Twenty-seven minutes late, and we haven't even got out of town yet!" Morgan glanced in the rearview mirror to make sure Denker had turned the corner behind him.

"Oh, who cares? So they'll cast disapproval on us as we trail in late, but they already disapprove of us anyway. At least we're putting in an appearance; that's all that counts. Oh, look!" Celia interrupted herself gleefully. "It's Sybil. Morgan, stop!" She reached over and honked the horn.

"But we don't have time," he insisted.

"If you don't stop, she'll think you're a bigot."

"Hell, she wouldn't have known who it was if you hadn't blown the damn horn."

The subject of discussion was a statuesque, strikingly handsome Indian woman. She strode the sidewalk with a dignity that bespoke great pride—almost arrogance. Had the flowered smock top and corduroy Levi's been replaced by a fawn skin shift, she would have been the picture of Nez Perce royalty. As it was, the blood of great chieftains and beautiful princesses did grace her veins, but in the present-day white man's world, her status meant nothing. She ignored the honking of the truck horn and kept up her haughty pace. She was used to that and much cruder attempts to divert her attention towards casual admirers.

"Sybil! Sybil Horn!" Celia called, and the woman stopped, slowly turning her head. The marble contours of her olive-skinned face melted to a smile as she saw who addressed her.

"Celia, how are you?"

The truck didn't quite come to a full stop. With Celia hanging half out the window, it crept slowly along the curb. Right behind was the Rambler station wagon, inching along in time. Mr. Denker at the wheel might not be quite sure where he was going, but he clearly put utter faith in his native guide and seemed to take great pleasure in viewing the scenery before him. Not once was his trust swayed by the fact the truck, too, bore out-of-state plates. Perhaps he was so lost he thought he was in Idaho.

Celia talked fast because it was obvious Morgan was not going to wait. "We can't stop right now. A few minutes late for a meeting, and the old man's all hot and bothered. Will you be in town long enough to meet us for lunch later?"

Sybil nodded.

"Good. How about Macy's at one o'clock?"

"All right," was all Sybil had time to say as the truck pulled out. She waved at her friend, still precariously half-in, half-out of the window, and even let her smile linger long enough to include Mr. Denker. He more than enthusiastically waved back.

SYBIL HORN and Celia Bolt had known each other for many years. They first met when Celia responded to an ad the Indian woman had placed in a local horse breeders' magazine. At the time, both were in a similar situation, struggling without much capital to build a good horse ranch, but Sybil was aided in this endeavor by her ambitious young husband.

Fate had dealt them a bad hand, and they had lost a good stallion, a proven Appaloosa. The horse had become ill and was down in the course of a day. The vet's examination revealed a severely twisted intestine. "Torsion" was what the vet called it. Whatever it was called, it was irreparable.

Desperately needing a stud to cover the mares that spring and lacking the funds to purchase one or pay a stud fee, they advertised for a trade—a proven stallion of good quality, or the use of same, in exchange for a promising but yet unproven three-year-old champion mare or pick of next spring's crop of foals.

Celia had read the notice in *Tri-State Appaloosa Breeders* and felt investigating was worth the sixty-five-mile drive to Mock-onema, where the Horn ranch was located. She had a quality stallion already, Sir Pepper Pot, but he had been servicing Blood-stone mares for seven years. Celia's desire was to introduce a fresh bloodline to the ranch, a stallion she could breed to the daughters of Pepper Pot. What transpired was a trade. Blood-stone's ten-year-old stud became the property of the young Indian couple, and the three-year-old son of Horn's dead stallion became the reigning monarch of Celia's ranch. The colt's name was Conquering Joseph. As it turned out, both parties were sure that they got the best end of the deal.

But more than horse trading came about as a result of the ad. Upon first meeting, a spark of friendship was ignited between the stoical, hardworking Indians and the optimistic city-bred girl. They were drawn into kindship by the strange series of coincidences that could lead people from such different backgrounds to an identical station. The road from Celia's ranch to the Horn's became a familiar thoroughfare for both as they took advantage of every opportunity to exchange visits. And not only their common interest in horse breeding was discussed at these meetings. Far from it. Among the three of them, they solved the problems of the world as they sat sipping spirit-laced coffee around a late-evening dinner table or spread their Sunday picnic lunches on the lush pasture lands.

It was Stoner Horn who solved the major problem of Celia's world. It was he who invited an only slightly successful rodeo rider to dinner one Friday evening, bringing the gathering to an equal number. Neither Sybil nor their other dinner guest, Celia, questioned his motives, for Stoner was known as an overly kind collector of strays and homeless, down-on-their-luck misfortunates. But with his good-heartedness came an equally keen perceptiveness, and the young Indian recognized the bulldogger as much more than a vagabond.

Stoner never thought of himself as a Nez Perce matchmaker, but he wasn't totally surprised when Morgan Kyles returned from walking a thoroughly smitten Celia Bolt to her car that evening and announced his plans. He had agreed to work for Celia once the rodeo season ended for room and board and whatever she could pay him in wages. Despite Sybil's wary theories that Kyles might turn out to be a psychotic ax murderer or even worse (Stoner was hard-pressed to think of anything worse than a psychotic ax murderer), the arrangement turned out to be ideal for both parties. Morgan Kyles never returned to the rodeo circuit.

Stoner and Sybil's life together wasn't destined to be so enchanted. The following summer, Stoner was struck with a crippling virus that left doctors puzzled and helpless. He died a month later, after his short but complicated illness had drained his wife of all capitol available and plunged her into the despair of debt. It was not her own people but Celia she turned to at this time. Celia saved her from cracking under the strain of grief and brought her back to the point of caring about life and accepting death.

With encouragement from Celia and Morgan, the young Indian woman began reeling in the broken lines of her life. She decided to put her years of animal experience to use and applied for a government job with the Department of Agriculture. Her application couldn't have been submitted at a better time. Various pressure groups were demanding the state hire more women and minority members. Sybil was both.

So, for the past four years, she had been working as a livestock inspector throughout the state. The job involved long hours and extensive traveling, but for a single woman with no commitments, it was ideal. Not enough years had passed since the death of her husband, and the demanding schedule was appreciated. But she was glad for the layover in Colfax, which was allowing her time to visit her in-laws and now offered the added pleasure of seeing her good friends again. Sybil was anxiously awaiting their one o'clock engagement.

SID DUTCHENS POUNDED his gavel on the table as if he were driving nails. With a booming bellow that shook the walls of the small Whitman County 4-H Fair Grounds meeting hall, he called the attention of his fellow club members. It was easy to see why Sid was presiding chairman of the Palouse Valley Saddle Club.

"All right, now, folks. Let's get started. We've waited long enough for Miss Bolt, and it just don't look as if she's coming today." Sid's coarsely accented words were propelled through thick, perpetually cracked lips. When it wasn't the heat of the summer or the cold blasts of winter that chapped them, it was Dutchens's maddening habit of biting at them as if he were trying to nibble the fleshy protuberances down to size.

"But Celia and Morgan always come, Sid," Nora Potter chirped. Her thin, pinched face, sharply pointed nose and chin, and eyes that darted back, forth, up, and down while she spoke reminded one of a nervous little chickadee. "And Celia knew we were going to elect committee members today. She wouldn't miss that."

An unidentified groan erupted from the back row, followed by the unmistakable stutter of Jacob Anderson. "D-D-Damn! If I'd remem-mem-membered th-th-that, I'd a-a-a stayed home today."

"Hell, Jake. That wouldn't have done you no good. We'd have voted you in as chief announcer anyhow."

"G-G-G-o to hell, S-S-Sid," retaliated Anderson, but the room exploded in laughter. No one, not even Anderson, took his affliction seriously.

When the merriment subsided, Dutchens again called the meeting to order. "Now we've waited a good forty minutes for those two, so I say let's get on with business."

Once more, it was Nora Potter to the defense. "But Sid, you know how far they have to drive. And Saturday morning traffic in Colfax is always so bad."

"Oh, come on, now, Nora. Sid there drives just as far as Celia and Morgan." This from Carla Fairfax, an attractive but aging blonde who sat in the front row and who had swung around on

Nora Potter, causing the latter's eyes to flick crazily around the room.

"Farther, really," added Dutchens, always eager to expound on just how much he did for the sake of the club. "My ranch is on the east side of the Bloodstone ranch, so I have another ten miles to come. But I don't lie around in bed all morning!"

Grant Castor, tall, gangly, with a hook nose and a clammy complexion, sneered and interjected, "You don't sleep with Celia Bolt, either." Grant was extremely preoccupied with sex and sexual activities. He made a point of riding only stallions.

Fran Castor, Grant's muscular, almost masculine wife, delivered a not-too-loving tap on Grant's bony arm and announced in a tone not unlike that of Tug Boat Annie's, "Why don't you shut up, you horny old goat?" But Castor merely rubbed his arm and laughed loudly at his own joke. Much too loudly to hear the lack of any other laughter, in fact.

For the third time, Sid Dutchens almost dented the table with his gavel. His fleshy face was slightly reddened. "Can it, will ya, Grant?"

"If I could can it," Castor managed to gasp between snorts of braying laughter, "I'd make a million."

At this point, Fran Castor began pounding on her husband's arm with real desperation; the assault was sufficient to distract Castor from his preoccupation with his own humor. He swung around on the woman with a touch of menace in his voice. "Now, Frannie . . ." The rest of his threat was aborted as he caught sight of Celia and Morgan Kyles making their way down the aisle of the meeting hall.

"I'm sorry we're late, everyone," Celia apologized as she slid into an available seat, "but it doesn't sound as if our tardiness put a damper on the festivities."

Morgan had no response but merely melted into a straight-backed chair, propped one booted foot on one denim-clad knee, and proceeded to make himself as inconspicuous as possible.

"Oh, no, Celia, honey. Grant has been entertaining us quite admirably." Carla Fairfax aimed a charming smile in Celia's direction, and Celia thought to herself, *Eastern society certainly has no monopoly on sophisticated bitches.*

"Now that everyone is here, I'm calling the meeting to order." Dutchens's booming announcement interrupted the war of smiles Celia was engaged in with the flaxen-haired, aging beauty. "Perc, you want to come up here and read last month's minutes?"

Percy Ludwin, secretary of the club, responded by gathering together what appeared to be a ream of paper and hurried up to the podium. Ludwin taught shorthand and bookkeeping at Colfax High School. He was an inoffensive slip of a man, always attired in a white dress shirt and red string tie, and although the local school boys took great delight in questioning the masculinity of the slight teacher, he came across as being more asexual than anything else. Despite their ridicule, Percy Ludwin displayed nothing but patience toward his students and was considered one of the finest teachers in the school system. Even the die-hard hecklers, once actually assigned to one of Ludwin's classes, would eventually succumb to the magic the man wove. He made students want to learn; made the knowledge of double-entry bookkeeping or the use of shorthand characters seem like the keys to new worlds.

He approached his stable of fine Appaloosa horses with the same training attitude. He lacked the personal fire and dynamism necessary to produce contest horses or racers, but the horses he bred and trained were well-known for their gentleness, even spirits, and confidence in their riders. They were generally thought of as the finest pleasure mounts to be found.

Second in importance only to his beloved horses came Percy's position as secretary of the Palouse Valley Saddle Club. It never occurred to him that the job was a thankless one that few of the members wanted; it probably wouldn't have mattered even if it had. It was almost power he felt when, on the first Saturday of every month, he could stand before the entire membership of the club and relate to them, word for word, the statements they had made the month prior. From the library of minutes kept in his home, he could find the exact date and under what circumstances a certain club member had called another a "son of a bitch" or he could produce a colleague's verbatim declaration that was later contrary to his or her behavior.

Not that Percy ever caused any trouble with this power of his, but he certainly relieved any club member of the denial, "Why, I never said that." Of course, when Percy Ludwin read his minutes, he didn't bore the membership with lengthy accounts. He summarized drastically, reporting only the essentials and highlights of the previous gatherings.

"Last month's meeting," began Percy Ludwin in his quiet, gentle voice, in direct contrast to Sid Dutchens's bellow, "was called to order at 9:30a.m. by Chairman Dutchens."

"*Pssst*, Celia." Sparrow-faced Nora Potter was trying valiantly to get Celia's attention, whispering to her from two rows back and, at the same time, peeping apprehensively around the room as if in fear of admonishment. When her attempt succeeded, Nora went on in a nervous whisper. "I'm so glad you got here. I made them wait for you, you know."

Celia acknowledged with a smile, then turned back to face Ludwin. But Nora's whispered conversation had not ended. "You haven't forgotten, have you? What you promised last month?"

For one terrible moment, Celia *had* forgotten. She let so much of Miss Potter's chatter pass in one ear and out the other. What was it she had promised her last month? If indeed she had actually promised. Nora had a way of making things sound so dramatic. Celia hated to resort to the schoolgirl tactics of "talking in class," but the slight frown of puzzlement on her face saved her.

"Remember, Celia? The Awards Committee."

At this point, Morgan pulled himself upright in the metal folding chair and glanced around, irritated but curious as to Celia's source of concern. When he realized that it was Nora Potter causing the distraction, his disapproval was not to be disguised. He glared accusingly, and Nora, in turn, sat back in her chair, fingers fluttering over her mouth and her nervous little birds' eyes looking up towards the ceiling. She was definitely not one of Morgan's favorite personalities. But Celia felt sorry for the older woman even though she felt great relief at Morgan's rescue. Besides, she had suddenly remembered her very one-sided conversation with Nora the month past. She had agreed to nominate Nora as chairman of the awards committee. With one final half twist behind her, she flashed the thoroughly cowed woman a cheering grin and an "okay" sign.

"A vote was taken. The decision was affirmative. The annual Palouse Valley Saddle Club Open Horse Show will be held this year on Saturday, October 5, with a rain date of Saturday, October 12. The meeting was brought to a close by Chairman Dutchens at 11:30 a.m." Percy Ludwin completed his quiet oration and returned to his seat. His obligation for the morning met, he planned to sit out the duration of the meeting in silence, taking his shorthand at a furious pace as usual.

Once again, Sid Dutchens's bulky frame appeared behind the podium. "Now. Anybody got any old business they want to talk about? Pauline."

Pauline Sire, heavyset, mustachioed, with bushy black brows over mysterious black eyes, swarthy, almost gypsy-like in appearance, took the floor upon being recognized. Her voice was a surprise. One would expect her speech to be thick with a Slavic accent, but she spoke with great eloquence. Her enunciation far surpassed that of the chairman.

"Mr. Dutchens. I have some information that should be made known to you and this membership. After spending a great deal of time and expending an even greater amount of energy consulting the numerical and astrological charts, I've uncovered a rather alarming situation."

Pauline had the full attention of her audience. She was known to most of them as Sister Sire, the only professional palmist within a 200-mile radius of Colfax. It was hard to believe that these solid westerners, most from sturdy pioneer stock and proud of it, who were overly blessed with the virtue of logic, could yield enough believers in the power of the occult to provide a living for a palm reader. But for Pauline Sire, her living was more than ample. She worked by appointment only and required a stiff fee for her services, as dubious as these services might have seemed to many. But believers or not, when Sister Sire spoke, people listened. Her black-eyed gaze encompassed whole congregations; the sparkling movements of her bejeweled fingers hypnotized.

"Well, come on, Pauline." Sid Dutchens, number one on the list of Sister Sire's unbelievers, was the first to tear his own pale blue eyes away from Pauline's commanding stare. She had paused purposefully, and the dramatics had had their effect. Everyone was practically on the edges of their chairs, and yet, if questioned under normal circumstances, all but a couple would adamantly deny any interest in astrology.

"The situation is one of an alarming nature, impending destruction that may affect any one of you." Pauline appeared to be addressing each and every one of her audience personally.

Celia looked at Morgan and rolled her eyes in mock terror; Nora Potter gasped melodramatically; Grant Castor swallowed hard, his gargantuan Adam's apple going up into his throat and disappearing momentarily; Sid Dutchens looked the perfectly serious Pauline "Sister" Sire straight in the eyes and uttered, "Balls!"

Almost as quickly as the words came out of Sid's mouth, the atmosphere of the room changed. Only a few giggled, and a few more sighed, but everyone relaxed. The sound of tense muscles once more returning to an "at ease" position was almost audible. It was as if an assailant had been holding a pistol on the audience, but when he pulled the trigger, instead of a lethal bullet speeding from the barrel, a flag saying "BANG!" popped out.

"Yeah, Pauline." Bruce Tanner followed Chairman Dutchens's example. "What do you mean, 'impending doom?' Jesus, you sound like some 1930 vampire movie." He curled his upper lip to expose his teeth and made a strangling motion with his hands. Most of those who weren't already chuckling broke into laughter.

Pauline Sire, however, merely curled the corners of her thick lips into the trace of a smile while her gypsy eyes flashed. She was used to being laughed at, used to having her predictions ridiculed. When one had as much confidence and faith in herself as Sister Sire, the approval of others was not a prerequisite for peace of mind.

"You may see humor in the situation now, but I pray you do not come to see the gravity. Listen to me, follow my advice, and we will be spared."

"Oh, for God's sake, Pauline," uttered the fast-becoming-annoyed cowboy who was sitting behind her, "cut the crap and out with it. We're not one of your clients paying you by the hour, you know."

"All right. I'll tell you once and once only. If the show is held on October 5, it will bring doom to one or more of us in this room today. All signs point to it. It is not a prediction, it is a fact. Change the date or don't, the decision is yours, and the responsibility lies on your heads. As for myself and my stock, we will not be competing in your disaster." Sister Sire rose from her chair and left the meeting.

"Huh?" was the eloquent reply from Jacob Anderson, so momentarily confused he managed to get it out without stuttering.

Low mumbles of conversation bespoke the other members' equally bemused condition until finally, Sid Dutchens dealt the table a mighty swat and announced in his booming chairman's bellow, "She's nuts! That's not a prediction—that's a fact!"

"Oh, my," fluttered Nora, "oh, my, we can't possibly, we just can't possibly change the date." Her fingers worked excitedly at her face. She was in a definite quandary.

"Oh, Nora," Carla scoffed in true disgust. "Of course, we won't change the date."

"But you heard her, Carla. You heard what she said."

"If you believe anything that black-haired fantasy spinner says, then that's your problem. The same for the rest of you." Carla released Nora Potter from her merciless stare to encompass the entire membership. "The date is October 5; that is old business decided last month. Now, let's get on with new business."

If there was a soul in the meeting hall who doubted the finality of the decision, if there was anyone who let Pauline Sire's comments send a shiver up their backs, they did not have the courage to buck Carla Fairfax's cold disdain. The meeting continued.

"CELIA, I'm so glad to see you. It's been months." Celia and Sybil embraced in the manner of good friends. Their greeting lacked the controlled, compulsory peck on the cheek employed by cool society women. Instead, each threw her arms around the other and hugged enthusiastically. Macy's was a casual diner and none of the cowboys who were crowded in for the lunch hour disapproved. Several would have loved to join in on the ceremony.

The two women secured a booth and began exchanging pleasantries. "Why didn't you tell me you were going to be in town? How long are you staying?"

"It was an accident that I'm here anyway. I just got in this morning. Due to the unscheduled death of a colleague, I had to pitch in for extra duty."

"Was he a friend?"

Sybil laughed. "Not hardly. He was a bastard." Many would have been taken aback by the woman's frankness and apparent lack of compassion. Celia, however, was cut from the same fabric and felt no shock at all. If you couldn't stand a person when they were alive, you shouldn't eulogize them when they are dead.

"Well, how's the old man?" It was Sybil's turn to question.

"Still horny as ever."

"No. I mean Joseph, not Morgan."

Both women laughed heartily. It was strange how they could involve themselves in crude language and humor, work at traditional men's jobs, express themselves aggressively and with assertiveness, and generally possess so many masculine traits, and yet retain the beauty, grace, and dignity of their sex. They were strong women without being hard; they had strong emotions without being flamboyant. They were totally androgynous.

Even stranger was that they appealed to the predominately male clientele. These were men who held the dated opinion that there are two types of women: those you marry and those you have fun with. But for some reason, both these women occupied a third, totally foreign place in these men's esteem. They would no more think of making the traditional "pass" at them than they would be inclined to remove their hats and scuffle their boot toes in the dust in search of conversation. Most of them would have given a lot to be eating their lunches seated next to and joining in on the easy talk at that attention-receiving booth.

"Joseph is the Old Man, Sybil. Morgan is The Man. The former is doing well. The latter is going to be coming through that door any minute now, and he's pissed off at me, to say the least."

On cue, Morgan strode through the entrance and let his eyes rove around the crowded restaurant. He nodded a restrained greeting to a few familiar faces but exchanged words with no one. He spotted the booth where Celia and Sybil were seated and began a nonchalant stroll toward them.

Several of the men jealously stared when they realized the newcomer's destination. When Sybil jumped to her feet and threw her arms around Morgan's broad shoulders, and planted a kiss on his weathered cheek, the spectators looked away. It wasn't fair. What did he have that they didn't? He wasn't even good-looking! Morgan, on the other hand, was embarrassed and would have gladly traded away the kiss for a bowl of Macy's famous chili.

Morgan Kyles was the stereotypical cowboy personified. He kept a firm hold on his emotions almost continually. He hated hellos and goodbyes. It would constantly mystify Celia how Morgan could run into an old friend from the rodeo circuit whom he hadn't seen for years and just shake hands. Even if they took in a few night spots and treated themselves to copious amounts of beer, they would never knock down the wall of reserve between them. They'd part again, not knowing if or when they'd ever meet.

It wasn't the masculine thing to do to tell another man how you really felt about him or to openly display your feelings for a woman. Slapping a waitress on the posterior or shouting out the window of your pickup to a good-looking but unfamiliar woman was okay, but at all times, men like Morgan Kyles must not let it be known that he had a softer side. It was only when he was with the woman he loved that he let his true self peek through the tough, macho hide. It was because of those rare, tender moments that Celia loved him so, and because Celia loved him and he made her happy, Sybil loved him too.

"Celia tells me you're pissed off at her." Sybil began the conversation as frankly as before. Morgan's presence didn't alter her behavior at all.

"Did she tell you what she did to me?"

The waitress appeared. Harried, blowing black hair out of her eyes with a well-placed puff of air produced by ridiculously positioned lips, she requested the orders.

"Three chilis, ladies?" Morgan asked.

"Not for me," Sybil quickly cut in. "I inspect meat for this state, remember. A grilled cheese sandwich and a chef's salad, please." Her black eyes twinkled, and even Morgan smiled. The waitress was untouched by the humor, however. Lunch at Macy's was a killer.

"Don't you wish you were still slinging hash?" Sybil said to Celia after the sour-faced waitress limped off with the orders.

"I wouldn't mind it," Morgan put in. "She wouldn't be getting me into these awkward positions if she was."

"Why, Morgan," Cellia said sweetly. "You've never complained about 'awkward positions' before."

"Hey, lady, can't you clean your mouth up?"

"Aww. Tell Sybil what the mean lady did to you."

"As if it isn't enough that we have to attend those damn meetings every month, now she's volunteered us to head up a committee."

"That's right." Celia had a touch of satisfaction in her voice. "We—Morgan, that is—is in charge of the advanced promotions committee."

Morgan groaned anew and slid deeper into the bench seat. "As if I don't have enough to do, running your ranch, Miss Bolt."

"Oh! Aren't we self-sacrificial? There's no reason why we

can't contribute a little to the show. We walk off with enough blues every year."

Suddenly Morgan bolted upright and pointed an accusing finger at the lady across the booth. "Now, wait just one minute. I've done my share of contributing. I served on a committee last year—you can't deny that."

"How *could* I have forgotten? You did work on awards last season, didn't you?"

"Yes, how could you have forgotten that, Cel? It seems to me you're expecting a little too much from Morgan here." Sybil felt she had to get in her two cents' worth. She had missed her friends badly and was comfortable in their presence despite what might appear to be an argument.

"I guess it slipped my mind because you only worked on the committee one day," Celia said to Morgan. The smug look on his face vanished as Celia turned to Sybil. "Sid Dutchens was the chairman, and my man stormed out of Dutchens's living room and hasn't been back since."

"I was willing. It's just that Dutchens is the most unreasonable son of a bitch on Earth."

"Not like you, honey. You're so logical and easy to get along with." But despite her sarcasm, Celia reached across the table and put her slender hand over Morgan's.

He pulled it away and scowled.

"Please don't be angry, Morgan." Celia's voice lost the bantering tone, and the sincerity of it touched the cowboy. He couldn't remain angry. Their hands touched once more, and, with his free arm, Morgan encircled Sybil and shook her lightly. "Damn. I'm a sucker for pretty ladies."

Lunch arrived. The same unhappy waitress distributed the dishes wordlessly. There was an awkward silence at the table. One never seems to want to talk while a stranger is serving a meal. It becomes more painful when one realizes that the stranger doesn't particularly enjoy serving.

After the waitress had left, Celia was the first to speak. "It's really not going to be so bad. Jake Anderson and Perc Ludwin are on the committee with us. You know Jake, Sybil, he's the rodeo stock contractor from the valley. The fellow with the stutter."

"Sure, I know him. Stoner and I pastured some yearling calves for him one winter. He's a nice enough fellow. I'm not familiar with Ludwin, however."

"I don't think he's ever been familiar with any woman," said Morgan.

"Morgan, I don't think that's nice," Celia rebuked him. "He's a very sweet man and a good horseman, too."

"Sweet maybe, and I ain't denying he's good with horses, but that don't make him a man."

"That must mean he doesn't have a chest full of hair, and he doesn't chew tobacco, cuss a lot, and wear dirty Levis," Sybil said.

"He's a schoolteacher, so at least Morgan can't argue with him," Celia said. "Neither would understand the other's vocabulary."

Everyone laughed, even Morgan. Sybil's teeth flashed white as she bit down on her cheese sandwich. Morgan thought how sad it was she had no man. A good-looking, strong woman like that needed a man to share with.

Suddenly, Sybil stopped chewing her sandwich. She swallowed thoughtfully. "What did you say you were in charge of? Advanced promo?"

"Right. What do you have in mind?"

"Morgan, you're always bitching about the club. About how bigoted the members are and how it isn't against the rules for an Indian to join, but they'll make it damn hard on him if he tries."

"Yeah. So?"

"Well, this is your chance to do something." She put her

sandwich on her plate and momentarily forgot about it. She used her hands as she talked; there was an edge of excitement in her voice. "Why don't you spread your notices to the Indian breeders? There's a lot of good Appaloosas on the reservation. Both old blood and new, strong blood. Calvin could talk it up, and I could pass the word around the state."

A slow grin made Morgan's face almost handsome. He looked at Celia for her approval. It had become a habit, and sometimes, he hated himself for it. She was grinning, too.

"They'd have a fit," Celia said deviously. "I can just picture Carla Fairfax's face now. Oh, Sybil! What a perfectly fabulous idea."

"It's only fair," Morgan said. "The Club runs around claiming they've got the best horseflesh in the area, but we seldom compete out of the club. Eighty percent of the participants at our so-called open show are club members, and when we go to other shows, we flood the entries."

"You don't have to give us a rationale. Does he, Sybil? He just wants to see Sid Dutchens get beat by some Indian kid on a horse that's never seen the inside of a barn and never eaten anything but grass."

"Sure, that too. I'd love to see some of the annual winners taken down a peg or two. But I'm serious. I'd also like to see this trading around of blue ribbons stopped. I know there's good stock outside of the Club, and I know that a lot of that stock was bred, raised, and trained by Indians. Sybil, if we get some posters and handbills printed, could you pass them out?"

"No problem. And like I said, I'll recruit Calvin's help, too."

Celia frowned slightly. "Do you really think he'll help? I mean . . ." She left her words hanging and shrugged her shoulders.

"I know what you're thinking—that he wouldn't want to get involved in a white man's game. There's plenty of prejudice on both sides, and my big brother is as bigoted as any two members of your club."

Morgan interrupted. "Maybe so, but Calvin's got a reason."

"Reason or not, he's not going to pass up a chance to show up a 'paleface.'"

"And I can't wait to see him do it." For the first time since they had left the ranch that morning, Morgan was truly happy; and for the first time since longer than he could remember, he was excited.

CHAPTER 4

CANTAR STIRRED in her straw bed apprehensively. Her nostrils dilated as she sifted through the odors in the air, and although she detected nothing alien, the hackles rose on the back of her neck.

Snuggled into the straw beside her, a tiny form emitted a whimper. Even at the tender age of one week, before his eyes were open and while his world still consisted of a small nesting box and mother's warm milk, he could sense the change in his dam's mood. Cantar immediately aborted the growl that was forming deep in her chest, and the hair on her back once again lay flat. With all the tenderness she possessed, as tenderly as any human mother would soothe her baby, the bitch caressed her pup with strokes from her tongue. Soon, the other pups awoke, and Cantar began grooming them as well. Once awake, all three clamored for food, and with some helpful shoves from Cantar's nose, they blindly groped for and quickly reached their mother's nipples.

For a few minutes, she relaxed. The tension that had sparked in her from the time she heard her master's truck leave the house, the nameless uneasiness that had mounted in her until she had almost growled audibly into the empty air, momentarily subsided. With her pups suckling greedily at her breasts, all motherly instincts were at their peak.

But the strongest instinct of any mother is to protect her young, and once more, the threat of evil was airborne. It was nothing she could smell despite the incredible sensitivity of her nose; it was nothing she could see. But it was there.

Cantar trusted her senses. She trusted them because they were infallible. She was cunning and dedicated to self-preservation. Had she been free-born and raised, no trap, gun, poison, or snare would have claimed her. She would have been the kind of superiorly elusive wild creature that ranchers hate and admire at the same time. Men would have surrounded her with stories, both real and imagined. The Indians, those that still revered the past, would have cherished her. But she was none of these things because Cantar had given herself to a man.

Three years prior, Hal Town, a bronc rider friend of Morgan's, had visited the ranch for a convalescent stay. He had brought with him a magnificent Airedale bitch, Delilah. She was a good stock dog, and word of her ability circulated. Then, to everyone's horror, she disappeared. Morgan feared she had been shot or gotten caught in a trap. With the help of neighbors, the entire county was scoured for any sign of the dog, but there was no luck. It became obvious that she had been stolen. Morgan's friend had to return to the circuit, but he still kept a small hope that his dog would show up. Morgan promised to keep looking.

Months passed, and the following April, a shaggy but familiar creature crept cautiously up to the ranch house late one evening. Delilah was none the worse for her adventure and apparently had not spent the winter entirely alone. Hal's Airedale was, without a doubt, pregnant.

Hal fairly flew back to Idaho to recover his dog. She was as overjoyed at the reunion as he was. Through speculation, Morgan pieced her story together. Knowing the bitch would not have left Hal, they assumed she had been stolen. Then, she either escaped from her abductors or, upon refusing to work for them (Hal claimed Delilah wouldn't work stock for anyone but himself), she was dumped. With the loyalty and perseverance peculiar only to man's best friend, the dog began making her way back to the last place she had seen her master.

Along the way, she had come in season and might have been aided during the harsh western winter by her mate. It seemed unlikely, though. Breeding behavior in domestic canines has lost its practical side, and most dogs would have just loved and left her. But the fact remained that Delilah was healthy and fat and had adjusted well to her situation.

A few days later, the Airedale presented her owner with four pups. As soon as they were born, Morgan was able to fill in the questionable part of Delilah's adventure. He had seen enough coyote pups in his lifetime, and even though their mother was Airedale, the littermates bore the stamp of *Canis latrans* all over them. Delilah must have encountered a solitary dog coyote, either a young one with no mate or a widower, just in the time of year when the urge to mate was strong and during the few months when the male coyote is fertile. A desperate, love-sick dog coyote would choose even an alien mate over none at all, and in typical coyote fashion, he would have formed a bond of protection and camaraderie with Delilah. Either he had been killed, or the Airedale's too-many-centuries-long devotion towards man forced Delilah to leave him. If the latter were true, there was a sad and lonely coyote somewhere howling his grief over an unfaithful wife and the loss of his children, whom he never saw.

Hal wanted to destroy the litter, for they were not only useless to him but potentially dangerous. Typically, a coyote is a shy creature who survives by his wits, not his brawn. His fear and distrust of man are innate, and no man has ever been attacked by a non-rabid coyote. But an animal with enough domestic dog blood in his veins, particularly as powerful and aggressive a dog as an Airedale, would not be intimidated by man as would a coyote and would not have the cultivated taboo of not biting the hand that fed him, as would a dog. The threat and liability of keeping such a creature around wouldn't be justified. Three of the pups were drowned before they could even nurse.

Sometimes, Morgan Kyles's logical mind betrayed him. On occasion, very few occasions, he went romantic. That April morning had been one of those occasions. He kept the only bitch puppy in the litter. He named her Cantar, which meant "to sing" in Spanish.

"Do you know what they are, Celia?" he had said while he stroked the day-old puppy's blind face. "They're freedom. Other ranchers may shoot them or trap them, but I'd never do that. It would be like trying to trap a piece of the wind or sun. And maybe she'll stay tame enough, and maybe, just maybe, she'll learn to love me, and it'll be like having a piece of freedom." Celia had put her arms around him then, and later they made love in the sweet-smelling hay. She had never loved him so much.

Cantar grew into a strikingly handsome creature. Morgan remarked that Delilah must have met a Samson, for at eighteen months, the coydog weighed ninety-five pounds, almost double the size of any female coyote Morgan had ever seen or heard of. She had the wiry coat of her dam, but the color was a mixture of reds and browns and blacks. Her face wasn't as sharply pointed as a coyote's, and her bone structure was heavier. While the entire physique of a coyote bespeaks speed, Cantar was more powerful and solid.

And the dream that Morgan had dared to put into words had come true. With fathomless devotion, Cantar had claimed Morgan as her own.

Coyotes are one of the least fickle of all animals. They will choose a mate and remain together for life, hunting, playing, and raising families, unless death takes one of the pair. Only then will the suffering partner pick a new mate. Morgan was Cantar's mate, and she defended him with a possessiveness that went beyond a dog/master relationship. There was enough domestic breeding in her to render her trainable (for experts claim that coyotes are virtually incorrigible not because of a lack of intelligence but because of an overabundance of it). The domestic breeding also quieted the highly strung, constantly agitated nervous system of the coyote. As a result of that perfect blending of blood, she feared nothing and no one, and yet could be controlled by a simple word from the man she loved. The coydog made the ranch her possession and protected it because it was hers, not because it was her job.

Her relationship with Celia was a sore spot for the pretty ranch owner. The animal merely tolerated her but would not accept Celia's friendship, let alone her mastery. Should Morgan and Celia be together in Cantar's presence, the coydog insisted on placing herself between the two. At all other times, Cantar remained aloof but never aggressive toward her, making Celia feel less like a source of irritation and more like a nonentity. Conversely, the situation pleased Morgan in a childishly egotistical sort of way.

Cantar's puppies had been sired by a cross-bred cattle dog that Morgan admired for its uncanny herding ability. He hoped that further dilution of the coyote blood would produce animals that were a little more doglike without being servile. Several neighbors had requested a pup from the litter, but Morgan was going to be very careful in placing them.

Cantar had lain with her head in Morgan's lap while she strained to whelp the three babies. In her single-minded way of reasoning, they were Morgan's puppies because he was the mate of her choice. She had tried to kill the smaller cattle dog twice before she finally accepted his mounting, and only then because

Morgan stood beside her and kept her from whirling on the anxious but willing male. And now, this danger she sensed was stirring the primitive warning system in her brain because her mate was gone, and she alone had to defend their family.

Cantar suddenly jumped to her feet, spilling her three pups off of her nipples and sending them toppling to the nesting box with confused whimpers. The odor was strong now, and it was the odor of man. It was not Morgan's scent, which would have been welcome, nor was it Celia's, which would have been ignored. It was a strong, unpleasant odor that filled her with disgust.

Cantar crawled under the barred door of the shed, dragging her full breasts in the dust. Morgan had dug out the space so it was just big enough for the bitch to enter to tend her babies, but he could still keep the shed locked. She crossed the distance between the shed and the barns, running hard and low and quietly. She gave no warning.

The boy's name was Sparks. Not even his friends, if that was what the relationships could be called, knew if that was his first name or last name or a nickname. He was tall and thin and unhealthy. His teeth were bad, and his skin was sallow. He was sixteen years old. He had never met his father and hadn't seen his mother in four years. He supported himself by stealing, and he got his enjoyment by drinking cheap whiskey until he slipped into oblivion. All Cantar knew was that he was on her territory and that he smelled evil.

She came up behind him as he worked with bolt cutters on the padlocked barn door. He hadn't heard her, so the shock almost outdid the pain when the bitch hit him in the small of his back. He was pushed into the barn door from the cannonball impact, and the collision with the wood split his cheek and broke his nose. But he didn't fall, and that perplexed the coydog. She backed off for an instant to study this adversary.

If there had been time, the boy would have been frightened.

As it was, his reasoning powers not being overly developed anyway, he reacted with animal instinct. He turned, so his back was braced against the door, and he gripped the bolt cutters firmly in his right hand. He raised his left arm protectively in front of his face. His lips curled back, exposing yellow, broken teeth. Blood streamed from his lacerated cheek, but he didn't seem to notice. A high pain threshold often accompanies a low mentality. It was difficult to determine who appeared more savage.

The shed, now devoid of protection, was the target for Spark's two companions. The ringleader and self-proclaimed brains of the group was a young giant. He called himself Crabs. He boasted of once having beaten to death an Indian girl from the Coeur D'Alene Reservation who gave him a dose of the little parasites—this when he was only fifteen. Nothing was ever proven, nor were any charges made because young women disappear from the reservation all the time and are never heard from again. They usually make their way to bigger cities to become prostitutes. But Crabs swore, even after three years, that he could still find the place where he buried the girl's body. Whether or not his friends believed his tale was of little consequence; they didn't dare dispute him. Besides his massive bulk and unmatched strength, Crabs was a monster, a dangerous, brutal psychotic. Cruelty was his ruling attribute, and not even his parents or his companions were immune.

The group's final member was a seventeen-year-old Indian boy. Crabs, who usually hated Indians, had met and taken a liking to the younger boy when he saw him in Rigsby's Pool Hall several months prior. Crabs admired his skill with the cue stick. When some of the local hustlers plotted to send this newcomer back to where he came from, Crabs came to his rescue. The boy had said his parents, both alcoholics, were dead. "I ain't running with no stinkin' Injun," Crabs had told him. "From now on, you're a Wop."

So Crabs took Wop home with him and instructed his thoroughly cowed mother and father that there was now one more mouth to feed. He even offered the young man the hospitality of his thirteen-year-old sister's bed, but Wop declined. "A faggot!" Crabs had spat, and the relationship almost ended there. But he thought of the money to be made in hustling pool and sneeringly acquiesced. "If I can pretend you're not an Injun, I guess I can pretend you ain't no goddamn fairy. You ever touch me—you won't have no pecker!"

The three—Crabs, Sparks, and the Wop—lived on petty thievery, pool -hall money, and what they could bully out of Crab's father's meager paycheck. They often talked about going to Spokane, but Crabs knew that in Lewiston, he was in charge. In Spokane, he feared his power would fall to a bigger gang. He had planned this raid on the Bloodstone Ranch, hoping for a big enough haul to finance a few weeks of riotous fun in the city. If things went well, maybe they would stay.

Crabs knew there were no hired hands on the Bloodstone. He knew the ranchers would be gone that morning, and he knew that the big dog that usually guarded the place would leave with them. She and the ugly guy were inseparable. He had flirted with the idea of pulling off the robbery at a time when Celia was there alone. She was pretty enough to make even that queer Wop want to take his turn with her. But it was too risky, and the ranch owner wasn't some Indian broad who could be used without anyone caring. He decided it was better to stick with tools and tack and small machinery. They could always be fenced. Then off to Spokane, where there were enough women to keep him happy.

"Wop, you can get under there. See if there's anything good, then we'll break the door down to get it out." Crabs was trying to talk the smaller-framed Wop into crawling under the door to the shed where Cantar's puppies were.

"Hell, man, are you crazy? That mother of a dog is probably in there. Her tracks are all over the place!"

"Don't be an asshole. You know she goes everywhere with that Kyles guy. Get under there."

Haltingly, Wop obeyed, because he knew if he didn't crawl under the door of his own volition, he would be stuffed under by his companion.

"What's in there?" Crabs called impatiently only seconds after he saw Wop's boot heels disappear.

"Tools and stuff. An air pump. Some welding junk." The reply was muffled by the thick door.

"Let me in. Hurry up."

There was a rattle of chains. "I can't, man. The bar is locked to the brackets." Then Wop unlatched and opened a window on the side of the shed. "You'll have to come through here."

It was a tight squeeze for Crab's 270 pounds. He was angry when he finally got inside. He hated to look ridiculous and usually compensated for his own folly or shortcomings by taking it out on the closest person around.

"Hell, this stuff is shit," he snarled.

"Crabs, you said Peterson wanted tools. He told you he could always unload mechanics' stuff."

He glared at Wop. "I said, this stuff is shit."

"It looks good to me. A lot of it looks new."

"What the hell do you know about tools? You Mr. Goodwrench all of a sudden?"

Crabs would have normally berated his companion a little while longer, then started dropping the tools out the window. They were good enough. But as he glared at Wop, he saw the nesting box in the corner of the shed. "Hey, look." He pushed by the smaller youth and walked towards the nest. "It's that dog's pups. Looks like a pile of rats."

Wop wasn't interested. He was only relieved that Crab's anger was diverted. Crabs picked up one of the pups in his hamlike hand. "Like a friggin' rat," he repeated. Then he began to squeeze the week-old baby. It made only one tiny whimper before the air was crushed from his body, and the bones of his rib cage crackled. Fluids dripped from his orifices, and Crabs threw the barely recognizable form to the dirt.

"Jesus, Crabs!" the astounded Wop cried. "What the hell did you do that for?" He was used to the cruelty of his bully companion, and he knew it would only anger him more, but Wop was sickened by the pitiful rag on the floor of the shed.

Crabs laughed. "'Cause they're rats. Here, stomp a rat." He threw another pup at Wop's feet. It hit the hard ground with a thud and squealed once before Crabs jumped towards it and smashed its fragile skull with his heel. Then he picked up the last puppy.

Wop couldn't contain himself any longer. He knew he'd pay horribly for daring to dispute Crab's authority, but he swung hard at the bigger youth. Crabs deflected the blow and, by hooking a foot around Wop's ankle, flipped the boy to the ground.

"You'll pay for that, little faggot." He had his foot on Wop's throat and was applying just enough pressure to let the Indian breathe. "Pretend this is you." He held the remaining whimpering pup in a giant paw and began to twist its blind little blunt-faced head in a circle. Wop could hear the snapping of the tiny bones and cartilage, and he felt the bile rising from his guts. He knew if Crabs didn't take his foot from his throat, he would drown in his own vomit.

Cantar sprang through the open window like a brown lightning bolt—growling and snarling in a mad frenzy. Almost three times her size, Crabs fell beneath her maniacal attack. Three bodies scrambled on the floor of the shed, each trying to gain their feet.

Cantar was the fastest. She ripped into the first thing she could reach, which was Wop's thigh. He screamed as she tore through the muscle, and he clutched blindly at Crabs for some sort of support. The giant seized the opportunity for escape and pushed the youth away. With speed belying his massive size, he crammed his bulk through the window, and it slammed shut behind him. He could hear his companion calling to him and the frenzied sounds of the dog.

Somehow, the boy managed to reach a heavy wrench on the bench close to him. He swung at Cantar's head. It was a solid blow, but the dog didn't relinquish her grip on his thigh. She ground her teeth even further into his flesh. With desperate strength, he struck again. This time, she staggered back a few steps and shook her head. It gave Wop precious seconds to save his life. In too much shock to feel the terrible pain in his leg, he climbed onto the workbench and then jumped for the rafters that supported the shed. Scrambling for a seat, the revived Cantar leaping and snapping at this dangling body, the boy called on the reserve of strength that comes in moments of complete desperation.

After a while, Cantar ceased her wild leaps. She seemed to know she could not reach the boy perched above her. She nosed her dead puppies. Tenderly, she put them in a pile and groomed their ruffled fur. Over and over, she returned to the pile, once even lying down and exposing her milk-gorged nipples to them. But they didn't awaken, and after repeated fruitless efforts, she kicked some dirt over the pile and returned to it no more.

Then she sat beneath the pale, weakening boy who clung to the rafters and lifted her heavy muzzle towards him. Mournful and low, the howl of grief poured forth until it ended on a quivering note that made the boy tremble. Drops of blood spattered on the dirt floor below him, and he could feel his grip on the rough wood growing weaker. Fear and pain and loss of blood were causing him to lose consciousness.

With the terribly tenacious patience of her kind, the coydog waited.

CHAPTER 5

"THAT'S FUNNY," said Morgan, giving the pickup's horn another sharp tap.

Celia laughed and slapped him affectionately on the knee. "You think all your women should come running when you toot your horn, Honey. I swear you're jealous of those puppies." She leaned over to kiss his cheek, then slid out of the truck. "I'm going to get changed, then let's take the two Mechling colts for a ride before it gets dark."

"Sure. Bring me a beer, will you?"

"Yes, dear," she answered happily as she walked to the house. Celia's mind was on the events of the afternoon, and she was already anxious to get started on their plan of action. She expected no trouble with either Jacob Anderson or Perc Ludwin. Jake did a lot of business with Indians, and rodeo was a sport where a person was judged solely on how well he competed. Race and social class seldom entered into it. As for Ludwin, there were few people with a more generous and charitable attitude towards his fellow man. The first committee meeting was scheduled for mid-June, giving Morgan and Celia time to prepare their publicity ideas and time for some feedback to trickle in from the reservations.

For the hundredth time, Celia wondered about that strange quality in people that makes them act one way as individuals and another when they are part of a group. Aside from a handful of die-hards, most of the club members showed no prejudice in their day-to-day lives. They dealt with Indians both socially and in business. But an Indian being invited to join the club or an Indian competing in the event of the year! Unheard of! And why? Not so much because everyone was dead set against it, but more because it just had never been tried. It just had never been done before.

Celia was convinced that, after an initial ruffle, their plan would be welcomed. She had that much faith in the basic goodness of her fellow members. She also felt that a merging of the two factions could do nothing but benefit the Appaloosa as a breed. And after all, wasn't that supposed to be the most important issue, the horses themselves?

"Celia!" Morgan's cry interrupted her musing. He sounded like thunder, and Celia felt a stab of fear. "Celia! Call the Sheriff!"

My God, she thought, *what can be wrong? What could make him sound like that?* She dialed the County Sheriff's office, and it seemed like minutes before anyone answered.

"County Sheriff's Office."

"Celia Bolt, Bloodstone Ranch. Could you send someone right away? I'm afraid we've got some trouble out here."

Celia could hear papers shuffled. "What's the problem, Miss Bolt?"

"Christ," she muttered to herself. "I'm not sure. We've been gone all day, and when we got back, I came into the house, and my partner stayed outside to check the livestock. He just yelled for me to call the sheriff."

"Do you think it's an emergency?"

"I don't know." Celia's voice rose in frustration. "I don't think he'd ask me to call if there wasn't a real problem. He's not the kind of man to panic. Please send someone—oh, my God!"

"What is it, Miss Bolt?"

"I just heard Morgan positively roar, and our dog sounds like she's killing someone! Please hurry!"

Celia threw the receiver in the general direction of its cradle and ran for the kitchen broom closet, where she kept her .30-30. There was no need to check; she knew the magazine would be full, and there would be a shell in the chamber. Morgan always told her, "If you're too scared to keep a gun loaded, you'll be too scared to use it if you have to."

Morgan's angry, unintelligible cries, all but muffled by Cantar's animal fury, goaded Celia toward the shed. A voice in her head kept pleading, *Keep calm,* but the panic infiltrated her shouts of, "I'm coming, Morgan."

She burst through the open door of the shed, her chest heaving from the frenzied sprint. Her rifle lay poised across her arm, but in the confusion of the violence that assaulted her, she had no idea where to point it.

In the rafters of the shed, beyond Morgan's reach, perched a pale, terrified youth. He clung to the main support with the same desperation with which a frightened child clings to its mother. His trouser legs were soaked with blood; blood smeared the boards he stood upon. His eyes were dazed with fright and pain and shock, and Celia knew he would tumble from his sanctuary soon enough.

Below him, leaping in a senseless, ceaseless fashion and bellowing as her powerful haunches propelled her to the zenith of her leap, was a crazed Cantar. Her face was bloodstained, as were her shoulders and back. Celia could see the churned, bloody earth below the boy—the smell of his life dripping from him inciting the crazed dog to even greater efforts.

And the most horrible sight of all, as animal crazy as his dog,

Morgan was drawing back his arm in preparation to throw a heavy hammer at the boy. Celia couldn't understand what he was shouting, and he wasn't aware that she was standing behind him. But she knew if he knocked the boy from his perch, Cantar would rip him to shreds.

Adding her voice to the din, she screamed, "Morgan! No!" and threw herself at his arm. Unrecognizing, he swung toward her, and for one terrible second, she thought he would strike her with the same violent strength aimed at the intruder. She didn't duck or flinch. She met his eyes unblinkingly. This was the same man who had made love to her so tenderly this morning, and now he was trying to commit murder!

Morgan lowered his arm. His face did not soften, but his shoulders slumped noticeably. He snarled a command at Cantar, and the dog quieted. She stood below the boy, her hind legs quivering from the exertion and her red tongue lolling over her porcelain teeth.

Morgan tossed the hammer to the ground, and as she followed its fall with her eyes, Celia saw for the first time the small pile of ravaged pups. She looked up at Morgan and then at the boy, weaving precariously. "What in God's name is going on?" she whispered.

Morgan took the rifle from her clenched fingers. She no longer feared he would turn it against the boy, although after viewing the violence against the puppies, Celia understood why he would want to. He wrapped his arms around her, and Celia, as she pushed her head into his hard shoulder, swore she could feel a sob shudder his frame. Was he sickened by this act of cruelty, or was it the terrible act he would have committed if she had not stopped him? He held her until the Sheriff arrived.

Cantar had to be locked away in a secure box stall when the authorities got there. The strangers, the recent taste of blood, and the savage events of the day had all left her highly agitated. Morgan feared she would lose control and someone would get mauled. She ceased her barking and replaced it with long-drawn howls, the eeriness of which made everyone a little more tense in an already too-tense situation.

The Sheriff radioed for an ambulance as soon as he saw the condition of the boy, and while they were waiting for it, they tried to talk him into descending.

"Look, son," said Roy Gilberman. "What you've done and what your punishment might be isn't the question right now. You're in tough shape, and we better get you to a doctor. You lose much more blood, and you won't live to see a judge."

"No way," the boy answered weakly. The defiance had long since drained from his voice. He looked directly at Morgan and added, "He'll kill me, man." Then with the last of his strength, "I don't want to die."

Celia turned to Morgan. "Maybe you had better leave, hon. He's scared to death of you, the poor kid."

"Poor kid! Celia, that 'poor kid' is psycho! I just buried those pups. Maybe I should dig them up for you to take a better look!" Like that of his dog, Morgan's anger was a time bomb, and his presence was hampering progress. "Okay, I'll leave." He shook off Celia's comforting hand and stormed from the shed.

Sheriff Gilberman found a ladder and propped it up against the bloodstained rafter. Wop didn't attempt to pull away, nor did he fight when the Sheriff eased him to the ground. All the fight had gone from the boy. With Morgan and Cantar both gone, he was willing to surrender.

Half-delirious, he babbled to the Sheriff, "I don't care what you do, just keep that dog away from me." Then his eyes flickered and started to roll back into his head, but as he sank heavier into Gilberman's arms, he saw Celia's face. Concern? Was she really concerned about him even after what she believed? Why should she care? With his last words, before he sank into unconsciousness, he said to her, "Lady, I didn't kill those dogs. I tried to stop him. Jesus, lady, I couldn't have done that."

Celia followed the ambulance to the hospital and, while the boy was being admitted, pressed formal charges against him. Since he carried no identification, the Sheriff merely listed him as:

John Doe

Male, Am. Ind.

(?)Approx. Age 16

Gilberman felt confident that he could find some background on the boy and if he had any accomplices. He was charged with criminal damage to property, trespass, and malicious mischief. Celia shuddered at the thought of the mangled pups. Somehow, "mischief" just did not fit the bill.

It was past dark when the paperwork was finished, and Gilberman told her she could leave. The doctor had refused to let anyone question the prisoner until morning, so the proceedings ground to a halt. From the pay phone in the courthouse, Celia called Morgan, who sounded every bit as tired as she.

"I've got a pot of stew cooking," he told her. "Hurry home, babe. I love you."

As she drove through the night, she couldn't help remembering the boy's words, the pleading in his voice when he told her he hadn't hurt the dogs. "I tried to stop him," he had said. There had to have been someone with him.

Morgan's stew was delicious, and she enjoyed the meal, much to her surprise. Bone-tired and fuzzy-headed from the many and varied events of a too-long day, Celia still savored the rich, meaty fare. What a marvelous man she was in love with. On top of everything, he could cook better than she could!

"I guess I went a little crazy today, didn't I?" he said quietly as he dished Celia seconds.

"I don't blame you. That was a pretty savage scene you walked in on."

"That's no excuse for losing control like I did. Celia, I would have killed that kid if I'd gotten ahold of him. Or worse yet," his voice dropped even lower as he sat back down in his chair, "I would have let Cantar finish him off, and that's no way for anyone to go."

"Honey, don't beat yourself over the head for something you could have done—but didn't." She lay down her spoon and walked around the table to encircle Morgan's shoulders with a comforting hug. "It's over now, and everything's going to be all right."

BUT EVERYTHING WAS NOT ALL RIGHT. From the bowels of the night came the mournful howl of the one who had lost so much that day. The howl of a coyote can express so many moods. At times, it is an explosion of joy and comradeship. At other times, it communicates with a mate or hunting partner. But the meaning of Cantar's grief-wracked cries was unmistakable. No, everything was not over, and it was *not* all right. She had lost her family, and she meant to have her revenge.

Morgan stiffened in Celia's arms. "A hell of a way to go," he repeated.

"Morg." Celia cuddled her head into his neck. "That boy. He wasn't the one who hurt Cantar's pups."

"What do you mean? How do you know?" Morgan twisted around, so he was looking directly into Celia's eyes.

"When we got him down out of the rafters—Morgan, he was really hurting. At that point, I don't think he cared if we sent him away for life. He was barely conscious. But just before he passed out, he looked me right in the eyes, just the way you're looking at me now. He said, 'Lady, I didn't kill those dogs. I tried to stop him. Jesus, lady, I couldn't have done that.'

It was an effort to get that out, but he held on until he told me."

"So, he's innocent by his own testimony?" Morgan shrugged and turned away. "I thought you had some real evidence."

"That's real enough for me. I can't get it out of my head—the sincerity in his voice. It's like he didn't care what else we thought about him, except he wanted me to know that he wasn't capable of that kind of cruelty. There was someone else with him, someone who *was* capable of such a thing. I'm going to the hospital tomorrow and talk . . ."

"No, you're not!" Morgan came to his feet angrily. "This thing has upset us enough already. Let Gilberman take care of it. That's his job. Yours is to run this ranch. You're not a social worker for some renegade dog killer. I'm going to bed. Are you coming?"

Definitely not the time to discuss anything logically, Celia thought. "I'm coming," she said. "As soon as I clean up the kitchen." But to herself, she added, *I won't have time before going to town in the morning.*

CELIA LEFT for the hospital while Morgan was doing pasture chores. She knew he would be angry but decided she would rather fight him about it when she got back, hopefully, armed with some information.

Sheriff Gilberman had not arrived yet, and it took Celia's most charming smile to gain admission to the boy's room. He had regained some color, his face no longer the ghastly pale Celia had last seen. His black eyes were belligerent, and his mouth a sullen line. *He could be a really handsome boy if he didn't look as if he had a vendetta against the whole world,* Celia thought.

His injured leg was elevated slightly, and under the covers,

Celia could see the swath of bandages wrapping it. “No wonder your room isn’t under guard,” she said lightly as she sat down in the straight-backed visitors’ chair. “You couldn’t get anywhere on that bum pin.”

She got no response, only a deeper frown.

“But then, maybe your buddies could spring you. Steal a wheelchair and wheel you out of here.”

“I don’t have buddies, lady.”

Celia dropped the light, bantering tone and drew closer to the boy. “Then who was the ‘him’ you told me about last night? The one you tried to stop? Who was he? You’re right. He can’t be much of a friend if he left you there—maybe to die.”

“Well, I ain’t dead, am I?”

Defiance, hatred, scorn—how could anyone so young develop such an attitude? “No, son. You’re not dead. And you can thank me for that. I saved your skin last night, so I feel you owe me a few answers.”

“I don’t owe anybody.”

Celia paced across the room, then whirled on the boy. “Listen, you little creep. I’ve never laid eyes on you in my life. I’ve never done one thing to hurt you. But you break into my place, destroy my property, and upset my life. In my book—you owe me.”

The boy set his jaw and turned his face.

A real tough guy, Celia thought. “Why did you have to kill those pups? How sick can you be that you’ve got to torture some defenseless creature in order to make yourself feel good?”

“I told you, lady. I didn’t touch those damn dogs. I ain’t some kind of a freak.” The boy sighed in exasperation. “Listen, that friend of yours with the hammer last night. I mean, he was one scary dude. But lady, what he was going to do to me ain’t nothing compared to what’d happen if I squealed. I ain’t stupid, lady. I wouldn’t be around today if I was that stupid.”

“No. You’re real smart. That’s why you’re in a hospital bed

with your leg chewed to pieces and a jail sentence waiting for you when you get out of here."

"But I'm still breathing. That'd stop real soon if I told you what you wanted to know."

"The police could protect you. I'd drop the charges against you if you'd testify."

"Police! Jesus Christ, lady, you think they'd care? If I got wasted, I'd be just one more dead Injun."

So that's it, Celia thought. She had seen so many young Indian people turn sour on the world, using the excuse that the white man never gave them a chance, so they wouldn't have to try. She'd seen them turn to drugs and alcohol and crime, always claiming that they were forced to it by an uncaring white society. But she had also seen people like her friend, Sybil Horn, and plenty of other Indians who succeeded in life and were proud of their Indian heritage. She knew the burn-outs were weak and probably would not have made it no matter what color they had been born. And for some uncanny reason, she felt this boy did not belong in that class.

"Where are your parents?" She felt a new line of questioning might be more in order.

"I don't have any."

"Oh, come on now. Everyone has parents—unless you're a mushroom."

"Huh?" For just a second, the boy dropped his reserve, and a true look of puzzlement crossed his face.

"Didn't you ever study biology? You know—mushrooms are a fungus. Reproduce by spore. They just sort of appear."

"I didn't get as far as biology." The sullenness had returned.

"Okay, here's an easy one. What's your name?"

"Al."

Celia was jolted for a second. She really did not expect an answer to any of her questions.

"Al, my name is Celia Bolt. I hope you already knew that. I'd feel terrible if you decided to rob my place and didn't even bother to learn my name."

"We knew your name. We knew a lot about you. We were even thinking about hitting the place when you were there —alone."

This is some sort of a test, Celia thought. *Play this right, and maybe I won't lose him.* Looking very calmly into the boy's defiant eyes, she said carefully, "I don't think you would have taken part in anything like that, Al. I don't think you have that kind of brutality in you."

Al lowered his gaze and said tiredly, "Lady, you don't know anything about me."

"I know your name. And I know you're an Indian and, for some ungodly reason, you think that's a crime. And I know you dared to challenge someone you're terrified of in an attempt to save that litter of pups. I think that for having met you just last night and under very adverse circumstances at that, it's quite a lot to know about you."

The boy did not answer. He continued to look at the bare hospital wall. Then he said, very quietly, "I'm sorry. I'm sorry we picked your place to hit, and I'm sorry I couldn't stop him from wasting those pups, and I'm sorry I can't tell you anything more."

"Can you tell me who your folks are? I'm sure they're worried about you."

"My folks are past worrying. Dad left when I was five, and Ma drank and screwed herself to death before I was thirteen. I lived with my grandma for a while, but she got so nutty she didn't know who I was sometimes. One night, she tried to stick me with a hunting knife, so I left. I can't tell you anymore, lady. I really can't."

Celia reached out to touch his shoulder. "Al, I'd really like to help you. You may think I'm just some bleeding heart, a do-gooder, but I have my reasons. Someday, maybe I'll tell them to you. But for now, I'd just like to say I'm willing and able to help you out. All I want from you is some cooperation. You don't have to tell me who your friends are; you've just got to try to cooperate."

"How? What do I have to do?"

"I'm not sure yet. I have to make a phone call first. I'll be back shortly."

Celia started to leave, but Al's call stopped her. "Lady, I sure don't know what you've got in mind or why you'd want to help some dumb Injun kid. I've never trusted anyone in my life, and I can't say I trust you now. And I'm warning you—no matter what I promise—you better not trust me."

There was no threat in his voice, and his face was devoid of the earlier sullenness. In its place was an earnest and honest appeal, a need to be listened to. And, perhaps for the first time in his life, someone was actually listening.

CELIA TAPPED HER FOOT IMPATIENTLY. She hated being put on hold, being treated like a mere client when she was actually a friend. *The secretary should know me by now,* she fumed to herself.

Finally, the familiar voice came over the phone. "Hi, Celia. What can I do for you?"

"Hi, Mike. I guess you heard we were burglarized last night?"

"Yeah. Heard it on the morning news. They didn't steal my horse, did they?"

Celia laughed. She remembered the day J. Michael Peadot had tried to buy Bloodstone Ranch from her, and the many times that he had made good his promise to be her friend. He had purchased two horses from her over the years and currently had one in training.

"No, Mike, they were only after quality merchandise." The gelding Celia was training for the lawyer had been acquired elsewhere. "Anyway, the reason I'm calling is about the break-in. We've got one of them—a young Indian boy about sixteen. Cantar caught him, and I guess it goes without saying he's in the hospital now."

Peadot grew serious. "Kid's lucky he's not in the morgue. I tell you, Celia, that animal's a liability."

"Come on, Mike, stick to the point and lecture me about liabilities later. I need your advice on the best way to handle this thing. I think I want you to defend the boy."

"What?"

"He's so young, and I have a feeling he's been kicked around all his life. He has no family. If I press charges and he's convicted, they'll send him someplace where he can really learn to be a criminal. It seems like such a waste."

"Then why don't you drop your charges?"

"Because then he'll waltz away from this scot-free and just go out and do it again."

"Celia, I'm not really sure why you called me."

"I want to know if I can follow through on the charges and have him released into my custody."

Mike sighed. "You're serious about this, aren't you? Does Morgan know what you're planning?"

"No. I haven't discussed it with him yet. But I know he'll go along with it. He's a real champion of the Indian cause, you know."

"I bet. You know this kid isn't some horse you're taking on to train. If he's sixteen or seventeen years old, he's probably been leading a life of crime for ten years—if he's like most of the Indian kids around here."

"Michael, you haven't even met the boy. You're just putting

him in a neat little category before even giving him a chance. I tell you, there's something different about him. And don't you forget—I'm a damn good judge of character."

"Okay, okay. I also know that you're stubborn as hell, and you're going through with this no matter what anyone says. So, why don't I save myself a lot of trouble and just give in now?"

"Now you're talking, Mike. I'm going to contact Sheriff Gilberman and see when we can meet with him. I'll call you back."

Celia started to dial the county sheriff's office but hung up the phone when she saw the big man walking down the hospital corridor.

"Miss Bolt. I'm a little surprised to see you here."

"I guess I may as well tell you now, Sheriff. You'll find out soon enough. I got the jump on questioning your prisoner."

"The Indian boy? Did you find out anything?"

"A little. And I didn't even have to use brutality."

"Well, ma'am, I'd tell you most anything you wanted to know about me, too, without too much arm twisting."

There was a brief silence while Gilberman looked for some response from Celia, but she only looked at him with that same friendly smile she greeted all men with. There wasn't much of the flirt in Celia Bolt, only a sincere charm that brought most men to her assistance. "I didn't do so badly for myself, either. I'll buy you a cup of coffee, and we can compare notes."

Seated in the hospital commissary, Gilberman curled his big hand around the Styrofoam cup. "I talked to the Russell Fulkersons this morning. It seems our boy lived with them for the past several months. He was a friend of their son Ted, but they didn't know much about him. They said he called himself Wop, which sounds like a pretty stupid name to me."

"Did you get a chance to talk to Ted?"

"No, but I've had a few run-ins with Ted in the past. Big, mean kid. Hangs out at the joints down on Mendell Street.

That's where he met Wop hustling pool. Anyway, he and another boy left for Spokane last week, and his folks haven't heard from him since. As far as I'm concerned, that one can stay in Spokane.

"The Fulkersons were a pretty pathetic couple; they seemed scared to death, and I'm sure half of what they told me was lies. They said that this Wop kid was staying there still, and they were afraid to tell him to leave. Then there was some talk about their thirteen-year-old daughter and a statutory rape charge."

"Did you talk to the daughter?"

"Nope. She was somewhere else, too."

"Sounds like sort of a vague family."

Gilberman laughed. "Vague is right. But I wouldn't count on any kind of testimony from them. They're obviously really frightened of that boy."

"Sheriff, I've talked to the boy. I didn't get too much out of him other than his folks are dead, and he was living with a grandmother until she went off the deep end and tried to kill him. And he's scared of something, too—or should I say some*one*? I'm willing to bet it's the same someone that's got the Fulkersons spooked."

Gilberman smiled patronizingly. "You're quite a police woman, Miss Bolt."

"Oh, not really. I just recognize a victim when I see one."

Gilberman drained his coffee and rose. "I think I better go question that poor victim myself."

Celia rose, too, and said hastily, "Is there a chance I could talk you into holding off on that questioning?"

"Not hardly, ma'am." The patronizing note was gone from the Sheriff's voice. He was getting a little annoyed at the woman, pretty as she might be.

"But he won't tell you anything. He's a tough character, and even if you try to scare him, I think he's more scared of what will happen to him if he talks.

"Look, little lady. Do you know what 'obstructing justice' is?'

"Sure, but I'm the one pressing charges, so it seems to me that I would have some say."

"It seems to me, Miss Bolt, that you should do your job and let me do mine. You called me, remember?"

"You've got me there," Celia conceded.

"Right. And it's not just your complaint. There's been an increase in petty theft and break-ins in the county over the last several months. I'm not going to let a possible suspect ride 'cause you suddenly feel sorry for him."

Celia waited outside the door while Gilberman conducted his inquiry. She could hear the Sheriff's voice, although she couldn't quite make out the words. As the questioning continued, she could hear his muffled tones grow louder in volume and angrier—much angrier. Not once did she hear Al respond. Maybe it was because his sneering words were not loud enough to reach her ears, but it was more likely that he just wasn't answering.

Twenty minutes later, Gilberman burst through the door. "Are you still here?" he exploded at Celia.

"Sheriff!" hissed a nurse. "This is a quiet zone, and I'll thank you to keep your voice down."

He clumped angrily down the hall. Sheriff Roy Gilberman was beginning to wish he hadn't gotten out of bed that morning.

Celia hurriedly ran after him. "What did you find out?"

He shot a disgusted look at Celia over his shoulder. "You know what I found out. Nothing. Not a goddamn thing. It's like talking to a corpse, except a corpse's eyes are blank, and that kid's got more hate in his eyes than I care to think about. We'll see how eighteen months in the county juvenile farm sets with him."

Celia did not feel as if it was the proper time to propose her plan, but she held her breath and blurted, "Sheriff, I've talked to my attorney, and he's willing to defend the boy. I want to have him released into my custody."

That stopped the big man cold. He slowly turned around and stared at Celia in disbelief. "Miss Bolt," he said carefully and icily, "you are insane—and I'll never allow it."

"If you fight me on this, I'll drop my charges, and you won't have anything to hold him on." *That's a mistake,* she thought the second the words left her mouth.

"And I'll have you cited for harboring a vicious dog, and I'll see you pay every penny of that bastard's hospital bill."

Now there were two nurses and a doctor converging on the arguing pair, hushing them threateningly.

"Look," Celia began again at a much lower decibel level, "why are we fighting each other? We both want the same thing."

"I'm not so sure about that. I'm beginning to wonder what it is you *do* want."

"Well, look at it like this. If we do it my way, you won't have to appoint an attorney for the boy at the county's expense, and you won't have to pay for his keep for the next year and a half in an institution where he can only learn to perfect his illegal techniques. If he's in my custody, he's off the streets, he'll be learning a trade, and if I can gain his confidence, we might even find out who his buddies are. That's what I want, Sheriff Gilberman. I want the person or persons who were responsible for that terrible act of cruelty at my place last night locked up somewhere where they can't hurt anyone anymore. I want the person responsible for the kind of fear that Al and the Fulkersons are feeling put away."

Gilberman had listened very quietly. "You just might find out more than you want to know," he said. "They may show up late one night armed to the teeth to finish the job—and you better not come crying to me when they do, Missy."

"Does that mean you'll go along with my plan?"

"That means I still think you're nuts. How are you going to control him, keep him on your ranch?"

"Do you remember that big guy with the wild look in his eyes last night? The one that was all for knocking the kid off the rafter with a brick and feeding him to the dog?"

"Sure. Kyles."

"He's my foreman. He's the law on the Bloodstone Ranch, and the dog is his deputy."

Gilberman sighed deeply. Was there a note of defeat in the sigh? "Who's your attorney?"

"Mike Peadot."

"Good God. I couldn't afford that guy if I was on trial for my life."

"We're sort of friends," Celia repeated sweetly. She could afford to be sweet; she knew she had won.

"Never again," Gilberman vowed. "Never again will I try to figure out a woman." He abdicated. "Okay. Have Peadot at my office after lunch. We'll work out the details." With a final shake of his big hands, he walked away from Celia.

Now to get Al to agree to this and to call Mike and . . . Before the sheriff was even out of sight, Celia was already scheming up a way to break the news to "the big guy with the wild look in his eyes."

CHAPTER 6

"LET'S get one thing straight. My name is Celia Bolt. Not 'Lady.' Call me Celia, or Miss Bolt, or ma'am, or even 'Hey You!' But I have a nineteen-year-old broodmare named 'Lady,' and we don't resemble each other in the least."

Al's expression did not waiver; he was a study in disinterest. He wore a new denim work shirt, and his new blue jeans were split at both seams to accommodate his bandaged leg. He sat on an upturned bucket in the tack room, his crutches on the floor beside him and his leg stretched out in front.

"So, what am I supposed to do with this shit?" Casually, the boy lifted a jumble of heavy work harness with his foot.

"Let's get something else straight. I'm no prude, and sometimes my language is pretty ripe. But I know how to talk correctly in correct company. I have a feeling you've mastered my first talent already, but not the second. I want you to practice cleaning up your mouth, especially in front of ladies."

"I thought you weren't a lady."

Was there just a hint of a twinkle in Al's somber eyes? Could it be this was becoming banter and not just outright spiteful defiance? Celia certainly hoped so. *God* how she hoped, because the last week had been hell, and she desperately needed a ray of hope.

Morgan had been livid when Celia proposed her plan. He had shouted threats and thrown curses just thinking about the boy. Then he began a torrid inquisition of Celia's motives. Was she having an attack of White Man's Guilt? If that was the case, there were plenty of Indian kids around who could use some help. Ones without a history of crime. Or maybe she was having motherhood desires. Maybe all these years claiming she did not want a family, that her work and her horses and Morgan were enough for her, had been lies. Well, if that was what she wanted, a child, Morgan could certainly help her out. He had grabbed her to him roughly, and Celia had slapped at him. They did not sleep together that night.

In the morning, Morgan had voiced the cruelest theory of all. Perhaps she was grooming his replacement. After all, the boy was good-looking and not much younger than Celia than she was than Morgan. He had said, "You always tell me you like to get them young and break them to your needs."

"My God, Morgan! I was talking about horses!" she had screamed in shocked rage.

"Horses. Lovers. What's the difference? You hold both of them between your legs. But I'm warning you, Celia. Don't try to squeeze too tight; you might get spilled."

Morgan had not pulled his highest trump; he had not said he would leave if the boy came to the ranch. Celia held herself in tension every time they spoke for fear he would confront her with such an ultimatum. But for the past few days, they had spoken only a few words to each other. The lack of companionship left an aching void inside her and gave her time to think.

Celia found that not even she could define her intentions clearly. She had told Al that she had her reasons, but what were they?

Morgan had been wrong when he suggested guilt was her

motive. Gratitude was closer to the truth. Years ago, Bloodstone had helped a lonely young woman and made possible for her a life she now held as precious as a jewel. But if she wanted to help someone to in some way repay Bloodstone, why pick this wild, irreverent boy who held everyone in contempt, including his own mother and himself?

There was more to it than that, more than she had ever told her old mentor, Bloodstone, or even Morgan. They did not know of the wealth and position that had been Celia's prison just as surely as this Indian boy was trapped by the poverty and despair of his once-proud heritage. Still, there was more, and this was what puzzled Celia. Morgan's claims of maternal instinct and the indecent sexual reference had hurt her deeply, but they had not held one drop of credibility. She had a "feeling" about the boy. How do you explain "feelings"? One afternoon, Celia even thought of having Pauline Sire visit the boy's hospital room—but she never called the woman.

Then Al was actually and legally released into her custody for a period of eighteen months, and her period of quiet reflection was over. In its place was frustration—total and complete. Morgan spoke to her even less and began sleeping in the barn in the room that was intended for Al. Al, equally uncommunicative, had to sleep on the living room couch as he and his crutches could not yet navigate the tiny, twisted stairway that led to the cabin's loft. Celia found herself lying awake all night, unaccustomed to sleeping alone and, to her disgust, fearful of the stranger she had fought so hard to bring into her home.

The most frightening component in this nightmare of conflicts was Cantar. Morgan had promised to keep the coydog in control. He did this not out of concern for the boy but out of a sense of flagging self-pride. With the rest of his world crumbling, it was the last power he felt he had left. As soon as Celia brought the boy home, Morgan ordered him out of the truck. Fighting hard to control his terror, Al stood motionless while

Morgan walked around him, touching him and saying to the menacing creature at his side, "Ours, Cantar. Ours." He looked the boy in the eyes and explained, "She won't hurt you." Then added with icy clarity, "Unless you give her a reason."

On this, the morning of Al's second full day on the ranch, Celia decided to put him to work. A heavy harness had lain in a crate in the tack room in tangled disarray since Bloodstone's days, and Celia wanted it cleaned and conditioned. She also decided she was not going to coddle the boy any longer, and the first thing she would put an end to was his infuriating habit of calling her "lady." She had not bargained on attacking his street language in the same conversation, but as it turned out, it was not such a bad idea.

"You're supposed to take it apart, unbuckle all the buckles, and start working this oil into it." She handed him a quart container of neat's foot oil. "By the time it's supple enough, you'll be supple enough to learn how to put in on a horse."

Al looked less than thrilled. "Maybe I'll send it back to the reservation and have all the old squaws chew it for you."

Was this an attempt at humor or a cynical slander of Indian life? Celia wished she could quit analyzing every word he said and quit choosing hers so carefully. The tension was destroying her. "I see you're not as ignorant of Indian customs as you claim to be."

He shrugged.

"Well, if you need me, I'll be within earshot. We're halter-breaking foals today. Oh, by the way, in your spare time, I want you to read this." Celia pulled a thin paperback book from her vest pocket and handed it to Al.

"What's this?"

"It's called a book. I know you didn't get as far as Biology, but you did learn to read, didn't you?"

"I can read; I ain't a dummy." Begrudgingly, Al held his hand out to take the book.

"I know you're not. That's why I want you to read this. You're going to be working on this place for quite a while, so you ought to learn a little about these animals you're working with."

"*Know The Appaloosa Horse.*" It would have been impossible to read the title with any less emotion in his voice. "A horse is a horse."

"Have you ever ridden? Were there any horses on the reservation where you grew up?"

"You've got to be kidding. The only horse I've ever been close to was in my grandma's stew pot."

"I'd like you to read it. Not all horses are alike."

Celia turned to leave, hoping she had gotten the last word, but the boy said softly, "Neither are all Indians." It was the same quiet tone he had used in the hospital when he told her not to trust him.

The sadness in his voice touched Celia deeply. She did not turn back to face him; she did not want him to see the emotion in her eyes. "Neither are all whites," she said. She got her last word.

MORGAN WAS UNSADDLING a chunky gelding at the barn when Celia found him. The roan was breathing hard, and steam rose from his shoulders and haunches into the nippy morning air.

"Charlie got fat and lazy over the winter, didn't he?" she said lightly.

Morgan scowled as he pulled the heavy saddle off of his horse and swung it onto the corral fence. A nosey filly inside the corral grabbed the stirrup leather in her teeth. Morgan flung his arm angrily and yelled at the little horse. As agile as a fawn, the filly spun on her hind legs and whisked back to her friends.

There was a wild splash of color in the corral—thirteen foals, all yearlings and no two alike. Morgan had spent the early morning rounding them up from their winter range, several hundred acres of tough mountain pasture land. Although they had been handled since their birth, a winter of freedom had sparked their spirits, and they were as fleet and elusive as the prong-horned antelope who sometimes shared their graze. Morgan, Cantar, and Charlie had put several hours' hard labor in to bring them to the home corral. But once inside the fences, the yearlings calmed. This was their home; most had been born within sight of the ranch house, and they had never been given reason to fear it.

For the next few months, the foals would stay close to the ranch. They would learn the simple lessons of babyhood. Once again, they would be taught to submit to the halter and lead rope, stand quietly when tied, and be mannerly during grooming and hoof care: in general, how to behave like the proper young creatures they were bred to be.

Then they would learn new lessons. They would be introduced to the lunge line. Their reckless racings over the winter range would be reduced to easy, flat-footed walks in an endless circle around their trainer. They would feel weight on their backs for the first time, a thick pad held in place by a snug surcingle. And, perhaps the most important lesson of all, they would learn the meaning of "whoa." No matter where they were or where they were headed, at what speed, or in what frame of mind, when these babies heard the command, they would learn to stop.

A horse's mind is not complex, and he is not capable of much intelligent thought. He is prone to panic and, like all highly gregarious animals, he is a great one to follow the leader, even if the leader is heading over a cliff! But if he is taught a command and taught it completely, particularly a verbal one, it will reach him even through his otherwise scrambled, frightened brain. In times of terror, the familiar command will calm him, for a horse is more comfortable with obedience than chaos.

All these things the young animals would learn through patience and kindness. It was Celia's way, and it had become Morgan's. So Morgan could not miss the disapproving look Celia flashed at him. But she held her tongue. "I see Flora is just as curious as ever," she said instead of the rebuke that had wanted to come out.

"Don't start on me, Celia. I'm in no mood."

"I didn't say a word!"

"You tell me my horse is getting soft. Is that supposed to be a compliment? 'How nice, Morgan. You and your horse are growing old together.'"

It was going to become an argument, after all. The only way she could prevent it from being a full-scale shouting match would be to turn her back and walk away. But there had been too much of that already. Too much silence. Too many of the wrong words and too few of the right ones. She was not going to back down, but she also did not know what the right words were. She loved this man, but she had no idea how to reach him.

"I've done me a day's work already, boss-lady. This old man's going to town."

Then there was no time for words. With a resounding smack on the rump, Morgan sent his horse into the stall, and then he was gone. The pickup roared into life and spun down the lane, Morgan at the wheel, punishing the machine with a heavy foot and hand.

He knew if he had stayed and tried to work the yearlings, he would have punished them, too, perhaps done more damage in one session than a lifetime of kindness could heal. He hated himself when he acted like this. Words came out of his mouth without control. It was like there was a terrible stranger inside him, forcing him to say and do hateful, hurting things.

As he jammed the truck into high gear, he knew he had to come to grips with this stranger. He had to find out who he was and why he would not leave. He would find this out today, or he would not come back.

CELIA SPENT the day on the verge of tears. She kept herself busy with the yearlings, but she could not keep her mind off of the morning's conflict with Morgan. She spent at least thirty minutes with each foal: haltering it, handling it, grooming and picking up its feet, and leaving it tied until she caught the next one. Flora, the black filly with the white blanket, had kicked her in the thigh when she tried to pick up her off hind foot, and Celia had allowed the pain to bring the tears coursing down her cheeks.

She took a break in the early afternoon and fixed Al and herself sandwiches. The boy had been working hard on the harness, but Celia said nothing as she interrupted his labor to serve him lunch. She did not know how much of the argument he had overheard, but he was the last person she wanted to discuss her troubles with. To tell the truth, he *was* her trouble.

Celia took two bites from her sandwich. It tasted like cardboard. She fed the remainder to Cantar, who consumed it greedily. She either liked the taste of cardboard, or the problem was not in the roast beef on rye but in the dry, angry lump that lay in Celia's throat.

At 5 p.m., Al crutched over to where Celia was working. He quietly watched while she groomed a solid-looking horse colt. She picked up each of his feet in turn, softly crooning all the while. The colt obviously enjoyed the attention and spent a good deal of time nosing Celia's hair while she was bent over. Finally, she took the halter off and shooed the friendly foal away. She turned to Al. "Yeah?"

"I got that thing all tore apart. I sure hope you can put it back together again."

"I can."

"And I took all the silver stuff off and shined it up."

"Uh-huh." Celia was making no effort to communicate.

"Some of it may need another dose of oil tomorrow. It soaked it up like a kid with a soda." The boy looked down at his hands, half disgusted with the grime that had worked into his skin and half surprised that he had actually done an honest day's labor with them. "Can I have some more of that roast beef for supper?"

"Sure. I won't be eating. I've got some more work to do out here."

"I bet you wish you'd never seen me, don't you?"

Once more, the tears started to spill. Celia bit her lip hard. "Right now, yes. That makes me a real bitch, I know."

Al shrugged. "Doesn't bother me any. Can I clean up?"

"Al, this isn't a prison. You don't have to ask permission to take a shower or have a glass of milk. Treat this place like you would your own. That means with respect, okay?"

"I got it. Make sure to put the toilet lid down, hang up my towels, and wash my dishes, right? I may have been born in a tipi, but I'm not a slob." He was grinning.

Celia smiled too, and for the first time all day, she did not feel like she was going to start crying. "I'll be up in a while, and maybe you can save me one slice of the beef."

Much to Celia's surprise, Al turned out to be a chef. When she came in after chores, she was hit at the door by a delicious aroma that wiped away all doubt about whether she was hungry or not. She traced the fragrance to two pans simmering on the stove. One held three slices of roast beef, paper thin, covered with a rich-looking mushroom gravy. Celia fished out a plump mushroom and popped it in her mouth, savoring the delicate flavor of the sauce. The other pan contained sliced carrots in butter, which Celia also sampled without the aid of silverware. She found the note just as her stomach was beginning to rumble.

> *Hey you, I didn't think you'd mind if I used these mushrooms.*
>
> *They don't have any parents, you know. – Al*
>
> *P.S. Don't call the cops. I just went for a walk. Sorry your old man is crazy.*

Celia folded the note and glanced around the kitchen. It was as neat as a pin, and so was the bathroom, as she found out when she went to draw herself a bath. A clean, dry towel hung on the rack, and the tub sparkled. "Well, I'll be damned," Celia said out loud. As she poured a capful of bubble bath into the steaming water, she added, "Just when you think things have hit rock bottom, you get a break." She lowered herself into the foamy tub and continued her monologue. "You had better not be conning me, kid."

The meal was as delicious as it smelled. She was cleaning up her dishes when Al walked through the door. "Hi," Celia greeted lightly. "Where did you learn to cook like that?"

To her despair, Al was back to his usual sullen self. "What's the matter with you? I've been gone two hours. I could've walked right off this place."

Celia's hands stopped their movements. Poised over the sink, they dripped suds into the dishwater. "I guess that never occurred to me."

"Well, it should have. I'm not one of your ponies, you know.

You can't pat me on the head and feed me some sugar and expect me to follow you around." The boy was trying to work himself into anger.

"I don't believe this. You're actually mad at me because I trusted you! That's ridiculous!"

AL'S FACE TWISTED. Inside him, a battle was raging. He wanted to say something cruel to her; he wanted to hurt her. But the hate, his longtime ally, was deserting him. And that scared the boy worse than anything else. "I'm going to bed," he said, finally. He limped off to the living room, his body tired and his thoughts confused.

He lay awake long after Celia had turned off the lights and made her way up to the loft. When her restless tossings and turnings ceased, and he was sure she was asleep, he crutched to the kitchen. He opened the refrigerator door slightly; he wanted a beer. He had not had any since the six-pack he and Crabs and Sparks had drunk the morning before they hit this place. They would not give him any in the hospital.

Earlier, there had been two cans of Olympia. Celia must have had one with her supper. *And she left one for me,* Al reasoned. He reached for the can, and his hand trembled—just slightly. "God damn it," he swore softly. He licked his lips; the old fears chewed at him. They sank their fangs into his mind with more tenacity than the big dog had savaged his leg. "God damn it," he said again, and his slender hand closed over the can.

He squeezed his eyes tightly shut. Why hadn't he left today? He'd had plenty of opportunity to just hike off. And why had he found himself whistling as he worked on the harness? And why had he left that stupid note? Why? What the hell was happening to him? For the third time, he swore to himself. Then he released the can. As an afterthought, he grabbed a jug of milk, poured himself a large glass, and drank it all without taking his lips from the glass. Then he went back to his couch.

Al was not sure of the time, but he had been soundly asleep for several hours when he heard Morgan's truck pull up. The big man let himself in and walked quietly to where Al feigned sleep. He shook the boy with surprising gentleness and whispered, "Get up, kid. Hate to change plans on you in the middle of the night, but you're sleeping in the barn from now on."

Al rubbed his eyes. "Huh?"

"Come on. There's blankets out there already. You can make it real homey tomorrow." All the while, he was shoving clothes and crutches at the boy.

Finally, Al's head was cleared of the slumber webs. "Oh, I get it," he said, his arms full of clothes.

"Yeah," said Morgan, a touch menacingly. "You get it. And you say one more word, you even blink funny, and you'll be wearing these crutches. Got that?"

Al slipped into his shirt and pants and, carrying his boots, left to claim his room in the barn.

CELIA COULD SMELL the whiskey on Morgan's breath. Morgan seldom drank whiskey; it altered his moods too much. She shuddered and pulled the covers more tightly around her. *One of three things happens when he drinks whiskey,* she thought. *He gets sad, he gets mean, or he gets horny. Well, if he thinks he can waltz into my bedroom after treating me so cruelly all week and just hop on like everything's all right . . . and with that boy downstairs listening to the whole thing! That'd really boost the old drunken macho ego.*

She could see his long, lean frame as he bent over, taking off his clothes, and in spite of herself, the familiar desire began to take over. Her hands relaxed on the sheets. *No way,* she kept on thinking, but she watched as he stepped out of his jeans. *Jesus Christ, Kyles!* she screamed at him silently. *How could you accuse me of calling you soft? There's not one thing about you that anyone could call soft . . . except maybe your head.*

And then he was beside her, the smell of the whiskey stronger but his words gentle. "Honey, I know you're awake. I sent the kid out to the barn. Can I get in with you?"

She did not trust herself to speak; she did not want to give in too quickly. She nodded her head.

"Is it okay . . .?"

That did it. Her heart melted. That night five years ago, he had stood at the foot of her bed. Bare-footed, bare-headed, bare-chested—the first time she had seen him devoid of his cowman's garb. "Ma'am, I know this is kind of sudden, but is it okay if I make love to you?"

She rolled up on her elbow. Her face was only inches above his, her hand on his stomach, her fingers beginning to explore the bristly forest of his hair. "It's okay, Morgan." He was back in her bed. They could make everything good again.

"No," he said, still soft and gentle. The whiskey was not putting the words in his mouth; it was just giving him the courage to say them. "Is it okay if we *don't* make love? I've got to talk, and I can't let it get all mixed up with the way you make me feel when we're loving." He touched her cheek with a cupped finger, then eased her into the crook of his arm. He took her hand and placed it on her own stomach. "Be a good girl and let me say my piece, and don't interrupt. Then if you still want me . . ." He left his words hanging for a moment before continuing.

"I've been a real varmint these past few days. I've been mean to everything and everyone I've come across. When I left here today, I was scared, Celia. I could have hit you this morning. Do you know how close I came? I pushed my horse and those babies harder than they deserved. It's just luck they're all okay. But I guess I don't have to tell you how awful I've been. What I do have to tell you is why. I was jealous, babe. I was jealous of that boy and the way you took to him. He's a thief and who knows what else, and it made me mad that you'd bring him here and put the ranch and yourself in danger. And I couldn't think of why you'd do such a crazy thing, so I made up reasons that'd hurt you. Then I started believing them myself."

He was quiet for a few minutes, and Celia thought he had finished. She stirred in his arms.

He began again. "I was no damn good, Celia. When you met me, I was no damn good at all. I ran out on a fine woman. The only thing she ever did wrong was to get herself knocked up by a restless cowboy and then try to turn him into a hardware salesman. I left her with two kids to raise while I bummed my way around rodeos, and if I did make any winnings, I pissed them away instead of sending them home to her. I crossed my friends and treated all women like whores. I couldn't even keep a horse. I had a good little bulldogging pony about eight years ago. I won top money on him at Scott's Bluff, then I holed up in a motel room with two broads and a case of bourbon and forgot to water him. I left him in the trailer in the Nebraska heat for two days." Morgan's voice cracked, and he put a large hand to his face.

"Please stop. I don't care . . ."

"No!" It was the closest he had come to shouting. "I'm going to finish. I want you to know just what kind of slime I was. I didn't have any friends left. Maybe I never turned thief like your Indian boy, but I was no better. Then I met you and came to work here. You didn't preach at me or try to tell me how rotten I had been. You just smiled that cute little-girl smile at me, handed me a pitchfork, and said, 'Let's get to work,' and I did. I didn't change because you asked me to; I changed because you figured I was a good man already, and I couldn't disappoint you.

"You got that way about you, Celia. People and animals both want to please you. And unless he's a whole lot badder-assed kid than I was a bad-assed rodeo bum, that boy will come around, too. And you're not helping him out for any reason other than you're the best God-damned female that God ever made. I know that for a fact, and I'm mighty proud to share your bed. I ain't saying I'm going to fall all over that kid from now on, but . . ."

Celia's hand was on his mouth. Her fingers crept back on his stomach and resumed their interrupted search. "Morgan," she whispered. "Please me. Please me now."

AL DID NOT MIND the barn. The cot was more comfortable than the couch had been, and he liked the feeling of privacy. There was a Dutch door that opened up into the alleyway of the barn. The top half was open, and Al found he liked the sights and smells and sounds he was exposed to.

There were three mares stalled in the barn. They were all in the final stages of pregnancy, a fact evident even to Al. The boy could hear them moving their swollen bodies restlessly around their stalls, grumbling softly to themselves. Occasionally, one of the yearlings in the outside corral would whinny shrilly, perhaps questing for the freedom it had enjoyed just a short while ago. Each time, it would be answered by a deeper, more mature whinny from a short distance away.

Al could detect the calm wisdom in the horse's voice as it comforted the youngster. He could not help but think of the idol of his own childhood, his Uncle Franklin, who had never tired of his adoring nephew's constant barrage of questions. To the difficult ones, or at least the ones that were too difficult for a five-year-old to understand the answer to, Uncle Franklin would always reply, "That's just the way it is, kid." Uncle Franklin—a red man killed by a yellow man while fighting a white man's war. But maybe he was out there, telling a frightened baby to take it easy because "that's just the way it is."

Al shook his head. He must be getting goofy, comparing his uncle to some stupid horse and putting words in their mouths, to boot. That milk must have screwed up his head worse than a bottle of cheap wine would have. Still—maybe Celia was right. Maybe all horses weren't alike.

Almost against his will, he picked up the book she had given him. He had folded it over and stuck it in his jeans pocket that afternoon, so it was still with him. He laughed scornfully as he studied the cover of the thin paperback. A stern-looking Indian sat astride a greyish horse, and both he and his mount were bedecked in their finest regalia. *There's a white man's Injun for you,* Al thought. *Who is that dude?*

He flipped through the first few pages until he found the text explaining the cover photo. *Jesse Redheart, great-grandnephew of Chief Joseph*. Once again, he emitted a scornful laugh. *Chief Joseph and the Nez Perce. All my life, I've heard about the great Chief Joseph. The only thing we're famous for is getting beat.*

But despite his sarcasm, he read the first chapter on Appaloosa heritage. Before Al fell asleep in the early morning hours, he had digested two remarkable ideas: horses could be just as different as people, and the Nez Perce had accomplished a lot more in the course of history than just being defeated.

CHAPTER 7

FOR THE SECOND time in less than a day, Celia was having a meal cooked for her. She awoke to the smell of coffee and the sound of Morgan clanging and lumbering his way through breakfast preparation. He sang an Ed Bruce tune at the top of his lungs, and Celia thought it was the most beautiful sound she had heard in days. *He's murdering that song, but God, it's great to hear him happy.*

He interrupted himself to yell up the stairs, "Better get on down here, Cel. My world-famous frijole omelet is about done. And you best come dressed since there'll be three of us for breakfast."

The meal was a complete success. Al, though not loquacious, was also not his usual sullen self, and he went a long way toward gaining Morgan's respect by asking for extra salsa picante for his omelet. When the dishes were cleared, and everyone was lingering over their final cup of coffee, Al even instigated some conversation.

"Those young horses that you've got in the corral—what's going to happen to them? Do you start riding them now?"

Morgan almost choked on his coffee. “Boy, you are green, aren’t you?”

Celia hastened to the boy’s rescue, but there was no need. Al bristled slightly, then gained control and said evenly, “Yeah, I’m green. And I’m never going to be anything else if I don’t ask questions.”

Morgan sobered. He shot a raised eyebrow look at Celia. “That’s fair,” he conceded. “Those thirteen little ones out there, they’re all yearlings—one year old or close to it. On this ranch, we don’t climb on a colt’s back ’til it’s a good two years old. Even then, it’s still a baby. It’s still growing, and its bones aren’t set yet. We won’t work a horse hard until it’s a four-year-old and full-grown.”

Celia cautioned, “You’ve got to watch it, though. Remember that is the Bloodstone Ranch philosophy of horse training. If you go telling people these practices as if they were gospel, you’ll get hooted at.”

“Why?”

“Because a lot of ranchers think it’s silly to wait that long,” Morgan said. “Sid Dutchens, he’ll rein or cut with a three-year-old. He’ll win all he can on them and not care if they’re crippled up by five. And he’ll breed a two-year-old filly if her bloodlines are good, but her confirmation stinks.”

“I don’t think I understand. What’s rein and cut?”

“I think you’re jumping the gun a little, Morgan,” Celia said. “We shouldn’t be indoctrinating Al in our practices until he knows the terminology.”

Morgan sighed. “I was just getting warmed up.”

“He never misses a chance to lambaste Sid Dutchens. He’s our neighbor to the east.”

“And if you’re lucky, you’ll never meet him. Now, to get back to the yearlings. We’re going to keep them close for a while. We’ll try to work them every day and get to know them. All the horse colts, that’s the males, will be gelded. You know, castrated. That is unless there's one or two that look like they have breeding potential. In my opinion, a stallion's only good for one thing, and we've already got our herd sire on this place. I don't like riding one, and I don't trust one."

"Please note," Celia interjected, "he said 'opinion.' There are people who ride stallions competitively and even for pleasure, and they swear by them."

"I got off-track again, didn't I?"

"Just a little." Celia was so pleased with the easy conversation that she hated to interrupt, but she wanted Al to know the difference between fact and personal opinion.

"Anyway, after the gelding, we start taking a real critical look at the babies. We like to keep out a couple to show. Sometimes, there's a bunch of them that's show material, but with just Celia and me to do the handling, you can't campaign too many head. We usually end up selling half of them as gentle yearlings well into their education. They're the culls, the rejects. Although most of our culls are better than some people's prime stock."

"Is that opinion?"

Morgan gave the boy a narrow-eyed stare. "Calvin Trueblood says you're one hell of a pool player. Is that opinion?"

Celia perked up her ears. So Morgan had been talking to Calvin. That must have been interesting.

"I don't know Calvin Trueblood, but he must know me. That's a fact. I'm better with a cue stick than most. But I don't play anymore."

"He said you and some fat buddy of yours about got yourselves killed at the Cigar Store in Mockonema a few months back. Folks in that town don't take kindly to being played for suckers. It's one thing to have talent and use it to best others in a fair contest, but it's another to pretend you're something you ain't in order to take their money."

This is it, thought Celia. *Will he fight back, or will he take it?*

The boy's eyes blazed. His hands curled tightly around his coffee mug. "I said I don't play anymore."

It was Morgan who broke eye contact. "Good decision," he said gruffly.

Celia's hand touched his knee and squeezed him affectionately. She knew the gruffness was all for show.

To play pool, you've got to have good hands," Morgan continued. "Quiet, light, sensitive but strong. You must have good hands."

Al loosened his grip on the mug and stared at his hands. "I never thought about it."

"To be a good horseman, you've got to have good hands, too. You want to be a horseman, kid? Or do you just want to put in your time here and then go back to—whatever?"

Al had expected trouble from the big man or resentment. He'd never expected these overtures of friendship. He stammered, "I—I don't know."

"Well, you finish up with that harness, then come on down to the corral. Even with that bum leg, you can help work the yearlings. We'll see if you're cut out to be a horseman or not."

When the boy left, Celia drew a long breath and then said, "I love you, Morgan Kyles. You are the best man I've ever known. But what's this about talking to the Truebloods? When did you do that?"

"Yesterday. I was feeling so bad about myself that I went over there. I figured the only person I knew with a worse opinion of me than I had was Calvin."

"Calvin doesn't think you're such a bad guy—for a white man, that is. So, what did he say?"

"That he knew of the kid, and he'd seen him around some of the pool halls in Colfax and Mockonema. He and this big mouthy kid tried to hustle Springer Jones one night, and Springer just nearly took both of them apart."

"The mouthy one, that'd be Ted Fulkerson. If you're looking for the monster who killed Cantar's pups, I'd say he's the one."

Morgan grunted. He did not want to be reminded of the incident. It was enough that he was giving the boy a chance; he did not have to forgive him, as well. "I also talked some business with Calvin. I told him about your idea to bring some reservation people to the show this fall. As expected, he thought the idea stunk. He doesn't want to compete against those people any more than they want him to."

Celia was disappointed. She had hoped for a different reaction. "But," Morgan said with a grin, "being the persuasive fellow that I am, I changed his mind. There's just one stipulation. He wants an endurance race added to the competition. He says most of his people can't afford $200 show halters and $1,000 pleasure saddles and fancy outfits. The contest events are fine with him, he feels they stand an even chance, but he wants one event that really puts the Appaloosa in the 'ancient limelight.' I swear that's the exact words he used. Sometimes that guy talks funnier than Perc Ludwin."

"I suppose he means something that calls on the same abilities of the Appaloosa that made him so popular with the Indians."

"Yeah, that's what he meant. And since we couldn't have a buffalo hunt as part of the show bill, I picked up a couple of books on the sport that explain the rules and judging and how to set up an endurance ride. I don't think it matters if it's sanctioned or not. What do you think?

"I think you're fantastic."

"Not so fast. I'm going to let you approach the club with the idea, and I have a hunch they won't be as enthusiastic as you."

"I can sell it to them," said Celia confidently. "What else did Calvin say while you two were getting drunk on his whiskey?"

Morgan actually blushed. "He said you were the only good

white woman he ever met, and I had better get my ass home and apologize to you."

"Now *that* is one smart Indian. And I sure liked the way you apologized."

Morgan returned the friendly knee squeeze Celia had given him earlier that morning. "Let's get to work before that young buck has all our colts broke for us."

"And I sure like the way you're treating Al. Thank you for helping him."

Morgan frowned slightly. "I'm not helping him, Celia. I still don't trust him, and I'm not sure I even like him. I'm giving him a chance to help himself."

"That's all he needs."

They went to work.

AL'S first day as a horse trainer was a miserable failure, at least to his way of thinking. He was kicked twice and got his toe bruised by a sharply stomped little hoof. Towards the end of the day, the spirited filly, Flora, managed to get her lead rope twisted around Al's crutch and then bolted, sending him flying. At that point, the boy was ready to quit, but Morgan chided him. "Look, kid. These are just babies, and they've just come off of the range. They're not wild, but they miss their freedom. It ain't personal; they ain't kicking at you because they don't like you. It's the restraint they're kicking at."

"But it's me that's getting hurt personally," complained Al as he struggled up on his feet and regained his crutch.

"Well, right now, you're not your most agile. In another day or two, you'll be getting along on that leg a little better, and you can dodge."

"Oh, come on, Morgan," Celia said. "In another day or two,

none of these babies will even want to kick. These are sensible, well-bred animals, Al—and I wouldn't give a nickel for one that didn't show any fight, but I wouldn't keep one around that didn't respond to gentle mastery. And I'll tell you, the best of the bunch is that little filly that just spilled you." Flora was now picking her way back to the people, stepping carefully so as not to trip herself on the lead rope. "She's full of good sense and spirit, and there isn't a mean bone in her body."

Al picked up the dangling lead rope and talked quietly to the mincing filly. "Easy, little girl," he said as he stroked her black neck. "I'm not afraid of you even if you did try to kill me, so don't be afraid of me."

Morgan and Celia fell back and busied themselves with another yearling; the boy's conversation was private.

"She says you're the pick of the lot, and you're going to settle right down and behave yourself and forget all about being free." The filly flicked her ears to catch the soft murmurs. She pressed closer to the boy, enjoying the gentle caresses, and let her head droop. "Is that right? Would you give up so easy?"

As if answering, Flora suddenly threw her well-shaped head in the air and barely missed hitting Al on the chin. Once again, she jerked the lead from his hands, burning the unprotected flesh as the rope slipped through his grasp. Whinnying shrilly, the filly raced to the fence, pulled up at the last minute, and stood tensely, expectantly. The other yearlings rushed to join her. Cantar, momentarily forgetting her sulking, self-appointed vigil over the Indian boy, ran in circles around the babies, yodeling excitedly.

"What the hell!" Al cursed, nursing his smarting palms.

"Damn," swore Morgan. "I'll bet it's Folly. Must be a fence down somewhere."

The words were no sooner out of his mouth than a lithe horse sprinted over the small hill. He paused for a moment, enjoying the commotion his appearance was making, then galloped hard at the fence. He slid to a stop, his chest lightly pressing on the boards, and lowered his head to greet the mobbing yearlings.

"We won't get any more work done today," said Celia. "Not with Uncle Folly here. Let him in with his babies, and we'll take him back out tomorrow and find the break."

Morgan opened the corral gate and whistled. The red horse responded immediately, galloping around the corral and slipping gracefully through the opening. He was short, not much taller than most of the yearlings who crowded around him. They nipped at his neck and haunches and dipped their heads to mouth his legs. They lightly rose in the air to box with him.

He was the color of a copper penny. Most of his winter coat had shed, and he shone in the late afternoon sun. But unlike the corral full of yearlings, he was a solid color. He had no white blanket, no white spots, not even a flecking of white, save for the thin blaze that traveled down the center of his small but excellently chiseled head. Al knew that whoever this newcomer was, he was no stranger, yet he was different from every other horse on the ranch.

Morgan grumbled about the inconvenience and set about putting brushes and halters and lead ropes away. Cantar resumed her slinking watch over Al, who did his best to ignore the coydog. Celia, not as upset as her partner, clapped Al on the back and said, "Come help me do chores, and I'll tell you about our visitor—Uncle Folly."

Uncle Folly. Could this have been the comforting voice of last night? That gentle whinny that brought to mind his own beloved uncle? Al pushed the thought from his head. He was really getting silly about these animals. He was going to have to watch himself.

Celia started the chores in the barn: graining, watering, haying the pregnant mares, and picking out their stalls. She examined each one for signs of impending labor. All the while she worked, she told Al the story of the red horse, with occasional interruptions to instruct the boy on one task or another.

"You haven't met the lady that started this whole thing rolling. Her name's Baby Box, daughter of Chico's Medicine Box. She was my first horse, a present from the man who built this ranch. Here, rinse out these water buckets, then fill them. You can hook the hose over there. When Baby was four years old, I bred her to our old stallion, Sir Pepper Pot. A year later, Folly was born, not a speck of white on him except for his blaze. Sometimes an Appaloosa grows into its color, but not Folly. He'll be five on the thirtieth of May, and you saw him. His registered name is Chico's Folly, the only mistake my mare ever made. Every foal out of her since then has been as flashy as a pimp's Caddie."

"I've never been lucky enough to see one." Al carried the first water bucket back to her.

"I'll hang them back up. These ladies are a little grouchy this close to foaling. Anyway, that's pretty flashy. Chico's Fluorescence, Flora, is her last year's foal by our stallion, Conquering Joseph. Folly's beautiful as far as performance, intelligence, manners. Did you see that sliding stop? And how quickly he came to Morgan's whistle? And he's well-built if you want a horse that's just barely a horse. He's only 14.2, the breaking point between a horse and a pony. That's just fifty-eight inches at the base of his neck, the withers. He's got all the Appaloosa characteristics except the color. So, he's pink-papered."

Celia noticed Al's furrowed brows as he handed her the second bucket. "Read the book; it'll explain. We broke him and trained him, but we couldn't show him, and I couldn't bear to sell Baby's first colt. So, he became our resident 'nanny.' When we wean the babies and turn them out on the range, he runs with them. He protects them and shows them how to get through the winter. He leads them to where we put hay, and if a really bad storm comes up, he brings them to the barns. Usually, when we bring in the yearlings in the spring, he runs with the two-year-olds for a while, but he's always been real attached to his little sister, Flora, and I guess he found a gap in the fence, so he came to see her."

"I heard them calling to each other last night. Here's the last bucket. Do you ride him at all?"

"Thanks. Not much. Hand me that pitchfork, will you? We have enough to do to ride the horses in training. We don't have time for pleasure rides. He's very gentle, and we usually put inexperienced people on him because he takes such good care of his riders. We'll run him back out with the two-year-olds tomorrow. He can stay with them for a while. In a few weeks, we'll know which yearlings we want to sell and which ones we want to keep out to show. The rest will go back on the range for another year's growth and another year of Folly's tutelage." The last few words were muffled as she was squatting practically underneath one of the brood mares. Celia stood up and eased her back with her hand. "This one's time is about here. The wax on her teats has softened, and she's dripping milk."

"When will she have her baby?"

"Amiga, here, is a strange one. Most mares will foal within twenty-four hours after coming into their milk. She's always held them. It might be two more days before she foals. We'll keep an eye on her, though. Will you fill the stock tank for the yearlings? The hose'll reach. Morgan and I have to ride those two colts for the Mechlings. They're picking them up day after tomorrow."

"Sure."

"Then I'll make you a deal. You can clean up first, which means you get first crack at the hot water. Better soak a while to take the sting out of the kick you got. *If* you'll throw us together some supper. I've got plenty of talents, but cooking has never been one of them, and you did such a good job last night. I'll even do the dishes."

Al was wrestling with the hose. “That sounds fair to me. What do you want to eat?”

“Up to you. There’s a full pantry. And while you’re at it, you might look through the freezer and see about defrosting something for tomorrow night?” Celia lifted her voice, making the last statement more of a question.

“I don’t mind cooking. It’s one of the few things I’m good at.”

Celia turned back to the mare. “By the way, you did well today. Even Morgan was impressed. It’s not so bad, is it, Al?” She did not want to see his eyes. The day had gone so well; she did not want to ruin it by seeing his dark eyes flash with scorn.

But the boy answered cheerfully. “It beats the hell out of prison, even if I have this dog stepping on my heels. Come on, Warden.” He limped out of the barn, dragging the green hose and whistling for Cantar, who slunk along behind him.

AL SORTED through the cans on the pantry shelves. He had a flair for creating interesting dishes, and he was truly happy when working in the kitchen. Cooking gave him the same feeling he once got from playing pool, back before he had to learn to “lose” convincingly.

His mother had taught him how to make delicious meals out of next to nothing. Dotty George used to talk about her days at the reservation school, how she stood at the stainless steel range in her freshly starched apron, her gleaming black hair neatly braided, stirring a pot of nutritious stew or kneading bread dough. She was in love with Samuel, the best basketball player in the school, and they were going to get married when they graduated. They were going to build a house and have a family, and she was going to be such a good wife and mother and homemaker. She would show him the book, the one her Home Economics teacher gave her for being tops in her class: *The Complete Betty Crocker Cook Book,* hardbound.

She would tell him these things, her words slurred and thick. Her dull eyes would close when she tried to remember those days. Her hair was no longer neat, her clothes no longer clean and pressed. Her face was bloated but her body frail, almost emaciated. The young Al would follow her directions or, as he grew older, read the simple recipes in the book and fix their only meal of the day. "It's good," his mother would say, but she could eat only a meager amount, spilling even part of that down the front of her greasy dress. Then she would turn to the homemade wine, the "firewater" she laughingly called it, that the men would bring her at night when Al was supposed to be asleep.

Yes, she and Samuel had married two weeks after graduation. How happy they were, how ablaze with hopes and ideals. But there was little call for a good basketball player, no work for her man. So she had to cook and clean in other people's houses, and care for other people's children. When Al came along, she only took a few weeks off work. Even so, Samuel was angry about the doctor's bill. "Why couldn't you go out in the field and drop it? That's what the old ones used to do," he had said.

She started back to work before she should have, but hers was the only income. Samuel would watch his infant son during the day, taking him to the smoky pool halls where he spent his time. But in a few months, Dotty lost her job. People complained she was getting sloppy and not moving the furniture to clean underneath. When Samuel found out, he severely beat her, causing her to bleed from her womb. They could not afford another doctor's bill, so Dotty healed at home. She was never the same after that. She lost all her strength. Dotty and Samuel George had no more children.

Al found himself grasping a can tightly as if he was about to throw it. Why was he thinking about them now? Just when things were starting to look okay, why was he picturing her in his mind?

He read the label. Pink Salmon. How about salmon stew? That was one of his grandma's specialties. Except she made it with mackerel but still called it salmon. A couple of times, she used salmon cat food, but if you didn't think about it, it tasted just fine. He remembered the recipe well.

He put some potatoes and carrots on to boil and drained the salmon. He picked out the little round white vertebrae and peeled the dark skin from the pink flesh, and laughed sardonically as he thought of his grandma's reaction to such wasteful behavior. She could never afford to throw away the bones or the skin. "They all add flavor," she would rationalize to the boy.

Al placed the waste on a tin plate and opened the kitchen door. Just as he thought, Cantar waited there. She growled softly as he presented the treat to her. "Have it your way," he said as she sniffed the present warily and then pushed the plate away with her nose.

When the vegetables were tender, Al made a paste of the salmon liquid and flour and thickened the vegetable broth. Then he broke the fish into chunks and added it, a can of peas, and some milk to the pan. He seasoned his creation and set the burner on low to keep it warm.

Al turned to the refrigerator once again. To make a meal out of soup, you had to have a good salad, too. He found half a head of lettuce, a green pepper, and an avocado. Wouldn't his grandmother have gone nuts over these supplies? The very thought of fresh vegetables out of season! He threw the greens together and grated some cheese over the top before tossing it a final time.

To complete the meal, he needed some good, heavy bread. Al looked through the cupboards and cabinets and in the pantry, but all he could find was a loaf of commercial white bread. "Fluffed up sawdust," his grandma would have called it. There wasn't time for anything fancy, but he could whip up a loaf of beer bread in a few minutes. Without all the fuss and bother of raising or kneading dough, he'd have a delicious loaf in just a little over an hour. It was also one of his grandma's favorite recipes. He could remember Dotty saying, "Make mine without the bread, Ma," then laughing as if it were the funniest thing she's ever said, no matter how many times she had said it.

Al mixed flour, salt, baking soda, and sugar together. Morgan must have brought a case of Olympia home because the refrigerator held ten cans of chilled beer where there had only been one last night, and the opened case was on the floor of the pantry. Al opened one of the cans and poured it over the flour mixture, making a puddle of suds. He cracked an egg into the liquid, mixed the egg into the beer, and then stirred the whole bowlful together into a sticky dough. This he poured into a loaf pan and set in the oven. He stepped back with an air of finality. Supper was prepared; he was ready for a hot bath.

He put his mixing bowl in the sink and ran a little water in it. He picked up the beer can to throw it away and heard the slosh of liquid. Out of habit, he tossed down the last swallow, grimacing at the warm, bitter taste.

That was how his father had drunk beer, warm, out of quart bottles. The Georges didn't have a refrigerator, and beer was cheaper by the quart. Al lifted the can to his lips a second time. It was empty, and he scowled. How clearly he could see his father, sitting in their only living room chair, pouring beer into a glass while he hummed quietly to himself, bringing the glass to eye level and peering at the amber liquid, then emptying the contents in slow swallows. The longer he sat, the slower the process became until he fell into a heavy snoring slumber.

Al had crushed the empty beer can without realizing it. Just as unconsciously, he pulled the tab on another can. Yeah, that was how Samuel George had spent his days, drinking warm beer and talking to himself, and falling asleep. That was all Al remembered about his dad except for those times when he would disappear for days, Dotty would cry a lot, and the living room seemed empty, as if someone had taken the furniture away. And he remembered him coming home again and how he would yell at him, and how he would hit Dotty and make her cry even more. And he remembered how he went away one time and never came back, and Dotty and Al took their chairs and their cots and the rest of their worldly goods and moved in with Dotty's mother—Bess Aspenleaf.

Al realized he had crushed another beer can and dropped it on the floor. He stared at the crumpled waste; he did not even remember finishing the second beer. He was going to stop. He was going to lie in a hot tub and let the steam drift these bad memories away. What was it his Grandma used to say? Steam purifies. Bess was always saying stuff like that, talking about the Old Ways. Al used to get pretty sick of it, although he did love his grandma. But what good did it do to talk about the Old Ways? They were gone, and if there ever was any truth in them, it was gone, too.

He bent to pick up the can but instead took a third one from the case. In a dreamlike state, he watched himself open it and take a reluctant swallow. It was an insult to his taste buds, a bitter gall that filled his head with bitter memories. He saw his mother getting ugly and hard. Saw her taking up his father's vigil in the old chair. Heard her voice turning mean. Felt the slap of her hand when he did not get out of her way fast enough. He remembered the men who would come to the house who talked too loudly and laughed too quickly—laughed at all the wrong things. He remembered saying to Bess Aspenleaf, "You're her mama. Can't you make her be good? Can't you make them stop coming here?" And then that can, too, was empty, and he poured another.

He remembered when the men stopped coming, when Dotty George became too sick to laugh with them. That was when they had to eat cat food and pretend it was salmon. He remembered the night he found her in her cot. The blankets were soaked with blood; the mattress was soaked with blood. After she was gone, Bess talked about the Old Ways more than ever.

Al's head was starting to ache. He felt beads of sweat on his face. His stomach churned; he was dizzy. He tried to pick up the cans. How many were there? Didn't matter. No one would notice a few missing beers.

He staggered across the room, tripped, and caught himself on the countertop. He had staggered that night. The night he had come home drunk for the first time, and Bess Aspenleaf had come at him with a butcher knife. There had been a weird light in her old eyes. She had called him by his father's name. She had sworn at him. "You turned my daughter into a whore!' she had screamed. Al had run from the little shack. He ran and never returned.

He could not run now, not even if his life depended on it like it did that night. His legs were rubbery. "Shouldn't drink warm beer," he admonished himself. "It'll make you drunk too fast. That's what did it. I'll just have a cold one. That'll clear my head. Just one more. No one will notice."

"M-M-M-M. SOMETHING REALLY SMELLS GOOD."

"Cel, honey, looks like we may have hired ourselves a first-class cook. Christ Almighty, I swear that smells like fresh-baked bread!"

"Al! Hey, Al!"

Morgan grunted slightly as he pulled his boots off. "He's probably in the tub. The kid worked pretty hard today. I'll bet he's tired."

Celia lifted the lid from the pan and inhaled. "This smells

like some kind of fish stew. And that *is* a loaf of bread in the oven.

"Want a beer, hon?"

"No thanks. I'll have a Coke if you'll fix it for me."

Morgan opened the refrigerator door. "Looks like our boy Al isn't so straightlaced. There's a couple of beers gone."

Celia pouted her lips a little. "I rather doubt that drinking is within the rules of his parole. He is only seventeen."

"Ah, a beer or two after a hard day's work never hurt anyone. These Indian kids start drinking booze as soon as they get off their mama's tit."

"Yeah, and half of them are serious problem drinkers by the time they're Al's age."

Morgan sobered a bit. "You're right. Why don't we have a talk with him? I don't see anything wrong with a beer for supper, but no more. Okay?"

Still frowning, Celia crossed the room. "I don't know—" Her foot hit something metallic. Glancing down, she saw the trail of discarded beer cans. "Morgan, I think Al might be a member of the half with the problem. There are six empty beer cans on the floor. He didn't even bother to throw them away!"

"Al!" Morgan yelled. Then more quietly to Celia, "Go look in the living room for him. I'll check the back."

She heard Morgan's angry bellow not a half-minute later. "God damn little bastard!" Then some splashing and Al's feeble protests, and more splashing and muffled, watery responses.

Celia sighed a troubled sigh. It was going to be a long, uncomfortable night.

CHAPTER 8

"MR. KYLES! MR. KYLES!" The voice was high and scared and excited.

Morgan bolted upright in bed, instantly awake. The covers fell from him, leaving his chest bare. Beside him, Celia stirred and murmured softly, "What is it now?"

It had been a long, uncomfortable night. She had not fallen asleep until after two a.m., and now, with the first grey streaks of dawn beginning to light up the window at the foot of the bed, she was being rudely awakened. The intruder was Al, and as Celia gathered the blanket up around her naked shoulders and tried to wrestle free from the peaceful hold of sleep, her first clear thought was that she wished she had never begun this crusade.

Yesterday, when it finally looked like the three of them were going to be able to get along, Al had gotten unconsciously drunk and almost drowned in the bathtub. There had been a lot of yelling and accusations, followed by Al's thick-tongued denials that he was drunk. Morgan had ended up hauling the boy, still insisting that he'd had only had one beer, out to the barn and dumping him on the cot to sleep it off. But here he was again, like a bad penny, standing at the foot of their bed and robbing them of what little sleeping time there was left.

Suddenly, none of that mattered. "It's the mare, the one you called Amiga. She's trying to have her baby, and she's got trouble!"

Morgan leaped out of bed and grabbed his jeans. Celia was not far behind, unmindful of her nakedness. As she slipped into a flannel shirt that had been hanging on the bedpost, her thoughts raced. *Horses can put on a pretty good show when they're foaling. There's probably no need for alarm. The kid's never seen a foaling before; how would he know if there's trouble?* Still, she said, "Morgan, you go with Al to the barn. I'll call Doc Mac."

Morgan was already pounding out the front door, and Al was maneuvering himself carefully down the staircase when Celia's phone call made connections. "Waha Vet Service," answered the still-sleepy voice.

"Hi, Julie. This is Celia Bolt. Sorry about the early morning call, but we've got a mare in trouble."

"You're not the only one this morning. Harold's up in Potlatch. Uterine prolapse in one of Halber's prize Simmentals. O.B.?"

"Yeah. Morgan's checking her out now. I'll call back with a little more information after I talk to him."

"Okay. I'll get Harold there as soon as I can. Get her up and walk her. That'll delay the foaling."

"Thanks, Julie." Celia hung up the phone and finished dressing hurriedly. For just a second, she let herself reflect on the dedication of Dr. Harold McClutchan and his wife, Julie. They were no strangers to being jerked from their beds at all hours of the night. Emergencies were their daily fare, and Celia hoped that this particular case turned out not to be an emergency.

By the time Celia got to the barn, Morgan was rinsing his arms in a bucket of water. Dressed only in jeans and boots, his bare chest and arms goose-pimpled with the chilly dawn air, his teeth chattering, he had a look of hopeless vulnerability about him. He shook his head sadly. "Not good, hon. Its head is tucked under its body and between its front legs." He indicated the straining mare on her side in the stall. "She's fatigued herself, but there's no way in hell she can push it out."

At that moment, the mare was seized with a contraction. Her vulva dilated, and Celia caught just a glimpse of two tiny hooves. Amiga grunted and lifted her head from the straw. Her white-rimmed eyes started from their sockets; her lips pulled back from her teeth in pain. The contraction relaxed, her head fell heavily to the straw bed, and she heaved with exhaustion.

"Jesus! Can't you do something for her?" Al said. His face was pasty. Celia wondered if it was the aftereffects of the previous evening's drunk or the sad plight of the helpless mare causing the near-hysteria in the boy.

Morgan was briskly rubbing his arms with a gunny sack. "Is Doc coming?"

"He's in Potlatch. He won't get here for at least another hour."

"Great. I can't get the little bugger into position. About the only thing that'll help her now is a cesarean."

"Let's get her to her feet. Al, grab her halter. Morgan, help me. Maybe if we force her to walk, we can delay the labor until Doc gets here."

"We're not going to delay anything. Labor's too far progressed."

Celia yelled angrily, "What the hell do you want me to do? Just sit here and watch her rip herself to pieces? Get her up!" She slapped the mare on her sweaty haunches. "Get up, Amiga. Come on, ol' girl."

With much shouting and pushing and pulling, they got the mare to her feet. She staggered, her knees buckled, and she tried to go back down. Morgan slapped her, forcing her to walk. Celia went to Amiga's head and urged her on, but the mare was in too much pain to respond to her masters' voices. Gripped with the next contraction, her yellow teeth closed over Celia's arm.

With a scream of pain, Celia ripped her arm from the mare's hold, tearing the thick sleeve of her jacket. Teeth raked long, red furrows. Celia lost control of Amiga's halter, and the tortured mare reared and pawed at the air. When she landed, her legs could not hold her, and she crashed to the cement alleyway of the barn. Her legs flailed wildly.

"Watch out!" Morgan warned. "She can kick just as hard lying down as standing up."

Celia was holding her injured arm. The tatters of the shredded sleeve dangled. Tears of pain and frustration rolled down her cheeks. The mare banged her head on the cement. "Morgan, if we can't help her, we've got to put her out of her misery. Doc'll never get here in time to save her."

Amiga grew quiet. There was no sound except the groans and rasps of her labored breaths. "I'll get the gun. Honey, your arm's bleeding. Al, take her to the house."

Al's pallor had taken on a shade of green. Even amid the confusion, Morgan had sensed a change in his attitude towards the boy. It was not the hangover causing the anguish in Al's face and eyes. He was crying for the mare—quietly but profoundly. This was not a person who could find pleasure in the pain of another living creature. Then, with a gesture of maturity that belied his own security, Al put his arm gently around Celia's shoulder. "Come on. He can take care of this. Let's go see to your arm."

Celia jerked away from Al. "No," she said determinedly. "I've known this old lady longer than I've known Morgan. The least I can do is be with her."

Morgan shrugged. "I don't want to argue with you. I'll get the gun."

An awkward silence hung in the barn. Amiga's breathing

eased. Celia knelt beside her and smoothed the lathered neck. "Easy, baby. It'll all be over with soon." She sobbed once, gently. "I sold one of her foals once for ten thousand dollars. Can you believe that? I've made money on every foal she ever dropped. But this one's going to kill her."

Morgan came back into the barn. He motioned to Al, and the boy helped Celia to her feet. He aimed the barrel and started to squeeze the trigger, but the mare exploded violently. She surged to her feet and lashed a hind leg in Morgan's direction. He scrambled backward to avoid the kick. In the throes of another labor seizure, Amiga strained powerfully.

"Good God! It's coming out. It may rip her wide open, but the little bastard's coming out. Break open some straw around her. Hurry!"

Three powerful expulsions later, the foal protruded from the mare as far as its hind legs. With a final groan, Amiga sank to the straw as if in slow motion. She was fatigued beyond the limit of her endurance. Morgan helped ease the foal the rest of the way from her exhausted body. Her torture ended, and her form shuddered one last time.

"Is she dead?" asked Al.

Morgan held his hand on her chest for a full minute. "Yeah. She must have jerked around enough to cause the foal to shift positions. But it just wore her down too much. She was one of the older brood mares, one of Bloodstone's. She had to be twenty years old. Her heart just gave out."

Celia intoned softly, "She was all heart, this mare. She gave her all even though it killed her."

There was a hushed moment, a quiet respect for the passing of a fellow creature. Celia and Morgan continued to kneel by the dead mare, the touch of their hands comforting their own sadness now.

Al bit hard on his lip and turned away. There was a strange burning in his eyes. He knew they were tears, but tears denied for so many years were too painful to shed. Like a noxious weed cut back time after time, never allowed to reach its growth but never severed at its roots, the tears drew their strength from resistance. Each time they were refused an outlet, they grew more bitter. Surely, he could not let them fall now, not in front of this man and woman whom he still did not trust.

So, he did what he had been doing since the night his mother died. He got angry. He lashed himself with accusations. If he hadn't drunk so much the night before, if his sleep hadn't been drugged, he would have heard the mare earlier. He could have gotten help for her. He might have saved her and her foal.

The foal! For the first time, he realized that the tiny head that had forced its way from the membranous sac was making very lively motions. "The baby! It's alive!"

Celia looked up at him. "For now. You can't raise an orphan foal. Not one whose mother dies before nursing him even once."

"But we can feed him," Al protested.

"Celia's right, kid. The first milk, the colostrum, has all these antibodies in it. It protects the foal from all sorts of infections. You can't give it anything in a bottle or through a needle that will match its importance. Besides, a baby foal sucks about a thousand times a day. We're running a ranch, and there aren't enough hours in a day to fool with it."

"I can do it. I'm out here in the barn at night anyway. I can feed it every couple of hours." There was an edge of something that was more than excitement in the boy's voice.

"It won't work. Even if he survives, he won't be any good. A hand-raised foal is always poor. There's just no room for sentiment in the horse business."

Silence once again. Al watched raptly as the foal fought for its independence. It freed itself of the clinging, viscous sac, then lay quietly, resting. Al noticed the constriction starting to take place in the navel cord, like a piece of trick photography. Within a few minutes, the foal began to struggle to its feet, and the cord broke off neatly at the constriction. It was all so perfect, except for the fact that the other participant in this drama was dead. When the little fellow did gain his footing, there would be no welcoming nuzzles, no full udder offering its rich, warm nourishment.

"Don't tell me that," he said. He was watching the foal, but he addressed Celia and Morgan. "You, Mr. Kyles, you're standing there a hair away from bawling, and you, Celia, your arm must be killing you, and you're sitting there petting a dead horse. So don't tell me you don't have any sentiment."

He lifted his head then and stared at Celia. "I've done you wrong from the beginning, but you're giving me a chance. Look at him." The little foal was attempting to rise again. "Look how much he wants to live. Don't you think he deserves a chance? His mama died to give him that chance. You said yourself how good her foals are. Please, Celia. Let me try with him."

Al's voice had risen with passion, but his final plea was almost whispered. It was too much; he was telling them too much and exposing himself too much. "All my life, I've watched things die. It's not pretty, but I got used to it. But I've never seen anything get born."

"I should put a bullet through its head right now and save us all a lot of trouble," Morgan said, hoping the gruffness would cancel out the tell-tale glisten in his eyes, "but if you want to try . . . Celia, go up to the house and phone Doc. Ask him to come as soon as he can and bring some more Foal Lac. And if there's any colostrum in the bank, please bring it. Then you stay up there and wash that arm really good. I'll drive you into town a little later to have it looked at. Al, go with her and get a bottle of iodine. We've got to treat this baby's navel stump."

Alone in the barn, Morgan allowed himself one more touch of the sentiment he said he had no room for. He closed Amiga's eyes and whispered, "You're running with Chief Joseph's herd now, old girl." Then he took an appraising look at the foal. It was a pale yellow, which would probably deepen to dun like its dam. On its rump were large white patches, irregular in shape. One of them looked like a handprint. "A 'Gambler's Hand.' That's what we'll call him. Gambler, for short."

Al was back in a few minutes. He had abandoned his crutch and adopted a stiff-legged hopping gait that took him from place to place in reasonable time and left both his hands free. Now he was carrying a shirt and jacket in one and a plastic pint bottle of iodine in the other. He handed the clothes to Morgan and asked, "What do we do with this?"

"Pour it over the end of the cord to disinfect it. Infection can enter the foal through the stump and travel all through it." He gently encircled the foal's body and held it still. "Go on, use the whole bottle. Soak it good."

Al managed to get as much of the orange liquid on the foal's navel as he did on his hands. "Celia got a hold of the vet's wife. She said he was done up north and headed here. He doesn't have any colostrum."

"Shit. That means this fellow'll be subject to every bug that comes along. We'll have to keep him loaded up with antibiotics until he can build his own defense. How's Celia's arm?"

"It's hurting her more than she's letting on."

"Amiga would have sooner died than hurt anyone. She was just out of her head. Getting born involves a hell of a lot of pain. And that's only the start of it. Sometimes living hurts too damn much."

Al said nothing.

"Is that why you went one-on-one with that case of beer last night?"

"People say when they drink, it helps them forget stuff. It never works like that for me. The more I drink, the more I remember all the . . . well, all the things I don't want to remember. Until I finally can't remember anything, and I just black out."

"This foal is going to have to be fed every two hours around the clock. We'll help you as much as we can, but at night he's your responsibility. How do I know you won't start drinking and forget him? I'm not going to lock up the liquor and watch you night and day. This is no prison, and I'm no jailer."

"I guess you don't know. I guess you'll have to trust me, that's all."

"I'll trust you the day Cantar trusts you." Morgan waved his hand at the ever-watchful coydog. She had been a quiet spectator in the early morning's drama, her gaze forever shifting from her master to the boy she was assigned to guard.

Al could not understand why the familiar anger was not rising in him. He opened his mouth, expecting a hot retort to spew forth. Instead, in a voice that did not sound like his own, he said, "All I want is a chance to prove you both wrong. And I want to save this foal. Now, are you going to help me?"

Morgan suppressed a grin. There might be hope for the kid after all. Together, they began to gather the necessary supplies. They had half of a drum of Foal Lac, a powdered mare's milk replacer, three nursing bottles, and several nipples. Morgan stressed the importance of cleanliness time after time. Infection was their main enemy: the bottles had to be sterilized between feedings, only enough formula was to be mixed for each feeding, and the bedding had to be kept fresh.

By the time Morgan had explained the fundamentals, the foal had managed a shaky stand. Together, they maneuvered it into a newly bedded stall away from the chilling body that had been its mother. He showed no fear and curiously butted at Al and fumbled at the boy's untucked shirt tail with his rubbery lips. "You're his mama now, kid," Morgan said. "May as well try to feed him."

When Dr. McClutchan's truck rattled into the lot, it was full dawn. Morgan hailed him from the barn, and Celia came to greet him with her arm swathed in a white wrapping. Briefly, she described what had happened, and he advised her in no uncertain terms to see a doctor for her injured arm.

"I will, I promise. As soon as I hear your prognosis."

"I can tell you now it won't be good. Hard birth. No colostrum. Land's sakes, you two don't have the time to hand-raise an orphan." Harold McClutchan loved animals, but after twenty-three years in a tough, demanding country practice, he had learned to see his patients through a detached, practical eye. Yet even he felt a twinge of emotion when he entered the barn. Amiga had been a fine mare and always an amiable patient. It hurt to see her sprawled in the alleyway and to know that later that day, she would be no more than coyote fodder.

"Over here, Doc. Look at this little bugger." Morgan spoke quietly so as not to disturb the foal. But it would have taken a lot more than a little noise to interrupt Gambler's first meal. Al held the bottle at the same height as Amiga's udder would have been, and the little yellow foal sucked greedily.

"Doc, this is Al George, our new hired man. Raising this baby is going to be his job."

McCluthcan knew differently, of course. He was aware of all the happenings three counties wide. "Hi, son. You've got your work cut out for you, you know."

"That's what these two have told me. But he's cooperating. Isn't that half the battle?"

Doc grunted. He did not believe in false hope. What he did believe in were his training and his medicines, and he set about planning his part of the battle. He filled a syringe with tetanus immunization and another with antibiotics. When Gambler had finished his meal and, full-tummied, began merely playing with the nipple, he injected him. Then he lubricated his gloved hand and probed the foal's rectum to remove the meconium, the hard fecal balls. He brought several packets of powders from the back of his truck and gave very explicit directions concerning feeding, medicating, and care. His instructions continued as he walked back to his truck and climbed in. “I’ll stop by tomorrow and see how he’s doing. I’ll bring another drum of milk replacer with me. Celia, you get that arm looked after—today.” He punctuated this final command by slamming his truck door shut.

“I will. I’ll go right after chores.”

“By the way, if you had a nice, gentle companion for that orphan, it’d help out a lot.” He started the engine but continued giving instructions as if he were consulting over an office desk. Harold McClutchan was not one to stand still. “It needs a lot of nuzzling and comforting to keep its interests stimulated and keep its bowels moving right.”

“I know, but we haven’t a barren mare on the place. The three in the barn were the last ones to foal, and the remaining two aren’t the type to accept a strange baby. I’ll call around today and see if any of the neighbors have something.”

His final and possibly most important instructions were an afterthought. “Don’t overlook that misfit gelding of yours. He’s the best nanny I’ve ever seen,” Doc yelled over the noise of his coughing engine. The truck was badly in need of a tune-up, but like its owner, it rarely stayed in one place long enough. “Give him a try!” he called as he clanged away.

Celia returned to the barn for another look at the foal. It would be a dun, she was sure of that, with white splashes on its rump. She remembered Amiga’s other dun colt. As a five-year-old, it had finished third in the state finals in both reining and pleasure. She had never raised a more versatile colt. She hadn’t the time nor the money to campaign him as he deserved, so she’d sold him. Two years later, he finished in the top ten at the national finals in both events. If this colt turned out to be . . . but what was she thinking? The chances of this colt surviving even a month were slim. She realized how tired she was and how much her arm hurt.

Her depression deepened when she found that Al had lapsed back into one of his quiet moods. She and Morgan discussed

Doc's visit and planned the day's schedule around the new inconveniences—her necessary trip to the doctor and the colt's timetable. When asked a direct question, Al grunted a response, but he offered nothing to the conversation.

Finally, Celia suggested they try Doc's advice about putting Folly with the baby. Morgan was skeptical, but he started out the door with halter in hand to catch the gelding. Before he got too far, Al called his name.

"What?"

The boy's face had a look of pain as if it was taking all his effort to say the next words. "You told the Doctor I was your new hired man."

"So?" Morgan was puzzled. "What did you want me to say—you were the new owner?" His sarcasm was gentle.

"No one has ever acted like I was worth taking notice of before."

"Then maybe you've been meeting the wrong type of people." Morgan had an easy half-grin on his face, contrasting with Al's tenseness.

A battle raged inside the boy. These past several days had thrown him into a state of emotional turmoil. All the excuses he had used before had been negated. *Why try? No one will ever give me a chance 'cause I'm just a dumb Injun.* It had been easy to live that way, expecting nothing from himself or anyone else. But here were these two people who were willing to give him a chance. What was this excuse now?

He had once told Celia not to trust him. Then just this morning, he had practically begged Morgan for his trust. And these damn horses. Why were they getting to him so? Why did he want to tie himself to the impossible task of raising this foal when even the experts gave it little hope?

They were both watching him expectantly. What should he say? That he had changed his mind? *"Put the foal down. I don't want the job."* Or should he try the truth?

"I guess if you're going to be introducing me to folks, I might as well tell you my real name. It's Alicut. My grandma named me."

"That was Joseph's brother, wasn't it?" An obscure fact but one that Celia remembered from a history book she once read.

"Yeah. My grandma never could get it straight that the war was over, and we lost."

Morgan had been expecting much more. He dismissed the confession lightly. Names didn't mean much to him. "You know your problem, kid? You've let too many assholes convince you that being an Indian is something to be ashamed of."

"I've never had any reason to be proud of it." He was not ready to tell them the rest, not quite yet. Not ready to tell them how the only job his father could ever hold was sweeping floors, and the only reason he took it was for beer money. Not ready to tell them how the white men who came to his mother always called her squaw, and they only came in loud, drunken groups. Not ready to tell them how he let Ted Fulkerson call him Wop and how he pretended he was Italian. Maybe all that would come out later.

"Sweet Jesus," Morgan whispered in mock drama, "don't let Calvin Trueblood hear you talk like that."

"Who is this Calvin Trueblood?" Al asked as Morgan walked out.

"You'll meet him soon enough. Maybe even this weekend. I think Alicut is a good name. It's strong."

"It's still just Al, okay? And you better get to town. I'll help with the chores. Are you sure you want to make the drive yourself? You don't look so good."

"I've made longer drives in worse shape. I'll be okay."

The boy's concern warmed Celia despite the pain in her arm. There was just no telling about the way things worked out. A few hours ago, she was ready to give up. Now, more than ever, she was convinced everything was going to be fine.

CHAPTER 9

FOLLY TOOK to his task splendidly; within a few minutes, most of Morgan's skepticism vanished. The red gelding nosed the baby all over, smoothing its rumpled baby fur with gentle caresses. Gambler's belly was full, so he did not exhibit instinctive exploration for an udder. Morgan worried how Folly's patience would hold up if Gambler did try to nurse from him, but then he remembered that weanlings were the gelding's specialty. He had seen scores of foals, just separated from their dams, insistently put their heads in between Folly's hind legs, and never once had he seen the red horse kick. Gently, but just as insistently, he had pushed the demanding heads away. Gambler would learn, if he lived long enough, that comfort and warmth and security were offered by this surrogate mother, but milk came in a bottle.

All his immediate needs satisfied, Gambler crumpled to the straw for a nap. Folly stood over him; his head drooped so that his muzzle touched the baby reassuringly.

Morgan and Al watched for a few minutes. Celia had left after satisfying herself that Doc's idea, like most of Doc's ideas, was going to work. She had shrugged off Morgan's demands that he drive her to town, saying there was too much work to be done to spare both of them.

The two, man and boy, were awkward together. Morgan wanted to say something, wanted somehow to convey a desire for friendship to the Indian, but he was at a loss. He was all right giving orders or advice, but the situation called for neither. It was a moment for sharing, just as Al had shared the secret of the name he found so shameful. But Morgan was no good with words.

"We've got to call him something," said Al, breaking the silence.

This was his opportunity. Even before telling Celia, he would reveal the name. "I've already named him. Of course, we won't send in the papers yet. We'll wait to see if he makes it."

"Well, what is it?"

"Gambler's Hand. Gambler, for short. See those spots that look like a handprint? A Palouse Indian by the name of Sam Fisher from out Washington way discovered how to get that fancy marking. He brewed some powerful medicine, dipped his fingers in it, and painted the pregnant mare with a handprint. Of course, not everyone can do it. It requires special Indian magic. Nature must have done it on little Gambler here."

Al chuckled. "You think you've got everyone believing you're a real hard case. Saying there's no room for sentiment in the horse business. Hell, Mr. Kyles, you're an ol' cream puff."

Morgan snorted, but he had achieved his purpose. The tension eased between the two of them, and they set about the morning chores like a team. They fed and watered all the stock and then fed themselves. By that time, Gambler was due for another bottle. While Al attended to the foal, Morgan used the tractor to pull Amiga's carcass to the end of the lane. There, the rendering truck would pick it up, hopefully within the day.

Then they fell into the previous day's routine of working the yearlings. Al's first pick was Flora. Perhaps she sensed a change in the boy's attitude, or perhaps she had decided to behave, but he haltered her, curried her, and picked up all four of her feet without incident. "Celia's right," he said. "She sure is a dandy."

Morgan was pleased by how fast the boy was catching on. He hated to categorize people, but he had never met an Indian that wasn't good with stock if he wanted to be. "It's not going to be hard to figure out which ones to show this year: Flora and that white colt with the red spots. His name's Blood Jewel, but we call him Lep."

"Short for leopard, I bet."

"Yeah." Morgan crinkled his eyes suspiciously. "How did you know that?"

"Celia gave me a book to read. I've only thumbed through it, but I know a white Appaloosa with spots all over its body is called a leopard. And I read that story about Fisher. I thought it was sort of dumb," he paused, then added, "at the time."

"Hmph. He's a well-put-together horse, and the flash will catch the judge's eyes, so they can see how well he's put together."

"He's flashy, all right. As flashy as a pimp's Caddie."

Morgan laughed. "You've picked up one of Celia's back-East expressions. I'll bet you've never been within a hundred miles of a pimp's Caddie."

No, but I lived with a whore, Al almost said. But he bit back the words. He was not going to be chained to the past any longer. "Is that where she's from?"

"Yeah. But she doesn't like talking about it much. I guess we all got things we'd rather forget."

Had Morgan read his mind? So, he wasn't the only one with secrets. They worked in silence, but the awkwardness was gone.

Celia returned mid-afternoon, her arm properly bandaged and in a sling. There had not been any real damage done, but the support of the sling helped ease the ache. She let the men finish the day's outside chores while she fixed an early supper. It amazed her that she was able to stay awake after the short night, the eventful day that had started too early, and the powerful pain pills the doctor had given her.

The men came to the table hungry and full of talk. The topic of the colt and how well he was doing dominated the conversation. For the first time, Al showed animation in his words and gestures as he told Celia how the foal came by his name.

"I hate to break up the party," Celia finally said as she suppressed a yawn despite the interesting information, "but I'm beat. The Mechlings are going to pick up their two colts in the morning," (another yawn) "and I've got to get some sleep. By the way, I ran into Lacey Trueblood while I was in town. She said she'll get her dad out here this weekend to talk about the show and the race. Good night, you guys."

Celia's yawns were contagious. By the time she climbed the stairway to her bedroom, the men were also feeling the tiring effects of the day. Al located an alarm clock to take to the barn with him, but before he left, he said to Morgan, "There's that name again—Trueblood."

"Yeah. Lacey is Calvin's daughter. And it looks like you'll get to meet both of them."

"I guess I'm not one to talk, but 'Lacey' sure sounds like a dumb name to me."

"Not if you've seen her. She's just a little thing—as pretty and delicate as lace. But tough! That little lady can ride anything with four legs and a mane. She's about your age. She graduates this year, anyway. If I were you, I'd start right now trying to figure out how to impress her."

"Na. Women are just more trouble. I've got enough problems as it is."

"You're right about one thing. Women can be trouble. Not the good ones, though. You can't live without the good ones."

Al set his alarm for the next feeding, then tried to sleep, but it was no use. Physically, he was worn out, perhaps too tired to sleep. His leg was throbbing from the demands of getting along crutch-less. He kept going over the events of the day. He couldn't believe it had been less than twenty-four hours since he was first awakened by Amiga's cries of pain.

He picked up the paperback Celia had given him and began reading the second chapter. He read slowly and had to pronounce some of the more difficult words out loud. He learned how the Appaloosa, almost eradicated after the defeat of Chief Joseph, was brought back into the limelight and made a recognized registered breed through the work of a handful of horse lovers—Claude Thompson, most notably. He read about the anger Thompson felt over the misuse of the breed, and he recalled Morgan's adamant stand on never misusing any horse. Just as he was starting chapter three, his alarm rang.

Al was getting used to the feeding routine, although this was the first time he would be in charge all by himself.

Wait a minute. Not quite by himself, for there was Folly. The little sorrel gelding whickered softly as Al emerged from his room. Then he snuffled at the foal, waking him from his deep slumber. Once Gambler was awake, he was hungry. He began pushing into Folly, the gelding moving away from him and calling in more insistent whickers as if to say, "Feed this kid, will you, please?"

Al giggled to himself and said, "I'm coming," then immediately felt foolish for talking out loud to the horse. He opened the stall, and Gambler stumbled toward him through the thick straw. He grabbed at the nipple and began feasting.

Folly eased closer to the boy, and for a few seconds, Al had to fight a tendril of fear that was grabbing at him. For several days now, he had worked with the yearlings. He had been kicked and stepped on and knocked down and survived all that. He was beginning to feel some degree of mastery over the young horses. But Folly was no yearling. Al had never stood next to a fully grown horse before, except for the confusing and frightening experience with Amiga that morning.

Folly pushed out his nose and blew hot air over Al's face. The boy froze. Again, the gelding inhaled this new one's scent; again, he exhaled the warm breath that smelled of sweet hay.

Al noticed a strange tingling that started somewhere in the pit of his stomach. With a comfortable grumble, the gelding lowered his head to begin smoothing Gambler's baby fuzz. He groomed the foal with long strokes of his tongue, and Al could hear tiny gurgles coming from Gambler's stomach. He knew that meant the foal's digestion processes were in full swing.

Holding tightly to the near-empty bottle with one hand, he laid the other on Folly's muscular neck. The tingle that was vibrating his own belly spread up his arm. So vibrant and vital and warm and alive, rock-hard flesh covered by satin-smooth skin.

For a moment, his eyes stung; but he wiped away the tears of emotion before they could gather, set his jaw, and felt a flush of pride creep over his face. He belonged! He was accepted, he was needed, and he belonged!

CHAPTER 10

JYMME MECHLING WAS A BEAUTY; there was no denying it. At sixteen, she could turn the head of any man. Her innocent face, framed in blond curls, was contrasted by her surprisingly mature body. Despite her age, there was nothing innocent about Jymme Mechling.

Morgan felt the girl's green-eyed gaze on his back as he saddled the two colts. "How come you're out of school today, Jymme?"

"I just asked Daddy if I could come along to pick up the horses. Daddy never tells me 'no.'"

"I'll just bet he doesn't." Morgan looked back over his shoulder at the girl and grinned. "I'll just bet no one tells you 'no' too often." Morgan liked Dave Mechling, even though he didn't approve of the lenient way he had with his daughter. Dave had more money than he knew what to do with, and since his wife's death five years earlier, he had dedicated the greatest portion of it to satisfying his daughter's every whim.

Jymme let her mouth fall into a pretty pout which erased the innocent look in a flash. But she didn't have time to answer. Her father walked up behind her, slapping his expensive gloves on his designer-jeans-clad leg. "How about it, Morgan? Ready to show us what you did with these two colts?"

"Sure thing, Mr. Mechling. The grey has turned out to be a real sweetheart. Jymme'll look great on him. I can practically guarantee you'll clean up in pleasure classes with him." As good as young Miss Mechling looked, she was even more stunning on a horse. She rode with a flawless style. "The roan is a little hotter. He needs a lot of hours under saddle to settle him down. Let's you and me take them out in the timber, and when we get back, we'll let Jymme do some arena work on them."

"I won't be doing much pleasure riding this year. Now that I have my license and my own truck and rig, I'm joining the rodeo association—WPRA."

Morgan shook his head. "I don't understand why all you pretty little girls with boy's names want to go rodeoing. Besides, you don't want to run barrels with either of these two babies, not this summer. They need another year of growing before you put them through a season of gaming."

Jymme flipped a blond curl back from her face. "Oh, I'm not going to use one of them."

Morgan had a flirting desire to pull her off of the fence and give her a good smack. He and Celia had spent two months training two of the finest three-year-olds the Bloodstone Ranch had to offer. The grey already had his halter championship, and a season of campaigning with a rider as competent as Jymme Mechling would put a pleasure championship on him as well. And the spoiled little girl had disdainfully referred to the colts as 'them.' Dave Mechling shifted a little in his ostrich-skin Nocona boots.

"If we had known you were interested in gaming, we would have picked out a different horse for you," Morgan said.

Mechling quickly leaped to answer. "No, Morgan, don't worry. We still want them. We'll be doing some showing; this rodeo is something Jymme's just got in her head."

"Besides," interrupted the girl, "we've already bought a barrel horse from Mr. Dutchens."

Morgan didn't answer for a few seconds. He cast a disapproving glance at Mechling, who had the good grace to shift a little more. He knew why the girl had gotten rodeo in her head. Rodeo was where the men were. Not the local boys, the solid stockmen who had to live in the area; rodeo was the home of the drifters, the wild men who didn't have to worry about their reputations. How well he remembered. "I wish you luck, Jymme. But I think after three months of it, you'll find rodeoing ain't all it's cracked up to be."

"Not if you don't win, Mr. Kyles. And I plan on winning." She swung off the fence in one graceful movement and dismissed her red-faced father with a casual wave of her hand.

The men mounted the colts and took off through the gate at a quiet walk. Jymme wandered into the main barn and found Al cleaning stalls. "Hi," she called. "Where's Celia?"

Al emptied a forkful of soiled straw in the wheelbarrow and then leaned on the pitchfork. "She's up at the house. There was an accident yesterday, and she got a little shaken up. Morgan let her sleep in."

Jymme sat down on a bale of hay and crossed her slim legs. There was no look of concern for Celia, no question in her eyes as to the severity of the 'accident.' "You must be that Indian boy on parole. My dad says you're a thief and maybe even a rapist."

Al laughed, then stabbed at the straw again. "Then why didn't your dad tell you to stay away from me?"

"Well, I sort of made up the rapist part, and my dad lets me do what I want." She leaned back and smiled provocatively. Her breasts strained against the fabric of her shirt. "Come to think of it, you'd never have to rape anyone. I'll bet any girl would just love to fall into bed with you."

Holy Christ! Al thought. *What did I tell Morgan last night? That women were just trouble. This here's trouble with a capital T.*

"What about it? How much of a real desperado are you?"

Forcing a smirk, he answered, "I was framed."

"Damn. I was hoping I was talking to a real outlaw." She dipped her head and looked up at Al through her long lashes. How often had she practiced that coy gaze in front of her mirror? How often had she achieved the desired effects?

To say Al was uncomfortable would have been a gross understatement. His muddied memories of his mother laughing and grappling in the dark with strange men had left him with a twisted concept of sex. He viewed sex and even marriage as victimization. And he knew who was the potential victim in this little scenario. "Sorry," he answered, "no outlaw, just a dumb Injun."

Jymme reached for the top snap of her shirt and pulled on it slowly. "Sure is hot for May, isn't it?" The top snap gave way, followed by the next two. "Aren't you getting hot?"

The boy could see the swell of her breasts, milky white against the tawny tan of her upper chest. He wondered how she had gotten tan so early in the year. Then he checked himself, wondering how he could be thinking about a thing like that when he was so close to personal disaster. What if he did reach for her? Would she scream bloody murder loudly enough to send him to jail? And what if he didn't? Would his rejection anger her into causing trouble for him anyway?

"You sure don't talk much. Come on, why don't you put that ol' pitchfork down and come over here with me."

"Look, Miss Mechling, I've got work to do. I wish I had the time, but with Celia hurt, there's too much . . ."

She was on her feet, walking slowly towards him and reaching out her hand to place an elegantly manicured finger on his lips. "Maybe it's better when you don't talk. You've never had a white girl before, have you?"

He thought of Ted Fulkerson's little sister, dim-witted and pimply-faced, used and abused for so long by Ted's friends and even Ted himself. He had been disgusted by her pathetic advances and furious at Ted's attacks on his manhood because he refused to sleep with her. But Jymme Mechling was a bewitching beauty, mocking him and exciting him at the same time.

"My daddy and Mr. Kyles won't be back for another half-hour. The way you're shaking, that'll be plenty of time. Why don't you just relax and enjoy yourself?" She extended her other hand and laid it lightly on his belt buckle. "But don't relax too much."

Al stepped back quickly, embarrassed and angry at the effects this girl was having on him. He knew she was just toying with him; he was convinced of it. So why was he shaking, as she had so clearly pointed out?

"I-I-I've got to go feed the colt. I told you, I've got no time." He turned his back on her and walked away, holding his breath and hoping she'd say nothing.

"Morgan found time when I was here last."

He spun around. "That's a lie!"

"Is it? When we came to pick out the colts, Daddy and Celia rode out to bring them in from the pasture, and we were alone for over an hour. He's nice, but I'm not that crazy about older men, at least not that much older. I get a real kick out of guys like you—first-timers."

Al felt the flush burn his face. He was tired of the humiliation and angry enough to speak his mind despite the consequences. "You'll get a kick out of me, all right. I'll kick that sweet little ass of yours all the way home if you don't knock off that shit. I don't care how good a screw you're supposed to be. I'm not risking this job for a piece of used tail."

Jymme slapped him, hard, and her face turned evil. But before she could spit venom, Celia's voice reached them from just outside the barn.

"Al," she called.

"I'm in here."

Jymme snapped up her blouse and glared at him. His face was still red from her blow.

"Oh, hi, Jymme. Al, Doc's on the phone. He's coming out to check on Gambler but wants to ask you a few questions first. Go on up to the house and talk to him. Jymme'll help me finish up this stall, won't you, honey?"

As he made his escape, Al could hear the pleasantries exchanged between the two. *What a phony little bitch,* he thought. She had been right about one thing. He had never had a white girl. He had never had any girl. And he decided right then and there he'd rather be celibate for life than give a woman a chance to confound him so totally ever again. As for Morgan—he had almost started to like the guy. *Can't trust anybody.*

Al finished his report to Dr. McClutchan, then headed back to the barn for Gambler's meal. Jymme and Celia were sitting on the arena fence, talking in low voices. By the time Al fed the colt and cleaned the stall, the men had come back. He had no desire to face Jymme again, so the boy hid out in the tack room and worked on the old harness that had been soaking in neatsfoot oil.

Morgan was angry, but he was trying to control it. His anger intensified while he watched Jymme work with the grey. The animal was a perfect pleasure horse. He jog-trotted around the arena, his head beautifully set and his body flexing athletically. Jymme rode him just as perfectly, except for the scowl on her face. Instead of the look of concentration expected from a pleasure rider, she was making no attempt to hide her discontent.

"Bring him over here, Jymme," Morgan finally yelled.

"I haven't even loped him yet," the girl shot back.

"Nope, and you're not going to." Then he turned to Mechling. "I'm sorry, Dave, but we can't sell you that horse."

Mechling cleared his throat nervously. "I'm afraid I don't

understand. We've already made the deal. I've paid down on both of those animals."

"I know that, and we'll refund what you put into the grey. The roan is still yours if you want him, but I can't let the grey go if he isn't going to be used."

"What do you mean, man? He'll be used. Jymme isn't giving up showing."

"That's not what Jymme says," Celia broke in. "She says she's just interested in barrel racing."

Morgan breathed an inward prayer of thanks. Celia was backing him up. He had no right to speak for the ranch without talking to Celia first, but she was behind him anyway. "You want a gaming horse, that roan is your baby. Give him a couple of years and some decent training, and he'll beat anything Sid Dutchens ever dreamed of owning."

Jymme swung down out of the saddle and threw the reins at Morgan. It just hadn't been her day. "I can't believe you're letting them talk to you like this, Daddy. I don't want either of these plugs, and I'm going home." She flounced off toward the car, leaving her father stammering with embarrassment.

"I don't want my money back. I want both colts. Jymme will like them when we get them settled in. You know kids."

"Yes, I know kids. They're fickle. And I guess Morgan and I don't want to sell a horse that good to a fickle little girl."

Dave Mechling was defeated. His daughter was honking the car horn and revving the engine impatiently. "This is the most ridiculous excuse for a business deal I've ever encountered. But if my daughter doesn't want the horses and you two don't want to sell them, I must be crazy for arguing. You can refund my down payment by mail." Shaking his head as if in a daze, he joined his daughter in the car, and they sped away in a shower of gravel.

Celia watched the car pulling the empty trailer as it wound around the curves of the long drive. "Well, partner, we've dug our graves this time. That down payment is already spent, and I was counting on the balance for about two dozen necessities."

"God, Cel, I'm sorry. But this colt," he stroked the grey's neck, "he's one of the best. If that spoiled little brat won't put the championship on him, then we will." Then he put an arm around Celia and drew her towards him. She nuzzled into his neck, and he kissed the top of her head. "I'm a real ass, aren't I?"

"No." Her voice was soft and husky. "You're just a romantic. A dashing, sentimental, poverty-stricken romantic. By the way," she pushed away from the circle of his arm, "who do you think is going to campaign our little colt? You're too big for him, aesthetically speaking, and let's face it, I just don't do the same thing for a horse that Jymme does."

"That's bull, babe. You can ride rings around her."

"I know that, but riding doesn't have that much to do with showing pleasure. The trick is to get the judge to look at your horse at the right time."

"Then explain why Marian Hodge is the most consistent pleasure winner we know."

"Because she is so ugly, the judges keep on looking at her to see if she's for real. Oh well, we aren't really in this business for profit anyway. We'll give it a go."

"Here comes Doc," Morgan said, changing the subject. He knew how much they needed the money, and even though Celia was trying to make a joke of it, he was aware of her disappointment. *She must love me a lot*, he thought. She had the final say and could have shot him right out of the saddle in front of Mechling. But she hadn't. "I'll put the colts up. Where's Al been all morning?"

"I imagine he's holed up somewhere well out of Jymme Mechling's way." A knowing look passed between the two.

Dr. McClutchan was pleased with Gambler's condition but guarded in his prognosis. The first twenty-four hours were the most crucial, and the veterinarian praised Al for his job so far. The Indian boy fairly glowed with pleasure while Folly stood close by, bobbing his head impatiently. "He wants his share of the credit," interrupted Al. He laid a hand on the sorrel's neck. It was a casual gesture as if the boy and the horse shared secrets that no one else understood.

"The horse talk to you now, does he?" said Doc.

"They're far better company than a lot of people I've met." It suddenly occurred to Al that he found nothing foolish in admitting he spoke to the animals, and it was close to impossible to believe he was ever afraid of the sorrel horse. "What about putting them outside, Doc?"

"That'll be fine as long as it's warm and dry. And make sure there's some shade. That sun is awful strong for this early in the year. I would imagine the gelding is going a little stir-crazy, being cooped up in a stall."

"Maybe so, but he takes to his job well."

"He's not the only one," said Celia. She had remained quiet during Doc's visit. She figured Gambler was Al's project, and he was the one to ask the questions and answer Doc's. But she had to let Al know how proud she was of him. She wished she could have followed up her observation with a friendly pat on the arm, but she knew she couldn't pull it off with the same easiness the boy had expressed towards Folly.

"Keep up with the medication and keep doing what you're doing. I'll check by next week. In the meantime, let me know if he so much as sneezes."

"Yes, sir."

Celia walked Doc to the truck. His happy chatter drifted back to Al as they left the barn. He was fastening a lead rope to Folly's halter ring when Morgan walked up behind him. "Doc says the little fart's doing great."

"Yeah." Al's mood darkened. Aside from another confrontation with that spoiled little blonde, the last person he wanted to see was Morgan.

"You going to put them out in the paddock?"

"Yeah."

"Need some help?"

"No."

"Getting pretty sure of yourself, aren't you?"

"Is that bad?"

"I guess not. Not as long as you don't take on more than you can handle."

"I can handle myself."

Morgan rocked back on his heels and ran a big hand across his face. "Celia tells me you ran into a little trouble with the Mechling girl."

"Don't know what you're talking about. Celia wasn't anywhere around this morning."

"Celia knows what Jymme is like. She knows a lot more than you think."

Al shot out hotly. "Really? Does she know about you and that little tease?"

"What?" The accusation hit the big man like a hammer.

"She told me about you and her. Said you found time for her and couldn't understand why I wouldn't."

"That's crazy, and if you believed her for just a second, you're just as crazy. That's a pathetic little girl's lie. I've never cheated on Celia yet, and if I did, it wouldn't be with a piece of jailbait that was going to shout it all over the country. To risk losing Celia, it'd have to be something really special—and I'm not sure anything's made that special."

"Well, if she means so much to you, how come you don't marry her? How come you just make a whore out of her?"

Morgan drew back his arm. He was not going to slap Al like a man would slap a kid who had smarted off one time too many.

He was going to punch him, punch him the same way he would punch a man who had insulted him in a bar.

But Al glared at him, unafraid and not ashamed of what he had said. "Go ahead, Mr. Kyles. Hit me. I've been beat on by better men than you."

Morgan let his arm relax. "It ain't your fault, and I'm not going to hit you. What do you know about sex anyway, except maybe what you've learned on the streets? And if you don't know anything about sex, how could you know anything about love? About the kind of love Celia and I have? I ain't going to hit you, but if you ever lay a word like that on my woman again, I'll knock you cold. And that's all I've got to say about that."

THE REST of the week passed without much incident. Gambler grew strong and flourished under Al's care. He spent his days frisking in the paddock as only a baby colt can. He would play furiously—a little yellow whirlwind running on stilt-like legs—then crumple into a heap in the spring grass to sleep deeply and untroubled. Folly was always there, of course, acting as a bumper board for the colt, who had not yet learned how to put on brakes. And more and more, the Indian boy came to love both horses. He realized that he had never been happier and had never felt so content and pleased with himself.

Saturday morning arrived like a blazing summer's day. Al was working with the pen full of yearlings. After another week's training and Doc's visit to do the gelding, the majority of them would be turned back on pasture. Lep would be left a stallion, and he and Flora would remain to be groomed into show shape. Two other horse colts had been selected to go to a consignment sale in early June.

Al was lunging a filly, cueing her to go from a walk to a trot, then stopping her with the command of "whoa." Morgan had shown him how to fasten the lunge line, how to handle the whip, and how to be patient and not push the babies past their mental or physical capabilities.

As Al was making the yearling change directions, a silver pickup drove up the lane. It stopped at the house, and two people got out—an Indian man in work clothes and high-browed black hat and a young Indian boy.

The truck was clean and simple. It wasn't decorated gaudily like some of the young Indians had a leaning towards. There were no naked squaws or anti-white-man slogans painted on the sides. It also wasn't rusty and blowing blue smoke the way the older men would let them get. There was a single red pinstripe narrowing down the sides of the truck. The door of the driver's side read:

TRUEBLOOD'S
CLEAR WATER RANCH
KAMIAH, IDAHO

Underneath was the portrait of a Hereford bull.

So that's Calvin Trueblood, thought Al. Then what happened next was so unexpected, so unbelievable, that Al's lower jaw dropped.

Cantar had been lying near the corral, watching Al as had become her custom. Ever since the boy arrived at the ranch, the coydog had kept a relentless vigil over his every move. Al couldn't turn a corner without walking into her silent green-eyed stare. It had unnerved him at first, her patient sentry, the desire in her tensed muscles that he make a wrong move, but these last few days, he had resigned himself to her constant watch. He had begun talking to her because even if she wasn't in sight, he knew she was close by, listening. But when the silver truck came on the scene, Cantar abandoned her post and ran to greet it.

The younger of the two visitors was the first to speak. He dropped to one knee and exclaimed in a high, excited voice, “Hiya, Cantar! Hiya baby!”

That was when the miracle took place. From a slinking shadow, the coydog transformed into a capering picture of total abandon. She cocked her broad head to the side and yapped and yodeled in a strange language of pure joy. Even stranger because Al had never seen the animal act in any way other than formidable, and this behavior was puppyish.

Soon, the man took part in this happy ceremony. He squatted beside his companion and spoke to the coydog in words that did not reach Al’s ears. She was almost groveling before him, lapping at his hands. Then she leaped to her feet and opened her huge mouth. The porcelain teeth sparkled in the morning sun. With the greatest of care, she grasped the man’s chin in her teeth and shook his head gently. The big Indian’s hands stroked Cantar’s neck. It was plain that this was a ritual of some sort—a display of mutual respect and affection.

Morgan opened the front door and greeted the visitors enthusiastically. “Right on time, Calvin. Come on in. Got the beers cold.”

Cantar ran to her master and gambled around his feet as if she was trying to include him in the greeting ceremony. Morgan kicked at her good-naturedly, and the coydog grabbed his boot in her mouth and tugged at it. The younger Indian laughed, a light, silvery laugh, and for some reason, Al, who had been watching the entire procedure, felt a strange emptiness.

He turned away from the three friends, clicked to the filly, and was determined not to feel the desire to join in their camaraderie. He heard their boots as they climbed the steps to the porch, and their voices disappeared when the front door closed.

“That filly must be out of Miss Kitty.” The voice came from

behind him and made Al jump. In his attempt to block the visitors from his mind, he hadn't realized that the boy had walked to the corral. "She was one of Mr. Bloodstone's mares. All her foals have that mature look about them and a real no-nonsense disposition, like the way that filly's working."

Al stopped the filly, then followed the lunge line out to pet the animal. She stood patiently but tipped her ears in the stranger's direction. "Are you Calvin Trueblood's boy?"

The youngster laughed that same silvery sound. "Thanks a lot."

Then Al recognized his mistake. This was no boy, but a girl —a young woman, really. She was slender and, like her father, dressed in work jeans and a flannel shirt. But up close, not even the comfortable cut of her clothes could hide the gentle swell of her hips below the tiny waist, the soft rounding of her breasts. She laughed once more, reached up to remove a cap from her head, and a sunlit-rippled shower of black hair cascaded down her back. The laughter spread across her face and twinkled in her almond-shaped eyes. "Dad would have loved that. Actually, I'm the closest my folks ever got to having a son."

Al was a little red-faced with embarrassment. To cover, he turned his back on the girl and spent twice as long as necessary removing the halter from the filly.

"Was I right? Is she Miss Kitty's yearling?"

"I don't know," he answered flatly. "I've only been here a short time. I don't know all their names yet."

The girl ducked through the fence boards and walked towards Al. "Mine is Lacey." She extended her hand and shook his. Her grip was firm; her slim, warm hand surprisingly strong. "And yours?"

He liked her. He liked her right away, and it scared him. Women were just trouble. But when he looked in her dark eyes as he let the handshake linger just a little longer, he knew there was no trouble in her. "Al George," he said, "and I've heard a lot about you and your father."

"I'll bet you have. Morgan and my dad have this running battle going. But if one of them is in real trouble, the other one is always there to help. Dad says Morgan is the only white man he trusts."

Trust. Why did he feel he could trust her? The whole thing was crazy. There was no such thing as love at first sight. He wasn't even sure there was such a thing as love at all.

"Can I see the orphan foal? Morgan said you were in charge of him."

Al fumbled for a response. His words weren't coming out right. Everything was phrased awkwardly. She must think him a fool.

He bumped his head climbing through the fence boards. Then, as he followed the graceful sway of her body as she walked towards the paddock, he totally lost track of what he was trying to say. It was like drinking too much beer.

Somehow, he managed to climb the paddock fence and call the two horses to him. Folly reached him first, and like magic, the presence of the gelding cleared the boy's head. Feeling the press of the sorrel's body against him, Al regained his confidence. The horse's strength flowed through him.

He told Lacey the story of the foal's stormy beginnings. Emotion choked him for a few seconds when he related how Amiga lost her life but saved that of her son, and he wasn't ashamed. Proudly, he told how Gambler had accepted him as a nursemaid. He explained how the colt got his name, and in completion, he gave credit to Folly. He had never talked so much in his life. He had never felt like this in his life.

The girl listened intently, smiling and nodding her head at intervals. "Quite a story," she said when he had finished. "If that had been at our place, Dad wouldn't have given the little guy a chance. We're a cattle ranch, you see, and all we have are working horses. Dad doesn't believe in keeping anything that doesn't pull its own weight or anything that creates extra work."

"Gambler will be worth it, someday."

Lacey smiled, and a look of extreme maturity came over her. For a moment, she reminded Al of a cross between Celia and, incredibly enough, his grandmother. "I think he's already worth it. I saw how you lit up just talking about him. Anything that gives a person that much pleasure is priceless."

Al had a crazy urge to grab her hands in his and blurt out, "Tell me everything about yourself. Tell me your entire life story." He was saved from such an impulsive act by Calvin Trueblood's deep voice calling to his daughter.

"That's Dad. It's time for me to do my thing for the sake of Indian rights." But there was no sarcasm in her words. "Can you come to the house with me? I'd like you to meet the big chief."

Al hesitated a minute. He wasn't sure how much Lacey knew about him, but he was sure Trueblood knew plenty. How would the Indian feel about his daughter even speaking to someone like him? But when Lacey touched his arm and urged him to go with her, all doubts vanished. He had a feeling that if this girl wanted him to run through fire, he would.

They walked slowly to the house, and Al had time to ask the biggest question in his head at present. "What did you and your dad do to make Cantar act like that? Any other truck pulls up here, she's ready to chew first and ask questions later. Even people she knows, like Dr. McClutchan, she threatens. And I thought she was going to rip the seat out of Dave Mechling's Kenny Rogers Specials." He chuckled when he thought of the picture the two of them had made, Cantar circling the man and the man spinning on his heels to stay facing her. But that mental image was soon replaced by one of himself grasping the blood-slippery rafters of the barn and fighting not to lose consciousness. Cantar was anything but humorous.

Lacey's forehead creased into a frown. "So, you've met Jymme Mechling. Came to pick up their two colts, no doubt."

"Yeah." Al hadn't intended to bring Jymme into the conversation. "But Morgan changed his mind and wouldn't sell them."

"Good for him. I hate that little tramp. Did she try to come on to you? What a question. Of course, she did. You wear pants, don't you?"

"Lacey." It was the first time he had said her name. Morgan had been right. It fit her perfectly. It wasn't a 'dumb' name at all. It was glorious. "I don't want to talk about Jymme Mechling. I'd be real happy if I never saw her again. I want to know about you two—you and your dad—and what went on with Cantar."

"We were just greeting each other like wild coyotes do. Sometimes we really carry it to extremes, and we all have a howl together."

"But your dad—she grabbed his face with her teeth."

"Sure. That's what coyotes do to each other if they're really friends. It's like kissing."

"I still don't understand. Why doesn't she act like that with anyone else?"

"Oh, that's simple. You see, our clan totem is the coyote."

"What's a totem?"

The girl looked at him with utter surprise. "Every family has a totem in our tribe. It's the object from nature that they identify with—their guiding spirit. Didn't your family have a totem?"

Vaguely he remembered the words of his grandmother from years ago. She would try to tell him those ancient things, and he never wanted to listen. Did she ever tell him about such a thing?

"I can see I've got some educating to do. Stick with us, Al George. We'll make a proper Indian out of you."

Celia, Morgan, and Calvin Trueblood were seated comfortably around the kitchen table. The men had beers, and Celia was drinking coffee. When the two young people walked through the door, Celia was struck by the difference between their last visitors, the Mechlings, and these favorites of hers. She had known the Trueblood family for as long as she had known Sybil Horn. They were a hardworking, close-knit, fiercely proud people, Calvin almost reaching the point of militancy at times. They weren't wealthy, but they did such a good job managing what they had that they were considered the most reputable tribe members on the reservation. Calvin lacked the proper family background to ever become chief, but there were no tribal decisions made without his consultation.

Lacey, though still very young, was the most likely to follow in her father's footsteps. She had been a partner in the ranch work ever since Celia could remember. She had a feel for horses and cattle—for all livestock—and was an influencing factor in the ranch management. But most importantly, she was a girl with a purpose. Like Jymme Mechling, she was bright, attractive, and talented. Unlike the blonde, she used her intelligence to do more than manipulate others. She had a goal, and she was dedicated to it.

"Want a beer, Al?"

Al looked at Morgan with just a hint of surprise. He hesitated only a fraction of a second. "No, thanks," he answered pleasantly. Then he stepped forward and extended his hand to the Indian man, who had been eyeing him speculatively. He was proud of the new crop of callouses on his palm. "Hello, Mr. Trueblood. I'm Al George, and I'm glad to finally meet you after all I've heard about you."

Morgan raised an eyebrow at Celia as if to say, *What's come over this kid?*

"Lacey, would you like a Coke?" Al asked after the handshake.

The girl answered affirmatively, then pulled a chair up to the table. She grinned at her father, whose face still wore the same expression. "Dad says your club might sponsor an endurance race at your annual show this fall."

"Not exactly. Your daddy said our club will sponsor a race if we want his cooperation in our little scheme."

"That's my dad. Master of the art of persuasion." She interrupted herself to look up at Al and take the glass from his hand. "Thanks," was all she said, but she scooted her chair over so he would have room to sit beside her.

"I belong to the Southwest Idaho Trail and Distance Riders Association," she went on. "I didn't race but a couple of times last summer—we don't have the time or money to go to many rides—but I joined because it's about the only competition Rain will behave herself at. And also, it's the only competition that Dad thinks is a fair evaluation of the working relationship between horse and rider. Anyway, I know some of my club members would love to help organize the ride and work the vet checks. And we could bring in a vet from Meridian who is strictly a livestock man except for his work with endurance horses. He steers clear of show stock. That way, all the officials would be neutral.

"I don't think you should even try to sanction the ride. You want to make it a race for beginners. You don't want any point-seekers signing up. The only thing is, you can't hold the race on the same day as the show. With a fifty-mile ride, depending on the trail and conditions, the winning time might be as fast as three and a half hours, but it might be as long as ten hours before everyone is accounted for. It's going to take one whole day."

"We could move the show to Sunday. It always used to be on Sunday until a few years ago. Or, we could have the race on Sunday. That is if we can talk the club into sponsoring the ride."

"Oh, Celia, I hope you can. I have a lot of friends who have good horses, but what can they compete in otherwise? They don't have fancy equipment; they're lucky to even own a saddle.

Something like this is custom-made for them. And when it comes right down to it, what kept Chief Joseph and his people two jumps ahead of the cavalry? The endurance of the Appaloosa. In fact, Apps are the only breed really giving the Arab a run for the money in distance racing."

"Okay, okay, you've convinced me." Celia knew that young Trueblood was every bit as proud of her heritage as her stern-faced father. But she enhanced her facts with humor, charm, and captivating vitality. She was the finest representative her tribe could ask for. "Now, are you willing to make a club appearance and convince the rest of the members?"

"Sure, if they'll let me in the meeting.'

"They'll let you in, all right," Morgan assured her, "and once you're there, hit them with a challenge that they can't refuse. We'll get this thing rolling even if we have to shame them into it."

"The next meeting is two weeks from today. If you'd like, Morgan can pick you up Friday night. We leave pretty early Saturday morning."

"I can spare her," volunteered Calvin. "Now, I want to see this year's crop of babies, even though it kills me to see all your good grass wasted on horses."

"You're a cattleman, through and through, aren't you? Come on; I'll saddle you up a roan three-year-old that could be your next all-around cow pony. That sorry old gelding of yours can't have many more years in him. And Lacey—I've got a pretty little grey gelding that's got your name stamped all over it."

"Grey Ghost and Red Rider. The two you didn't sell to the Mechlings," exclaimed Lacey.

"You got it. Tell your old man to mortgage the spread, and he can buy them for you."

Calvin threw down the last swallow of beer and got to his feet. He was tall, much taller than most Indians, and his stony face glared down at Al almost accusingly. "Are you coming, too?" he asked.

Lacey turned her smile on the boy. "Please ride along, Al."

His heart almost ached. He could picture how she would look—her slender body swaying with the horse's moves, her black hair lifting in the breeze. "I can't," he said with sadness. "It's time to feed Gambler." He couldn't bear to tell her the truth. That he'd never been on a horse before, and the very thought of it was frightening.

"That's too bad. I'd like to stay and help you with the colt, but Joseph's always been one of my favorites ever since my Aunt Sybil owned him. I can't pass up an opportunity to say 'hi.'"

Even after they had all ridden off, her words stayed in Al's mind. And when they returned from the ride and made their goodbyes, her face remained with him. It hovered around him as he did his daily chores—her black hair tousled and her cheeks rosy with exhilaration. The sound of her laughter tinkled in his ears, and the thought of her smile warmed his heart.

At supper that evening, he emerged from his cloud of reverie and asked, "How long do you think it would take me to learn how to ride?"

CHAPTER 11

"LESSON NUMBER ONE: you're in charge. You give the commands. Even though a horse will test you, it expects direction. Never let a horse buffalo you."

"Gotcha," said Al. Celia was holding Folly's bridle reins, and the boy was rubbing his hands nervously on his pant legs.

"Lesson number two: With this horse, forget lesson number one. You'll have to ride for a lot of years before you know as much as he does. He won't take advantage of you, and he won't do anything to hurt you, but if you let him, he'll make a horseman out of you. Now, mount up."

A little of the color drained from Al's face. "What? I mean, he doesn't have a saddle."

"So?"

"How do I stay on? What do I hold on to?"

"Riding is an art of balance. The saddle has many purposes, but the main one isn't to give you a handle to cling to. The only way you'll learn to be a good rider is by learning how to move with the horse—and the best way to do that is by riding bareback." Celia threw the reins over Folly's neck. "Indians mount from the right, cowboys from the left. Folly doesn't care, so take your choice."

Al managed a weak smile. "I guess I'll stick with the winners." He approached the sorrel's left side. "I don't mind telling you I'm scared stiff."

"Never, never let a horse know you're scared. Horses don't like fear. They frighten so easily themselves, they don't want their riders frightened, too. Use my leg as a step up." She squatted on one knee and offered her bent leg as a platform.

Al's injured leg was still weak, and lack of confidence robbed him of his coordination. His mount was clumsy. Once on the horse's back, he was surprised by the slickness. He had the uncomfortable feeling that he was going to slide off the other side. He pictured himself slipping beneath Folly's hooves and being stomped into an unrecognizable pulp.

"Relax, Al, relax." Celia's words broke through his tragic imaginings.

"How do I pretend I'm not scared?"

Celia laughed. "By not speaking until you can control that quiver in your voice. Speak to your horse, but only in a calm tone. It's okay to be scared, but keep the fear contained. Don't let it pass into your hands, legs, or voice." She slapped his knee firmly. "Loosen up your legs, and you'll quit sliding around. And don't clutch so hard with your hands. Those reins are there to help you communicate with the horse, not for balance. Folly's not going to let you get hurt. Trust him."

Slowly, the tension began to drain from the boy. First, he slackened the reins and let his hands rest on Folly's withers. Next, he released the death grip his legs held on the gelding's barrel. The ramrod stiffness of his back eased. Traces of a smile crinkled at his lips. "Still on top," he said proudly. The sorrel breathed a deep sigh of obvious relief, and Al's smile bloomed. "I had him worried, didn't I?"

"I told you he'd take care of you. I don't want to scare you all over again, but if you'd have clutched like that on most horses, they'd have thrown a fit, not to mention you. Just sit on him for a while. If he wants to move, let him. He can't wander off." She indicated the confines of the small arena. "I want you to feel comfortable on him."

Al nodded his head. There it was again. That strange feeling that came over him every time he touched the red horse. Had his muscles not been so tense, he would have felt it the instant he was astride. The humming audible only to him. He couldn't begin to explain it to anyone even if he wanted to, which he surely didn't. They'd think he was crazy if he told them how this horse charged him with life and confidence. It was just a horse—just a horse—just a horse . . .

Smoke. Smoke was everywhere. He could taste its harsh dryness. It stung his eyes. And the pain in his side was unbearable. He wanted to cry out at the pain, but he dared not for fear they might hear him. Surely they would find him anyway. And if they didn't, the flames would. He couldn't run, for where would he flee? Then, through the cover of the thick smoke, he saw an outline. It approached him quietly, placing one muffled hoof step after the other. Why hadn't it scattered with others when the nightmare began?

"Al. Al, are you all right?"

The boy cleared the smoke dream from his head.

"You were swaying. Sort of weaving. Are you okay?"

"I'm okay." Then, more definitively, "I'm okay."

AL HADN'T THOUGHT he could bear the two weeks before he would see Lacey again, but he had more than enough to keep him busy. Time passed rapidly.

Every day, he practiced his riding. He no longer needed assistance in mounting. His lean, young strength and agility served him well, and he was soon swinging onto Folly's back with style.

He found his rate of progress to be governed by the horse. When Folly thought it was time to learn how to sit a trot, he trotted, and it was beyond Al's power to make the sorrel gelding perform any other gait. Falls were frequent, but they no longer frightened the boy. He soon realized that Folly would never step on him, and he found that by forcing himself to remain loose, the spills didn't hurt. He could have saved himself from some of the falls by clutching the sorrel's sparse mane, but he elected to play fair. As a result, his balance and coordination improved daily.

Celia tried to stay out of the way, and Morgan, whose teaching techniques tended to be excessively vocal, always found some chore to do that kept him far from the arena when Al was riding. She helped Al with the things that required verbal instruction: proper application of the tack and care of the horse before and after the ride. But she kept to her original premise that Folly was a better teacher than any human could have been, and Al learned more and faster on his own.

So, he wasn't unprepared, just pleasantly surprised when the gelding collected himself into a lope one morning, abandoning the steady trot he had been subjecting the boy to for the majority of a week. He was flying. Not working at it like a hummingbird but soaring like a hawk on a wind current. He felt like he and the horse were one and that he could no more fall from the sorrel's back than he could fall from a rocking chair.

But he was wrong. After two turns around the arena, Folly switched back to a trot. Al lost his precious balance and thumped into the dust. He eyed the gelding suspiciously. "You did that on purpose, didn't you?"

If a horse could laugh, Folly did.

Al told the story at supper that night, and Celia told him it was Folly's way of saying it was time the boy became a more active member of their partnership. From now on, it was Al who must decide when to go, at what speed and in what direction, and when to stop. She promised to help him with his cues the following day. She also emphasized that it would still be a while before he was ready for a saddle. But not to worry. Lacey would be more impressed with him if he rode Indian style.

On Monday of the second week, Dr. McClutchan spent the morning at Bloodstone gelding the yearling horse colts. One at a time, all the colts except Blood Jewel were put under mild anesthetic, and Doc bent over them, scalpel in hand, to remove their testicles. Al's job was to sit on the colts' necks to prevent them from lifting their heads and to protect the animal's eyes, which had lost their blinking reflex due to the anesthetic, from dust and the bright sunshine. He grimaced during the first two geldings, but by the time the third colt was ready to be operated on, he got over his squeamishness and took an interest in the only slightly bloody procedure.

As Doc was drawing his blade along the colt's scrotum, Al hesitantly asked a question. Instead of Doc telling Al not to bother him, which Al feared might have been the answer, Dr. McClutchan began to explain his surgical technique. By the time the morning's work was completed, Al felt more like an assistant than a hired hand.

Doc's final job before leaving Bloodstone Ranch was to examine the miracle foal—the orphan that shouldn't have looked so fat and healthy because, as everyone knew, orphans, if they live, are poor doers. Even Doc abandoned his usual caution and issued his educated opinion that Gambler's Hand was, indeed, out of danger.

On Thursday, Morgan and Celia decided it was time to return the yearlings to the mountain pasture. They separated out the nine youngsters that showed promise but lacked the maturity or flash that would make them early halter winners. Morgan invited Al to ride along. It would be the first time the boy had ridden outside of the arena, and Al wasn't sure he was ready. But when Celia reminded him that Lacey would arrive on Friday, and if she asked to go riding, she wouldn't be referring to the corral, he accepted.

Morgan, on his gelding, Charlie, and Cantar did all the work. Al was busy just staying aboard and trying not to look clumsy. The yearlings had to be driven the first mile; they kept trying to circle back. Even after they resigned themselves to leaving the ranch, they continued to call to the four yearlings left behind. Their whinnies, however, were not as plaintive as the anxious cries of Gambler, who was being left for the first time in his young life. Folly, on the other hand, appeared to be enjoying his brief release from the responsibilities of nurturing.

ON FRIDAY MORNING, Morgan loaded the two young geldings that were designated to be sold at the auction, along with a two-year-old filly and a gelding of the same age that hadn't matured up to expectations during the winter. He was to leave them with a friend in Craigmont who would add the four to his stock and haul the whole lot to the sale in Boise on Sunday. Then he would pick Lacey up at Clearwater Ranch and have her back to Bloodstone in time for supper.

Al spent the entire day fluctuating between excitement and dread. What was it Morgan had said, that he should be trying to figure out how to impress the girl? He had to admit, everything he had been doing for the past two weeks was in preparation for Lacey's return visit—if not to impress her, at least to prevent himself from looking foolish.

He perfected his flying mount onto Folly's bare back until he looked as good as any trick rider. He groomed Gambler's baby fuzz to perfection over and over again. With Celia's help, he studied breeding records until he knew at least the names of the ranch's broodmares as well as the history of some of their more successful offspring. In the few hours of spare time he had each day, he tackled the books Morgan had purchased on distance riding. To his surprise, his reading skills improved. He didn't know if it was because of the constant practice or because he actually found the material interesting. But none of this readied him for the actual second Lacey jumped down from the truck and greeted him in her silvery voice.

She was still dressed in her school clothes. They were plain enough not to disguise the vibrant life they covered. Her hair was feathered softly back from her face, and there was just a hint of makeup accenting her features. Al felt his heart fly to his throat, preventing him from saying a word to her. *I'm such a jerk,* he admitted to himself. *Every day she looks like this. Guys are probably falling all over her at school. What would she possibly see in me?* Then he screamed mentally at himself, *Say something, you dummy!* Finally, he stammered out a "Hi! That couldn't have been less convincing if he had planned it that way.

Lacey didn't seem to notice his predicament. A cloth gym bag dangled from her shoulder. "If I change real fast, do you think we'd have time for a ride before supper?"

Al didn't trust his voice this time. He shook his head affirmatively and watched her run lightly into the house.

"I've never heard such witty conversation in my life," laughed Morgan.

Al blushed. "Go to hell," he mumbled. Then, more to himself than to Morgan's grinning face, he added, "I'll probably fall off the goddamn horse."

"No, you won't. You'll do just fine. I'll saddle the Ghost up for Lacey. You go get your horse."

"Maybe I better not go. I've got to feed Gambler in a couple hours and—

"Go get your horse. You think I'm going to let you be rude to a guest? And Monday, we're going to start bucket-breaking that colt. We can't run a ranch on his time schedule."

Lacey changed and was ready to mount up in less than five minutes. She wore a pair of Levi's, much newer and better-fitting than the pair she had worn the first time Al met her. Her T-shirt read, "I'm High on Herefords," and had a Hereford stencil on it similar to the painted head on the Trueblood's truck. She wore a denim jacket covered with colorful patches, and her hair hung loose.

"Don't ride too close to the mountain pasture," Morgan cautioned them. "I don't want any of those babies following you back." Then, as Lacey mounted the grey gelding, Morgan made a stirrup out of one big hand and boosted Al to Folly's back. The boy's gratitude was obvious. At this point, he wasn't sure he remembered how to get on. "And no racing, Miss Trueblood." He emphasized Lacey's name. "I don't want that little gelding ruined for pleasure." Once again, Al mentally sighed his thankfulness for Morgan's perception.

They rode quietly at first. Lacey suggested the direction, and Al merely grunted a reply. A half-mile from the ranch, they came to a gate, and Al slipped to the ground to open it. He led Folly through the opening, closed the gate, and then decided to break the ice by mounting with his sure-to-be-noticed flying leap. He gathered himself tensely, laid a supporting hand on Folly's withers, and swung his right leg over the gelding's back. With a decided lack of dignity, his momentum carried him over the other side and deposited him in an untidy heap on the ground. Folly turned his head and looked at the boy with mild curiosity. Al prayed for the ground to open and swallow him—but it didn't.

To make matters worse, Lacey began to laugh. It was just a

giggle at first, hidden behind her hand, but soon it erupted into the laugh that Al remembered so well. He knew he couldn't lie on the ground forever, so he got slowly to his feet and began brushing himself off as Lacey said, "I'm sorry, Al. It's just you looked so funny, and Folly, the look he gave you!"

"You want to hear something really funny?" Al's voice was miserable with self-pity. "Last time you were here and asked me to ride—I'd never been on a horse until that next day. I didn't want to admit it to you. I guess I just wanted to—to—"

"To impress me?"

She was going to laugh at him again; he knew it. Why did he ever think he could pull off this charade?

"Look at me," she demanded. "Do you think I always look like this when I ride? Look at these jeans." She stood in her stirrups and reached behind her, trying to pull some slack in the fabric that covered her buttocks. There was none. "They're killing me, they're so tight! I like to ride in pants that are at least a size too big. That way, I don't have to worry about splitting them out. And this jacket—do you know how hard I've worked to win these patches? I never wear this thing if there's a chance I'll get it dirty. And do you know how long it's going to take me to brush my hair out tonight? It looks great flying on the breeze, but the snarls are murder. I usually pull it up under a cap, but the last time I did that, you thought I was a boy, remember? I wanted to make sure you didn't make the same mistake again."

"You mean you were trying to impress me?"

"Is that so hard to believe?"

Al mounted his horse, not quite as stylishly as he wanted but with confidence. "I just don't know why anyone as pretty and smart as you would care what I thought."

"I guess you've probably had a lot of girlfriends. I know about you, why you're here, and I know that boys like you—well, girls are attracted to boys like you. You're exciting."

"Is that why you wanted to impress me, because you think dropping out of school and cheating folks at pool and stealing and drinking too much is exciting?"

"Oh, no, I think that's dumb, really dumb. But I'm not like most girls. What I like about you is what I see now and what Morgan's said about you."

Al scowled. "I pretty much know what that's been."

"No, you don't, or you wouldn't be making such a face. Morgan was pretty mad about you at first. I remember when he came to talk to my dad about it. What a night! But he says he's never seen anyone take so naturally to ranch work. And I can tell myself. I've seen how well you've done with Gambler. Most boys aren't interested in horses. All they care about is cars and trucks and acting big and getting girls to—you know."

"Sounds familiar."

"Particularly the 'you know' part, right? I'm not willing to do the things a lot of girls do to get boys interested in them. The clothes they wear, the smoking and drinking and drugs, and the way they talk! There are seven girls in my class who are pregnant and a couple from the junior class that won't be coming back in the fall because they'll have babies. And not one of them has a husband. I've got plans for my life, and I can't afford to mess myself up. But that doesn't mean I don't appreciate a handsome face."

Lacey clucked to the gelding and urged him into a gentle lope. Al loped along beside her, delighting in the way he moved in unison with his horse. At one point, he glanced over at the girl and was struck by her beauty. She wasn't cute or even pretty. She was the most beautiful thing he'd ever seen, and he couldn't believe the words she had just told him. He promised himself he'd not make her lose her high opinion of him.

Suddenly, she laughed out loud and slowed Ghost back to a walk. "When I was four years old, I asked my mom what the difference was between a stallion and a gelding. You know what she told me?"

Her humor was infectious. Al grinned. "What?"

"That a stallion could be a daddy, but a gelding could only be an uncle."

For just a few seconds, Al found himself wondering what it would have been like to have grown up in a real family. A loving family. "I didn't even know what a gelding was until I came here. I mean, I knew what one was, but I just figured that there were male horses and female horses. I didn't realize the third sex was so popular. What made you think about that?"

"I've known all about bulls and cows and what they did since I could talk. I've discussed breeding and heat cycles and infertility and all that kind of stuff with men since I was ten. I never got embarrassed over any of it. But I've never discussed sex, I mean people sex, with a boy before. How come I feel like I can talk to you?"

"I guess I've just got one of those faces. Tell me about these plans of yours."

"You really want to know? You won't think I'm bragging?"

How could he tell her that listening to her voice was such a pleasure that he didn't care if she was reading the phone book? "Go ahead, tell me."

"Ever since I can remember, all I've ever wanted to do was work with animals. At first, people thought I'd grow out of it—it was just the tomboy in me. But here I am, fully grown, well, almost, and still crazy about animals. Dad's always made it clear that there was a place for me on the ranch, but I want more than that. What I really want is to be a veterinarian, but that takes at least six more years of schooling and a lot of money, not to mention brains and connections. I've worked towards it all my life—taking the right courses in school, keeping my grades high, getting as much experience as I could—never dreaming I'd actually get the chance."

"What chance?"

Lacey took a deep breath. "No one knows this yet except my folks and the school board. I wasn't going to tell anyone until my graduation party next week."

"So, I have to wait to find out?"

"No. But what I'm going to tell you—I want you to know that it's not because I'm just showing off or something. It's because I'm so happy, and I can't think of anyone I'd rather share this happiness with."

Al wanted to reply as honestly as she had spoken. He tried to say, "I'd be proud to share your happiness," but it wouldn't come out of his mouth. "You haven't even told Morgan or Celia?"

"No."

His thoughts raced and collided headlong with each other. For two weeks, he had dreamed of her. He had pictured her in his arms, and twice, in the pleasure of sleep, he had seen her coming to his bed dressed only in her radiant smile and shimmering black hair. He had awakened, trembling with the thought. And now, she sat on her horse proudly but so vulnerable. For all her strength, he could sense her frailness, and he didn't trust himself not to hurt her. He was only just learning how to deal with his own feelings; he wasn't ready to be responsible for someone else's.

"Maybe you had better wait to tell me then. That is if I'm invited to your party."

She smiled weakly. "You're invited. Come on, let's give these horses a little run before heading back."

Dinner conversation was lively. Morgan told a few jokes that bordered on off-color; Lacey told the latest news from the reservation, and Celia made everyone rehearse their lines to be spoken at the Saddle Club meeting the following day. Al didn't say much, but he responded with interest and was proud of the fact that he understood the terminology and finer points of distance riding. His eyes seldom left Lacey's face. A few times, when their gazes met, she rewarded him with a smile.

They all elected to turn in early, and for a third time, the Indian boy's sleep was disturbed with dreams of misty passion. He awoke, confused and unsure of himself, and was almost relieved when Morgan, Celia, and Lacey left for the day. He was alone with the horses—a simplicity he had come to love.

Cantar had changed markedly in her attitude toward Al. She still eyed him with suspicion if he spoke to her, but she no longer went out of her way to keep watch. She accepted him as she would a piece of furniture. Because she had learned to trust his presence as the correct thing, she let him assume the duties of guarding the ranch while the master was away that Saturday morning. Close to noon, Al saw her trotting off toward the mountain pasture as if she had a definite purpose. He called out a farewell, and she glanced indifferently at him over her shoulder.

The sun had started its downward swing when a rusty white car chugged up the lane to the ranch house. It was in bad shape, both mechanically and aesthetically, and Al wondered what kind of business its driver could have at Bloodstone. He couldn't explain why the little hairs on the back of his neck started to tingle as he watched the sad vehicle pull closer, couldn't understand his apprehension until the motor came to a final stop and Ted Fulkerson lumbered out of the car.

"Hi there, Wop. Long time no see."

The anger rose in Al's throat until he could taste the bitterness of it. The past humiliations. The verbal abuse. Leaving him, perhaps, to die. But the fear was there, too. "What are you doing here, Crabs? I heard you were in Spokane. Where's Sparks?"

"I spent some time in that piss-pot of a city. Sparks bought a rap up there, and he's sitting it out in their stinking jail."

You probably sold it to him; you probably left him holding the bag the same way you did me, you lousy maniac, he thought. But he didn't have the courage to say it.

"That's why I'm here, buddy. I need a new partner, some new wheels," he slapped the flaking once-vinyl roof of the aging car, "and some dough. I figured you could help me with all three."

"I don't get paid anything for working here. I'm here instead of in the slammer, like Sparks."

"I don't see any bars, Wop. You could leave any time you wanted. Looks like you fooled that good-looking bitch and her old man real good."

"I kind of like it here."

Fulkerson laughed. It was as evil a sound as Al had ever heard. Even from ten feet away, he could smell the rottenness of his breath and see the sadistic flash of his eyes. "You like it here! What'd they do, Wop? Cut off your balls like they do to the horses? Make a gelding out of you? 'Course, that wouldn't really be necessary, you being a fucking fairy already. Let's see, pervert. Pull down your pants, and let's see if you've got any balls left."

Fear pushed away the anger. It was all Al could do to stand and face the monster. His voice quavered slightly. "They'll be back soon now. You'd better get out of here, Crabs."

"That's just it. I can't get out of here. I've got shit for a car and no money. I'm hiding out at—you don't need to know where I'm at. You'd blubber your guts out to the first cop you could find. They've got you trained, all right. You just be at the old gas station outside of Clarkston Sunday at midnight. Come in something that'll get us to Seattle."

"I can't do that. They'll find out for sure."

Crabs whined in terrible parody. "Oo-oo-oo, I'm so scared they'll catch me." He narrowed his eyes and glared fiercely. "You'll be there, you understand? You double-cross me, and you'll wind up worse than dead." Then he laughed again, but there was no humor in the terrible sound. "These little horsies you seem to like so much—you don't show up, and something real sad just might happen to one of them." Crabs leaned down and picked up a stone from the drive. With deadly accuracy, he tossed it towards the paddock where Folly and Gambler were quietly grazing. It struck the little yellow colt on the rump, and Gambler sped around the paddock in fear. The laughter grew louder and more unsettling. "See you Sunday, Wop."

MORGAN and the two women returned later in the afternoon. Al was busy with the evening chores and didn't bother to greet them. He was feeding Gambler when Lacey came to say goodbye. She had her cloth bag over her shoulder, and she looked so young and innocent that his heart ached for her.

"I've got to go. We're shipping cattle Monday, and Dad needs me to help separate them tomorrow. Otherwise, I could have stayed the whole weekend."

Al didn't answer.

"Don't you want to know how I did today?"

"It's not my race. I don't care." He had hurt her enough, but he couldn't stop. All the shame he felt for himself was turning his words into hot bullets. "I've got more important things on my mind than horse shows and parties. I lead one of those exciting lives, remember? And why don't you grow up? You can't play with horses all your life."

She left the barn, tears of betrayal glistening in her dark eyes.

Al didn't go to supper. It was late when Celia came to his room, and she had a worried look on her face. He had prepared the lines; he knew exactly what he was going to say to her. He just wished he knew what he was going to do on Sunday.

"What's going on, Al? What's wrong?"

"You think something's wrong just because I didn't rush out to say 'hi' and ask how your day was.? Maybe I don't give a fuck how your day went."

"I thought you were taking an interest in this thing. I thought you were taking an interest in Lacey."

"Her! What a kid. All she can talk about is horses. I wanted to get in her pants, sure. But after I realized what a jerk she was —" He shrugged his shoulders.

He had hit a nerve. Celia's worried look was chased away, and in its place was one of disgust. *Go on, hate me!* Al thought. *Tell me I'm a no-good bastard. Then I can leave tomorrow and not feel bad about it.*

"Something happened today. I want to know what it was. This isn't you talking, Al."

"What do you know about me? Remember what I told you in the hospital? I told you not to trust me—right? So what do you do? Go off for the day and leave me in charge. How frigging dumb can you be? I could have run off with—everything!"

Celia took a long, ragged breath. How could it be starting all over again? She calmed herself. "I know you wouldn't do something like that. Maybe you don't care anything about me or Morgan or even Lacey. But I know one thing for sure, Al. I know you care about Gambler. There's no way in the world you'd run off from him."

For just one second, Al felt like giving in. He wanted to hide in her arms and tell her everything. It was so tempting. Instead, he said, "Don't be so sure about that."

Again he heard the startled snort as the rock hit Gambler's flank. The terror of an unknown assailant had goaded the colt into a frightened, stiff-legged gallop to nowhere. Ted Fulkerson's psychotic laughter boomed in his ear.

CHAPTER 12

Sleep eluded Al that night. For the first time in three weeks, he wished fervently for a drink, for lots of drinks, for enough drinks to put him into that blank world where nothing mattered. He rose to give Gambler his morning feeding. The colt was so perfect. The enormity of a perfect little life that existed because of him struck him like a blow. The responsibility was too much.

He cleaned the bottle and haltered Folly, letting his hands work with the routine but letting his thoughts wander. He could get the keys to the truck; that was no problem, but how could he get his hands on any money? He knew enough about the ranch workings to realize there was very little money to be had.

Suddenly, his thoughts were forced back to the present. Folly pushed his face into Al's chest with enough force to hurt. "Hey, you big lug. What are you doing?" He looked the gelding in the eye, and for a second, he felt fear. There was too much understanding in that liquid orb. Or was he just seeing his own reflection too clearly? Was it a gesture of farewell when he threw his arms around the horse's neck and buried his face in its harsh mane? He inhaled the clean smell, the clean, pure smell of horse. So why did he also smell smoke? He clung to Folly for support . . .

The pain was still there. The terrible pain. But the horse dropped his head to touch his shoulder. He could see, even through the smoke, the thin white blaze on the horse's face. "Simiakia," he whispered through the pain and fear, "you have come for me. Give me strength." He tangled his hands in the horse's mane and slowly pulled himself to his feet.

As yet, they had not been seen. He could hear the shouts of triumph, the cries from the blood-hungry soldiers, and the horrible sounds of agony when they found a still-living victim. Soon, they would be at his tipi. Soon, they would find the body of his beloved wife, and even in her death, they would ravage her once-proud beauty. Soon, they would be upon him. Fear gave him strength, the strength he needed to pull himself onto the pony's back.

"Too short," they had always laughed. "He is too short to be a buffalo pony, and he has no spots. Give him to your wife to use as a carrier of packs." Now most of them were dead, and their proud buffalo ponies were scattered like leaves in the wind. He lay across the horse's neck and whispered in his ear, "I'll not fall from you, Simiakia. Help me."

"I think we had better talk." Morgan's hand was on his shoulder. It was a firm grip but not unfriendly. "I just got a call from Sheriff Gilberman. He said Ted Fulkerson was back in town, or so he had heard."

"So?"

"Don't pretend with me. We know he was in on what happened here. He and another boy, Randy Chortney, robbed a pawn shop in Spokane. Only there wasn't enough money to suit them, so they beat the owner half to death and raped his wife."

"What are you telling me this for? I sure as hell wasn't in on it."

"Al, he was an old man. His wife was seventy-two years old. Before they were through, they'd used a wine bottle on her."

Al felt like he was going to be sick.

"How can you feel any loyalty toward him? He's a monster. My God, I can't understand why you would try to protect him."

"Because I'm scared of him, that's why. Because he said if I didn't help him, he'd kill me, and he'd—he'd hurt the horses."

"Why do I get the feeling that the last thought scares you worse than the first? I knew he had to have been here. The things you said to Celia and the way you treated Lacey . . . I knew you wouldn't change back overnight."

"She probably hates me now."

"No. There's no hate in that girl. She'll understand."

Folly shifted his weight restlessly. A decision had to be made. "I was supposed to meet him tonight at the abandoned gas station on the edge of Clarkston. I was supposed to swipe your truck and enough money to get us to Seattle."

"Ha. That kid's got a real imagination," Morgan said humorlessly. "I'll call Gilberman back and see how he wants to handle this. You coming up to the house?"

"If I'm welcome. I might as well tell you, Mr. Kyles, I was going to do it."

"To save the horses, maybe, not your own hide. Just for the record, if you're going to act like a man, you might as well talk to me like one. It's Morgan."

GILBERMAN DIDN'T COME to the ranch. He was afraid that Fulkerson might be watching the place. Instead, he met Morgan in Lewiston and outlined his plan to trap the fugitive. After dark, a deputy would come out to the ranch and would drive the green pickup to the meeting place. Morgan suggested using Al, but Gilberman scoffed. "Like as not, that kid'll drive off with your truck and the Fulkerson boy both. Leopards don't change their spots, Kyles. You raise Appies—you ought to know that."

Morgan hated the word "Appy," and he wasn't overly fond of Roy Gilberman. "That's where you're wrong, Sheriff. *Appaloosas,*" he enunciated the word, "can change color every spring shed."

"I'm not arguing technicalities with you. Deputy Read is the kid's size and color. Have him wear some of the Injun's clothes,and by the time Fulkerson gets close enough to realize his mistake, it'll be too late. The plan can't miss."

But it did miss. Morgan, Celia, and Al sat together in the ranch house living room, drinking coffee and not even trying to talk. At 2 a.m., the flashing light of the sheriff's car appeared in the window.

"He got away; we lost him," said Gilberman apologetically while he fingered his stiff-brimmed hat in his hands.

Al turned pale. "How could you lose him? He's the size of a moose. Sweet Jesus, how could you have fucked it up?"

Gilberman was in no mood for criticism. "Listen, snot nose. You're not off the hook. I'm not so sure you didn't warn him."

"Don't be ridiculous," Celia snapped. "I know everyone's tired and disappointed, but let's not resort to name-calling. Honestly, Al wants him caught as badly as you do, as badly as Morgan, and I want to see him behind bars."

The sheriff put his hat back on. "I'm sorry, Miss Bolt. It's been a long day, and it scares me to think an animal like that Fulkerson kid is in my county. If you folks hear anything, let me know. 'Night, now."

He left, and the room was uncomfortably silent. Finally, Al said, "He'll be back, you know."

"Maybe he won't. Maybe they scared him off."

Al looked at Celia as if she were something he couldn't quite get into focus. "Where's he going to go? He doesn't have any money, and that car he had can't last much longer. No, he'll come back here even if it's just to finish with me. You don't know him."

"Then you're sleeping in the house for a while. And we're all going to be extra careful."

The boy shook his head. "I can't do that. I can't leave Gambler. Morgan, don't you remember what he did to Cantar's pups? He enjoys doing things like that. Someone's got to stay in the barn."

"It's not going to be you. I'll stay out there, and I'll have the rifle with me. And Cantar. If anybody's got a score to settle with Fulkerson, it's her. By the way, where was she yesterday when he came?"

"She took off toward the mountain pasture. I've noticed her sneaking up there a lot these past few days."

"So have I," added Celia. "In fact, she didn't bark at the Sheriff's car. She must be gone now."

Morgan frowned. "Can't have that. I'll shut her in the barn with me when she comes back." He got the rifle from the closet and put extra cartridges in his pocket. "Keep these doors locked, okay?" He kissed Celia good night. "Love ya," he said softly.

Celia shivered when he walked out the door. She pulled her cardigan more closely around her. "Do you really think he'll come back?"

"Yeah. Maybe not tonight; probably not tonight. He'll figure the cops are still here. But he'll come back. Do you have another gun?"

'I've a handgun. I keep it in my dresser, but I've never shot it."

"I wish you'd get it out and keep it by your bed—loaded. And tomorrow, practice with it a bit. If he shows up, don't be afraid to use it on him."

" I couldn't shoot anybody."

Al stared at her in disbelief. "You'd shoot a rabid dog, wouldn't you? He's every bit as dangerous as one. Believe me, you wouldn't be able to talk him down. He used to brag about killing an Indian girl, and I was never sure if it was the truth or not. But after what he did in Spokane—I guess if he could do that, he could do anything. Please, Celia. Promise me. Don't give him a chance. If he hurt you, I'd—"

"Hey." Her voice was quiet and calm. "Take it easy. We'll all stick together, and we'll be okay. I'll keep the gun by the bed."

"And you'll use it if you have to?"

"I'll use it. Now, I'm going to try to get some sleep, although, after all the coffee I've drunk tonight, I doubt if that's possible. See you in the morning."

She climbed the stairs to the loft. Al watched her and waited until he heard her open her dresser drawer and rummage through it, then close it again, before he turned out the lights. He lay on the couch and pulled the Afghan over himself. In a few minutes, they were both asleep.

AL HADN'T PLANNED on sleeping. When he awoke, he was surprised that it was light enough to see the clock on the fireplace mantle. It was almost time to feed Gambler.

With the dawn, he felt safer and much more brave. As he was slipping his stockinged feet into his boots, the only clothes he had bothered taking off the night before, he thought that his smoke dream was returning. He smelled the unpleasant tang, but the pain was missing, and his mind was much too aware of his real surroundings to be one of his mysterious visions. As he pushed his heel down into the second boot, he realized that he wasn't imagining anything.

Following his nose and sniffing like a dog, he crossed the kitchen and reached for the back door handle. "Ow!" he exclaimed and drew his hand back. He grabbed a kitchen towel and wrapped his hand. Once more, he grasped the handle and threw open the door.

The entire back porch was in flames. The door was blistered and scorched and ready to burst into flames as well.

"Celia!" he yelled in a voice that would have wakened the dead. "Fire! There's a fire out back!" He turned away from the heat and was running towards the telephone and almost collided with Celia.

Her face was pale, but her voice was steady. "Get Morgan. I'll call the fire department. Then hook up the hose. Hurry!"

The barn was a sufficient distance from the house that the commotion hadn't awakened Morgan. He had fought off sleep most of the night and, with the approach of dawn, had felt he could safely close his eyes for a few hours.

"Morgan, wake up! The house is on fire!"

The big man sprang to his feet. He, too, had removed only his boots when he laid down, and he didn't stop to put them on. "Back porch. I'll get an extra hose."

Al was frantic, but not so much that he had lost his head. He knew that Crabs was at the bottom of the whole thing, but there was no time to investigate. There was no way the fire department would arrive in time to be of much help. If the ranch house was to be saved, it would require immediate action.

Folly whinnied, and even Gambler was moving restlessly around the stall. They could smell the smoke. Then Al noticed that the stall wasn't latched. Another trick? No matter. It wouldn't do to have panic-stricken horses running amok during an emergency. He swung the coiled hose onto his shoulder and ran to the stall. "It's all right, guys. You'll be okay."

The blow from behind sent him crashing into the solid door and face-first into the straw. The acrid odor of urine, the ammonia smell, cleared his head and saved him from fainting. He lurched to his feet, his sense reeling, and had trouble focusing on the leering giant who blocked the doorway.

"No, they won't, faggot. They're not going to be okay, and neither are you. You're invited to a wiener roast, and guess whose wiener we're roasting?"

He held a pistol in his hand. It looked like a police revolver, and Al swore at the ineptness of the Sheriff and his whole department. None of this should be happening. He had done his part.

"I told you not to cross me, didn't I? You're going to die, and it's going to hurt—a lot." He picked up a red can and began splashing its contents on the stall door and in the straw. Gambler pressed against the back of the stall. His white-rimmed eyes were wide with fright, and his nostrils dilated at the rank smell of the gasoline. "You'll all fry together, and they won't be able to tell the horse meat from the chicken shit. Go ahead and yell if you want. They won't year you. They're too busy trying to save the house. Pretty smart of me, starting that other fire. And pretty smart of me to show up after first light—just when you thought you were safe again. I'm a fucking genius."

Crabs threw the gas can to the side. He kept the pistol trained on Al while he shoved a ham-sized fist into his pants pocket. He pulled out a book of matches and managed to light one without letting the barrel waver from the Indian boy's direction. He touched the lit match to the red ends of the others in the book, and he held the small torch in his free hand.

"See you in hell, fairy. Keep a seat warm for—"

The sound came from hell. It was a snarl of insane anger that could not have come from the throat of any living thing. The pistol exploded in Crab's hand.

Al heard the hum and felt the terrible sting. It sounded like an enraged bumble bee. He stumbled backward and was saved from falling by the solid mass of the sorrel gelding behind him. Then, everything went black for an instant.

The screams of despair wailed louder in his ears; the smoke encompassed him like a buffalo robe until he could scarcely breathe. He could feel the heat of the flames. They were traveling through the very center of the fire. He clung to the horse as he would have clung to a messenger of the gods. Perhaps that was it. Perhaps that was why the pony had returned. The Great Spirit had sent it to carry him safely back from the land of devils.

For almost a lifetime, they fought the flames. And when he swore his strength was spent, the smoke cleared. He could breathe again. He slipped from Simiakia's back to bathe his face in a quiet mountain pond.

CHAPTER 13

"He's coming to."

Faces swam in front of his eyes.

"How do you feel, son?"

The words sounded like they were being played at the wrong speed. Al tried to sit up, but gentle hands pushed him back onto the soft pillows and replaced the cool compress on his forehead.

"Not so fast, now. You've a nasty gash on your head. Nothing permanent, but you won't be riding any broncs for a day or two."

He didn't recognize the features that hovered over him, nor the slow-motion voice, but he suddenly remembered the fire. "The horses? The barn?" he tried to exclaim. Instead, it came out as a weak plea.

"They're all right. And we've still got a roof over our heads." That was Celia's voice, coming from somewhere above his left shoulder. He had so many questions, but he couldn't make his mouth form the words. He began drifting off into the twilight world again, with only fragments of words and snatches of sentences penetrating his consciousness.

"Better off here . . . Don't want to hospitalize . . ."

"Wake him?"

"Blood pressure . . . Call me."

Then he sank into blackness once more.

Celia woke him every few hours all through the day. She attached the blood pressure cuff like she knew what she was doing and wrote the readings in a notebook. She would murmur simple questions—ask him his name or ask if he knew where he was—and when he would answer, she'd let him fall back asleep again. He didn't wake on his own until the sun was setting and the living room was bathed in comforting shadows. He smelled food cooking and was aware that his stomach was growling.

Slowly, he got to his feet. He stood for a few seconds while a wave of nausea swept over him and then washed away. He walked into the kitchen, careful to put his feet down softly. Any sudden movement brought the waves crashing back against his head.

Celia stood at the stove, stirring something that smelled delicious. "Hi," he said weakly. Then he lowered himself into the nearest chair.

"Good. You're back among the living. I was just about to wake you to see if you'd like some soup. Do you know how long it's been since you ate last?"

"Do you know how long it's been since I've been hungry?" he countered. He didn't want to come right out and ask what had happened. He was not sure how much he wanted to hear.

"It's all over now, Al. He won't be hurting anyone ever again."

"The last thing I remember is him lighting a match and saying something about meeting him in hell. Then there was an awful sound—almost like a scream. The gun he was holding on me went off, and I felt the bullet crease my head. I fell backward, but I don't think I actually fell. That's it." It was a long speech. His throat was dry and tight. The last words had to be pushed out of his mouth.

"Morgan went back to the barn to look for you. I manned the hose. As you can see, we'll need a new back door, and the stoop is totally destroyed, but it's nothing compared to what could have happened. By the time he got there, the Fulkerson boy was face-down in the straw, surrounded by flames. Cantar was ducking in and out of the fire, biting and slashing." She stopped stirring the soup and shut her eyes tightly. "He said he didn't know what was worse—the terrible sounds she was making or the boy," she paused, "screaming in agony. My God, I'm glad I didn't see it."

Al felt nausea again, only this time it centered in his gut, not in his head. "It was her, then, who hit him. She got her justice, didn't she? But how did I get out?"

"It was the God-damndest thing I've ever seen." Celia and Al had been too caught up in their conversation to hear Morgan entering. The big man stood framed in the doorway. He stared at Al with something akin to admiration. "I couldn't even see you; the flames were shooting so high. I could hear Gambler; he almost sounded like a baby crying. The hose was gone from the barn hydrant, and I was fixing to tear myself away to get another one. The whole time, I kept on saying to myself that it was hopeless. Whatever and whoever was inside that stall was a goner. I was pretty unnerved, what with all the noise and the smell of—" In deference to Celia's wan face, he didn't finish the sentence.

"Anyway, I was spooked enough that I didn't believe what I was seeing at first. Those flames were like a wall. No horse that ever lived would have come through them. But here comes Folly, leaping like one of those trained lions you see in the circus, jumping through a flaming hoop. Right behind him, like he's tied to his tail, comes Gambler. And holding onto Folly's mane, sort of dangling to him, is you. The two horses went running out of the barn.

"I figured there was nothing you needed that was as important as getting the fire in the barn put out, so I got another hose and fought the fire until the department fellows showed up. That's when I went looking for you. Folly was standing in the paddock. Gambler was with him. And you—you still had your hands wrapped in his mane. It was all I could do to pry your fingers loose. Dr. Rahter was here, he came with the ambulance, and he said he's never seen anything like it. You were out cold, but your hands were still working."

"I don't remember any of it," Al lied. He remembered the agonized cries, the heat of the flames, the smoke, and the horse's calm strength. It was more than just a dream; he knew that now.

"There was no structural damage to the barn. No horses were hurt. Cantar got some burns but nothing serious."

"And Crabs is dead," finalized Al.

"Yeah, he's dead. Maybe I could have pulled him out in time. Maybe I didn't try hard enough." There was just a hint of guilt in Morgan's voice.

"No, Morgan, nobody could have helped that boy." Celia meant so much more than what her words said. Then her voice lightened. "Some good news for you, Al. Gilberman said that in light of what happened, all charges against you will be cleared from the books, and the custodial period has been reduced from eighteen to six months. There's just a little legal hocus-pocus to go through, but when six months are up, your record will be clean."

"It was the least he could do," Morgan growled. "He didn't bother to tell us that Fulkerson was armed, with one of his deputy's revolvers, no less. He couldn't have botched things any worse if he planned it."

Al wasn't listening to Morgan's tirade. He was thinking about what Celia had said. He had less than five months left to serve. Then he'd be free, with no claims on him.

He wondered what he would do then.

THE RITES of graduation had taken over the ancient rites of passage into adulthood—at least for the Trueblood family. Had she been born two hundred years earlier, Lacey would have ceased being a girl and become a woman by the age of thirteen. The event would have been marked by a special celebration and banquet and followed closely by her marriage. By the age of seventeen, she would have had a family started and been the wise counselor of her warrior husband. As it was, her graduation from high school, the first of Calvin and Madeline Trueblood's three daughters to do so, was the symbol of her first step into the adult world.

One hundred and eight students from the reservation graduated from school that spring. For some, it was a welcome escape from a barely tolerated prison. For others, the diploma represented a passport to the outside world. For far too many of them, it was a day like any other. It meant nothing in particular. For Lacey Trueblood, however, it was the most exciting day of her life.

She had abandoned the traditional cap and gown and was dressed like a princess in a doe-skin dress decorated with porcupine quills and feathers. It had been in her mother's family for generations, passed lovingly from mother to oldest daughter. Some may have thought it pretentious, but Lacey chose to honor her people on this special day. In her valedictorian speech, she talked of commitment, not only to the future but to the past, as well. She spoke names from history that many of the audience had never heard of, and she concluded her talk by quoting the famous words of Chief Joseph: *Hear me, my chiefs. My heart is sick and sad. From where the sun now stands, I will fight no more, forever.*

"Our great forefather did not mean that to be the end of his struggle. He never stopped fighting—not in spirit. He knew the uselessness of battle. He knew our people were outnumbered and out-armed on every front. He knew to continue the war would have been sheer suicide—the end of the Nez Perce as a nation. But with his inner strength and wisdom, with his patient appeals to his captors, with his words that will live forever—he was victorious. He still lives in each of us. We have each won a battle on this proud day. We have won it for him—and because of him, we will continue to fight."

The party held in Lacey's honor that evening was the biggest event the reservation had seen in a while. Madeline and her many sisters had spent the greater part of the week preparing a bountiful menu. The modest ranch home was decorated with ceremonial trappings. The guest list included all of the governing heads of the reservation. In spite of the fact that there were other parties going on that evening, all who were invited opted to attend the Truebloods' function. Many of the students floated from party to party, but those who appeared at the Clear Water Ranch were prepared to behave with respect and not get involved in post-graduation exploits.

White faces were few and far between at the festivities. Those who were in attendance were very honored to be there, including Morgan Kyles and Celia Bolt. Even more honored, if not a little uncomfortably so, was Alicut George—a boy fast approaching manhood and plunged into the middle of a world he had long tried to deny.

"She's the most beautiful thing I've ever seen," whispered Al to Morgan. Lacey was involved in a circle dance with several other young people. She was stomping her moccasin-clad feet in time with rhythmic drumbeats. Her hair hung loose and appeared to have a life of its own.

"She's an eyeful, all right." Morgan ran a finger around his collar. He wasn't used to the starched tightness.

Celia, on the other hand, had become another person as soon

as she donned her formal clothing. She was surrounded by three distinguished-looking tribesmen and was laughing politely at a story one of them was telling. She wasn't aware of it, but Morgan felt dismissed by her easy gregariousness. He felt out of place and clumsy. Together, he and Al stood in the corner in mutual pity.

"She's ignoring me," Al convinced himself. "I had my chance, and I blew it."

"She always does this," said Morgan. Neither was concerned that they were discussing totally different "she"s. "Watch her. She'll dance with every man here."

"She's danced with seven different guys since I've been watching! And I can't even dance."

"Pretty soon, she'll come swishing up here and say, 'Morgan, aren't you having a great time?' And half the men in the room will have their eyes on her. How the hell can I be having a great time, standing here like a stuffed pheasant and her flirting with everybody? Here." He pulled a small flask from his inside vest pocket. "Want a drink?"

"What is it?"

"Jack Daniels, black." Morgan took a small, secretive sip. "Damn good stuff."

"Yeah, I guess I'll have some."

Al reached for the flask, but Morgan did not let go of it right away. He looked the boy in the eye and made a startling discovery. He did not have to look down on him anymore. Could he have grown that much in a little more than a month? Or was the boy just standing a little taller? "You can have as much as you want, but I'll tell you, there isn't a whiskey made that'll make you feel any better than holding that pretty little lady in your arms."

Al pulled his hand back. "I can't do that."

"Sure, you can. You just waltz on up to her the next slow

dance they play. You don't have to be no Fred Astaire to stand out there and sway."

"And if three guys are there in front of me?"

Morgan laughed. "No way. None of these kids have got the guts to slow dance with Lacey. Not with her old man watching."

"Great. You trying to get me scalped?"

"Calvin won't do anything. He's just got everybody thinking he would."

"I'll make you a deal, Morgan. Next slow dance, I'll ask Lacey if you'll ask Celia."

"But I don't dance! I never get out on the floor unless I'm drunk, then I start stomping toes."

"You said it. You don't need to be no John Travolta to slow dance."

Morgan watched as his woman executed a fancy two-step with Eddie Trottinghorse. She was looking up into the handsome Indian's face. "She can do it all. She's at home anywhere; she fits in any place. How'd I get so goddamn lucky? 'Cause I know, no matter how many good-looking men she dances with, how many intelligent conversations she gets into tonight, she's coming home with me. Sometimes, I just stand and wonder—why'd she pick me? No, boy, ain't no whiskey in the world can compare with that."

The song ended. There was a burst of applause, and then people started shouting out requests. The fiddle player stepped forward and quieted everyone with a wave of his hand. Slowly, he drew the bow over the strings and began a heartfelt tune, an old standard. Older couples who had chosen to sit out the faster dances began to drift toward the dance floor. Morgan poked Al in the ribs. "I talked myself into it," he said. "Let's go."

Lacey was standing by the punch bowl. Her face was flushed from the exertion of the last dance. She glowed the way any woman would when she was the center of attention. As Al approached her, another man touched her on the arm. Al caught her eye quickly. "Lacey," he was as breathless as if he'd been dancing, "would you like to dance?"

Lacey looked startled. She turned to the older man, who smiled magnanimously. "I was about to ask Miss Trueblood for this dance, but I think she'd much rather be your partner. You're quite a hero—so I hear, young man."

Al took her in a stiff-armed position and steered her crudely to the fringe of the dancing mass. "Remember the horseback riding? I'm as new to this as I was that."

"I thought you were still mad at me. I thought you'd never ask me to dance."

"I don't like crowds. This is your night, and everyone wants you. Besides, I thought you were mad at *me*. I said some pretty cruel things."

"But you didn't mean them, did you?"

Al grinned and relaxed his arms a little. He was catching the easy rhythm of the tune. "I like you just the way you are. Celia and Morgan told me how you acted at the Saddle Club meeting. I was so proud of you. And your speech tonight! You had everyone in tears. I've never heard anybody talk like that before."

"I can talk like that about things I know and understand—like horses and cattle and Indian history. I'm very proud of being an Indian, Al. It's my heritage. As a people, we have lots of problems, but I meant every word I said in my speech."

Could she see into his soul? Could she see the shame that fermented there?

"Did they tell you I'm now the first official full-blooded Indian member of the Palouse Valley Saddle Club?" The child-like excitement was back in her voice.

"They sure did."

"Some people weren't too pleased—Chairman Dutchens, especially. But I fulfilled all the requirements. I live within the geographic boundaries, I own at least one registered Appaloosa of breeding capabilities, and my application was nominated by a member in good standing and approved by a simple majority of the members present at that meeting. Morgan was so surprised. He's always complained about how prejudiced the club was. This was one time I think he was glad to be proven wrong."

"Speaking of Morgan, look at him." The big man was weaving gracelessly with Celia held tightly in his arms. His face was buried in her hair. "He's worse than me."

"I wonder what he's saying to her?"

"I don't know, but I bet it has nothing to do with horses."

Lacey's pretty face fell into a disappointed frown. "That's what I'm trying to tell you. I can chatter on for hours about things I know, but I'm tongue-tied when I try to . . ." Her words hung on the air.

"Try to what?" Al shook her gently.

"Try to tell you how much I like you." She blurted it out, then the rest came, as if a plugged hose had suddenly been cleaned of debris, allowing the water to flow rapidly once more. "All week, all I could think about was you. I wanted to go see you after the fire, but I was afraid to. When I was supposed to be preparing for graduation and this party, I kept wondering if you'd come. Didn't you see me looking for you when I was giving my speech? I don't know what to say to a boy like you when we aren't talking about horses. Part of me is terrified of you, and part of me . . ." The water ceased flowing; the hose was empty.

Sometimes I just stand and wonder—why'd she pick me?

Al pulled her closer and gently encircled her in his arms. He could feel the rapid beating of her heart against his own chest, and he was surprised at the way her head rested so conveniently against the hollow of his shoulder. By the time the dance had ended, he trusted himself to speak.

"Do you remember how you were going to tell me about your surprise, and I wouldn't let you?"

"Yes."

"Would you tell me now? I know you're going to announce it soon, but I'd like to hear it first."

"Let's walk out on the porch," she said conspiratorially. They held hands more like children than lovers and strolled outside. It made no difference that several pairs of eyes were watching the young people—some not entirely approvingly.

"Several weeks ago," she began, "I was informed by the state that I had won a full scholarship. I applied to the University of Idaho in Moscow last winter, hoping we'd find some way of raising the tuition by fall. This scholarship took care of that worry, and my Aunt Sybil's in-laws, the Horns, live in Moscow, so I didn't have to worry about housing. I could come home on weekends easily, and Moscow is closer to Lewiston than Kamiah is. I didn't realize how important that part would be when I applied."

"So you're going to college."

"That's just part of it. I always knew I'd go on with my schooling if at all possible. U of I has an excellent agricultural school, and Dad insisted on me attending. So many new techniques have been developed since he graduated. But the best part came a week ago. I found out the Thursday before I came to Bloodstone. Al, the reservation is going to fund my way through vet school!"

The enormity of it overwhelmed Al. He was still stunned by the realization that Calvin Trueblood was a college graduate. In his life-long struggle to belittle his own people, he had overlooked those who had achieved. Now this tiny girl dressed like a Nez Perce princess, this girl who fit so perfectly in his arms, was telling him she was going to be a doctor.

"There's a fund tended by the treasurer of the reservation. It was started more than seventy years ago by the first of our tribe to receive a professional degree from a white man's school. Phillip Looking Glass was a lawyer. When he graduated, he turned down an offer to work at the capital and instead came back to the reservation. He realized our people could be so easily cheated because we didn't understand the law. For forty years, he was the attorney for our tribe. And he started this fund to help other young Nez Perce go to school. Every so many years, the board chooses a student with promise and finances their college career. The only stipulation is that when they graduate, they return to the reservation and work for a salary. The number of years of service varies with the amount of money that has to come out of the fund. Many of the graduates never leave the reservation.

"My first two years are already paid for by the state. What's important now is that I do the kind of work in my pre-vet studies to get accepted at Washington State in Pullman. Incidentally, Pullman is just across the border from Moscow. I don't even have to leave my neighborhood. Al, are you happy for me?"

After all the honor and personal accomplishment, she was still concerned with how he felt about her. *Why'd she pick me?* "I'm just having trouble understanding all of it. Remember, Lacey, you're talking to a guy who quit going to school when he was twelve."

"I know that. And that's why it's so important to me that you care."

He could have kissed her then; it seemed the most logical thing to do. But Calvin's no-nonsense voice called to her from the doorway. "Lace, your Aunt Sybil is here. And you'd better get ready for your announcement."

"Al, you've got to meet Sybil." She took his hand and started to take him back to the party.

"Young Mr. George will be along shortly. I want to talk to him first."

"Daddy . . ."

"Go ahead. I'm not going to bite him."

Reluctantly, Lacey left. Al watched her thread her way

through the crowd until she disappeared. Calvin drew a pipe from his breast pocket and began filling it from a leather tobacco pouch. "I don't know if you are aware of it or not, but my daughter has been chosen to receive a very special honor."

"I know. And I know what a special person she is."

"Do you? Do you really know what it takes to become a success in our world? I knew your father, son. He was a good boy but a fool. Don't look at me like that. I'm not saying anything about him that you never thought yourself. And I've the right because we were once good friends. He thought basketball was the way off of the reservation. He made two big mistakes. Know what they were?"

Al shook his head. It was always hard for him to picture his father playing basketball. Just drinking.

Trueblood held a match to the pipe and sucked hard enough to create a sufficient draft for the tobacco to light. "The first was thinking that any good school was going to offer him a scholarship. He was a star here, but no college takes any stock in that. Our schedules aren't tough enough. What's our competition? But his biggest mistake was wanting out too badly. The answers don't lie out there."

"How can you say that? Lacey's leaving—you're sending her away."

"But she's coming back. If we Indians can't learn to stand tall among our own people, we don't deserve the respect of the white man."

"Let me get this straight. Are you telling me to stay away from your daughter because of what I am and what my dad was?"

"No." Trueblood sucked reflectively at his pipe. "I'm just telling you she has plans, and I'm not going to let anyone interfere with them."

"Mr. Trueblood, I don't mean this with any disrespect, but I think you're underestimating me, and I'm damn sure you're underestimating your daughter." Al turned to leave. It wasn't the older Indian's voice that made him stop and turn back; it was the name he called him.

"Alicut. Do you know what the first step is in gaining respect?"

"I'm sure you're going to tell me. You seem to have all the answers."

"It's learning to respect yourself. When Samuel George was about your age, he lost that respect." There was no smile on Trueblood's face, but he looked as if he wasn't far from one. "Maybe his son is just finding it."

CHAPTER 14

THE FIRST MEETING of the Advance Promotion Committee met on the following Thursday evening at the Bloodstone Ranch. Morgan chaired the committee, and members Jacob Anderson and Percy Ludwin, plus interested party Sybil Horn, made up the balance. At the same time, a second committee meeting was being held in the kitchen of the ranch house. Celia was in charge of this group. The club's newest member, Lacey Trueblood, was on the roster, and so was a fairly new member, Hank Mattingly. The purpose of this group was to draw up plans for an endurance race to be held in connection with the annual show. Possible race courses, entry requirements, cost of a race veterinarian and assistants, rules and awards—all the details were to be worked out on paper and presented at the next Saddle Club meeting, at which time the members would vote on whether to include the race on the show bill.

Hank Mattingly was in his thirties but appeared much younger. His blonde hair and startling blue eyes gave him an innocent look, and his easy grin and quiet manner marked him as a gentle man. He had arrived in the Colfax area less than a year prior and had set up a realty office that specialized in ranch property. Mattingly owned two horses, nothing fancy, and mostly participated in Club trail rides but did not compete. He did not say much at the meetings, so most of the members were surprised when he volunteered for the race committee.

Celia learned more about Mr. Mattingly in the first five minutes of the informal gathering than she had in the year she had known him. He was originally from Portage, Wisconsin, where he also ran a rural real estate brokerage. There, he had belonged to an organization called UMECRA—Upper Midwest Endurance and Competitive Rides Association—and a splinter group, ApDRA—Appaloosa Distance Riders Association. He had competed actively in distance riding for more than ten years and had temporarily abandoned the sport in favor of establishing his new business. But he was excited about the prospect of a club-sponsored ride and had more help and suggestions to offer than Lacey herself.

Al felt like an outsider. He had agreed to fix clam chowder and corn muffins for after the business meeting, and he made himself quietly busy in the kitchen. But he was annoyed every time Hank Mattingly opened his mouth. Once, when the young man from Wisconsin and Lacey were bent over a diagram, the two heads almost touched. The bushy reddish blond and the shimmering raven-black hairs mingled before Al's eyes. Jealousy churned in his stomach until even the simmering chowder smelled sour.

"If they agree on the race, Hank, will you be riding?" Lacey's tone was friendly and pleasant, but to Al's distorted senses, it sounded coy.

"Oh, I don't know. I miss it, I really do. Back home, my gelding finished in the top ten in the heavyweight category six years in a row. One year, we were club high-point champions. He's a great horse, but I've let him get out of shape. I don't really have the time to work him back into it. And if I did, would it be fair? This race isn't even going to be sanctioned because we want it to be a race for beginners. I'd have no business bringing in a proven winner."

Al scowled at the braggadocio. "Big fucking deal," he said to the clam chowder.

"What about you two?"

"Not us," offered Celia. "This is a working ranch. Everyone's got their jobs. For the mares, that's being pregnant. The only geldings we've got on the place that are over five years—that is the minimum age, isn't it?—are Morgan's work pony, Charlie, and the old gelding I use that belonged to the original owner, Bloodstone himself. I don't think either one of them is endurance caliber. If we still have a gelding around here by the time he's turned five, he's just wasting our hay."

"That's why I never wanted to get into horse breeding. I'd have trouble selling an animal once I put my heart into it."

Celia shrugged. "It's a business, Hank, like any other. We raise them and train them for one purpose. It's nice to win with them, but you can't eat trophies. I get a charge out of campaigning a horse and showing him off, but I get a bigger charge out of selling him for a fine price to someone who'll enjoy him."

"And you, Lacey? Will you race?"

"I raced three times last year. I won the novice division twice, and I placed when I had to go open. Sure, I'm going to enter. What with working and having to save my pennies for college, it'll probably be the only chance I'll get this summer."

"I was going to offer to help you train, but it sounds like you must have a good formula already."

"I'm not sure about the formula, but I've got a good horse." She paused. "At least, I think she is. Some may argue about it."

Hank looked puzzled.

"You've got to know her horse to understand," clarified Celia.

Hey! I'm here, too! I'm not just the frigging cook on this place! Al was screaming inside. He thought if Lacey smiled at the Viking one more time, he'd soak his blond head in clam chowder.

Hank Mattingly was saved from a soup bath by the appearance of Jake Anderson in the kitchen doorway. "We're d-d-done out there. You three can g-g-gab all night, but we're going cra-a-a-zy smelling that chow."

"All right, let's eat," seconded Mattingly. Then Al almost lost control. While the other group was filing in, the blond touched Lacey's arm gently and whispered something to her. Lacey dipped her head, and her slim hand pushed the hair behind her ear. A sunlit smile spread across her face, and she put her lips close to him and answered.

Morgan was rattling soup bowls and telling one of his jokes in a booming voice. "So, the zebra comes to the cow and says, 'What do you do around here?'"

Al let the ladle splash into the cauldron. "Enjoy your soup," he snarled and went out the newly replaced back door, slamming it behind him.

He could hear Morgan continue in a mockingly feminine simper, "'I give milk for the farmer's children so . . .'"

"They don't even care that I left." He stomped out to the barn, kicking rocks as he went. Cantar had been under the new back porch and had started to follow him, but his strange behavior was too much for even the coydog, and she returned to her bed with a puzzled whine.

Folly greeted him with a soft snorting sound. "You're always glad to see me, aren't you, boy?" Al began to calm down a little. Gambler was stretched out in the clean straw, exhausted from a day of racing butterflies and trying to leap shadows.

Al took Folly's bridle down off the hook and guided it over the gelding's head. Then he led the horse from the stall, mounted, and slipped into the moonlight. Slowly, the evening's conversations drained from his memory. His body relaxed, and even the tense knot in his stomach began to loosen. He moved with the horse's easy gait; it was a natural thing for him now. Sometimes he felt he had ridden this horse all his life . . .

The pain was lessened; it was just a dull ache that only stabbed at him if he moved too suddenly. The horse carried him gently, far from the burning nightmare of the camp. Thoughts of his wife drifted in and out of his consciousness. First alive—singing to their soon-to-be-born child in her swollen belly, sewing his moccasins and telling him gossip, quick flashes of her white teeth when she would laugh. Then dead—the ragged round hole in her neck spoiling the perfection of her beauty. He weaved with the terrible pain of her death, a pain more agonizing than all the white men's bullets. The only strength he had left was that of the horse beneath him.

Thundering hooves brought him back to the present. "Al, will you wait?"

Lacey pulled up next to him. He didn't look at her, but he could hear Charlie's panting and the girl's sharp breaths. "He's not used to this kind of night riding, and I'm not used to such a heavy-footed gait. Where are you going?"

"Riding."

"Duh, that's obvious. Why'd you leave?"

"I didn't think you'd notice, mooning over that Viking like you were."

"Why, Al, are you jealous of Hank?"

"Didn't take you very long to get on a first-name basis, did it?"

"He's a very nice man; I like him. But he's thirty-five years old."

"So. Back in the old days, men couldn't marry until they had proved themselves, and then they'd take the prettiest young woman." My God! How did he know that? Was it something his grandmother had told him? How he used to hate it when she'd say, "In the old days . . ."

"Al, I'm ashamed of the way you acted, and if I didn't care so much, I'd of let you ride all night. But I want you to come back. Please. I've got to go home first thing in the morning, and we haven't even got a chance to be together."

"What were you two whispering about?" he demanded singlemindedly.

"I guess that would have tended to make you a little suspicious."

"More than a little."

"If you must know, he was asking about Aunt Sybil. He wondered if she was, well—available. If you had stuck around long enough, you would have seen some real charming on his part."

Al felt foolish. He was glad the moon wasn't any brighter, or she would have seen the crimson flush on his face. He had two choices: he could continue his wounded act and spoil what was left of the evening, or he could apologize and return to the ranch.

Lacey's hand reached out to touch his. The decision was made. The apology came easy, and the ride back was slow.

By the time they had put the horses away, and Al gave Gambler his evening feeding, the party was breaking up. They passed Jake Anderson in the yard. He waved goodbye, and as he climbed in his truck, he said, "'M-m-m-member now, Lace. You ever want to s-s-sell that dev-v-vil of a mare, call m-m-me. She'd g-g-go to the Nation-tion-tional finals for su-s-sure."

"I'll keep that in mind, Mr. Anderson. There isn't anything Rain likes better than throwing fellows, and I'd like to see her happy if I ever had to sell her."

"When am I going to meet this killer horse of yours?"

"I've been holding off on that. I don't want to lose you."

Laughing together, they stepped into the house. Percy Ludwin was preparing to leave. "I didn't get a proper chance to congratulate you, Lacey, on your scholarship."

'Thanks, Mr. Ludwin. I didn't realize news like that crossed state lines."

"When you're bright enough, everyone can see your light." It should have been corny, but Ludwin had such sincerity about him that it sounded like poetry. "I'm not suggesting you'll need it, but I do have some influence in the administration office at Pullman. It's my alma mater, you know."

"I can use all the help I can get."

"And you, young man. May I talk to you for a moment?"

Al was reluctant. The last time he was pulled aside, it was to be warned to stay away from Lacey. It was one thing coming from her father, but if this little squirt was going to tell him how he should leave the girl alone "for her own good," he'd not stand for it. He didn't want to ruin his evening all over again, but he stepped out on the front porch with Ludwin.

"I was wondering if you'd be interested in studying for the GED test to get your high school diploma?" Ludwin said without preamble. "Pardon my nosiness, but I asked Celia about your background, and it's a shame that a boy like you should be hampered by not having graduated."

Al was taken off guard. He had been all ready to defend himself, and the attack was not going to take place. In its stead was an offering of friendship. "I don't know anything about it."

"I teach a class two nights a week at the Colfax High School to help people prepare for the test. That's a little far for you to come, and with ranch work, it's hard to commit yourself to a set time. I could talk to Gregg Nie at Lewiston High School and find out when they start the classes again, or if you'd like, I could send you the self-study guides. You'd have to buy the books."

"I guess that'd be the best." Al pictured his six-foot frame crammed into a child-sized school desk, the rest of the students laughing when he made a mistake. "I never got along too well in the classroom."

"Good. I'll send you the information in the mail. The tests

are given every so often. I'll send you a list of test dates and locations. You can't take it until you're eighteen."

"Why are you interested? You don't even know me."

"Because I'm a teacher, young man. My whole life has been dedicated to helping young people educate themselves. Somewhere along the line, someone failed you, or you wouldn't have gotten yourself associated with the likes of that Fulkerson boy. Perhaps someone failed him as well, but the difference is that you had the strength to rise above that failure. I admire that, and I'd like to be a part of the realization of your potential. I must go now; it's a school day tomorrow."

Al whistled under his breath after saying good night to Ludwin. "I sure hope these studies aren't as hard to understand as he is," he muttered.

Lacey had poured a Coke for Al and was sitting on the small sofa, saving the vacant half for him. Hank was telling a Helga and Hanz joke in a perfect German dialect. Al found himself wondering how he could have misjudged the man. He seemed like a nice enough guy, especially since he was sitting close to Sybil now.

Al sat down and spoke up at the first chance he got. "Celia, when you were talking about the reasons why Bloodstone wouldn't enter a horse in the race, how come you left Folly out? He turned five in May, and he's got all the requirements for an endurance horse. He's small, he's got the lean muscles, not the blocky ones, he's been on the range all his life, and he's . . ."

"And he's pink-papered," interrupted Morgan. He wasn't sure what Al was getting at, but he was going to nip any ideas about showing the sorrel gelding in the bud.

"Wait a minute, Kyles. That's a term that disappeared in January of '83."

"Oh, no, Hank. Not on this ranch, it didn't," Celia said. "Morgan voted to break away from the Appaloosa Horse Club when they passed that new ruling. Please don't get him started on it."

"I'm not following this," said Al tightly.

"Being pink-papered meant that the horse had characteristics of an Appaloosa—striped hooves, mottled skin, sparse tail, white sclera—but no white markings."

"Like Folly?"

"Yes, Al, like Folly. The animals could be used for breeding stock but not entered in registered shows or other events. A lot of breeders complained that they had good horses going to waste or having to be sold as grade horses. It was vastly political, but as of January '83, these solid-colored horses are allowed all the privileges of their colored cousins."

"It's crazy," blurted Morgan, "to have to look at the papers to tell if the horse is an Appaloosa or not, just because some crybaby breeders weren't willing to take risks anymore!"

"I can sure see your point, Morgan. Back in Wisconsin, I had a friend that raced in UMECRA. Her little mare had all the characteristics of an App, flashy as can be, except the papers. So now she has to see solid-colored horses pick up the High Point Appaloosa trophies even though she outscored them. What a slap in the face!

"What you're trying to tell me is Folly is eligible to be in the show, but you won't let him," Al said.

"I took a stand, Al. It wasn't the most popular one at the time, but I held it. I'd look like a fool if I changed my mind now."

"Morgan, you're forgetting one thing. He's not your horse; it's not your decision."

A chill drifted over the living room. The boy and the man tried to out-stare each other, but neither would drop their eyes. When he said the words, Al did not realize what a sore spot they would hit. Having said them, he did not back down.

Finally, Celia spoke. "Al, Morgan speaks for the policy of the ranch. I'm afraid we couldn't enter Folly." But she didn't sound a hundred-percent convincing. She didn't even convince herself. Sometimes she got tired of trying to protect Morgan's male ego.

"Say, Al, if you're interested in trying it, I'd lend you my gelding. You do the conditioning. It'd be worth it to me to see him used." Hank was trying to revive the lost gaiety of the evening. He didn't want to see it end like this.

"No thanks, Mr. Mattingly. I guess it's not that important."

Al cemented the last brick in the wall between himself and Morgan by leaving the room.

AT FIRST, he thought it was another dream. He was having them so frequently he often did not trust his senses. But never in his sweet and hazy dreams of Lacey was she dressed so strangely, nor did she look so frightened or sound so unsure of herself.

The June night was chilly. Over her loose cotton nightgown, she had pulled a plaid wool jacket. Several sizes too large, it hung midway to her knees, and the sleeves hid her hands. Her bare feet were shoved into a pair of rubber boots that were small enough to stay on but looked ungainly and made a flopping noise when she walked. Her face was pale and distraught, her lovely hair tangled and tousled. Despite the queer assortment of clothing she wore, her voice shook with the penetrating dampness of the night air and perhaps with an inner chill as well. "Are you awake, Al?"

He sat up on his cot. "Lacey, what are you doing?"

She looked so much like a child who had had a bad nightmare. "I couldn't sleep. I had to—to talk to you." Her lower lip quivered.

"You goofy kid," he said gently. This wasn't like any dream

he had ever dreamt. He reached out to grab her hands. "You're freezing!"

"I didn't want to wake anyone. I found this jacket by the back door. I think it's Morgan's. And these boots—" She raised her foot and stared at the cracked and weather-abused boot as if she didn't remember putting it on. "I must look a sight." She was close to tears.

"You look like a little kid." He drew her towards him and pulled her onto his lap. "Like a scared little kid." His arms gathered her shivering body close to his bare chest, and she hid her face in his neck. After a few minutes, his own comforting warmth accomplished what the oversized jacket couldn't. She stopped shaking.

"It wasn't supposed to be like this," he said softly, his hands gently patting her back. "You were supposed to show up in the middle of the night like some kind of goddess and drift into bed with me. You weren't supposed to make me feel so—so—protective."

She pulled her face away from him and looked at him through lowered lashes. "I'm a big disappointment, aren't I?"

Tenderly, he pressed his lips to her forehead, then kissed both of her closed eyes. He tasted the salt tears. The emotions that welled inside him were so new. He felt responsible for her, the same way the tiny orphan foal had made him feel. She could affect him in so many ways with her simple, sweet manners. In his arms now, he was overwhelmed by her innocence and vulnerability.

"I don't think you could ever disappoint me. I pray that I will quit disappointing you."

"You frighten me, Al. The way you get so angry. In a way, it's beautiful, like a thunderstorm. But when the storm's over, and things have been destroyed, it's not beautiful anymore."

"I'm always getting mad and blowing up over something, in other words."

She nodded her head slightly. "Do you know how much you hurt Morgan tonight? He tries to act so big and tough, but he can be hurt, too. Just like you."

"I didn't mean it the way it came out, but after I said it, it was too late. I didn't know how to take it back."

"Just like Morgan, again. Can't you understand how he feels?"

"But I'm going to make him change his mind. I'm going to train Folly for that race, and somehow I'll get Morgan to change his mind. You've got to help me, Lace."

Lacey got to her feet. She slipped off the jacket and stepped out of the cumbersome boots. Shyly, she touched Al's face and traced the curve of his jaw with her finger. "I didn't come out here to talk about horses."

Her kiss was awkward, and it took him by surprise. Before he realized it, she was pressing against him, her hands hot on his bare skin. He embraced her, passion replacing the feelings of protectiveness that had consumed him only moments ago. Her breasts were soft through the sheer cotton of her nightgown. They yielded gently to his hesitant touch. Their lips met, tightly at first, then parting, tasting each other. His mouth found the hollow of her neck and her throat, and her pulse fluttered against his tongue like a tiny bird's wings. Her fingers slid across the flat muscles of his back, and she tilted her head, her eyes squeezed shut, her breath coming in sharp gasps.

He moaned. Not even in the dreams was she so warm, or did he want her so badly. He was nibbling her now, his teeth playing gently at the material that covered her breast. He laid his cheek on the cotton, and he could feel her nipple, erect and hard with her young desires, every bit as flagrant as his own. His hands fumbled for the hem of her gown and stroked the silkiness of her calf, her thigh.

She was breathing harder now, panting in his ear, pleading in urgent tones, "No, Al. Oh please. We shouldn't. We shouldn't."

Then, with an effort violent in its desperation, she leaped from his embrace. “I can’t, Al. I’m sorry.”

She was gone, leaving him aching with unspent passion, throbbing with the need for her. He lay back on the cot, his chest heaving. Was it only a dream after all?

The discarded boots lay on the floor where she had kicked them. He breathed her name reverently, and he slept no more that night.

CHAPTER 15

MORGAN LET OUT a whoop when he opened the manilla envelope. Celia was buried in papers, trying to make numbers match and worrying the end of her pencil because they wouldn't. She looked up, startled. "Don't tell me. Good news —finally."

"Damn right. Got the check for those four horses we sent to the consignment sale. You won't believe it."

"The way I have this figured, we need at least four-thousand-two to pay Dave Mechling back his deposit. He's been pretty patient about it, don't you think? And another two to pay this month's bill.

Morgan beamed. "I can beat that. The two yearling horse colts went for eight and eight fifty. The two-year-old colt brought thirteen-forty, and," he paused dramatically, "that filly that we both thought so little of sold for," another pause, "six-teen-seventy!"

"Morgan, it's finally happening." Celia sighed and laid down her well-chewed pencil. "Those weren't bad horses, just young and slow to mature. We couldn't afford to spend a lot of time on them. But our name carried them." She walked behind him and draped her arms over his shoulders, and rested her chin on top of his head. "Four-one-nine-four. Even with the commission taken out, we've got enough to get us through this month." She sighed again.

"If we weren't so damn unprincipled, we would refund about six hundred to whoever bought that filly. She just wasn't worth that much. I agree with you, our reputation pushed the bidding up, and I'm not sure how right that is."

"Morgan Kyles, I don't want to hear about principles. 'Unprincipled,' my ass. You're deluged with principles. I think you're trying to make up for all those years you spent as a rodeo bum. That filly was worth $1,670 to whoever bought her. Your principles, my love, cost us seven thousand dollars just a few short weeks ago. I'd rather sell one terrific horse like the Ghost for forty-five hundred than four mediocre animals for forty-six."

Morgan frowned. "I know, I know. I've kicked myself a hundred times for that, watching you sit over there, struggling with those damn books." He reached up to hug her. "And how come I'm getting the feeling you're setting me up?"

"Are you feeling sufficiently penitent about sending us into financial doom?"

"Yeah, yeah. You're mad about the kid, aren't you?"

"Honey, do I sound like I'm mad?"

"No. That's when you're the maddest."

Celia lowered her head to Morgan's shoulder and rubbed her cheek gently on him. She chose her words very carefully. "He didn't mean it the way it sounded. Morgan, nobody looks at the papers to see whose name is on them."

"Or whose name is on this check."

"Or whose name is on that feed bill or the gas bill," she countered a little too sharply. "You'd no more walk out on me and leave me with a pile of bills than I'd not back you up in a policy decision like I did Thursday night. You're as much a part of this place as I am. There wouldn't be a Bloodstone Ranch if you hadn't come along. The only reason Al said what he did was because Folly is Baby's first foal. He knows how special all of Baby's foals are to me."

"We'd look like hypocrites if we let him enter that horse."

"Hang your pride, Morgan! Haven't you watched the two of them? Folly's always been a good horse, but when Al's on him, it's like he's a different animal altogether. It just might be that Folly is the best horse Bloodstone has ever bred, but we've been so blinded by his color, or lack of it, that we've never noticed it. It took someone like Al to bring it out in him. What about his pride, Morgan?"

"Maybe the Club will decide against the race, and we won't even have to worry about it."

"That's a total cop-out and not worthy of a man of principles like yourself. And it won't mend the rift between the two of you. We were all three doing so well up until then."

"So, what do you want me to do?"

"Think about it. That's all I ask." She straightened up and kissed the top of his head, noticing the surprisingly large number of grey hairs streaking through the dark strands. *It's a bad age,* she thought. *Forty-four. A man likes to feel he's accomplished something by that time—he wants to have something solid to show for half a life's time of hard work. No wonder he's so sensitive.*

She thought back to the day Mike had her sign the title to Bloodstone Ranch. "Fee Simple Subject to Condition Subsequent," he had called her type of ownership. It was just a lot of legal jargon at the time, but it was to be the source of a lot of problems later—problems between her and the man she loved.

"The stipulation is you must remain the sole owner of the property. You can sell the ranch, but you cannot sell interests in it or pieces of it," Mike had explained.

"What happens if I take on a partner?"

"You can't. If the ranch becomes anything other than a sole

proprietorship, it can go back to Bloodstone's heirs. They have what is called a Right of Reentry. They can take you to court to get the property back."

"That's strange. Why in the world would he set it up like that?"

"I didn't know the old man well, but from talking to his lawyer and the other research I've done on him, I think I can answer you. His daughter, the one he hasn't heard from in so long, was once a fairly good horsewoman. She worked side by side with her dad, a lot like you did, until she met a student from U of I who turned her away from the horses. She became quite the 'prima-donna,' married the boy, who incidentally was very well put, and left her father."

"I don't think I'm very clear yet."

"Don't you see? He worked hard on you, Miss Bolt. He trained you in his theories and techniques. But you're a very young woman and very pretty, and I'm sure there is not a lack of suitors in your life. He was afraid one of these local boys would win your heart and then start running the ranch *his* way. If there's no possibility for anyone else to own interest in the ranch, it sort of does away with schemers. He'd rather see you sell outright than compromise the things he taught you."

Morgan finally spoke, bringing her back to the present. "I'll think about it," he said.

"And while you're mulling that over, ponder this for a minute or two. We've got the biggest three months of the show season ahead of us. I want to really pour it on. I want to campaign Ghost like mad. I want to put a halter championship on our young stallion; then, I want to sell him before winter. If he's as good as I hope, he'll pay next winter's feed bill. Flora has potential coming out of her ears. I want her in front of as many judges as possible. I want to put Red Rider in as many classes as we can this year, and next year he'll be one of the best junior reining horses in the state. I've never seen such reflexes in a colt. We've got . . ."

"Whoa, whoa there, lady. What kind of operation are we running here? Where's the manpower going to come from?"

"That's just it, Morgan. We've got Al for the summer, at least. He's more help than I dreamed he could be. And with a little sweet talk to Calvin, I think we can hire Lacey until school starts. Let's give it a shot, hon. Let's end up in three state finals, maybe even the nationals this year. Are you with me? Look at this check," she waved the yellow piece of paper. "If we can get almost seventeen hundred for a two-year-old that has never been shown just because she carries our name . . ." She didn't have to say anymore.

"I'm with you, babe." He put his arm around her waist and pulled her close. Still seated, he rested his head between her breasts and said very tenderly, "I'm always with you."

Oh, Mr. Bloodstone, Celia thought fervently, *if you could have known this good man . . .*

Close to noon, Celia went looking for Al. She found him lunging a fully tacked two-year-old in the arena. His face was set while he concentrated on the filly's movements, and he didn't realize Celia was watching him. She was analyzing him, really, noting his quiet, steady way with the young horse.

He hadn't been told this was his job. Celia had worked with him a day, showing him how to set the horses' heads and how to look for correct leads. Then she had said that the two-year-olds needed to be worked every day. The next thing she knew, Al had taken over the job. He sandwiched half-hour workouts for several of the colts and fillies in between his other tasks. That was the characteristic she appreciated the most in the boy. He was never to be found idle. He had that rare ability to see what needed doing and set to it without being told.

"Hey, cowboy! How about some lunch?"

"I'll grab something later," he called back. Maybe he had

seen her. Maybe he had been ignoring her the way he and Morgan had been ignoring each other.

Celia watched the filly a few minutes longer. She was a calm horse; she didn't fight her bit or the reins that kept her head set properly. She would make a good broodmare in a few years.

"I wish you'd come up to the house. Morgan's got something to talk to you about."

Al whoaed the mare, then walked out to her as she stood, easy and relaxed. "Who cares?"

"You would, I think, if you'd give him a chance." She watched him lead the horse to the fence. He took off the bridle, and she smiled approvingly as he eased the bit from the mare's mouth, then patted the animal as she pushed her soft nose into his chest. "Come on, Al. I've got to be in the middle of this silence game you two are playing."

"You're not in the middle!" The mare pulled back, not used to the reprimand in his voice. "You agreed with him, remember."

Celia walked over while Al calmed the confused filly. "None of this is really your business, but since you're being so quick to judge who's on whose side, I'll let you know how things stand on Bloodstone Ranch. Morgan Kyles saved this place for me. I was pretty desperate when he came along; I was a hair's breadth from selling out. He gave me hope, spirit, and the sweat off his back, and he never asked for anything in return—anything!"

She stared at the boy, daring him to make a remark that would cheapen the confidence. He continued to fuss with the mare. "Love isn't a strong enough word for what we share, Morgan and I. But one thing we do share is this ranch—its benefits, its responsibilities, and its policy-making."

He thought she was through. He swung the saddle off of the horse's back and laid it on the top fence rail, then hung the blanket, damp side up, next to it. In his mind, he had been counting the weeks left in his custodial period. He was getting ready to tell her how soon the two of them could have their precious ranch to themselves again. But she was not through.

"On the other hand, we don't always agree. I am often a little quicker to see both sides of an issue."

Was there hope? "Do you mean you don't agree with him—about Folly?"

"Let's put it this way. I agree that they shouldn't have done away with the pink-papering, but they did. As long as the rules have been changed, I don't see why we shouldn't follow them. I am reasonably sure I'd never take a solid-colored horse into a halter class, but I see nothing wrong with letting them perform."

"Then why didn't you say so that night?"

"Because, young man, you put me on the spot. You didn't mean to, but you knocked down a hornet's nest right on top of my head." Her tone changed, softened. She slowed down to think about her words. "In case you haven't noticed, I'm a woman. I may swear like a man sometimes, sweat and work like one, too. I compete in a man's world, and I want to be treated as an equal. I've fought hard for that recognition, but I like being a woman. I like the freedom of being feminine when I feel like it. I like the way I feel when Morgan puts his arms around me, and I don't even come up to his shoulder. God. I don't have any right to talk to you like this. You can't possibly understand."

He remembered Lacey, shivering in his embrace. He remembered how strong and protective he felt when he comforted her. He understood, but he said nothing.

"What I'm getting at is I'm not some kind of dyke who turns every relationship into a power struggle. What would you have thought of me if I had contradicted Morgan in front of everyone, if every time he made a statement, I jumped him? Why, how many shades of bitch would that paint me? Not to mention Morgan. How long do you think he'd put up with that? How long do you think any man who's worth having would?"

"So you let him have his way."

Celia smiled. "You're here, aren't you? That was a real toughie, but I finally got him to see it my way. A good deal of the time, he comes around to my way of thinking. I've got my ways; gentle persuasion, one might say. There are advantages to having been born female."

CHAPTER 16

SUNDAY WAS one of the longest days Al had ever lived through. Hours before dawn, he helped load the horses into the stock trailer. Morgan and Celia were taking Baby and her six-week-old foal, Flora, along with the Ghost, Sangre Hermano (the two-year-old son of Amiga, still a stallion and affectionately called Herman), and Red Rider to the show in Missoula, Montana. They would stop in Kamaiah to pick up Lacey at Clear Water Ranch and weren't expected back until late Sunday night.

Al had work to do, and he alone was responsible for the ranch, but instead of feeling good about the trust they were showing towards him, he cluttered the day with fretting.

Lacey was coming. She'd be spending the rest of the summer with them, a prelude to going away to college. Morgan had hung up the phone after talking to Calvin, crossed his heart with his fingertips, and held his right hand in the air. "I swear, that's what he actually said. 'Prelude.' Holy Christ. There ought to be a law against educating Injuns!"

He should be happy. He should be ecstatic. But he had not seen the girl since she had fled his room that chilly night. Would he have another chance? Would she come to him again? Would she let him this time? And—oh God, what would he do if she did? So he did chores and worked the two-year-olds and rehearsed over and over again in his mind what he would say to her.

At four o'clock, he decided to take a ride on Folly. He would be able to put a good ten miles on the horse before the evening's feeding.

He headed toward the mountain pasture at an easy lope. Al had come to trust the sure steps of his mount. The confusion of his personal affairs vanished for a time. It seemed impossible to worry when he was astride the red horse. At one point, he closed his eyes, dropped his reins, and held his arms outstretched. The clean smell of the grasslands swept over him, along with the muffled sounds of Folly's hooves striking the earth, the rhythm in time with his own body, and the far-off bark of a dog.

A dog! He pulled up and listened, trying to pinpoint the direction of the sound. It was misleading. The foothills rolled gently all around him, and vibrations bounced from one grassy mound to another. But somewhere close by, there was definitely a dog—perhaps two, unless it was the reverberations distorting the barks. There shouldn't be dogs on the pasture land. He knew the damage even one dog could wreak if it got in with the herd of yearlings, let alone a pack of them.

He rode to the top of the nearest hill, shaded his eyes from the setting sun, and scanned the area. He wished he had brought Cantar along. No dog would dare to invade her territory. He lowered his hand slowly, remembering why he hadn't brought the coydog. Early that afternoon, he had seen her trotting off in her single-minded way—in this direction.

He flipped his hand up over his eyes again as he spotted a flash of black against the greyish-green hillside to the west. If he hadn't seen the movement, he would have thought it a dark rock, so motionless was the black figure now holding. But knowing it wasn't part of the landscape, he could discern the legs, a russet color, and the long plume of the tail with a white tip. He could see the animal was not facing him, so the skillful act of hiding was not being carried out for his benefit. The dog was not even aware of its audience.

Al had to make up his mind whether to ride back to the ranch for a rifle or to call to the dog in case it was just someone's pet that had strayed too far. He was getting ready to ride closer when another, more familiar figure crested the hill. It was Cantar, slipping through the tussocks of grass as stealthily as a thief. "That dog's had it," said Al quietly. The strange animal was large, but Al had seen Cantar enraged. He doubted if any dog was her equal in battle.

The coydog crept along, swiveling her broad head, testing each placement of her feet so as not to make a sound. Al held his breath. His tenseness was making Folly shift nervously, so he slid down and ground-tied the gelding. Then he crouched low and advanced closer.

Suddenly, the black dog leaped into the air and bellowed. Al jumped inadvertently, and Folly tossed his head, snorted, and for a moment looked as if he was going to run off. It was more like the sound one would expect to hear coming from the throat of a bull, not a dog. Cantar, too, leaped and twisted so that she faced her adversary. She braced herself for what Al realized would be the contest of her life.

The black dog charged, mouth agape. Cantar spun away from his initial attack and nipped him almost playfully on the rump as he thundered by. Although outweighed by a score of pounds, the coydog was much quicker and much lighter on her feet. She lightly evaded a dozen passes, never launching an attack herself, content to let the aggressor wear himself out.

Her strategy worked. The black dog made a final charge, then flopped to the ground, panting. But instead of tearing into him, Cantar minced towards him, coyly cocking her head. She extended her muzzle, and the dog lapped at her with his lolling tongue. After he had caught his breath, the dog slowly stood up and sniffed Cantar—everywhere. While she stood statue-still, the black one investigated her face, the insides of her ears, her neck, all the time working his way back towards her slightly swinging tail—the only part of her body in motion. Then he (for by this time, it was very obvious the other dog was a male) slapped a foreleg over Cantar's shoulder and once more buried his nose in her ear. Then they separated and skipped—for it could be called nothing else—back over the hill and out of sight.

Al rolled onto his back and chuckled. "Why, that sly lady," he said aloud to Folly, who was carefully cropping grass. "So, that's where she's been trotting off to every day. She has a boyfriend. I guess she doesn't think much of the guy Morgan has picked out for her."

Then he closed his eyes and pictured the courtship play of the two canines. He thought how everything, everyone, had their tender sides: Morgan, with his explosive temper and gruff reprimands, could calm a frightened horse with ease; Joseph, the overpowering range stallion that would subdue a misbehaving mare with vicious, yellow-toothed bites, would gently nuzzle the same mare only hours later; and Cantar, the golden-eyed guardian of her domain. He had now seen her tender side. Then he thought of Lacey. He couldn't help it. Every thought that had entered his mind all day long somehow made its way around to the Indian girl . . .

She had been an offer from her father. Her mother was dead, killed in the same vicious slaughter in which he had lost his own beloved wife and unborn child. And now, her father was going off to die.

The old man had no teeth left, no strength with which to fight the soldiers. The scant flesh covering his ancient bones would not be enough to protect him from the oncoming winter. The fires of life were already dying in his tired soul. He had nothing left to offer his people, only the burdens his age and sickness made on them. That, and his daughter. His young daughter, whose coming-of-age banquet was canceled because of war. Through her, he could give strength back to his people—through the union of his daughter and the young man who had come to them on the red horse.

He did not think he wanted her. He could not gaze upon her innocent face without seeing his wife. He could not listen to the words she spoke without hearing the terrible death gurgles of his slain woman. But her youth and spirit overcame his own hesitations. When she came to his sleeping pallet, shyly lifting his robe and curling her strong body into his, he did what he thought he never could. His wife was gone, but he was still living, still a man and still a warrior.

She woke him in the morning, blowing the drifting scent of sweetgrass into his sleeping face. She had gathered tufts of it and placed them on the glowing embers left from the night's fire to make the tipi smell like the spring that was so far away. He could hear the hungry snorts of the horse he had left picketed outside—the horse that was too precious to be put in the tribal herd. The nickers and snorts became more insistent until they rubbed out his drowsy thoughts and brought him fully awake.

"Sorry, Folly," Al said to the impatient horse whose nose was hovering inches above his upturned face. "Guess I fell asleep. Almost dark. We'd better get going—huh?"

He mounted and returned to the ranch to be greeted by Cantar. Did she really have a smug, satisfied look on her face? He hurried through chores, fixed himself some supper, and then stretched out on the couch to continue reading the distance-riding books. He was getting into the chapter about saddles, realizing he'd soon have to begin using one, wondering what type he would prefer for distance riding, and just starting to say to himself, *Lacey can help me with that,* when he heard the truck pulling into the drive. The horses in the stock trailer were calling their greetings to the home place as he put on his boots and ran excitedly out the front door.

Celia climbed out of the driver's side of the cab. The reason for her driving became evident as Morgan approached him and threw his arm around the boy's shoulder in an uncustomary action. "Did we ever win big, boy," he said enthusiastically. His words were perfumed with Jack Daniels.

He felt another arm touch him, shyly slipping around his waist. He looked down at the tousled hair, the sleepy eyes, the slightly hesitant smile. "I wish you could have been there," Lacey said.

Celia called out sharply. "Come on, you three, quit romancing and get these horses unloaded."

"Coming, Mother," Morgan said, giving Al another affectionate slap.

It didn't take long once they all got to work. The six horses were soon bedded down. Everything that could wait until morning was left for later. Within an hour of arriving home, the four of them were scattered around the living room, unwinding before heading to bed. Morgan sat in his favorite chair, appearing to be falling asleep, but his eyes sprang open and his head snapped up every time he felt that Celia's or Lacey's narratives required editorializing.

Al was not familiar with winning. He had never known a winner or ever expected to be one, but he was hearing things that swelled him with pride. He had helped ready these horses for the show, and he felt part of the glory. While even Celia was thrilled at their good placings, Al was far beyond that. He was sprawled in a chair next to the table where the various ribbons and trophies had been put, and as he listened to the details, he frequently reached out to finger the starched frills of a rosette or the cool smoothness of a trophy.

The Ghost had been the big winner, ridden to first in youth pleasure by Lacey and, with Celia on top, first in Junior Horse Pleasure and Ladies' Pleasure and second in Open Pleasure. (At this point, Morgan offered his opinion as to the politics of the Montana judge.) He had also trotted off with the High Point Pleasure Horse award. Baby and her foal had won the Mare and Foal Class, and Herman had taken his class, with Flora coming second in hers. The only No Show of the day was turned in by Red Rider with Morgan in Men's Pleasure. The hot roan had insisted on laying back his ears and wringing his tail whenever another horse approached.

"But that's okay," insisted Morgan. "A cutting horse is supposed to keep his ears pinned. He's supposed to look mean."

"Do you win money for this?" asked Al, no longer afraid of showing his "greenness" in his interest in the sport.

"Not much. You get a percentage of the entry fee for first through fifth place, so the bigger the entry, the bigger the payback. We won enough today to pay our expenses and Lacey's salary for the week."

"And since you're so all-fired up, you can go along next weekend to Baker, and I'll stay home. The one time I showed today, I lost. It wasn't worth dressing up for. The rest of the time, it was, 'Morgan, do this.' And 'Morgan, do that.' 'Morgan, where's the hoof-flex?' and 'Morgan, will you zip up my chaps?'"

Celia gave him a playful clout over the head with a rolled-up show bill. "Life's tough all over."

"Yeah. Sure. I'd like to go." He looked at Lacey's smile. He knew he wouldn't mind in the least zipping her chaps. He'd actually look forward to it.

"Well, I'm going to bed. Got to make another trip to Kamiah tomorrow to get that Devil horse of yours, Lace."

"You knew the terms, Morgan," the girl countered good-naturedly. "If you wanted me, you had to take my horse, too." She yawned. "I guess I'd better turn in as well. Where am I going to sleep?"

"I thought we'd give you the office for the summer. There's a pull-out couch and a closet, and I've taken a dresser in there for you."

"Thanks. I guess you're like my dad. He has an office, too, but he does all his bookwork on the kitchen table. Well, good night." Then specifically to Al, "See you in the morning." He sought a message in her words, but as she walked away, he was afraid she meant exactly what she said.

Al's thoughts suddenly jumped back to his piece of news. "Morgan!" he almost shouted, stopping the big man's tired climb up the loft's stairway. "I almost forgot. You know how Cantar's been disappearing for hours at a time? I found out why. I went for a ride today out towards the pasture where the yearlings are, and I saw her and some strange dog. They were getting along real well."

Morgan was all interest. "Are you sure it was a dog? I can't believe she'd let a dog near her."

Celia was gathering coffee cups and suddenly sat them all down disgustedly. "I told you this would happen, Morgan. It had to have been a coyote. Now, what are we going to do with pups like that?"

"Hey—wait a minute, you two. I was there, remember, and it was no coyote. It was a dog. Black. Bigger than Cantar by a good twenty pounds."

Morgan rubbed his stubbled cheek thoughtfully. "Black, you say? Brown legs? Sort of a long, silky coat, and white on his chest and tip of his tail?"

"Yeah, that sounds about right."

Morgan laughed explosively. "That'd be Patch Hoyton's dog,

Brunus. If he knew it, he'd beat that fancy hound of his half to death."

"What's so funny?"

Celia explained while Morgan continued to chuckle. "Brunus is a purebred Bernese Mountain Dog. They originally came from Switzerland. Patch paid a pretty penny for him. They're advertised as being not only good stock dogs but death on predators. Patch runs sheep a little north of here, and he claims to have coyote problems, so he keeps the dog with the flock to protect it."

Morgan had recovered enough to continue the story. "Last spring, when I wanted to breed Cantar, I asked him about using Brunus, and he damn near threw me off his place. He said his dog didn't screw coyotes, it killed them." Morgan started to laugh again.

"That was in March, Morgan," said Celia, puzzled. "Why would she be in heat again so soon?"

"Don't know. Unless she came back in early to make up for losing her pups last time. But she'll have her litter this time, won't she? That dog of Hoyton's is one fine animal. And he's giving away for free what ol' Patch wouldn't sell."

By the time Al started chores the next morning, Lacey was already up and unloading the trailer. He hurriedly grained the stalled horses, then tried to stroll outside, his thumbs hooked in his empty belt loops. "Mornin'," he called casually.

Lacey looked up from her task. Her nose was smudged, and as she pushed her cap back from her head, she smeared it more. "Hi. I thought I'd get an early start. The sooner the trailer is ready to go, the sooner I can get my horse."

"You know you won't get Morgan going until after noon. He

had quite a load to sleep off. I'll give you a hand here, then you can help me clean stalls and put horses out. Deal?"

"Sure. Does this mean you're not mad at me?"

"Mad at you?" He was honestly puzzled.

"Yeah, for running off like I did the other night. You must think I'm a real child. I bet you're not used to girls telling you no."

"No," he said slowly. He wasn't lying. He wasn't used to girls saying anything to him. "But you're not just an ordinary girl. You're special, Lace. I don't mind waiting for you."

She sighed deeply. "My dad always said, 'Lacey, there's time for the boys later. It's your schooling that's important now. The boys will wait.' I always believed him until these last few weeks since I met you. Then I started wondering if my dad was ever seventeen. I sure hope he's been right all these years, 'cause I really like you, Al."

He felt it again—that overwhelming desire to hold her and shield her from anything harmful. He touched the tip of her nose and said, "You've got a dirty nose, kid." Then he helped her with the trailer.

Morgan didn't sleep as late as Al predicted, and by ten, he was ready to take off for Kamiah. Celia elected to stay at home and take care of the few necessary jobs. Otherwise, it was going to be an easy day for everyone. The three of them were in high spirits as they pulled out of the lane with the empty trailer clattering behind. They made one stop in town to pick up the mail, which brought enough items of interest to keep them talking non-stop, all the way to Clear Water.

AL RECEIVED a thick envelope with the return address of P. Ludwin. Morgan chuckled as he handed it to him, making a remark bordering on off-color, but Al ignored it. He was busy trying to think of the last time he had received a letter, and his memory failed him.

"Morgan, you're cruel. Mr. Ludwin is a nice little man. Why's he writing you, Al?"

The boy was suddenly embarrassed at the attention. He tried to slip the envelope into his pocket, but there was no way he could get away with it. "Open it," Lacey insisted.

He ripped back the flap and started to unfold the letter. "It's just something he was telling me about. Some way I could get my degree without going back to school. I don't know . . ."

Luckily, he didn't get a chance to finish. Saying he wasn't interested would never have gotten quite the same results from Lacey. She put her arms around him and squeezed him tightly. "Al. I'm proud of you."

"Hey, hey," interrupted Morgan, tapping her on the shoulder to break up the bear hug. "He's only got the letter. If you're getting this excited over that, I'm afraid to think of what you'll do if he passes. And remember—Calvin placed your virtue in my hands."

Lacey backed off and blushed. "I just think it shows a definite largeness of character, but I am proud of him."

"Whew! If that don't sound like your daddy."

"Look at this," wailed Al. "I can't do this. I can't even pronounce some of these subjects."

Lacey looked over his shoulder. "They're not so tough. I've got most of these books, and I can help you. Let's see the study guides."

She read a couple of the questions and reiterated, "See, I told you it wouldn't be that difficult."

Morgan was staring at her in amazement, almost forgetting to watch the road. "Not so tough! Little lady, I don't even understand what those questions are asking!" He hmphed and added,

"Common sense is more important than book learning, anyway."

"You're right, Morgan," there was a twinkle in the girl's eyes, "but when you fill out a job application, you never see a blank that says, 'Please list your common-sense quotient.'"

Morgan hmphed again. "The trouble with you, girl, is you've got too much common sense."

They continued to argue about the relative merits of an education, and Lacey continued to amaze them with the easy familiarity she had with the exotic and pretentious-sounding subjects. Before they realized it, they had arrived at Clear Water, where Al was to meet, for the first time, Spotted Rain, the horse that he had heard so much about.

Even though he had been working daily with horses for close to two months, Al was wise enough to acknowledge that he knew very little about the animals. He also knew enough to realize that the small mare he was looking at was unlike any other horse he was ever likely to meet. Lacey whistled, and the mare trotted to the fence and hung her head over the top rail so the girl could scratch her poll. "This is Rain, Al," she said.

For some inexplicable reason, Al kept his hands safely pocketed. Perhaps it was the eyes. The mare's white-rimmed eyes flicked over him almost disdainfully, then they fixed themselves on a spot somewhere above his head, totally dismissing his presence.

Morgan walked up to the corral, and immediately the mare pinned her ears flat against her skull. Lacey reprimanded her with a sharp word, but the only result was the easing of her ears. Hatred still shone in the dark eyes.

"Most dangerous horse you'll ever see, boy," said Morgan, and he was deadly serious. "I've seen evil horses at rodeos before, but most are dumb or scared. This animal is neither, and that's what makes her so bad. She's as smart as you are, and you'd never beat her or bluff her into being anything different than what she is."

With his newly trained horseman's eye, Al appraised Spotted Rain. She was small, about the same height as Folly. She was a rich red with snowflakes of white scattered all over. A white blanket draped over her rump, and large red spots dotted it. Her face was emblazoned with a perfect white stripe that sparkled cleanly. *Good color,* he thought, but he knew Spotted Rain would never stand a chance in a halter class. There was no roundness to her, no bulk. She was a greyhound of a horse. Her belly angled up sharply from a deep chest, so the line of her ribcage was just barely visible. Al had always thought that if a horse's ribs showed, it must be skinny, but skinny could never be used to describe Rain. Lean and tough, with long, flat muscles deeply defined in her shiny coat, she was the very picture of endurance and stamina. There was no part of this horse that spoke of decorative excess.

"Let her smell you, Al," said Lacey.

"Not on your life, kid," Morgan warned.

She shushed him almost rudely and coaxed the Indian boy again. "Go ahead. She'll like you. It's just overbearing, macho men who can't stand the idea of being bested by a horse that she hates."

"Present company included?" Morgan said.

"'Fraid so, Morgan. You and Dad and most of the men on this ranch."

"Most of the men in the country, you might as well say."

"No—that's not true. She likes Doc Holenback. That's Doc McClutchan's young partner," she added for Al's information. "He approaches her with enough respect. He doesn't try to force her to do anything; he asks her. And she likes that blacksmith from Kooskia."

"What she's neglecting to tell you, boy, is that the mare went through four farriers and almost killed one before they found one crazy enough to get along with her."

Al stepped closer. He remembered his first riding lesson, when Celia told him how a horse hated to sense fear in a person. But now, he was being told something different. This animal resented confidence. His confusion showed on his face. Rain inhaled his scent one time, then dismissed him again. She turned her face to Lacey, let her head droop, and enjoyed the caresses of the only person she truly cared for.

Madeline had lunch ready, and it was a pleasant meal. Lacey told her parents, much to Al's discomfort, about the study plans. Calvin nodded approvingly at the boy and lessened Al's embarrassment. After lunch, Lacey disappeared into her room to find the textbooks she had mentioned, and then she requested Al's help in loading some of her tack and her horse into the trailer. Morgan decided to have one more beer with Calvin. Neither had any desire to be anywhere near the horse, which Al thought was a little extreme.

On the drive home, Al prompted Lacey to tell him more about the horse that had everyone so in awe.

"We bought her at an auction as a yearling," Lacey began. "She came out of Montana. She's registered, but we've never seen her sire and dam nor heard of them. She was always different—a real loner, and even as a baby, never got spooked or silly about anything. I fell in love with her right away. I was eight years old, and it was my job to halter-break her. I found out you never got anywhere with her by force. She'd fight you to a standstill. So, I had to find ways of convincing her to do things. We got along just fine.

"The trouble started when she was a two-year-old. She was too small for Dad to break, so he had one of the hired men ride her for the first time. She fought until I thought the two of them were going to kill each other. That bastard ruined her mouth—it's as hard as iron now and almost everything else. Have you ever read the poem 'Bronco That Would Not Be Broken of Dancing'?"

Al shook his head.

"It's about a colt that wouldn't learn how to behave. He ends up fighting until he breaks his heart but never his spirit. Anyway—that was Rain. I finally begged and pleaded with Dad until he told the hand to forget it. He said he'd wait until she was a three-year-old and big enough for him to break.

"After she recovered from the horrible treatment the hand had given her, I started riding her. Just bareback, at first. Of course, my dad didn't know. She threw me plenty, but each time it was because I made a mistake. I tried to get her to do something she wasn't ready to do. I know it sounds like I spoiled her, and maybe I did, but I found if I just took my time and convinced her gently, she'd never refuse a second time. And something else came of that experience. I became such a good rider that there aren't many animals I can't ride now.

"By the end of the summer, I had her fairly well trained. When my dad found out, he was angry at first, but then he was just proud of me. I rode her all that winter, and the following spring, Dad decided he'd take over to teach her how to work cattle. The rodeo started all over again. Then one day, she threw him, and something inside her seemed to snap. She came after him, and I know she would have killed him if he hadn't rolled under the fence. He stormed into the house and called the killers. He said he wouldn't sell her to anyone else because their blood would be on his hands. I screamed and cried and begged him to give her another chance, but he meant it.

"That night, after everyone was asleep, I packed a saddlebag with clothes and some food, climbed on Rain, and started riding. Remember, I was only ten and pretty goofy. I had this crazy idea that I'd find some long-lost tribe still living wild on the reservation, and Rain and I would live with them. I rode all night, and at dawn, I was lost. I stopped to rest and to let Rain graze, but around mid-morning, we were hit by a late-winter blizzard. Mom and Dad had discovered I was missing, and they had everyone looking for me, but the storm was so bad by noon that the searchers had to give up.

"I was pretty scared and knew I couldn't last out the day, so I put my trust in Rain. I climbed on her bareback so it'd be warmer and wrapped myself in her saddle blanket, and tied myself on. I didn't even put a bridle on her because I knew I couldn't hang on to the reins. About nine that evening, Dad heard a horse whinny outside the front door. I had passed out by then, but Rain had brought me home.

"Of course, any question of selling her vanished. Dad made a rule that no one on the place touch her except me. He says he never worries about me when I'm on her. That doesn't mean she never gives me any trouble, but when it really counts, I'd bet my life on her. She's never let me down."

Everyone was quiet when Lacey was done. It wasn't a story she told lightly. The strained tones in her voice betrayed her. When she put words to the special relationship she and the outlaw horse shared, she risked ridicule, disbelief, and accusations of braggadocio. She found none in this hushed audience of an aging cowboy who related better to animals than people and a young Indian who was only just learning how to relate to anything.

Finally, Morgan broke the silence. "I think it's true with any good horse or at least any good horse that's lucky enough to find a good owner. Take ol' Charlie, for instance. Why, he'd trot down the road with anyone, but I can almost feel the relief when he knows it's me settling down in the saddle. And maybe you don't know it, Al, but Folly's more horse when you're forking him bareback than he's ever been for me or even Celia. Oh, for the good ol' days when all a man really needed to get along was a good horse and a good dog."

"Unfortunately, those days are gone now, Morgan. Even if

that storm hadn't come up, Rain and I would have had to go back home. There just weren't any wild Indians to be found, no matter how much I wished it. Do you remember that movie with Kirk Douglas, *Lonely Are The Brave*?"

"Yeah. I saw that. Douglas was a rambler who wouldn't admit the old days were over. He broke a buddy out of prison."

"Uh-huh. In the end, he thought that if they climbed this hellacious hill, they'd outrun the posse, but when he got to the top, there was a highway, and his horse got hit by a truck, and a cop had to shoot it."

"What a bummer," said Al.

"The real bummer is the fact you can't go back—ever," Morgan said.

"Hey, I didn't want to blow your day. Sure, you can't go back. I'll never be an Indian princess, and you, Morgan, you'll never get to boss a cattle drive. But we've got today, and we've got the rest of our lives, and we've the right to make choices."

For a "day off," the rest of the day was full. Lacey gave Al a lesson in sitting the stock seat. He found he disliked the saddle. He had trouble sensing the movement of the horse when the heavy barrier of leather was between him and the horse's back. Lacey assured him that he'd soon get the feeling for it.

Later, Lacey showed Al what was involved in a halter class. It surprised the boy that there was so much more to do than spruce the horse up and lead it in. He had to make sure it was standing squarely on all four feet, had to show off the animal's strong points without calling attention to its weak ones, and had to be busy with the horse without getting in the way of the judge. After he realized how much he didn't know, he feared he'd not be ready to show at Baker that weekend.

After supper, all four went for a quiet ride along the creek bed. The sunset was not brilliant but soft and muted, a hazy wash of colors melting into the horizon.

That night, as Al lay in bed, he felt a little like that calm sunset. For so long, he had been keyed up, feelings of guilt and confusion battling in him. He was worried about his relationship with Lacey and, in another sense, worried about the argument he had had with Morgan. But everything seemed fine now, and the tenseness drained from him.

The last thing he remembered before drifting to sleep was Lacey's voice saying, ". . . and we've got choices."

CHAPTER 17

AL FINGERED THE CRANBERRY SHIRT. He tried to look like he knew what he was doing, which he didn't, and he was too embarrassed to ask for assistance. He liked the way the material felt, but he was trying to remember all the things Lacey had told him to look for: Will it shrink? Does it need ironing ("Because I'm not going to iron it for you!")? "Get something that'll breathe; it gets awfully hot at a show." Then he remembered her saying, "Look for something red, Al. That's your color. You'll look terrific in red." And he was off in a dream world again.

"Can I help you, young man?" The sales lady startled him, and he dropped the sleeve of the shirt as if he had been caught in an illegal act.

"Ah, yeah. I'm looking for a shirt to, ah, show in."

"Show what?"

"Oh, ah—horses. I've got to show a horse next weekend."

He sounded like a simpleton, but the sales lady smiled indulgently. She was used to seeing these shy reservation kids who had never had a chance to pick out store-bought clothes. A lot of the kids would be well into their teens before they wore something other than big brother's or big sister's discards or church hand-outs. "The trend is to cottons now, but they require a little work—starching and ironing and all."

"I don't want that. What's this one made of?" He indicated the cranberry shirt, beginning to feel more comfortable. The saleswoman was a bit patronizing, but at least she wasn't looking at him like he was going to rob the place.

"That's polyester and rayon. It'll wash up nicely, and the wrinkles will just fall out of it if you hang it up damp. It's a very becoming shade for you, too. Is it your size?"

"I'm not sure."

"Would you like to try it on? And these jeans?" She picked up the pair of Levi's he had laid on a nearby chair.

"Sure." He took the shirt down from the rack and tucked the folded jeans under his arm.

The sales lady pointed out the dressing room and smiled as he walked in. *He certainly is a good-looking boy*. On impulse, she selected a silk bandana from a display case. It was navy blue, pinstriped with red, and it would be just the thing to set off those black eyes.

A few minutes later, Al emerged, looking like a new person. He grinned at Dorothy—that was what the sales lady's nametag read, and he was beginning to feel as if she deserved a name—and said, "Fits okay, doesn't it?"

"It certainly does." She didn't ask about the rest of his outfit. She knew the jeans and shirt were probably all his budget would allow. Still, she handed the bandana to him. "Try this on. It's the icing on the cake."

Al started to take the scarf from her, then he said, "No, I better not. I'm sort of borrowing the money for this, and I better not press my luck."

Luck? he echoed to himself. Was it just luck that had brought about this relationship he had with Celia? If it hadn't been for her, where would he be now? Certainly not buying a fancy western shirt and getting excited about going to a horse show. A horse show, of all places! And it was equally certain that he wouldn't be studying for his high school degree, nor would he be assured of at least two thousand dollars waiting for him in the fall—free and clear, earned by legitimate toil.

That was the big surprise that Celia had given him last night. She had been, and would continue, putting away $100 a week for him as a salary, and when the custodial period was over, it was his. In the meantime, he could draw on it for necessities, like these clothes, but he couldn't go overboard. That was why he had decided to accept Morgan's loan of boots and a hat. He grinned at how much of a tightwad he could be when he came about money honestly.

"Will that be all, then?"

"I guess so."

"I'll just take the tags off these and ring them up while you change. Unless you'd like to wear them?"

"No, ma'am. I'm a real sloppy eater, and right now, I'm going to lunch. I'd probably get ketchup on my new shirt."

Dorothy laughed and snipped the tags from the clothes. It was such a friendly sound. Al wondered if all these nice people had existed before, and if so, why hadn't he met them. Maybe they couldn't get by the chip on his shoulder. "I work for Bloodstone Ranch," he told Dorothy as he was retreating back into the dressing room. "Celia said to charge them to her account." He had his back turned so he didn't see the frown chase the jolly look from Dorothy Govington's face.

Al could hear the argument before he rounded the corner to the sales desk. He recognized Dorothy's voice, but it was a different tone than she had used with him. It was defiant and strident. "Walt, I don't know why people continue to do business with you. You are the most suspicious man I've ever known!"

"If it was up to you, there'd be no business. You'd extend credit to anyone."

"Celia Bolt isn't 'anyone.' She's an excellent customer. She pays her bill every month."

"Her bill, sure. But I don't think she'd be too happy about outfitting some strange kid."

"Don't be silly. If he was lying, would he have stopped at one shirt and one pair of jeans? Of course not. You know the old saying, 'May as well be hung for a sheep as a lamb.' I believe the boy, Walter, and I'm willing to pay for the loss if I'm wrong."

"It'll come out of this week's pay, mark my words."

Dorothy lowered her voice to a sly challenge. "And I'll bet you the price of one of those silk bandanas that you're wrong."

Al wanted to leave the clothes and sneak out the back door, but he knew if he did, it would be the same as admitting guilt. He owed it to himself and to his newfound champion to handle the situation, not run from it. He let the dressing room door reclose noisily and started whistling as he walked to the desk. "Do you want me to sign anything?" he asked innocently.

Walter Govington rolled his eyes, but his sister answered cheerfully, "Just this charge ticket. And good luck at the show."

"Thank you, ma'am. And thanks for your help."

He forced a jaunty walk out of the store, and by the time he was halfway down the street, he found he wasn't angry at Walter. In fact, he found he didn't even blame him. He might have acted the same way if he were a store owner. He was feeling extremely good about himself as he entered The Watering Place, took a seat, and waited for Morgan to show.

The Watering Place was a bar, but it had a reputation for serving the best Mexican food in Lewiston, a town known for its Mexican restaurants, and the hottest sauce in the county. Al bought a Coke and started reading the signs on the wall. He had never been in this particular spot, even though it boasted three regulation-sized pool tables.

The owner, LeRoy Bushberry, had a reputation for more than his tacos. He ran an honest place, and even Crabs Fulkerson had stayed clear of him. It was too early for the lunchtime crowd, and the bar was almost empty except for two men playing a game of eight-ball on the far table and a third leaning against the bar, talking to the skinny girl who was tending.

It didn't take long for the good feelings Al had cultivated all morning to wear off, and he began to feel uneasy. The big man at the bar was talking low, and the skinny girl kept up a monotonous giggle, but Al felt they were discussing something besides their love lives. The hair began to stand on the back of his neck. Finally, he slugged down the rest of his Coke and started to leave.

"Where you going, kid?" asked one of the pool players. "We kind of thought you'd want to play the winner—you being such a pool shark and all."

If there was ever a time to run from trouble, this was it. But something made Al stay, some new piece of self-pride that he had discovered not too long ago and that he had been polishing ever since. "If you fellows know who I am, you must know I'm sort of out of your league."

"Besides, Delmar," interrupted the one at the bar, "you should know the kid here doesn't play pool no more. He's got a new game now, don't you, boy?"

This was the dangerous one, Al realized. Delmar and his beefy-looking buddy at the table were just along for the ride. Again, he felt the desire to run. There was something in this thick-lipped stranger that reminded him of Crabs. But he held his ground. "I don't know who you are, mister, but you seem to know me."

"Why, I'm your neighbor, boy. I'm sure you've heard your boss lady speak fondly of me. The name's Sid Dutchens."

Morgan had once said he hoped Al would never have to meet this man, and now Al knew why. It was there—the same something that was in Crabs Fulkerson. The evilness, the cruelty, the desire to see others squirm. "I guess they never got around to telling me about you."

"I suppose it just slipped her mind. You must stay real busy out there all day. Tell me, what is it you keep busy with?"

Delmar and Beefy laughed as if on cue, and the skinny girl giggled her moronic giggle. Al didn't consider answering. He knew that whatever he said, it could be twisted into some kind of dirty joke.

"I hear talk that Celia's thinking about replacing her herd stallion," wheezed Delmar between guffaws.

"Now, that's not true. They've just imported a brand-new filly to keep the young stud busy. You know Celia. She likes to keep her breedings pure."

Al covered the distance between himself and Dutchens in a flash. The weeks of ranch work had toughened his wiry frame, and he swung at the older man's face, hoping to smash the thick, chapped lips into a pulp. He got one good punch landed before Delmar and Beefy grabbed him and pinned his arms to his sides.

Dutchens wiped the blood from his face. He was scarlet with anger. He had misjudged the boy and hadn't expected the explosion quite so soon and with such accuracy. He sneered. "Don't get me wrong, boy. I'm all for it. That Trueblood gal has just got too big for her britches. She needs drilling. Only way to keep a squaw manageable is to keep her knocked up."

Al was passed the point of caring if the odds were three to one or twenty to one. His arms were held tightly, but he lashed out with his boot and caught Dutchens just below the knee. He heard the girl's shrill cry of, "Get 'im, Sid!" and felt his right arm wrenched painfully behind his back.

"You little red bastard son of a whore," hissed Dutchens as he struggled to his feet and stood gingerly. He drew a buck knife from his pocket, held it in front of Al's face, and carefully opened the long blade. Then he grabbed a handful of Al's hair and pulled his head back at a dangerous angle. "You boys know what this kid is?"

He really wasn't looking for an answer, but Beefy jerked Al's arm up another inch and whispered, "A dead Injun?"

"Now, we wouldn't want to get carried away. I'm sure I'd be within my rights as a white man and a tax-paying citizen of this town to defend myself against this Injun slime, but I'm a merciful man. I believe this kid is a member of the Nez Perce tribe. You know what Nez Perce means, Jolene?"

"Nah, Sid. I try not to think about Injuns any more than I have to. What does it mean?"

"Pierced Nose. Ain't that right, kid? Back in the old days, these Injuns would stick a hole right through their noses."

"Sounds like a good idea to me. Then you could put a ring through it and chain 'em to a tree when they got all liquored up." Jolene was getting into the swing of things now. She was glad she hadn't called in sick that morning as she had contemplated.

"This little papoose seems to have escaped the blade—so to speak."

"Go on, Sid, stick 'im!" Spittle had gathered at the corners of Delmar's mouth.

Al closed his eyes. No matter what, he wasn't going to yell. No matter how much it hurt, he wasn't going to give these songs of bitches the pleasure of hearing him scream. He almost wished Dutchens would get it over with.

"Let him go, Dutchens." It was Morgan. "Let him go, or I'll slice you into little pieces and feed you to my dog."

Al felt a slight lessening of the grip on his arm. Jolene suddenly found a pressing responsibility in the kitchen.

"I said, let him go. You know I mean it. Delmar, and you, whoever you are—scram!"

The two were trapped, inferior subjects pressed between

their superiors. If there was any squeezing, they'd be the ones to flatten first. Delmar licked his lips and all but released his hold.

"Go on, get out of here," Dutchens growled. If he was going to back down to Kyles, he didn't want any witnesses. "Jesus Christ. We were just having a little fun."

Delmar and Beefy scurried past Morgan and out the door. Al stepped back from Dutchens and rubbed his shoulder. His eyes blazed. He was ready to take the man on, knife or no knife, and Morgan sensed it.

"Well, the kid isn't laughing, Sid, and neither am I." Morgan stepped forward and touched Al's elbow. "Get out of here. Go wait in the truck." After a tense silence, he added, "Please."

Al backed up slowly. He should have been scared; he knew that. He should have run for the door the second Dutchens's two trained monkeys released him. But the rage overcame every other emotion. The very thought of this disgusting piece of scum even mentioning Lacey filled him with righteous anger. He said nothing, but his eyes told Dutchens what the score was. And despite his bulk, despite his bravado, Sid Dutchens felt regret that he had ever begun this terrible thing.

Al left The Watering Place, but the look in his eyes didn't leave Sid Dutchens for many days to come.

Al waited in the truck for several minutes. His shoulder throbbed, and his scalp hurt. At one point, he began to tremble and couldn't stop his hands from shaking and his teeth from chattering. When Morgan opened the door, he jumped at the sound. They drove through Lewiston in silence.

Once they reached the highway, Morgan increased the speed and turned on the radio. Nervously, he kept switching channels. Finally, he turned the noise off and said evenly, as if he was fighting to control himself, "I'm not going to ask you what he said. I know that fucker too well. I can just imagine. Whatever it was, I'm sorry for it."

Al recognized the churning in his gut and knew its meaning all too well. "I'm going to be sick," he said almost apologetically.

Morgan slowed the truck and pulled off the road. Al hastily climbed out, and Morgan sat alone, drumming his thick fingers on the dash and wishing he hadn't held his temper so well. This wasn't the first time Dutchens had tried something like this. The man was a bully, and for too long, he had been allowed to get away with it because he picked victims that nobody really cared about.

But he'd made a mistake this time. A lot of people were beginning to care about this kid. He wasn't a loser, not anymore, and Morgan was determined that this senseless incident wasn't going to make him feel like one. He was trying to think of something to say that would tell Al how he felt about him, but he never would be good at talking about emotions. Frustrated, he turned the radio back on and was humming along with Waylon when Al got back in the cab.

The boy was pale, but he had stopped shaking, and he even managed a weak smile. "I guess I'm more scared now than when it was happening. I was too mad to be scared then."

"Al, don't let this change anything. Dutchens is an asshole."

"I know. The funny thing is, if this had happened a few months ago, I would have been sure it was because I'm an Indian. But now, I realize it's just 'cause, like you said, Dutchens is an asshole, and assholes come in all colors. Man, I can't believe I'm saying that. Me. The guy who used to pretend he was Italian—anything but an Injun. What's happening to me, Morgan?"

Morgan steered the truck back onto the highway. "One thing for sure. There are people who believe in you now. It has a way of changing a man. I ought to know."

There was no more prying by either of them. Their silence

showed the newfound respect they had for each other more than claims of affection ever could.

There was an unspoken agreement that they wouldn't tell Celia about the incident. Morgan doubted if she would find out. Dutchens would be reluctant to spread the tale since it didn't turn out as he had hoped, with Al begging for mercy at his hands. As they neared the ranch, Morgan pointed out Dutchens's lane, and Al made a mental note to stay clear of that particular property line on his rides.

"Oh, almost slipped my mind. I stopped by Govington's earlier to see if you were still there. You'd left, but Walt's sister —Dorothy—she said she had something for you." Morgan dug into his jacket pocket and pulled out a paper bag. "Free of charge, she said. I don't understand, I've done business at Govington's as long as I've lived here, and I've never got anything free. What gives?"

Al looked in the sack and grinned as he saw the navy-blue bandana. "It's like I said—bad guys come in all colors, and so do good guys."

THE SHOW in Baker on Sunday was preceded by one in Walla Walla on Saturday, and the decision was made to attend both. Flora, Lep, The Ghost, and Herman were all pre-entered, plus Chico's Fancy, a four-year-old mare, bred by Bloodstone but owned by the Janusiks from Winchester. Celia had been training her as a barrel horse, and this was to be her first competition. The empty place in the six-horse trailer was filled with extra feed and supplies since this was an overnighter.

Al was doubly excited. The shows were the prime reason, but he had another one—one he was embarrassed to admit. In his seventeen, almost eighteen years, he had never been out of the state. And now, in one weekend, he'd be in both Washington and Oregon. It wasn't like he expected to be in another world when he crossed the border, he doubted if the landscape would even change, but he was excited just the same.

As they were loading the horses in the darkness of early Saturday morning, Morgan pulled Al aside. "Sid Dutchens will be there," he said.

"I can take care of myself."

"Well, let's hope you've no reason to. Dutchens will behave himself. There'll be too many important people around for him to do anything else, so just take it easy."

"Yeah, yeah."

"And take care of my ladies—okay?"

"I will. Morgan, you sound like an ol' mother hen, you know that?"

"Hey, I'm entrusting you with an awful lot. Just don't disappoint me."

"Al, come on," called Lacey, her slight frame outlined in the glow of the truck's headlights.

"You'd better get going. Your girl's calling."

Al sandwiched himself between Celia and Lacey and straddled the gear shift. "Bring home some blue!" shouted Morgan. But as the truck ground into low gear, Al was thinking about what Morgan had said just before. Was Lacey really "his girl"? Was it that obvious?

The first morning's showing was impressive. Al showed Flora in halter, actually competing against Celia and Lep. The boy and the filly won, despite Al's profound nervousness. The filly was a natural show-off, and probably could have taken the class even if no one was on the end of her lead line. The only thing she couldn't do was understand the announcer.

Neither could Al, or so it seemed for a few seconds. His number was read off for first, and he responded only after the competitor next to him jabbed him in the arm. Celia had no trouble picking up on her number when it was announced third.

Once again, Herman captured his class. Sid Dutchens took second with a handsome leopard stallion, but the horse had a look in his eyes that bothered Al. It wasn't anything really glaring, not a look of dejection or ill health, but more a lack of confidence. Herman, on the other hand, shone through his expression. He was as gentle as a kitten and was never a problem in the way so many stallions could be, yet his eyes showed a freeness of spirit and interest in everything around him.

When Celia came out of the ring, Al threw an arm around her and squeezed her. "Nice going, boss," he said. Then he fastened the royal-blue ribbon to Herman's silver-studded halter. "There's some folks over there asking an awful lot of questions about him." He nodded his head in the direction of a young couple who were talking to Lacey.

"I recognize them. They were at the show in Missoula. By the looks of their clothes, they've got some money."

"By the looks of their car, they've got a lot. They came in a Ferrari. It's the kind of car I've always dreamed of stealing."

Suddenly, Al came very close to having his day ruined. A big, square-knuckled hand clapped down on Celia's shoulder. "Congratulations, Celia. I sure admire the way you handle that young stallion."

Al had to clench his fists tightly to prevent himself from reacting. He heard Celia respond in a pleasant-enough voice, but he didn't catch what she said. All he knew was that he had to walk away, or the sight of Sid Dutchens and the sound of his sly innuendos were going to be too much. "I'll take Herman to the trailer," he muttered and led the horse away.

Later, while the three of them were eating the lunch Morgan had packed in the cooler, Celia said conversationally, "I would have introduced you to Dutchens, Al, but he's such a jerk, I thought I'd spare you."

"Yuck," was Lacey's reply. Then she took a gulp of Pepsi as if to wash his thought away.

"We already met in town last week."

"Oh, if Morgan was with you, you probably got a really good impression. Those two hate each other."

"I think I've got him figured out. I know enough to realize that stallion of his has been manhandled."

"Listen to him," laughed Lacey after swallowing a bite of tuna-fish sandwich. "He wins one ribbon—or should I say the horse wins it for him—and he's an expert."

"Hey, I know enough to tell the difference between a horse that feels good about itself and wants to compete, like our horses, and a horse that's miserable." He shoved the remainder of his sandwich in his mouth, walked over to The Ghost, and began grooming the gelding's already flawless coat.

"Well, what's the matter with him?" Lacey said. "I was just teasing. You know, Celia, sometimes I get tired of having to watch every little thing I say to him for fear of hurting his feelings. Oh great," she interrupted herself, "look who's coming."

It was easy to recognize Jymme Mechling's silver-blue Toyota truck and matching trailer. She was arriving just in time for the start of the performance classes, and she had come to win.

Ghost performed consistent with his ability. He was entered in three classes, placed second in one and won two, plus he qualified for Reserve High Point Pleasure, quite an honor for a three-year-old. Al had worked off his resentment towards Dutchens. He decided the day was going too well to let one incident spoil it. He even welcomed a meeting with Jymme Mechling. It seemed years ago that she had made such a fool of him. He was so much older now, so much more sure of himself.

The meeting came while the arena was being raked in preparation for the barrel race. Jymme was jogging her gelding in the practice ring. Al sat on the fence, watching Lacey warming up Fancy. The blonde saw him, charged across the ring, and pulled her mount to a sliding stop just in front of him, spraying the fence and Al's jeans with sand.

"Hello, again."

"What are you doing here?" said Al casually as he dusted off his pant legs. "I thought you were a rodeo star now."

"Oh, I am. But I haven't forgotten my roots."

"Doing us a favor by showing up every now and then? Did you happen to see The Ghost clean up in the Pleasure Classes? I guess you must feel like a dope for turning him down."

Jymme frowned. "Pleasure is so dull. I like action. How about you? Getting any action from Miss Goody Two-Shoes?"

She wasn't going to get to him, not this time. "We have a nice working relationship."

"I'll bet that's a real case of the blind leading the blind."

"It's all in the touch," he countered.

Jymme leaned forward and rested her elbow on the saddle horn and her chin on her fist. "You've changed. I think for the better. Are you going to Baker tomorrow?"

"Yeah." Al looked past Jymme's pretty face to smile at Lacey as she trotted by.

"Where are you staying?"

"At the fairgrounds."

"That's where my horse is staying," scoffed Jymme. "I've got a room at The Blue Top on Highway 30. Room 120."

"Our stock is too expensive to leave unattended," said Al. "But after I get everyone bedded down, maybe I'll wander over that way." He didn't give her a chance to turn him down. He swung his leg over the fence and slid lightly to the ground. "Good luck in the barrels," he said over his shoulder. When his back was turned, he smiled with such relief that his face ached by the time he got back to the truck.

"What are you so tickled about?" Celia asked him.

"Just talking to Jymme Mechling."

"You finally got her number?"

"Yeah. How fast is that horse of hers? Can she beat Lacey?"

"It's one of Dutchens's animals. What do you think?"

"Maybe I'm wrong, and too bad Miss Trueblood isn't here to correct me, but I think that might be the difference. Fancy runs because she loves to. Dutchens's animals perform because they are forced to."

Al wasn't wrong. Both horses were fast, and both girls were excellent riders. But the difference was in attitude. Jymme flew across the time barrier, her bat popping on her horse's bunching hindquarters, with the fastest time of the day—except for Lacey's apparently effortless ride of one-tenth of a second faster.

After the barrel race, the Bloodstone crew packed up for the 150-mile drive to Baker. They stopped for a steak dinner on the way and didn't arrive at the fairgrounds until dark. That night, Al settled down in an empty stall on some hay bales. Lacey and Celia slept in the truck. The luminous dial of Al's alarm clock read 3:00 when he heard Lacey climb out of the covered bed of the pickup and pad softly into the darkness, her path proceeded by the pale beam of a flashlight. A few minutes later, he saw the light heading back.

Quietly, he slipped from underneath his blanket and stood in a shadow. As she walked by, he grabbed her. "Gotcha," he whispered in her ear as he encircled her waist with one arm and clasped his hand over her mouth to keep her quiet. But her wiry strength surprised him, and an elbow in his midriff made him let go of her and yelp in pain.

"Geez, Lace. I was just kidding," he moaned.

"Well, you scared me to death. I don't think it was very funny. Good thing I just came from the bathroom."

Al straightened up. "I see you weren't too terrified to defend yourself. I'll bet your dad taught you that move."

"Nope. That was just reflex. You're lucky I *didn't* use the move Dad taught me. What are you doing up, anyway?"

"I thought maybe we could—uh—celebrate a little. I mean, we're both winners, aren't we?" Al had regained his confidence. He put his arm around her again and pulled her close. "What do you say?" She was wearing the same nightgown she had worn that other night. He could feel her breasts crush against him. He had not only regained his confidence, he was charged with it.

"Stop it, Al," she protested, putting her hands against his chest and trying to push away.

"Come on, babe. We're a winning team." He covered her mouth with his. He hadn't kissed her since that night, since that first hesitant and painfully sweet instant. But it felt so different this time. He felt stronger, more demanding. His tongue sought an opening between her lips.

"Cut it out. I mean it," Lacey spat at him.

"What's the matter?"

"Don't be kissing me while you're thinking about her!"

"Her who?"

Lacey scrambled free and tried to straighten her nightgown. "Jymme Mechling, that's who. I saw you two."

"Don't be crazy. If I wanted her, I'd be there now. Blue Top Motel, Highway 30, Room 120. She made a point of telling me. She's a tramp, Lace."

"Yeah. She's a tramp because she'll sleep with you, and I'm a tease because I won't. What do you men want from a woman?"

"Holy crap, Lace. What's with you? You on the rag or something?"

She stopped smoothing the wrinkles from the nightgown. Her dark eyes narrowed. "That's disgusting. You sound like some street Injun."

"Maybe that's what I am, a street Injun. That sounds like your dad talking."

"You're damn right. And I'm proud of my dad's influence. Proud of being an Indian and proud of being a woman, and neither you nor anyone like you is going to make me feel differently. So don't talk to me like one of your gang-bang girlfriends."

That should have ended it. She should have gone back to the truck and left him to hitch to the Blue Top. That was what he wanted, wasn't it? But that wasn't what she wanted. She wanted him to hold her like he did that first night. Gently. She wanted to tell him about her feelings, her fears. And she couldn't do that unless he made the first move. She had done all the apologizing up until now, and it was time he made some sort of effort.

The Blue Top Motel wasn't what he wanted, either. All the swagger drained from his voice. "I'm sorry, Lace. I get so mad when you say stuff like that. I don't give a damn about Jymme Mechling. And she isn't a tramp because she sleeps with a lot of guys; she's a tramp because she brags about it. She doesn't care about anybody she sleeps with—it's just a contest with her. I care about you, and I wouldn't hurt you for the world."

"But what do you want me to do?"

"I want you to be my girl, Lace. I want you to act like my girl."

"You mean you want me to sleep with you?"

"No. I've felt like that girl in that play we've been reading."

"Pygmalion?" For the life of her, she could see no resemblance between Al and Eliza Dolittle.

"Yeah. And you're the professor. Everything we do is like school. It's you who taught me what to do at the show. You're teaching me about riding and helping me condition Folly. You're getting that fancy math and history and all that book stuff into my thick skull."

"But I thought you wanted me to help."

"I do—but that doesn't stop me from feeling dumb."

"Al," her lip began to tremble, and she looked down at her bare feet, "I'm afraid to learn the things you could teach me."

He couldn't tell her that the night he'd held her was the closest he'd ever been to a girl. That would kill the one aspect of their indefinable relationship that Al seemed able to control. He put a finger under her chin and tipped her head up. Her dark eyes were brimming with tears, and he felt that old desire to protect her. "Just be my girl. Quit trying to pretend we're only friends. Sometimes, you act like I'm your brother."

"Do you really think I'm not affected by you? Don't you realize I want to be your lover? But I'm scared, Al. That's why I try not to be alone with you, and when we are alone, I try to think about horses or history or poetry or anything except the color of your eyes and how strong your hands are and the way your mouth felt when—when—" Her words trailed off into a confused sigh.

"But why are you afraid of me? Lacey, I won't hurt you. I just want to please you."

"That's really easy for you to say. But what if I got pregnant? Then what?"

Pregnant. That thought never even entered his mind. Maybe he was a street Injun after all, and maybe he'd never be anything else. All he had been thinking about was how it would make him feel like a man. The possibility of pregnancy certainly never cropped up in his sweetly erotic dreams. But it was a fear that Lacey faced every time she felt desire rising. And it never even occurred to him. He could offer to marry her, couldn't he? Ha! How many times had a girl been promised that? How many girls did she know that had had their lives ruined by that false promise?

"Al. I've got six years of school ahead of me. And then I've got to work off the loan to the reservation board. All my life, I've planned for that. Maybe someday, I'll want a family, but a baby now would destroy me. And it would destroy you, too, if you stayed around."

The mocking words rang in his head. *Only way to keep a squaw manageable is to keep her knocked up.* Al felt disgusted. He didn't deserve her affection.

"I don't plan on being a thirty-year-old virgin," she continued, her spirit and sense of humor coming to the surface, "but I plan on being really certain, you know, educated, before I go to bed with a man. I'm not going to depend on the man to be responsible, no matter how much he thinks he knows or how much he cares about me. I am your girl, Al. I've been your girl since the night of my graduation party. And when I'm ready for it, I'll be your lover. I hope you can wait for me."

The next day, Al and Flora again won their class, and when they came out of the ring, Al all smiles, and Flora tossing her head and arching her neck proudly, a slim figure dashed from the ample audience.

The kiss that Lacey Trueblood planted on the handsome young winner was anything but sisterly.

CHAPTER 18

"YES, Connecticut. Can't you resign yourself to the fact that there is life east of the Mississippi?"

"East of the Mississippi? I have trouble admitting there's worthwhile life east of the Rockies."

Celia shook her head in mock disgust. "Don't tell me your 'principles' are going to prevent you from selling livestock to people from Connecticut."

"Oh, no. I'm all over that stuff. Let's go for it. When are they coming?"

"According to the letter," Celia unfolded the paper and read it again, "they'll be in the area tomorrow. There's a number to call in case we can't be here."

"What did Al say they drove? A Ferrari?"

"Yeah. How much do they cost?"

Morgan just snorted. "If you can afford a Ferrari, price doesn't matter."

For a moment, Celia was quiet. She had almost forgotten that a Ferrari could have been part of her destiny—or a Porsche or a Mercedes or Maserati, for that matter. She seldom thought of that other world, and when she did, it was painful. It wasn't the wealth she regretted walking out on, although the family fortune would have made life much simpler. It was the closeness of a family she resented being deprived of. It hurt to realize that she had never really known her parents, or they her.

"What's wrong, Cel?" The concern in Morgan's voice warmed away the pain.

"Nothing. I was just thinking."

"About Connecticut? That's where you're from, isn't it?"

"Yes."

"Well, maybe someday you'll tell me all about it. You don't know these folks, do you? What's their name again?"

"Stanton. Milford and Emaline Stanton. And no, I don't know them."

"That's not such a dumb question. Connecticut is a pretty small state."

"Yeah, about one-fifteenth the size of Idaho—but with four times the population. You can't think of the east with the same attitude as the west. In eastern society, people take precautions not to expand their range of acquaintances too far. They only try to know select people."

"Sounds like a pretty artificial way of life to me. No wonder you left."

"Left where?" Al and Lacey came breezing through the living room together, as they had been ever since the Baker show. Al was stuffing the last half of a sandwich in his mouth, and his question was muffled.

"Connecticut. That's where I'm from."

"Oh, yeah? I was just reading about an endurance race out there. I didn't realize people in the east were into that kind of riding."

Morgan cuffed the boy on the shoulder. "Have you noticed how you can take any conversation and turn it around to endurance racing? I'm getting sick of it."

Al ducked to evade another blow. "We're going to bring the

youngsters down from the mountain pasture now. Don't want the Stantons to have to ride too far to spend their money. See ya."

The two ran out the door, and Morgan watched them as they raced to the barn. Lacey was inches ahead, but at the last minute, Al grabbed her belt and held her back so he would touch first. Then they hugged briefly and almost playfully. "He's a good kid," Morgan said, "but if he gets that girl into trouble, Calvin'll kill him. And I won't interfere."

"They're both good kids. I've talked with Lacey, and they're behaving themselves."

"Oh, come on. What do you expect her to say? 'Why yes, Celia. Every time you think we're out riding, we're actually screwing each other's brains out.'"

Celia scowled. "She would tell me the truth. She's one smart little lady. She knows what she wants, and she won't let any mistakes get in the way."

"I'm just scared for them. I remember what it was like to be seventeen and in love for the first time." He watched while Al and Lacey cantered off toward the mountain pasture. He felt a familiar burning, still hot after all the years. "You doing anything for the next hour or so?"

Celia put her letter down. She had it memorized. "No. Why?"

"'Cause I was just thinking about how it feels to be forty-four and in love for the last time."

MILFORD AND EMALINE STANTON arrived at Bloodstone at nine a.m., precisely when their letter said they would. The morning was already warm, and the top was off on their Ferrari 275. They were dressed casually in jeans and slightly scuffed boots, a testimony that they had come to ride, not merely to nose around. Their clothes weren't the only thing that proved they were monied—old money—and not a member of the newfound-wealth set who were so careful to let everyone know how well off they were or just playing at being rich. The way in which Milford Stanton ignored the thin layer of dust on his automobile said he treated the car like a car, not a classic. And the direct way Emaline began the business proceedings made it clear generations of experience were behind her cultured, well-modulated articulations.

"As our letter stated, Miss Bolt, we are on a buying expedition. We have attended horse shows all over the northwest as well as visited several ranches in the three-state area. Yours is not the first we've seen."

"Your letter just said 'stock.' What exactly are you interested in? Young horses? Trained?"

"We raise hunter/jumpers, but we are seeing a growing interest in the Appaloosa in the east as an all-performance animal. We'd like to start a foundation herd of truly western-bred horses. The ones being shown now have obvious thoroughbred and Arabian influence. Too much of it. In fact, many look like thoroughbreds with spots. Milford and I feel that if you're going to switch to a different breed, you should go all the way. We like the Appaloosa the way it was bred back in the Nez Perce days, and I think it would cause quite a stir to show the horse people back home what Appaloosas are supposed to look like."

Milford Stanton smiled indulgently. "Emaline likes to cause a stir. She likes to be different."

Emaline let the affection she felt for her handsome husband creep through the business face. "It's not harmed us yet."

Morgan grinned for the first time since the Stantons arrived. He felt he finally had a handle on the attractive couple, and he liked them. He had been hesitant at first, a bit put off by Mrs. Stanton's aggression and Mr. Stanton's willingness to let her do most of the talking. But now he realized it wasn't a case of female dominance, just the fact that Emaline was a better talker. Not unlike Celia and himself.

He let his arm rest on Celia's shoulder. "You sure hit a note with me, Mrs. Stanton. The fellow that started this ranch, Gib Bloodstone, took real pride in being able to trace all of his foundation stock back to the Painter line. That was the line started by Claude Thompson when he set about saving the breed back in the early 1900s. That or the Sam Fischer herd. And as everyone knows, most of Sam's stock came straight from the old Nez Perce bloodlines. We've added a little Absarokee blood with our stallion, Conquering Joseph, but other than that, we're as pure as you can get."

"We've really been impressed with your young stallion. What is it you call him? Herman?"

"Not really a very flashy name," said Celia sheepishly, "but most people this far north aren't familiar with Spanish, and they mispronounce Herman anyway. Gib Bloodstone was from New Mexico and worked as a sheep herder as a boy. He spoke Spanish as well as English, and he gave a lot of his foundation stock Spanish names. We've tried to carry on the tradition. *Sangre Hermano*—Blood Brother."

Morgan cut in. "When Gib had saved enough money, he decided to start raising horses. The story goes that an old Navajo gave him a piece of advice. He told him that the Sioux were the finest horsemen, but the Nez Perce had the finest horses. So he came north to find them."

"We've seen some of the Indian horses in the area, and frankly, I've been very impressed. A little rough, perhaps, but solid horseflesh."

"Emaline's a real primitive," Milford explained.

"We've brought our yearlings and two-year-olds in off of the pasture. They'll look a little rough, too, I suppose, but you can't develop agility and surefootedness in an animal by keeping it stalled. Would you like to see them first?"

For the next several hours, the Stantons scrutinized the entire Bloodstone horse population. Al and Lacey scurried to catch individuals for closer inspections and saddled a few of the older animals for the easterners to ride. Morgan surprised himself by not being bored or getting fidgety, which were his usual mental states whenever a horse-trading session ran over half an hour. He was surprised at the thoroughness yet speed with which both Stantons examined the horses and admired the easterners' obvious knowledge of what constituted good animals. Both were picturesque astride, yet Morgan could tell they were more than picture-book riders. They were far from the spoiled, rich hobbyists he had expected them to be, and he decided he would be proud to let Bloodstone breeding be introduced into Connecticut by this capable pair.

Celia, on the other hand, was caught up in the irony of the whole affair. How did events turn so that she, the daughter of Waterbury's Roman Bolt, incognito in a little western town, barely squeaking out a living raising horses and living with an ex-rodeo bum, came to be giving a pair of descendants of Connecticut's founding fathers a full-scale tour of her meager establishment? Someday she would laugh at it all. Someday.

"Quite frankly, Celia," ("quite frankly" seemed to be one of Emaline's favorite expressions, yet its affectedness was tempered by the first-name basis both she and her husband had quickly adopted), "this is the most consistently admirable grouping of horses we've looked at. We've seen lots of individuals we've liked, but yours is the first ranch I've been to where I'm hard-put to find a horse I *don't* like."

"We breed for consistency," said Celia proudly. "You'll never know how thrilled I am to have you say what you just did. You two know horses probably as well as anyone I've ever shown my stock to."

Their eyes locked in mutual respect in spite of so many differences.

"The truth is, we need a stallion," said Milford, who was a little better at getting to the heart of the matter. "And I don't think we need to get in a corner and talk this thing over. We like your Herman, and we're prepared to offer a very fair price for him."

Celia held her breath. What was a 'fair price' to people who could afford to let a Ferrari get dirty? She couldn't believe her ears when Morgan cut in. *Please, God, don't let him spoil this deal,* she prayed.

"I know you've been following our show circuit, so I guess you're aware that Herman has won every class we've entered him in this year. He's qualified for the State, you know."

"We know that, Morgan," said Milford almost apologetically, "but a halter championship, even a state halter title, means nothing to us. We care about performance and attitude. Herman has the perfect disposition for a hunter/jumper—alert yet easily handled. It seems to be a trademark of your horses, and from what I've seen of Herman's brothers and sisters, it is an easily perpetuated one. We want your horse, but we'd like him now, not after the State. We have a shipping van leaving for Connecticut this Friday, and our offer remains the same whether he has won a hundred titles or not even one class."

"Whew, you sure put it straight out, don't you?"

"I was told that was the way you 'cowboys' did business," Milford said with a smile.

Celia and Morgan eyed each other. "I guess our next question is—what's your offer?"

"We have three places left in the van. That aged broodmare, Miss Kitty, and her filly, and of course, Herman. We'll give you $15,000 for the lot. With proper care, I think that mare has a few breedings left in her, and I can promise, producing or not, she'll live out her days pleasantly. What do you say?"

What could Celia say? Maybe Herman could win the State. Maybe he could win the Nationals. But how much would she have to spend to campaign him? And how much would he produce in returns? And how long before those returns started coming in? In comparison, here was a cash offer that would assure a comfortable winter.

In the end, she made the decision for Herman's sake, just as she had done several years prior for another one of Amiga's foals. In Connecticut, he would stand out like a beacon amongst those thoroughbred crosses. He'd show the east coast what a range-bred Appaloosa was all about.

"It's a deal," she said softly. "And, by God, I expect you to make a name for this fellow."

"That's part of the bargain," said Milford confidently. "We'll send you the news clippings."

"Lace, Al. You want to run the babies back up to the pasture? And keep an eye out for Cantar," said Morgan. "Let's the four of us go up to the house and settle this thing on paper."

In a flash, Lacey and Al were mounted bareback and herding the milling yearlings and two-year-olds out of the corrals. "I'm going to let Gambler follow," yelled Al as the little dun colt capered alongside Folly.

"Okay," Celia yelled back. "Take the rest of the afternoon off, but be home in time for chores." Now that the decision was made, she felt a little giddy, a little extravagant.

Her lightheadedness cleared when she saw Emaline uncharacteristically grasp Milford's arm. "Celia, have them wait a second. Oh, Milford. I've never seen anything like him."

Celia couldn't imagine what the easterner was talking about. She had examined every horse on the place. And where did that voice come from? The flat, no-nonsense business tones were replaced by something akin to a squeal. She called for Al and Lacey to wait. "What is it, Emaline?"

"That colt," she answered, this time a little breathless. "That little yellow colt. Where have you been keeping him?"

"That's Gambler, Amiga's last foal, the one she died delivering," said Morgan. "He's Folly's--the red horse's—buddy, and he stays in his stall most of the time. That is, when he isn't just running the place. Al hand-raised him. He's as tame as—"

"I want him," cut in Emaline, coming close to rudeness.

There was silence as Morgan looked at Celia, then they both turned their heads slowly toward Al. Gambler was standing alongside Folly, pricking his ears and stomping a little hoof impatiently.

"We've never thought of him as a sale possibility. He's become such a fixture on the place," explained Celia.

"What will it take to include him in the package? Emaline doesn't usually take such an instant fancy to any horse." Even Milford Stanton was seeing a side of his wife he'd never seen before, at least not since their baby had died. So seldom did she laugh anymore or show any emotion. Maybe this oddly marked little creature would bring a little sunshine back into their lives.

Amiga's legacy, Celia thought. As if her sacrifice assured his importance. Perhaps he had already saved one life in return—the life of a frightened Indian boy who had found a purpose in life in the helpless young foal. Could a price be put on his worth? "Sorry, Emaline. I don't feel the colt's mine to sell. As a matter of fact, I don't have the papers on him."

It wasn't a lie. They had held off sending in the registration until they were sure the foal would live and, for some reason, had not yet gotten around to processing the papers.

"I don't care. I can straighten out any registration red tape. Who does he belong to?"

"If he's anyone's," said Morgan, slowly, "he's Al's. Come on over here, kid."

Al flipped one long leg over Folly's neck and slipped to the ground. He handed the reins to Lacey and walked over. Gambler followed him, prancing along as if he had springs instead of bones in his legs. He kept playfully pushing his muzzle into Al's armpit, but when Al wouldn't respond, the colt gave up and ran back to pester Folly.

"Well, what do you say? Is Gambler for sale?" Morgan said.

"Why ask me? I don't have anything to say about the finances around here."

"That colt wouldn't be on the place if it wasn't for you. I'd have put a bullet in him the night he was born. He'd have been coyote bait. Celia just said she didn't feel like the colt's hers to sell, and he sure ain't mine. So what about it?"

Emaline looked anxiously at Al. "Young man, I don't understand what's going on here at all, but if you're the one I've got to bargain with, then let's get on with it. Will you take a thousand for him as is? No guarantees on registration necessary."

Al swallowed. "No, ma'am, I won't. You see, I don't know what he's worth."

"Will you take—"

Al held up his hand. It was no longer the hand of a pool player. He had calluses, and one nail was blackened. There was dirt ground into the creases of his skin that the strongest of soaps wouldn't wash out. "I don't know what he's worth as far as dollars go 'cause I just don't know that much about horses. I mean, I'm surrounded by fancy-assed show animals, and I pick me the only throwback on the whole place." He flipped his hand over his shoulder to indicate Folly. "I wouldn't take a thousand for Gambler or two thousand, either. If he were mine to sell, I wouldn't take any amount for him."

He looked at Celia for a reaction, and she flashed him a knowing smile. Glancing at Morgan, he caught a shrug giving him the go-ahead. He looked back at Emaline and continued a little stronger. "I like you, Mrs. Stanton. I've been real fascinated all morning, watching you and Mr. Stanton go over the herd, and I guess I'm a little jealous too, though, 'cause I've never had money. I'd give about anything to have a fancy car like that Ferrari. But I'm smart enough to realize that there's some things that just can't be bought. And I don't believe that a lady as smart as you can't see that. Gambler means a whole lot to me. He's the first thing I ever really cared about and the first job I ever did right. And I've got a feeling about him. Someday, he's going to be a lot more than just a pet. So if it is up to me, he's not for sale, and I sure hope you're not mad at me."

Emaline Stanton smiled sadly. Yes, there were things that had no price. She could afford to test how strongly this boy really felt about the colt and how much Celia and Morgan honored the boy's decision. She could afford to offer a price they wouldn't be able to turn down. After all, they needed the money; this was obviously a shoestring operation, and she had more than she could spend. Yet, all those dollars had done no good when the baby had been sick; all the money in the world wouldn't bring her back. Yes, there were things that had no price.

"Of course, I'm not mad. But I'll be in touch to see how he gets along. And if you change your mind, let me know." She reached for her husband's arm again and squeezed close to him. "I'm ready for that drink, Morgan."

Morgan mixed drinks cheerfully while Celia attended to the paperwork. "You were right about Miss Kitty," Celia called out to him from the office. "She was twenty-two last spring. I guess I just got in the habit of saying she was close to twenty." She emerged from the office, envelopes in hand, and extended them to Emaline. "But I know for sure she's back in foal now. Joseph caught her in her foal heat, and she's not been back in. I'll guarantee that."

"No arguments from us," Milford assured them. "She's in excellent condition, and life will be a little easier for her on our place."

"Don't pamper her too much," warned Morgan. "I had an old

horse once thought I'd do a favor for. Let him winter in off the range, and he just keeled over about mid-January."

Celia shuddered. He was definitely no horsetrader. But she sensed no apprehension in the Stantons' response.

"Celia's from Connecticut, you know," he continued. "She'd probably do the same thing if I sent her back to all that comfort and civilization."

Now she did wish she could kill him or at least silence him. "That was a long time ago." She tried to sound friendly but pierced Morgan with an icy glare. "And I didn't exactly spring from the lap of luxury," she lied.

"Really. Where are you from?"

"Union," she lied again. She remembered going through there once as a child on vacation. It was the first time she realized not everyone lived as they did.

"Oh. Then you're not related to the Bolts from Waterbury. My parents live in Waterbury, and my mother is on the Mattatuck Historical Society Museum guild with an Audria Bolt."

"No," she answered, then laughed nervously. "I'm sure I'd remember a rich relative." She felt the foolishness of the deceit but could do nothing about it. "Morgan, are those drinks about ready?" she asked, trying to change the subject.

He handed her a frosted glass and grinned apologetically. "Here you go." Then he lifted his glass slightly above his head, and in a rare moment of theatrics he said heartily, "Here's to Connecticut Appaloosas. May they never forget their roots."

CHAPTER 19

Bloodstone Ranch had never known a more glorious summer. It was one of those splendid seasons when there was a simultaneous sparking of all the elements of life. Nature set the stage by visiting the area with perfect weather. The days were a succession of sun-bathed gems, and the nights comfortably cool—blanket weather. Gentle breezes fanned the landscape daily, rustling the leaves and the grasses in a summer song, lifting the horse's manes and tails as they grazed. Unlike other summers, other blistering, brittle-brown summers, where the sticky fingers of humid heat squeezed the land in a slow death grip, the grass stayed green. The pasture remained a lush emerald carpet for the sleek horses to feed upon.

Once every week or so, the fluffy clouds would begin grouping together as if a meeting had been called. They'd close in on one another, piling into huge clusters, quarreling and shoving and growing angry. In vain, some unseen chairman would pound away on his gavel. "This meeting will now come to order!" But it never did. Each cloud would spill its contribution until it was spent. Then the meeting would break up, each bit of white fluff going its separate way and the mellow sun beaming once again, leaving the grass singing with dewy joy.

The fruitful summer meant more wealth for Bloodstone Ranch. Celia knew the pasture would last longer and the hay fields would produce more of the precious horse fuel that kept her animals warm over the long winter. For the first time since she took over the ranch, she wasn't spending her summer wondering how they would survive the winter dry spell. The money from the sale of Herman and Miss Kitty and her foal had swelled the bank account like never before.

Even without Herman, Bloodstone continued to shine in the show ring. The filly, Flora, couldn't be beaten, and The Ghost was proving to be everything his owners thought he could be. Both were qualified for the finals in three states, and Celia took delight in politely but firmly refusing to discuss all offers to buy them. Other summers, financial desperation might have forced her to part with them, but this was *her* summer. They would go to the finals in her rig and proudly show under the name of Bloodstone Ranch.

The orphan colt, Gambler's Hand, was also proving the stuff he was made of. The grit that gave him his chance at life, the fighting spirit of his great mother, propelled him like a whirlwind through each day. The gentleness and quiet intelligence of his father slowed him down just enough to make him watch each step. In size, he had more than caught up with his mare-raised siblings. He was the tawny color of autumn grass, and the dazzling white handprint on his rump remained as eye-catching as it was the day Morgan named him. In the show ring, he stood out among the other weanlings. The judges could not deny the show-stopping way in which the little colt handled himself. Confidence was his trademark. He had never known the comfort of a mother, a twenty-four-hour-a-day mother who existed solely for his benefit. As a result, he never experienced the trauma of being jolted from a mother's coddling. From the beginning, he stood squarely on all four of his little striped hooves.

Collecting the ribbons for the colt was a young man equally as self-confident. Al George had come into his own that summer. He had learned he was not a failure, and it was a wondrous discovery. He had tapped a communication line between himself and the horses he worked with. He was a natural horseman, and it amazed him that he could have spent his whole life never knowing the talents he harbored.

He had also learned that his success with horses wasn't an isolated fluke. He wasn't the scholastic failure that he had always assumed himself to be. Mathematics and the sciences, literature, and history were no longer undecipherable evil mysteries jeering at him from between the bindings of ominous volumes. He had mastered the secrets of study as surely as he had learned to master the young horses and teach them to do his bidding. He found, to his delight, that he enjoyed the hours he spent with the books and was confident of passing the GED in the fall.

He also found subtle differences creeping into his character. His conversations became easier; he no longer believed that everyone he met had prejudged him. His ability to express himself improved. He found it was no longer such a chore to repress the desire to use street language or poolroom phrases. He also found the desire to reach for a can of beer was quieted. He didn't want to fall into the black void of an alcoholic stupor anymore; he was afraid of missing even a single moment of the new life he was leading.

Gone, too, was the belief that he was an unloved person. The boy who had been deserted by his father and chased from the only home he had ever known by a knife-wielding grandmother, the boy who had allowed himself to be demeaned and humiliated by a bully in exchange for a semblance of friendship—that boy seemed as unreal to Al now as the great Indian chiefs had once seemed. He knew, now, about the beauty of friendship, the security of trust, the thrill of respect. He knew pride in himself, and it was almost the greatest of all his discoveries.

The greatest discovery of all was love. On the morning of his eighteenth birthday, Al George awoke and spoke his deepest feelings aloud. Lying in his cot, surrounded by the safe secrecy of the horses, he said, "I love Lacey Trueblood. Today I am a man, and I love her like a man loves a woman. Today I make a vow that someday she'll be my wife."

He dreamed of her constantly, not only at night but during the day when his hands were busy with some chore that left his mind free. Like the unsettling smoke dreams that had ended when Ted Fulkerson died, these imaginings were so real that Al would awake from them momentarily confused. The dreams were always of a lean, young, brave, and beautiful doeskin-clad Indian girl. They would make their love in the soft sheltering grasses, under the blazing starlit skies, or beneath a buffalo robe in a fire-lit tipi. But Al knew he was that brave, and the girl was Lacey.

The physical presence of his beloved was not accompanied by such mutual pleasure. Al still fumbled in his attempts to arouse passion in the girl, and she, in turn, mistrusted her passion. Al feared his eagerness would offend her; Lacey feared her refusal to give in to her own desires would anger him.

Al would hear himself saying things to her that he knew she had heard others say. They were the standard "lines" of the generations. Every man had uttered them at one time or another when his longing for a woman overtook his own sensitivities. More often than not, the girl who had always taken pride in her ability to take care of herself would dissolve in hopeless tears. "How can you say that?" she would whimper softly. Then "Don't you know how much I want you? Can't you wait for me to be sure?"

Al would feel like a brute, and he would melt at the sight of her tears. But it was not until the day he became eighteen that Al admitted the depth of his desires. He didn't want Lacey just as a lover; he wanted her forever. He wanted to make a life with her. So if the course of love was not necessarily smooth, it was true.

Romance was not restricted to the very young that summer. A frequent visitor to Bloodstone was Sybil Horn, and with her was usually Hank Mattingly. They made an intriguing couple, she slim and willowy and raven-haired and -eyed, he blonde and bronzed by the sun and thickly muscled. Their relationship lacked the intensity of Sybil's marriage. Unlike Stoner Horn, Hank was easygoing and charming but slow to motivate. It was obvious he wasn't pushing the young widow at speeds faster than she felt comfortable going.

Love, too, had found Cantar, and even if the union had not set any longevity records, the results had altered her life. The mysterious trips to the mountain pasture had ended, and Cantar began spending her days lolling around the ranch house with a self-satisfied grin on her canine face. She watched the riders come and go with no desire to accompany them. Her belly began to widen, and everyone knew it was not due to the lack of exercise.

Sometimes, a relationship can run a comfortable course for years, then one or both parties change, perhaps from a startling self-discovery, and the situation erupts. Often, the end result is the demise of the partnership, one partner just outgrowing the other. A happier consequence is the growth of the partnership itself, a new depth of feelings, and a new dimension of passion. Such was the case between Celia Bolt and Morgan Kyles that perfect summer.

Morgan had always been jealous, although he would have never admitted it to himself, let alone Celia. He lived with the resignation, somewhere in the back of his mind, that someday she would ask him to leave. She'd find another—younger, smarter, certainly more handsome, surely richer—who could give her what she deserved. He trod the line between resentment at not having a legal claim to the ranch and fear of abusing the privileges she granted him. He knew he was not good enough for her and could never picture them together years down the road, so he stubbornly steered away from anything that might hasten the inevitable breakup.

A great deal of the ranch's isolation policy changed that summer, with Al coming to stay, the hiring of Lacey Trueblood, and getting involved in the effort to make the annual Saddle Club Show truly an open one. Much to Morgan's surprise, he enjoyed the extra company and the additional live-in companions, and the involvement in a "cause," and he found that by sharing Celia, he wasn't increasing the chances of losing her.

The single event that convinced Morgan Kyles that he was not just a passing fancy in Celia's life until she could find something better took place the night Herman, Miss Kitty, and her foal left for Connecticut. There had been a quiet celebration, just the two of them, Al and Lacey, and Hank and Sybil. Morgan had drunk too much, which was understandable considering that $15,000 checks just don't fall into one's hands every day, and for a change, Celia, too, had a little more alcohol than she could handle. She told her companions the whole story: how she could never get along with her wealthy family, her wild days as a youth, her stormy walkout. They listened throughout the evening, too amazed to interrupt

But it was her last statement, when she took Morgan's supporting hand, stared up at him, and said as if they were all alone, "But there are no regrets because I found you," that rang in the big man's head over and over again. They had been together five years, and for the first time, he actually believed they might stay that way forever.

There was but one blemish that marred that otherwise flawless summer. For Al, second only in importance to his affection for Lacey was the new world he had discovered—the world of distance racing. He enjoyed the showing and working with the colts, but nothing compared to the unity between him and Folly. It was from the red horse that he drew his strength. And to his delight, it had been made official at the last Saddle Club meeting with a near-unanimous and very enthusiastic vote. There would be an Endurance Race held that fall on the Saturday before the horse show—Saturday, October 5.

Hank Mattingly had loaned Al an endurance saddle, Al had personally concocted a special mix to feed both the gelding and Lacey's Spotted Rain, Doc McClutchan had instructed the two young people in the use of electrolytes—everything pointed to the conclusion that Bloodstone's entry in the first Palouse Valley Saddle Club-sponsored Endurance Race would be Chico's Folly.

Everything, that is, except Morgan Kyle's blessing. There were no more arguments, but there were some painful moments. Painful for Morgan because he felt his opinion meant nothing to the boy; painful for Al because Morgan's approval meant so much to him.

And so it passed, one brief season in a lifetime of seasons. The mellow summer days shortened, and the smokey moon of September drew closer.

CHAPTER 20

LACEY WAS LIVID. Her dark eyes flashed with anger. "How could he do it? Willy Littledog went to school with me. He's one of the best horsemen I've ever known. There are plenty of reservation ranches willing to hire him. How could he sell out?"

"Money, Lace."

"That's bullshit." Lacey seldom swore, but she felt betrayed.

"It's not bullshit when your old man's out of work, and you've got three little brothers and sisters that are hungry."

"But to go to work for Sid Dutchens! You hate the man! How can you defend Willy?"

"Because it's not Willy I've got a gripe with. Dutchens is paying him three times what any reservation rancher could."

"But the whole idea of distance racing is to test you and your horse as a team. It's not fair to hire someone to condition your animal for you."

"It's not against the rules. Look, Lace, you can afford to be an idealist. You've got two parents that love you, a job, and you're going to school on a scholarship. You've never known what it means to be desperate."

Lacey drew a deep breath. "I guess I'm being a little unfair, too. It just makes me so mad. Sid Dutchens thinks he can buy anything and anyone."

'But we know differently, don't we? He might be able to buy a trainer, but he can't buy first place. Not in this sport, he can't. Just relax and quit picking on poor Willy Littledog."

The anger left Lacey's face like the passing of a storm cloud. "Since when have you started using words like 'idealist'?"

"Since I got smart. Just think. A few months ago, I couldn't even spell 'gradyouate.' Now I almost are one."

"You're a nut." She slapped at him playfully, then sobered, her arms creeping around him, her face seeking the comfort of his chest. "I'm going to miss you so much."

"Hey." Al took her shoulders in his hands and pushed her away, then tipped up her head so he could see into her face. "You'll be back on weekends. You don't think I'm going to keep that monster horse of yours in condition, do you?"

That wasn't what he wanted to say at all. He wanted to tell her how much he was going to miss her, too, how a part of him was going to die when she left with her father in the morning. He wanted to say just the right words that would keep her from going.

"This has been the most fantastic summer of my life. I don't want it to end."

He couldn't play fair any longer. "It doesn't have to end, Lace. You don't have to go to school. You could stay here. We could get married, start our own ranch."

She backed away from him as if he had hit her. Once again, her eyes flashed in the starlight, this time incredulously. "I—I couldn't do that, Al. It's what I've planned all my life. There are a lot of people counting on me."

He turned away and leaned on the corral fence. Folly snuffed at his hand, and he let his fingers stray over the gelding's soft muzzle. "Is it your dream, Lace, or your dad's? I don't think you know the answer to that yourself. What about me? Don't you think I need you? Who's more important to you? A bunch of old reservation bigwigs or me?"

"Talk about being fair—that question stinks. I'm not picking one over the other. You said yourself, I'll be back on the weekends."

"How long is that going to last? You'll be in a different world. You're going to meet new guys, smart guys, guys with money. Pretty soon—"

"Damn you, Al! How many times do I have to tell you? I'm not going to school to find a husband. I want to be a doctor, not some rich man's wife. I want it for me, most of all, and I don't give a damn if you think that's selfish. But I want it for my family, too, and my people. It's what I've wanted all my life! Stop mooning over that—that fucking horse, and look at me!" She was almost screaming now. "And I want it for something else, now. Something that didn't even exist a year ago. I want it for us. You and me—man and wife. You did just ask me to marry you, didn't you?"

"You and me—doctor and flunky, you mean."

She slapped him hard across the face, and the sharp sound made Folly snort and jump back from the fence. "I hate you when you talk like that. Like this summer never happened. Like you're still some street Injun. And if you think I'm going to start telling you all the reasons you have to be proud of yourself—then you're crazy. You want to be miserable? You want to believe I'm going off to school to find another man? Then go ahead. And if you think I'm going to start crying, you're wrong. I'm through crying over you, Al." She had to turn away so he wouldn't discover that she'd lied.

They were silent for several minutes. Folly walked cautiously back to the fence and stretched his head over the top rail. Al felt the horse's soft, warm breath on the back of his neck. Lacey's back was towards him, straight and proud, her shoulders lifting with each hard-drawn breath. She'd be gone in the morning; he wouldn't have another chance.

"Lace?" The fear was plain in his questioning voice. "Lace, I'm sorry. I'm just scared of losing you, that's all. But even if I do, even if things are never the same between us, I won't go back to being what I was. You've taught me a lot this summer. Not just about books but about other things. What it means to be an Indian. What it means to be proud of being an Indian. I'm not going to forget any of it, even if you forget me."

She still didn't turn around, but her back relaxed, and her shoulders stopped heaving. "If I came to the barn tonight, would you make it okay? I can't leave worrying about being pregnant. Can you take care of that?"

He was stunned. The half-playful tussles that had turned into frustrating arguments; the lengthy, moonlit goodnight kisses and shy gropings that had left him achingly sleepless; all summer long, they had teased without fulfillment. And now, on the eve of her departure, she was offering herself to him.

He thought guiltily of the small, foil-wrapped package he had purchased from the machine at the gas station in town. He remembered how dirty he had felt the day he'd brought it home and hid it in the most secretive corner of his room.

She faced him, her young shoulders once again square. "You've had other girls." It was more of an accusation. "You should know what to do." There was no softness in her voice. It was not a surrender; it was a challenge.

"It'll be okay, Lace." He started to reach for her, but Celia's voice from the front porch stopped him.

"Lacey! Your dad's on the phone."

Again, a feeling of guilt washed over the boy. He feared Calvin Trueblood not so much because of his physical attributes but because of the terrific hold he had on Lacey. Trueblood had been on the phone while Al was planning a way to get his daughter into bed. The timing was incredible and unfortunate.

"Coming," Lacey called. Then to Al, she whispered, "Tonight."

But she never came, even though the boy lay awake until dawn. Sleep overtook him about the time the sun was rising, and when he awoke later, she had left.

"SHE'S GOING to have to drop them soon, or she'll pop."

"That's what I like about you, Doc. You never try to confuse people with all that technical jargon."

Cantar lay on her side, her belly stretched as tightly as the skin on a bongo drum. She had sought the shady comfort of the barn alleyway where the leaf-cooled breezes could fan her, and she was panting slightly in the late August heat. She seemed totally unconcerned with her master's fussy ministrations.

"Look, Morgan. There ain't nothing you can do to make her have them any sooner and nothing you can do to keep her from having them when she's ready. Jiminy Gosh! You're acting like a nervous husband about to be a daddy for the first time."

Al was standing behind Doc and Morgan, leaning on a pitchfork. "As goofy as he is over that bitch, and if I hadn't seen her with that fancy sheepdog myself, I'd swear *he* was the daddy."

"You shut your mouth, youngster." Had Doc not been there, Morgan would have cursed a blue streak and sent Al flying, but there was something about the vet, perhaps his repertoire of cornball expressions, that made even the rankest of people watch their language. Morgan felt his cheeks grow hot, and he made a mental note to give Al a good kick in the pants later.

"It doesn't really matter who the daddy is, now. She's in charge, and she's taking her own sweet time. Just keep her comfortable. Lands!" he exclaimed as he looked at his watch, "I'm an hour behind. Gotta go!"

He climbed into his battered truck and disappeared in a cloud of blue smoke and driveway dust. "Only an hour behind is ahead of schedule for Doc, isn't it?" Al said dryly.

Morgan scowled. Nothing was going to keep him from being worried about his dog. "I'm going to tie her tonight. I don't want her wandering out into the middle of nowhere to deliver. After what happened to the last litter, I'm afraid that's what she might try to do."

"Yeah. Especially with me around, right?"

"Don't be such a dumbass. That's not what I meant at all."

But Al wasn't so sure that he wasn't correct. Cantar had come to accept him over the past four months, but by no stretch of the imagination did she like him. The boy had tried to pet her once or twice but was turned away by a cold glare in her yellow eyes. A few times, he had accidentally brushed against her and had felt her muscles tighten and saw the hair of her ruff raise slightly.

"No matter. I won't be poking around her nesting box. I'm too fond of my fingers."

Morgan fastened a heavy hay rope to Cantar's collar that night and tied the other end to a ring on the floor of an empty box stall. She whined nervously when he came to check on her before bedtime, and he assured her that everything would be all right.

In the morning, the frayed end of the hay rope lay in the straw. There were traces of blood on the raveled fibers, evidence of the coydog's toil. This time, she had found a mate on her own, and on her own, she would give birth to their pups.

For two days, Morgan was frantic. He wore out his good horse, Charlie, by riding the mountain pasture in search of his dog. He sat up through the night, hoping she'd return for the food he left out.

By the third morning, he had driven Celia to desperate means of seeking refuge. She and Nora Potter were driving to Moscow to pick up the awards for the Saddle Club Show, now only a month away. Nora's call had come before seven a.m., and Celia, who normally would have fabricated an excuse not to spend the day with the nervous little woman, jumped at the invitation.

Al, too, found a reason to leave after morning chores were done. Unlike Celia, who was sure that Cantar was safe, he felt guilty and pessimistic about the affair. He couldn't help believing it was his fault the dog left, and the worry in Morgan's face touched him more than he could admit. The big man fell into an exhausted sleep after breakfast, and Al left a note that he was going to take Folly and Rain for a ride and would keep an eye open for Cantar.

The spotted mare had become quite used to Al over the summer, and her affection for Folly was evident. She had even learned to tolerate Gambler's antics, which surprised Lacey. "Maybe there's some mother instinct hiding in that animal," she had exclaimed one day after watching Rain submitting to a rash of coltish foolishness. Since Lacey left, Al had kept the mare in condition by ponying her along behind Folly. Sometimes, he was tempted to ride her, but the idea was usually swept aside by a mental image of himself in traction. Still, he was flattered by the way the lithe little mare would come to his call and slip her head into the outstretched halter. Lacey was gone, and this spirited mare was his only link to her.

Al clung to the secure partnership he had formed with his horses because he was so unsure of his relationship with Lacey. She arrived at Bloodstone every Friday night, but Saturdays were occupied with showing, and on Sundays, she would return to Clear Water Ranch. It was agreed that she would continue this schedule until after the show season, then Rain would be shipped home to winter, and Lacey would stay in Pullman most weekends. The weather would start getting undependable, and studies would get progressively harder.

Nothing was ever said between the two young people about the unfulfilled plans of that last night. Al knew the telephone call from her father had broken what control he had had over Lacey. It seemed the two of them made an effort not to be alone. They talked, but it was always about horses or the weather, or the upcoming race.

But if Al had relinquished his hold on the vow he had made concerning making Lacey his wife, he did not betray the promise he had spoken on their final night together. He felt he had lost her, but he wasn't going to lose his newfound pride. Without her help, he continued to study; without her encouragement, he continued to find ways to improve himself. The GED exam was scheduled for early November, and by that time, his probation period at Bloodstone would have ended. He wasn't sure what he was going to do with his life, but he knew he wasn't going back to being a pool hustler. In the meantime, he did his job with a quiet maturity that masked the sadness he truly felt.

The sadness was more than a result of his frustrated love. The more he conditioned the misnamed red gelding, the more convinced he was that they could win the race. Although nothing more had been said since the night of the argument, Al had no doubts about being allowed to enter Folly. Morgan would back down, but Al knew the big man too well. He wouldn't attend Saturday's race. He'd have something to say about too much work needing to be done to get ready for Sunday's show —the *real* event.

Al left the ranch at an easy jog-trot. The spotted mare followed along eagerly, keeping the lead line slack. As was his custom when he trained, the boy swept his mind clear of all troublesome thoughts. He concentrated on the sound of Folly's hoofbeats and watched the muscles bunch in the little gelding's shoulders. He had long since outgrown the need to consciously ride with horses' gaits. Folly was an extension of his own body, and he no more had to think about moving in sync with him than he had to think about breathing.

It was easy for Al to lose track of reality when he rode. The life-like "smoke dreams" had disappeared, and the sensuous visions of the Indian brave and his woman had likewise ceased coming to him, but he would still retreat into a hazy, surreal world of timelessness. He and his horse and the endless sweeps of grass-covered hills, the rocky, scrambling bluffs, and the perfect blue sky—they were all that existed. And he wasn't Al George then. He had no name. His past lay somewhere in the smoldering ruins of a charred tipi; his future waited somewhere in the outstretched arms of a black-haired princess. And so he rode.

They had covered the twelve-mile loop of the training circuit, and Al had to look at his watch to see how long it had taken. He was pleased to see that less than an hour had passed. He swung out of the saddle and checked the breathing and pulse rate of both horses. Finding it well below the specified maximums, he smiled and slapped Folly's neck affectionately. A little more tentatively, he scratched Rain behind the ear. "Good guys. Now that you're warmed up let's do some real work."

For the next hour, they climbed the buffalo-hump hills that bordered the east edge of Bloodstone. Folly would lower his head and trot steadily up one side, Rain tripping lightly behind in a graceful feminine way that belied her true nature.

Then Al would lean back in his saddle and let the red horse pick his way down the other side. Not once did either horse misstep, even in the steep stretches where they had to sit on their haunches and slide for several feet.

Checking his watch again, Al pulled the horses up and dismounted. This time, they were breathing more rapidly. He let their heads drop and allowed them to graze for ten minutes before checking their pulse and respiration recovery. "Whew!"

he said. "You two are like a couple of machines!" In the short interval, their pulse and respiration had dropped sufficiently below the 68/68 criteria required before being allowed to advance during the race.

Al checked his girth, tightened it a notch, and had started to mount when he caught several figures out of the corner of his eye. At first, he thought it was a small group of yearlings or two-year-olds that ran loose in the hilly pasture. They often came close while he was training and followed along curiously for several miles.

But as they drew closer, he realized the horses had riders. There were three of them, still too far away for Al to recognize. Several hundred yards in front of them was a big, dog-like animal running clumsily and appearing strangely out of balance. Between the leading dog and the riders were two other dogs. Al could hear the men shouting, and although he couldn't understand what they were saying, the words sounded angry.

Whoever the riders were, they didn't belong on Bloodstone land and certainly not with strange dogs. That, in particular, bothered Al. Celia and Morgan had told him countless times the damage a dog-panicked herd of horses could do to themselves. With little hope of being heard, Al yelled and waved his arms. He had a niggling thought in the back of his head that he would feel a lot better armed with something other than the hoof pick hanging from his belt loop.

The riders didn't hear Al, but the dog in the lead slowed its pace a fraction and swung in his direction. With it heading straight at him, Al suddenly realized who the animal was. The whole story became clear in an instant. "Jesus," he swore, then flipped onto Folly's back and headed the gelding down the hill at a reckless speed.

It was Cantar running towards him. She was lumbering, really, exhausted and coming dangerously close to tripping, to dropping the precious bundle carried in her jaws. A pup. Her pup. Her only pup left from this, her second ill-fated litter. The other four lay scattered in bloody tatters around the entrance of the old badger hole she had used as a den, and the den lay one mile within the boundaries of Sid Dutchens's land.

Behind Cantar, coming closer with every leap and gaining even more now because they wisely chose to angle towards her new trajectory, were two range-bred curs, every bit as evil and bloodthirsty as the men who owned them. Bringing up the rear, cursing their horses and whipping them with rawhide quirts, came Sid Dutchens and two of his ranch hands.

Cantar wouldn't have made it up the hill. Her body, drained from delivering and nursing a litter of five, was pushed beyond its physical limits. It was only the stubbornness of her character that kept her going. But even that was leaving her now. Her eyes were glazed over, and she was running simply out of reflex, the way a frog's legs will continue to twitch while it hangs dead on a gig. But she had heard the voice, a voice she knew, and it pushed past the bleary mess that her mind had become and directed her toward safety.

Al's legs flew as he kicked at Folly's sides. Over and over again, he called the coydog's name. "Come on, girl," he shouted, "you can make it." Crazy anger churned inside him, transmitting itself to the raging gelding and the snorting spotted mare beside him. The curs were closing in on their stumbling prey, but before their teeth could slash Cantar's rump, she dove beneath the security of Folly's legs.

The gelding slid to a stop, hovering over the coydog, snaking his head at the dogs who tried to dash in to get her. Al quickly unfastened Rain's lead shank, and she swung around to protect the gelding's hindquarters. They stood the dogs off like wild range horses, striking with their steel-shod hooves and drawing their lips back in yellow-toothed, open-mouthed attacks. It was all Al could do to stay atop the red horse, yet Cantar lay beneath Folly, her breath bellowing, the pup slumped across her legs.

The bigger of the two dogs, a one-eared, wooly-coated dust-colored male, made a move on Cantar from Folly's near side, the one not protected by Rain. As quickly as a cat, the gelding twirled and struck dead on target with both hind legs. Al could hear the sickening crunch, and the dog flew ten feet through the air before thumping to the ground, his jaw and shoulder broken. The other dog retreated and came to its stricken mate's side, sniffing blood and growling softly. It was a stand-off.

Al didn't dismount. He sat on his horse, trying to calm him, but the shaking in his voice only upset Folly and Rain all the more. By the time Dutchens pulled up on his sweat-soaked stallion, both of the Bloodstone animals were foaming, too.

"What's the matter with you, Injun? You don't interfere when a man's on a varmint hunt." He ignored his maimed dog, who was whining piteously and feebly thumping his tail at his master's approach.

"She's no varmint. You knew whose dog she was."

"When she's whelping coyote pups on my land, she's fair game," Dutchens spat.

"When you're on Bloodstone land, you're trespassing." Folly had grown still. Between his legs, Al could feel the incredible power of the tense, sinewy muscles. Like it always had, the strength soaked into him. It strengthened his own body the way fire hardens steel. "Now I suggest," his voice was rock hard and careful, "you turn around and beat those nags of yours back through wherever you came from."

Dutchens reached down for the rifle he carried in his scabbard. "Don't be a fool, you dirty-assed little shit. There's three of us, and we've got guns. Back off and let my dogs finish with that cattle-killing varmint, just like they did her whelps."

"No, sir, I'm not going to do that. You could get by with killing Cantar, just like you get by with slicing up reservation drunks. But you can't get by with shooting me. I've got friends now, Dutchens. Friends that count. And, by God, if you so much as scratch one of these horses, any court in the state will have your ass. And we're not moving, not me and not either of these horses."

Dutchens turned purple-faced. He slammed his rifle back in the scabbard, clenched and unclenched his fists several times, then shifted his weight to his left stirrup.

"I wouldn't suggest getting off your horse, Mr. Dutchens. You know this mare's reputation. She's chased better men than you over corral fences."

"We ain't gonna let this little snot get away with this shit, are we, Sid?"

Dutchens exploded. "What the hell you suggest we do, Delmar? You want to crawl under that horse and drag her out?"

"Spiker! Take 'em!" Delmar yelled to the dog, but she only whimpered and sniffed at her mate.

"If you care anything about that dog, Dutchens, you'll get it up on your horse and to a vet."

"You shut the fuck up. I don't want to hear any more of your advice. You'll pay for this, Injun. Don't think this is the end." Dutchens whipped the rifle back out of the scabbard. He jerked off two explosive shots that ended the cur's misery. Spiker leaped back; Dutchens had to saw viciously at his horse's mouth to keep it from bolting.

Folly and Rain stood statue-still. Only the dark patches of sweat on their necks betrayed their nervousness. Al was afraid to speak, but when he did, the words were calm. He heard them as if they were coming from someone else's mouth. "You had better fix the hole in the fence you must have cut, and it had better be before Morgan and the sheriff come out to inspect."

Dutchens wheeled his stallion, struck at its flank with the quirt that hung from his wrist and galloped away. His two hands glared stupidly at Al for a fraction of a minute, then followed. Lastly, the dog, Spiker, nosed her dead mate one more time.

With her bobbed tail clamped close to her rump, she slunk off after the men.

"THEN I GOT DOWN, and she let me pick up the pup. I thought it was dead at first, but I could feel its heart beating real faint. Do you think it'll be okay?"

Morgan stroked Cantar's head and watched as the pup made halfhearted attempts at nursing. "I don't know. That whiskey and honey will spark it up some, but God only knows how far she had to bounce the poor little guy along. He'll make it, though, if he's got half the guts his mama's got."

"I don't mind telling you. I was more scared about reaching for that pup than I was when Dutchens pulled his rifle. I can't believe Cantar would trust me that much."

Morgan heard his own voice saying softly, "I'll trust him the day Cantar trusts him."

"What?"

"Nothing. I was just thinking how much better animals are at being friends. They don't get all hung up on pride and worrying about what other people will think, do they?"

"No, I guess they don't."

"Are you okay? I never even asked you that. You didn't get hurt, did you?"

"No. I'm fine, but I don't think I've seen the last of Sid Dutchens. He was more than mad, Morgan. I think he'd of killed me if he thought he could get away with it."

"How good is Folly, Al? Honest, now. Forget how much you love him, and tell me what his chances are in that race."

Al stared hard at Morgan. He saw the lines on the big man's face, the concern in his eyes, the gentle way he touched the coydog. "He's damn good. He'd win if he had the chance."

"Then you ride him, boy. You put him in that race, and you ride up that spotted stud's ass and right over top of that son of a bitchin' Dutchens. You and that mis-marked, pink-papered, runty little horse are going to win that race. And something else. I'm going to be there watching you do it."

CHAPTER 21

"I'M LEAVING. You sure you don't want to come with?"

"Yeah. I'm going to lunge Rain and Folly as soon as I finish chores. Then they can have tomorrow off."

"Are you getting nervous?"

Al bit his bottom lip thoughtfully. "This race is all I've thought about for so long now that I can't believe it's the day after tomorrow."

Celia stole a quick look at her watch. She was scheduled to pick Lacey up after her last class. "Have you been doing any thinking about what's going to happen after next month?"

Al grinned. "When I'm once again a 'free man'?" There was none of the old sarcasm in his manner.

"Not only a free man but an educated one."

"Don't go jumping the gun on me, lady. I haven't passed that test yet."

"I don't think that'll be any problem. I don't think there's anything in this world you couldn't do if you put your mind to it."

Al picked half-heartedly at a clump of dirty straw. He sighed but didn't answer.

"So what's bothering you, Al?" She leaned back on the open stall door and hooked her boot heel up behind her. She'd be late picking up Lacey, but she knew the girl would understand. "You got the world by the tail. You've got money in the bank, and you're working on a good reputation around here. You've got a terrific girl from one of the finest families in this state crazy about you. And yet, you've been acting so—so sad lately. I would have thought after all this time that we could level with each other."

He put down the pitchfork and assumed a position similar to Celia's. Nervously, he began to worry the dried remains of a blister on the palm of his hand. "What are two people supposed to do if they love each other? I mean, if they are really sure that they'll never want anyone else—ever?"

Celia chose her words carefully. "Well, they get married, I suppose. If the time is right."

Al scoffed. For just an instant, he had that old desire to hurt someone, hoping to lessen his own hurt. "When the time is right, huh? So what are you and Morgan waiting on? You two aren't exactly Romeo and Juliet, you know."

It worked. Celia straightened. "You're right. We're not a couple of teenagers fumbling in the dark. We know what we're doing. And what we do and why we do it is none of your business."

"Oh, sure. I'm supposed to pour out my soul to you like some mixed-up kid badly in need of therapy. Well, in case you haven't noticed, *lady*," (and this time the 'lady' was cruelly enunciated, a mockery of one of their first arguments), "I'm not a kid anymore. I'm a man, God dammit, and I've got you and Morgan to thank for it. So start treating me like a man, okay? You want me to level with you, start leveling with me. What is it with you two?"

Celia slumped back against the stall door again. She looked

defeated. "No one's ever had the nerve to ask me that question before."

"No one's ever asked you a lot of things. Not even people who are supposed to be your friends. You had to get drunk to tell us about your family. Jesus, Celia. You carried that story around with you for years. You never even told Morgan. Nobody has a right to be that tough."

"I couldn't face it. It was easier to pretend that I was never that poor little rich girl. You don't know what it's like . . ."

He shot away from the wall and covered the ground towards her in one stride. "Don't tell me I don't know. Little by little, I've told you everything—every fucking thing—about my dad, my mother. All of it. Because I trusted you. Because, God dammit, I love you, too. And now I'm as confused as I've ever been in my life, and yeah, I need to talk to you about it. But as an equal, for a change. So you start off, Celia. You've trusted me with this place, with your horses, with your life's work. I haven't failed you, have I? So go one step further. Trust me with your heart—okay? Why? Why don't you two get married?"

"Because Morgan's already married. He has a wife in Washington and two daughters who'd be a little older than you. They never got a divorce."

"But that must have been years ago. There's some kind of law about desertion, isn't there?"

"I suppose there is. If he bothered to check into it."

"In other words, you're afraid he wouldn't marry you even if he could."

Tears pricked the corners of her eyes. "I love him so much, Al. But he's always acted like he didn't believe it. That was one reason I didn't want to tell him about my background. It'd give him one more excuse to think I was too good for him." She blew her nose on the handkerchief Al had handed to her and gave herself a few seconds to recover. "Things have been so good lately. He's changed. He's more outgoing, more sure of himself around other people. He's got interests now, and I can't get over the way he's gotten involved in this endurance race. We get along better than we ever have. And I keep on hoping that maybe . . ."

"Maybe he'll walk through the door one night with a handful of flowers and propose, right?"

She laughed self-consciously. "Pretty corny?"

"No. It's not corny at all. If I thought I stood a snowball's chance, I'd do the same thing with Lacey. But you're right. We're not talking like situations here—you and Morgan, me and Lacey. You see, she *is* too good for me, and the longer she stays in that school, the clearer she'll see it."

"Oh, Al, that's not true. And if that's what you believe, no wonder you've been so upset. She's crazy about you."

"She's here for a day or so, and I've got to watch myself every minute. I want her so badly that I can't sleep at night." He laughed bitterly at himself. "Sounds like your typical horny teenager, doesn't it?"

"No . . . you don't have to defend yourself to me. Love—physical and emotional—they go hand in hand. Or at least they should. If you didn't believe that, you'd be calling on girls like Jymme Mechling. But you're so young, Al. And Lacey's even younger. Please give it some time."

She knew it wasn't enough even as the words came out of her mouth. It was trite, non-convincing. But that was all she could offer.

FRIDAY WAS LIKE A HOLIDAY. Calvin and Madeline Trueblood arrived early. Sybil and Hank Mattingly showed up in time for lunch. They brought their sleeping bags and announced their willingness to pit crew for Al and Lacey at the endurance race. Morgan broke open a new bottle of Jack Daniels, and by late afternoon, even Calvin had mellowed to the point of not questioning where his sister and her white friend planned on spreading the sleeping bags.

Morgan told the story of Cantar's rescue at least three times, embellishing the tale more glamorously as the level of the Jack Daniels dropped. The pup, now four weeks old, played himself into exhaustion with the company and spent most of the early evening sleeping inside Al's shirtfront. By eight o'clock, everyone was ready to turn in. The race was scheduled to begin at first light.

Lacey and Al confined their horses to stalls for the night, forking them extra high-grade hay and checking their tack for the tenth time. It was the first opportunity the two had to be alone and the first chance Lacey had to drop the artificial smile and forced good humor.

"Al," she said as she straightened the headstall on her bridle and rehung it in the trailer compartment. "I'm leaving school. I'm not going back on Sunday."

He didn't answer. At first, she thought he hadn't heard her, but when she turned to repeat herself, she saw him sinking onto a bale of straw, a look of disbelief on his face.

"Wh-what?"

"It's no use going back. I can't concentrate. I don't care about anything except—except being with you."

"What are you going to do?"

"Go away with you. Go wherever you want."

"But your family?"

She shook her head. "My dad will disown me. There's no way I can stay here." Then desperate enthusiasm crept into her voice. "Look, Al, I've got it all figured out. I have a little money. I can go somewhere to wait for you until your probation period is over. What is it? Another couple of weeks? Then you've got your salary coming from Celia. What with that and the money

Jake Anderson will give me for Rain, we'll have enough for a good start."

"Hold on. What's Jake Anderson got to do with this?" His legs weren't quite so shaky now. His head was clearing.

"He's offered me $3,000 for Rain. He knows there's not one cowboy in twenty that can stay on her eight seconds.

"You'd sell Rain?"

"Al. If you asked me, I'd sell myself."

This wasn't what he wanted, stealing off like two criminals, making her turn her back on her family and turn her beloved horse into an outlaw. Is this what he had driven her to? "Lace, let's talk this over."

"What's there to talk about? I'm losing you, Al. I know that. I'll get here some Friday night and find you gone. Or worse, I'll find you're with some girl who can give you what you need. I can't bear the thought of you with another girl, and I hate the girls you've been with before me. I dream about them sometimes. They don't have any faces, or else they all look like Jymme Mechling, and they're reaching out for you. I hate them."

Her eyes were dry. She had practiced this speech so many times she could repeat it almost emotionlessly. But to Al, it was a shock beyond description. He couldn't think of a reply; his senses were locked. He could offer her no encouragement or comfort. The one thing he could say was of the least importance to him. His only concern was for the future, but all he could assure her of was the past. "Lacey, there's never been any other girls. I've never made love to anyone."

The monotone never wavered. "Then I'll be the first. Soon. When we're safely away from here, I'll be the first."

Sleep was beyond question. Al walked his room restlessly, struggling with his conscience. Countless times he went to Folly's stall and laid his face on the little horse's neck, but the familiar strength was gone. The horse was just as firm, just as warm as always, but for the first time, an invisible barrier stood between them. He thought of the race only hours away and wondered how he would find the strength to see it through.

Shortly after midnight, Al's pacing was interrupted. The familiar smell of pipe tobacco told him who his visitor was. "Hello, Mr. Trueblood. You having trouble sleeping?"

"Yes, young man. As a matter of fact, I am. Sleeplessness has plagued me for several weeks now, ever since I got a call from the Dean of Women at Lacey's school."

Al lurched inside. "And?"

"And she informed me that my daughter, my straight-A daughter, was failing five of her seven subjects. She wanted to know what I thought the problem was."

"And you think I'm the problem, right?"

Trueblood sucked his pipe. "I didn't say that."

"You didn't have to. You've disapproved of me from the start."

"Alicut, you're a smart young man, and you've come a long way in a short time. But you've a ways to go. If I disapproved of you as strongly as you seem to think I do, would I have let Lacey spend the summer here? Use your head, boy."

"Look, Mr. Trueblood. I'm sorry Lacey's not doing so good in school, but maybe she just wasn't cut out to live your dream. Maybe she'd rather live her own life."

Trueblood struck his pipe on the palm of his hand. He cleared his throat a few times. The words came hard. "You can help, son, and I could help you."

"How? By disappearing? Are you trying to buy me off?"

Asking for assistance was foreign to Calvin Trueblood. The unfamiliarity showed on his face and in the uncertainty of his words. "That's the last thing I want. If you leave, she'll follow. She'll hate me, and I couldn't live with that."

Al felt close to victory. He saw the pain in the older man's eyes, and it spurred him on. "You know what you are? One of the most selfish men I've ever known. You're so full of your goddam Indian pride that you never consider how people feel."

"That's where you're wrong, Alicut. I understand feelings. I understand them only too well. And as for pride, how proud do I look now? You're enjoying this, aren't you? You've got me under your thumb. All I can do is try to explain and hope you'll overlook this power struggle we seem to have going on long enough to listen."

"I'm listening."

"I graduated from the reservation school twenty-three years ago. I wasn't as lucky as Lacey; I didn't have her brains. I worked like a dog to put myself through college, and during summers, I'd come back to the reservation to work. That's when I met a girl—a lot younger than myself, but I fell in love with her. She was a good student, an excellent student, actually. College material and a sure bet to receive a reservation loan if she applied. I asked her to wait for me."

Trueblood paused. He looked hard at Al as if seeking encouragement. The boy was silent.

"But she didn't. She was anxious to grow up. To get married. To start a family. She was so young she didn't realize how much time there really was. I lost her to a good-looking basketball player—a good friend. I think you know the rest of the story."

The victory turned sour in Al's mouth. Suddenly, Trueblood stopped being the enemy. Just as he had been speechless before Lacey hours earlier, he stood mutely before her father. He was sure he couldn't handle any more surprises. He longed for the solace of a good drink.

"Don't let history repeat itself, Alicut. I beg you. Give it time. You owe that to Lacey, to yourself. For the memory of your mother, give it time."

CHAPTER 22

"HOW DO we start this thing, Hank?"

"You just yell '*go!*', then stand back."

"S-s-sixty three rid-d-ders, you'd bet-t-ter stand back."

Everyone laughed. You couldn't help but laugh at Jake Anderson. Then Morgan sobered and slapped Al on the leg. He looked up at the boy tensely sitting astride the red horse. "You nervous?"

Al shook his head, then glanced over at Lacey and smiled. "What's there to be nervous about?"

The Truebloods, Hank and Sybil, Morgan and Celia, and Jake Anderson were crowded around the two riders. Rain's eyes were wide and white-rimmed with excitement, but Folly's evenness was keeping the mare in check.

"We'd better get to the starting line, Al," said Lacey after bending from her saddle to give her father a quick kiss. "I don't think Rain can keep herself from biting someone any longer."

The pit crew watched as Al and Lacey jogged to the mass of milling riders. "We'll see you at the first vet check," called Hank.

"Can't b-b-believe they're going to g-g-go fifty m-m-m-miles."

"Who's going to win this thing, Hank?"

"It's hard to say. Your boy Al has a good chance if he doesn't clutch up. Lacey's got a good horse, and she's had some experience. The girl from Princeton has a gamey horse, and that stallion of Dutchens's is promising."

"That stallion would win with the right rider." A soft voice invaded the group's conversation.

"I guess he should know," said Morgan as they all turned their heads to look at the slight, shaggy-haired Indian boy. "He trained that horse. Hello, Willy."

"So, you think Dutchens's stud can beat my daughter's mare?" Calvin said.

"Yes, sir, I do. I think he could beat any horse out there except maybe that sorrel of yours, Miss Bolt." Willy Littledog spoke quietly, his dark eyes unblinking. "I can tell about horses. You know that, Mr. Trueblood. I can see what's inside them."

"Kind of s-s-sounds like Paul-l-line Sire, don't he?"

"Who, by the way," said Morgan, "isn't here, I see."

"'C-c-course not. She pred-d-dicted gloom and doom, m-m-member?"

"What do you mean, Willy?" asked Celia. She studied the calm confidence on the boy's face.

"You don't really understand that horse. He's more than you've ever given him credit for. As for that stallion, he's a giver. But if you ask for more than he can give, if you push him, he'll blow apart."

"Why is it you're disclosing your boss's secrets, son?" Calvin said.

"I'm not working for Sid Dutchens anymore, Mr. Trueblood. He fired me the day before yesterday. Said my being around upset the other men."

"He waited until you got his horse in shape, though, didn't he, the son of a bitch."

Willy Littledog laughed weakly. "Damn right. Anyway, tell

Lacey that for me. Tell her that horse can't handle pressure unless he's got a hell of a calm rider on the reins. And that's not Sid Dutchens."

There was no more time for conversation. Grant Castor, in his exuberant manner, had yelled, "Go!" The mass of horses churned up the grass; sixty-three sets of freshly shod hooves dug in for traction. The head of a wild-eyed leopard gelding reared above the crowd, and his rider snatched at his sparse mane to stay aboard. Another frightened animal began kicking as other horses passed him. The young rider was thrown, and the last trickle of horses parted around the downed horseman. Undaunted, the Indian youth caught his mount and swung back into the saddle. With a whoop, he sped off, his horse's spotted rump soon disappearing over the first hill in hot pursuit.

Lacey and Al were in no hurry to take the lead; the breakneck speed of the front runners could not be maintained for long. They were content to lope along, secure in their footing and saving their horses for the rigorous miles ahead. They didn't speak, each trying to keep their thoughts on the race and not what lay beyond the finish line.

The first ten miles of the trail climbed a series of fairly steep hills. The inclines weren't any sharper than the practice hills Al had trained on, but the progression of cutting steel shoes and the slick cover of early morning dew slowed the pace a little. Their strategy worked. Lacey and Al began to pass riders without speeding up their ground-eating trot. As they neared the first-quarter check, they were among the front twenty teams.

The crew had water waiting for the horses and a cup of hot coffee for the riders. Sybil threw a blanket over Rain, who barely interrupted her greedy sucks at the water pail. Hank blanketed the sorrel horse, then laid a hand on Folly's neck. "He's barely broken a sweat. Neither has she. Look at the way some of these horses came in."

Al glanced around at the other racers. A few had been ridden poorly, pushed too hard up the steady inclines of the trail. The ones that were gasping for breath, the ones that were enveloped in the wispy mist of hot, sweaty bodies cooling in the frosty air, would surely be held the maximum time. Judging from the looks on their riders' faces, some had already been disqualified.

"Is Dutchens still in?"

Morgan was quick to answer. "He passed the pulse and respiration check about a minute ago. His horse looked strong but a little wild-eyed over all the excitement." Then he gave Al and Lacey the message from Willy Littledog.

Lacey listened soberly. "Let's go vet in now, Al. They're a little high but in no danger of not making the parameter. Then Dutchens will only be a minute or two ahead."

"And we'll be in position to start applying some of that pressure Willy talked about."

Folly and Rain checked out well below the maximum readings. The required twenty-minute rest period was spent caring for both horses, examining their hooves, and massaging their legs and backs so the muscles wouldn't stiffen in the cool morning air. At one point, Celia caught the worried look on Al's mud-stained face. She motioned to Morgan to work with Folly and drew Al aside.

"What's wrong?"

"Nothing. What makes you think—?"

"You're out of here in two minutes. We don't have time to play word games."

Al paused and looked at his watch as if to verify the time. "Okay. Something *is* wrong. I don't know if it's me or Folly, but I can't feel him. It's like we're not moving together."

"Al, you're just nervous. You'll relax this next quarter."

"No. That's when we've always been the closest, when I'm nervous or scared. That's when Folly has taken over. But not today," and as a whispered afterthought, "and not last night."

"He's only a horse, Al. Don't expect too much out of him."

"Come on, Al. We can leave in one minute. Mount up."

Al climbed into the saddle almost wearily. He looked like the race had already ended in defeat instead of just barely beginning. "That's where you're wrong, Celia. That's where you've always been wrong."

As they jogged away, she pictured the face of the other Indian youth who had said to her only that morning, "You don't really understand that horse."

The steady climb continued for the next several miles. What with the horses that were pulled at the vet check and those held the maximum time, Al and Lacey had become two of the frontrunners. They increased their speed out of the vet check, but once the spotted rump of Sid Dutchens's stallion was in sight, they slowed.

"It takes a lot more effort for him to get up these hills than for us. His horse is heavier, not to mention his two-hundred pounds of ugliness. If we hang back here just in sight, we'll put the pressure on his horse to set the pace."

"Like Willy said."

"Yeah. I want to win this, Al. I need to win." Her face was grim. There was no trace of the softness that had always touched his heart. How hard, how brittle, could she become?

At the eighteen-mile markers, the trail flattened. They had reached a plateau that stretched for miles, but instead of the terrain becoming more hospitable, it grew treacherous. Rocks of all sizes were scattered over the trail, and the trail itself was deeply rutted. Dutchens pushed his horse to a hard gallop. The sound of the stallion's shoes clipping rocks was like pistol shots.

"I'm not loping through here, Lace. Let that ass cripple his horse."

At first, she looked like she was going to argue, but then she pulled her eager mare to a trot. They wove around the rocks and boulders silently. At one point, they hit a slab of bedrock that required them to dismount and lead the horses. After two tedious miles, the trail broadened into a flat, grassy meadow.

"We'll make up time here," Lacey shouted. Rain needed no encouragement. She and Folly strode side by side, eager to stretch their muscles after the long climb.

Al stole glances at her face. The girl he loved—never had she been so beautiful as in the wild freedom of this place. She and Rain moved in unison, one in spirit and flesh. Could she really do it? Give up everything for him? Would she do as she said? Sell herself for him?

He felt sick with shame and confusion. The saddle was growing uncomfortable. Every step Folly took jarred him. Not even when they drew in sight of the leopard stallion did his spirits lift.

They slowed to a jog-trot the last mile and came into half-time only a few hundred feet behind Dutchens. Rain and Folly were already breathing normally, and after letting them drink, Lacey and Al presented them for their check, which they passed with readings only slightly higher than at the first check. But Sid Dutchens also passed easily, even though the big stallion was showing signs of fatigue.

"He's icing him down," Hank said quietly as he helped Al massage Folly's legs. "That brings his p's and r's down faster, but it's a false indication of how well the horse is really doing."

"We're pressing them like Willy said, and I can tell how much it bothers them."

"Well, keep it up because you're wearing him down. Keep him in sight but don't pass. By the way, you're a good ten minutes in front of the next horse. It's like the three of you are in your own race. The field was cut by seven at the first check, some for lameness and some that pushed so hard their horses couldn't recover in the time. I suspect we'll lose a few more at this one."

Morgan walked over to Al and offered him a candy bar. The

boy shook his head. It would take more than chocolate to cut the bitter taste in his mouth.

"What's it like out there?" the big man asked.

"Scary."

"Just let Folly take care of you, kid."

"Yeah. He always has before, hasn't he?" It took great effort to inject his words with confidence. "We're off in two minutes."

"This quarter will be fast," Lacey called over. "Hang around here to see what kind of shape the first couple of horses are in, then get to the next checkpoint."

"Yes, ma'am." Hank flashed his handsome Viking smile, then said to Al, "Between the horse and your lovely lady, I think you're in good hands."

Al wasn't so sure. Lacey set the pace, staying within sight of Dutchens but not challenging. A few times, they were close enough to see the nervous stallion trying to swing his head to look at them and to see Dutchens saw at the reins and hear him curse the horse. On occasion, Lacey would murmur something to her mare and stroke her neck, but she said nothing to Al.

Folly, too, was acting foreign. He was content to lope along behind Rain instead of positioning himself at her side. A few times, he lagged, and Al had to dig him with his heels. And yet, the gelding did not seem tired, only disinterested. Al was convinced the little sorrel horse had lost heart.

Less than an hour after leaving the half point, the three riders pulled into the final vet check. They no sooner stripped the saddles from the horses and threw blankets over them than Willy Littledog approached Al and Lacey's area. The Indian boy gestured to Al, who moved away from the group. They faced each other, both frowning, both very worried.

"What's going on out there, man?" A pair of field glasses hung from Littledog's neck. His words were accusing.

"What are you talking about? You were the one with the advice to hang back."

"Hang back, sure. But your horse looks beat. What are you doing wrong?"

"Me! It's not me. The horse is just giving up. He's earning his name, I guess."

Littledog's hands clenched into fists. Sparks flew from his eyes, and for a second, Al thought he was going to have to fight. "People have called me a traitor because I trained for Dutchens, and maybe I am. I had my reasons, and I'll have to live with them. But you've no excuse to betray that horse.'

"You're crazy, man. You're talking about him like he's . . ."

"You know what he is. Horses don't have much choice about who they belong to. The only thing they have a choice about is who they give themselves to. Like Dutchens's stallion. He's a brave horse with a shit for an owner. The only reason he's running is 'cause he's scared not to. I only hope he has better luck in his next life. But look at Lacey's mare. She'd run her heart out for Lacey. And then there's you and the sorrel horse. I watched you train, man, through these," he held up the field glasses. "It's like he waited his whole life to give himself to you. And today, it's like watching strangers. One of you is giving up, and it's not the horse."

"Al," Lacey's voice was brittle. "For God's sake, take care of your horse."

"Listen to her, man. Take care of your horse. The old days may be gone, but the best way for an Indian to find himself is still on horseback. I'll be watching you."

Hank Mattingly was cleaning Folly's feet when Al turned back to help. "Work on his shoulders, Al. Don't let them stiffen up. The last ten miles is straight downhill. And it's not an easy drop."

Al nodded his head. He was afraid to speak. Emotions choked him. He had thought it was only him, only his imagination, only nerves. He looked deeply into Folly's eyes, and all he saw was his own reflection. Littledog was right. Al had found himself with the help of this little horse. He had found what it meant to be Indian. Now he was preparing to betray that pride. And if destroying his own life was not enough, he was dragging her down with him. And this horse, who was so much more than just a horse. Had it really waited all its life for just the right hand on its reins, just the right touch of the heel? Was he proving that the little red gelding had waited in vain?

"Dutchens is taking his stallion to be checked. You'd better get up there," Hank advised.

The vet was just pulling the stethoscope from the stallion's chest when Al and Lacey approached. "Sixty-eight, sixty-eight. Not a breath or a heartbeat too slow. I'll let you go, but take it easy on this big guy."

"Sure," Dutchens mumbled and cast a hateful look at Al.

"What was Willy saying to you?" Lacey asked after the vet checked them through.

"Just offering a little advice." Then he touched her arm—the first time they had touched in weeks. "I just want you to know, Lacey. No matter what happens, I love you. I'll always love you."

Her eyes softened. They were so much like Folly's eyes. He could see himself so clearly in their warmth. On his neck, he felt a gentle caress—Folly's breath.

The twenty-minute required rest period was nearly over. Al was tightening the cinch, preparing to mount, when Calvin Trueblood ducked underneath Folly's neck. "This is the race, Alicut. Every step you take now counts. There is no room for mistakes."

"I know. And we don't plan on making any. You've got my word on that." The boy extended his hand. Trueblood hesitated for a second, puzzled, then grasped Al's hand firmly in his own. He held Folly's reins while Al mounted.

"There goes Dutchens," said Hank.

Al and Lacey could hold back their mounts no longer. "See

you at the finish line," Al called, and once more, they were in pursuit of the stallion's spotted rump.

The horses were fresh from their rest, and for the next two miles, they sprinted briskly. Al's whole body pulsed, like a hand when it's "been asleep," and then straightened so the circulation can return. It went through a tingling, almost painful period of coming back to life until he once again felt the blood coursing through him. The warmth had returned. He no longer rode his race alone. He laid his hand on Folly's neck, and it fairly buzzed with energy.

"Simiakia," he whispered, not knowing why but not questioning. Some things were never meant to be questioned.

The horses weren't ready to be slowed, but Al and Lacey had no choice. Just past the forty-mile mark, the trail once more became rutted and rocky and began a sharp descent. Dutchens continued to trot, leaning back in the saddle as far as he could.

"He doesn't care if he ruins his horse, does he?" Lacey said.

"We can't let him get ahead, Lace. We've got to trot, too."

"Okay. Let Folly pick his own way, but be ready to pick him up with the bit if he stumbles."

For the first time in forty miles, the gelding eased in front of the mare. He needed no encouragement to move steadily down the hill. Al leaned back to lessen the jarring on Folly's shoulders and to help the little horse balance.

They had traveled one treacherous mile when Al heard a cry and a clatter of rocks behind him and felt a shock that threatened to knock Folly off his feet. Cautiously, Al swiveled in the saddle. Rain was sideways on the trail, her shoulder leaning on Folly's rump. Lacey's face was white.

"She slipped. I almost went over her head. She threw her backside off-center to keep from falling on me."

"Are you all right?"

"Yeah." Her smile was weak. "Thanks to Folly catching us. Come on. We're wasting time."

They covered another mile in the same fashion before Lacey called to Al to stop. He turned to face her, half angered at the delay. "We can't let him get ahead, Lace." He could have bitten his tongue. The girl's dirty face was streaked with tears. She had to have been crying silently for the last mile.

"She's hurt." Lacey slipped to the ground and cradled the mare's head. "She must have really wrenched her back when she slipped."

"How bad?"

"Bad enough that I'm going to walk her the rest of the way down the hill." She looked up at Al. The love and pride in her horse shone through her tears. "If I asked her, she'd beat you and Dutchens both, even if it meant destroying herself. But we'll walk in. Heck, I'll probably still win my division."

Al started to dismount. "I'll walk with you."

"No!" she exploded. "Al, you can win this. All that's between you and the finish line is one fat son-of-a-bitchin' poor excuse for a horseman. You can't quit now. It's up to you to win it for all of us."

"So what's wrong with quitting? Last night, you were all for it."

For a second, she was shocked. Then, a slow smile crept over her tear-stained face. "Win it for me, Alicut George. Give me a victory to take back to school. There'll be other races for me and Rain." She stepped forward, and Al leaned from the saddle. He kissed her deeply, touched her upturned face with one curled finger, then trotted off.

He could hear Rain's outraged whinnies as he guided Folly down the hill. The gelding whickered softly a few times, but his ears were pointed forward, not back to catch the mare's plaintive cries.

"You don't want to leave them any more than I do. But we've got to. They're depending on us. They've put their trust in us, boy." Al kept up a constant murmur, concentrating on making each downward step a safe one. "Lacey and her dad and mom, Celia, and even big old Morgan. Hank and Sybil . . ." With every step, he recited a name, and with each name came a fleeting glimpse of a past kindness or slight: the cruel treatment both he and Cantar had received at the hands of Sid Dutchens; the simple way Doc McClutchen explained complex things to him; the owl-eyed patience of Percy Ludwin.

The names continued with the steady, unfaltering drum of Folly's iron hooves until the listening began to come from outside of himself. And then the names that bubbled from his lips sounded foreign but vaguely familiar. The pictures were of another era. A longhaired Indian brave sitting by a late-evening campfire, sharing fellowship and a bowl of antelope stew. A chubby grandmother making a pair of moccasins; when she laughed, she showed spaces where her teeth had once been. Yet, he knew this brave—at that moment, he knew him as intimately as he knew himself.

Al was riding on instinct now, raw animal instinct, as his perception of what was then and what was now muddied together . . .

It must not happen again. He could not lose two wives, two sons yet unborn to his world, two families. His adopted people, who had struggled so valiantly to outdistance the soldiers, lay camped just over the mountain pass. How badly they needed their rest. The children were starving; the old people exhausted. Even the brave spotted ponies were stripped to nothing save their iron hearts. And his wife, his woman who had once again given him a reason to live, grew closer to her time every day. Never would they be safe. Not until they reached the land to the north where the friendly whites lived. Yet the soldiers came on like evil shadows.

Between his legs, he could feel the strength of his pony. He could feel his mighty heart beating, coursing the hot blood through his body, like a mother whose heart beats for two, whose blood runs in the veins of her unborn child to nurture and give strength. The heart of Simiakia beat for him as well—for the blood of all of his people.

Ahead, he could see the army scout. He rode a long-legged bay horse, its belly full of army grain. The soldier's head burst with the knowledge that would destroy his people. He must overtake him, silence him. He must give his people time to escape.

The hopes of a nation traveled with the red gelding. From a tribal herd dominated by flashy spotted ponies, it was left to this one undersized, shamefully solid-colored horse to save them.

They reached more level ground: more level but equally as dangerous as the steep, rocky hill they had just sped down.

The trail was a narrow one. It had scarcely enough room for the two ponies to slip past one another. One misstep could send the horse and rider plunging to death on the sharp boulders below. To even glance down made him dizzy with fear, so he willed his eyes to close and willed his body to become one with that of his pony.

The soldier was out of sight around one of the blind corners. His lead was still great, and in less time than it takes to skin a mountain hare, the bluecoat would reach the meadowland. There, on the flats, his horse could outrun the battle-weary Simiakia. It was here, where the superior agility of his wildcat-quick pony gave the greatest advantage, that he must catch the army bay.

How could he have known of the second army scout lying in ambush above the path? How could he have known that this time, the Gods were not with him and his magic pony? They fell together, his pony silent and he, still clinging to the sparse red mane, calling the same word over and over again like an unvanquished death cry.

"Simiakia!"

"Okay, okay, you son-of-a-bitchin' heathen. Pass me, then."

Dutchens' words were snarled and brought Al to his senses. Only then did he realize he had been the one chanting wildly. And it was then that he admitted what he had tried to deny all along.

He was the Indian brave. It was not whimsy that had brought him together with this red horse to run this race. It was the justice of time. For generations, the two spirits had searched for each other, and now, on this narrow ledge, they were being given a second chance.

As in his vision, Al willed himself not to look down. He knew he had to pass Dutchens and the flagging stallion on the outside, and he did not need to see the consequences of a false step. "Passing," he called, then gave Folly free rein.

Nose to rump, then nose to shoulder. Almost neck and neck . . .

Suddenly, Dutchens jerked savagely on the stallion's outside rein. The big horse swung his head and shoulder towards the edge of the cliff. A lesser horse would have faltered, would have tried to stop, or would have swung wide from the gaping-mouthed stallion. For a lesser horse, the race, perhaps life itself, would have ended there. But the red horse was Simiakia, and he carried a warrior.

Like a wounded bull buffalo, he charged. He slammed into the stallion's shoulder and, despite his lesser weight, he knocked the horse off-balance.

The leopard stallion panicked as his front feet slid from beneath him. A cool hand on the reins would have saved him; a soft word of encouragement would have restored his confidence. Instead, Dutchens cursed anew and sawed at the reins. His own terror made him a dangerous weight in the saddle. He flung his bulk to the inside but only succeeded in unsettling the stallion's balance still further.

Al flattened himself to Folly's neck as the two snaked passed the thrashing stallion. Then, he reined his horse in and dismounted, hoping to quiet the frantic stallion from the ground.

But the horse was past the point of saving. He skidded in the loose shale, his eyes insane with fear. Before Al could grab the reins, the stallion pitched over the edge of the cliff. Dutchens made an attempt to throw himself from the saddle, but his efforts were fear-fumbled. The screams of the man and the screams of the stallion were impossible to separate as they both bounced their way to the valley floor below.

The last few miles of the course were no race for Al; they were a desperate rescue mission. He crossed the finish line, shouting for help, trying to explain all that had happened but unable to make the words coherent. The faces in the crowd were a blur. They looked threatening and hostile and closed in on him menacingly. He fought for consciousness, tensed up on his pony, and commanded him to break through the crowd. But gentle hands held Folly's bridle; gentle hands reached up and eased Al from the saddle.

Celia's voice reached the boy. "It's okay, Al. The ambulance has gone already. Willy Littledog saw what happened. He saw it all."

"He tried to kill me." The awful realization choked him. Then it was Morgan's arm around him, steadying him, keeping him from falling. He surrendered himself to the big man's protective hold.

THE AWARDS WERE PRESENTED by campfire light that evening. The mood was subdued. Word had come from the hospital that the Chairman of the Palouse Valley Saddle Club would live. His back was broken, and the extent of his spinal cord injury was yet unknown. It was being called a tragic accident, and certain members of the group wasted no time in relating Pauline Sire's forewarning.

Also whispered around the campfire that night was an account of Willy Littledog's behavior at the scene of the accident. Grant Castor rode in the ambulance that followed Littledog to the spot, and he said the boy acted "downright spooky." The stallion lay dead at the foot of the cliff, his rangy body twisted unnaturally, his leopard spots undiscernible from the blotches of blood. Littledog lowered himself cross-egged next to the stallion, placed a hand on each knee, closed his eyes, and began a soft chant. When the ambulance left, the boy was still there, and no one had seen him since.

Yet, these were horse people, and accidents were not rare to them. Men and women who spend most of their lives working with creatures of such size, disposition and unpredictability as horses learn to expect accidents. Although the mood was hushed, the crowd showed definite signs of anticipation when Nora Potter and Hank Mattingly stepped up to the firelight.

"Folks," Hank began as he set a cardboard box down, then straightened again, "what happened today was really unfortunate. But I hope it doesn't turn any of you against distance racing. Let's face it, it could have happened in a gaming event or even on a regular trail ride. Sid's only mistake was wanting to win too badly.

"On the good side, sixty-three horses and riders started this race, and fifty-two finished. That's very good statistics considering it was the first race for all but two riders. And I think everyone who participated in this race, as a racer or a crew member, has learned something today. Nobody gets through a tough course like this without realizing that he and the horse are partners. I hope the membership will see clear to make this an annual event.

"Now, I'm turning over this ceremony to Celia Bolt, the lady who chaired this project, to hand out the awards."

There was a polite round of applause as Celia walked to the campfire. While the crowd quieted, she looked out at the faces. Most were familiar, but even the familiar ones appeared different to her. There was Carla Fairfax, for instance, looking her usual elegant self. But Celia had seen her hours earlier, her blonde hair in disarray, her face haggard, as she was the second-to-the-last rider across the line. Celia had seen her legs, molded by expensive jodhpurs, buckle as she slid to the ground and overheard her tired but jubilant words of praise to her mare. Carla Fairfax would never again be a snob, as far as Celia was concerned.

And there were others that had proved themselves that day. They sat before her, red and white. Friendly adversaries only a few hours ago; weary comrades now. They had shared the rigors of the trail and could no longer deny their similarities. The value of the rigs that hauled their horses, the make of their saddles, the amount of silver on their chaps—those things were of little importance to these fifty-mile veterans. Celia was overcome with pride, not in herself for initiating the idea of bringing red and white together, but in this crowd.

"Before we start handing out awards, I'd like a word about the awards themselves. As you all know, Nora Potter was in charge of them this year, and since Nora's never been one to pat herself on the back, I'd like to say a few words on her behalf."

At this point, Celia had to snake out her hand to grab Nora, who was in the act of fleeing the firelight. The birdlike woman simpered and tried ineffectually to quiet Celia, but Celia held tight and continued.

"Maybe Nora's catching ESP from Pauline, or maybe she, like myself, just decided the importance of the Indian to the Appaloosa horse. You know, a lot of us have acted like the breed started with Claude Thompson, which is crazy. All he did was save what the Nez Perce had already developed. And as I look out at you tonight, Indians and whites, I hope I'm seeing the beginnings of a new Palouse Valley Saddle Club.

"Anyway, not knowing all this, Nora took it upon herself to offer a very different type of award this year. Nora's not much for standing in front of crowds and making speeches, but I think this year, she's shown her true feelings with her selection of trophies.

"Receiving the first of these special awards is our big winner from today's race. First across the line goes to Alicut George, riding a little horse I've always had a fondness for—Chico's Folly."

The Indian boy sprang from his seat next to Lacey. The wide grin on his face made him look so young, so carefree. Celia could scarcely believe he was the same boy she first saw clinging to the rafters of their barn. "Congratulations, Al," she said and kissed him lightly on the cheek.

Then she handed him the trophy. It was a bronzed horse, the indentations on the rump marking him clearly as an Appaloosa. From the lower jaw trailed a thin bronzed wire—the war bridle of the Nez Perce. Upon his back sat a warrior, naked to the waist, brandishing a bow. Al held the trophy out for all to see, and the firelight burnished the bronze.

"Before Al sits down, I've got a few other awards. This gift certificate from Govington's in the amount of $50 is the First Place Heavyweight prize, and Doc and Julie McClutchan and the Waha Vet Service donated this credit slip for another $50 to Best Conditioned Horse. Congratulations again, Al.

"Just one more thing. I know all of you in the club—actually, everyone in the three-state area--knows the stand Bloodstone Ranch took when the Appaloosa Horse Club decided to do away with pink papering. Since Morgan and I didn't want to appear hypocritical, we allowed Folly to run in this closed Appaloosa race under one condition.

"Technically, as of last night, Chico's Folly no longer belongs to Bloodstone Ranch. I'm afraid this is your last award of the evening, Al. Here are Folly's transfer papers, signed and dated."

CHAPTER 23

CALVIN TRUEBLOOD WAS NEVER one for surprises, so it was unusual for him to show up at Bloodstone on Wednesday morning. Al was working in the barn and wouldn't have known Calvin was there if he hadn't heard Cantar howling. The pup, Shakey, was joining in with a reedy young voice that broke every few seconds. Al smiled to himself, put down his work, and started up to the house.

"Hi, Mr. Trueblood. Morgan's not here, and Celia's out riding. Can I help you?"

"You're the one I came to see anyway, Alicut. I wanted you to go somewhere with me. When will Morgan be back?"

"Not for a week. He's got some personal business in Washington. Went to look up some family."

Trueblood grunted noncommittally. Al had no idea how much the Indian knew about Morgan's past.

"Celia should be back soon. I'm caught up enough to take off. Where are we going?"

"There's someone I want you to meet." He was vague and seemed eager to change the subject. "Lacey told me you'll be staying on here."

"Yes, sir. And I know she told you more than that. We're getting married. It won't be until she's through with her pre-vet and actually into vet school, but we are going to get married."

"She mentioned something to that effect."

Al laughed. "I don't know if I'll ever get used to the way you talk. I can't wait to hear what kind of line you'll have when the minister asks, 'Who gives this woman?'"

"I'm sure I'll say something appropriate. In the meantime, what are your plans?"

"I'll stay on at Bloodstone and learn all I can about horses."

"Cattle are more practical."

"Maybe so, but horses are in my blood. I've made a down payment on a foundation stallion already, and I'm working on a specialty reputation. I'm going to raise and train endurance horses. I've even got some rich connections out east."

He thought of the telegram he carried in his pocket. It had arrived on Tuesday. How the Stanton's got the information, he didn't know. It read:

CONGRATULATIONS STOP AVAILABLE TO
CONDITION TWO DISTANCE HORSE PROSPECTS
NEXT SPRING STOP CHANGED YOUR MIND ABOUT
GAMBLER STOP ADVISE STOP TELL CELIA ROOM
HERE IF SHE WANTS TO VISIT FAMILY STOP

EMALINE STANTON

Then he remembered, word for word, the conversation the telegram had started. How he had asked if he could buy Gambler and how Celia had told him the colt was already his. But he couldn't accept another horse from them. If he labored all his life at Bloodstone, he couldn't repay them for the gift of Folly.

So, they agreed Gambler was his in exchange for the back

salary he was due. Even then, Al insisted on more. If Gambler's Hand went to the Nationals, he would double the purchase price. When Morgan left for Washington Wednesday morning, he dropped the transfer papers for both horses in the mail.

Then there was the subject broached by Emaline's invitation. Did she find out Celia was lying, or had she known all along? It was only tentative, but Celia had made plans to visit Connecticut when the show season ended. Just to visit the Stantons, mind you, and see how Herman was getting along. And if she happened to find herself in Waterbury . . .

Once again, it was all tentative, but she might just run into someone to invite to the wedding that just might take place in January. Only tentative. Only tentative.

"Lacey told me you plan on purchasing that orphan foal."

"If you mean that orphan foal that's probably going to the Nationals in the weanling class, you're right."

"The amount of money you'll spend on that colt could buy a fine Hereford bull."

"We can't breed a Hereford bull to Rain."

"I think you're being foolish."

"There's a lot of things we'll never agree on, Mr. Trueblood. But there's one thing for certain. We both love your daughter."

The two locked eyes, and a truce was formed between them. When Celia rode into the yard, she found them both playing with the pup, treating each other as friends.

"Hi, Calvin. What brings you back so soon?"

"I wanted to borrow Alicut for the day. I'll have him back tonight."

"It's okay with me if it's okay with him. Where are you off to?"

"He won't say," Al said. "Maybe he's going to take me to the mountains for a manhood ceremony."

"It's something like that. Come on, get in the truck."

Calvin Trueblood was not one for idle chatter. They discussed the success of the show the previous Sunday, and then they were quiet. It was not an uncomfortable silence, however. Not until Al began to recognize the surroundings did he grow uncomfortable. Seeing the reservation where he grew up, the school that had been such a source of irritation . . . it all seemed part of a dream.

When Calvin finally stopped the truck, it was outside of a clinic. "We're here. She's very sick, Alicut. I've kept in touch with her. I'm the only one that still cares."

They walked inside, and Calvin led the way to a ward. He was greeted by several of the staff and seemed familiar with the place.

She lay in the hospital bed, frail and grey. Calvin pulled the curtains around them.

"Hello, Grandma. It's Al . . . Alicut."

The old woman's voice was weak, but her eyes shone with clarity of mind. "I know who you are. Do you think I'd forget my own grandson?"

He remembered the night so well, the night she drove him from the house with a knife and called him by his father's name. "I guess not."

"Calvin has told me all about you. I'm proud of you, Alicut."

Al looked at Trueblood with amazement. "I'm sorry I haven't come before, Grandma. I didn't know you were sick."

The old woman sighed. "I know. Young people these days have so much else to think about. It's not like the old days." Then she began to mumble in a language Al could not understand and then to sing a tuneless chant he remembered from his cradle days.

"She does that," explained Calvin. "She'll slip in and out. Wait a few minutes. She'll come back to us."

"Why did you never tell me?"

'Because you weren't ready for her, Alicut. You didn't know the questions, and you wouldn't have understood the answers. I'm going to leave you now. I'll be in Dr. Franklin's office."

Just as Trueblood said, Bessie's eyes came alive after a short while. She continued her conversation with Al as if she had never interrupted herself.

"Calvin tells me you work horses now."

"Yes. I'm good with them."

"Of course."

Al furrowed his brow, and the old woman laughed. "How many times did I tell you, Alicut? Your totem. The Red Horse."

"I don't remember." His voice trailed off.

"You never heard me. You hated the old ways. When I would try to tell you, you would shut your ears."

"Tell me now, Grandma. Why is our totem a red horse? We are Nez Perce. We ride spotted ponies."

"Hah! That is what they told him. The summer of burning grass. That was when he came to our tribe. Sick and weak, on a red pony so small no warrior would ride it. But he was a good man, and when our people joked at his pony, he would joke back. Simiakia, he called the miserable beast."

The word stabbed through his head. "What does that mean?"

She sighed again, this time with deep sadness. "Oh, Alicut. So many times I have told you."

"I was a different person then. I lived in another world where you couldn't reach me." His words were desperate. "Tell me just one more time."

"Simiakia. It means pride. Manhood. Belief in ourselves as Nez Perce. Such a name for a horse so unlike anything to be proud of.

"He took to wife a young orphan girl from our tribe. Joseph himself performed the wedding. Soon, they had begun a child. But life grew bitter. The white man wanted our land, and when we wouldn't give it to them in exchange for money, they began to chase us.

"For a long time, we ran, Alicut, and at our lead, scouting for us, at our tail, protecting us, among our old people, giving rides to those who had to rest, everywhere, was the warrior on his red pony. At night, he would tell stories about how his pony was magic, how the gods had made his pony so ugly that no one would want to steal him. He made us laugh. He made us proud. He made us forget our hunger.

"Then, one day, when we were resting for one last race to Canada, we spotted a bluecoat scout. He had seen us, and he wheeled his horse to run to General Miles to tell him where we hid.

"We could go no further, Alicut. We had to stop the soldier, or we would all be trapped. So, the young warrior leaped on his red pony. He told us his pony's magic was stronger than any bluecoat. But he never came back. The soldiers arrived instead. And the red pony was never found."

"Grandma, you talk as if you were there."

"The child that they had begun, the child that was born on the march to Oklahoma in 1878, she was my grandmother, Alicut. And she and my mother told me the stories over and over again, like I tried to tell you. They said my great-grandmother never again took a man. For the rest of her life, she waited for the young warrior to return on his red pony. Waited for him to return from his race. Oklahoma was hot and dry, but there would have been life for her if he had returned."

The old woman's voice was almost gone. "I must rest now, Alicut. Must rest."

"Yes, I know. I'll come back soon, though. There is so much you have to tell me. But before I go, you must hear this."

Bess Aspenleaf's eyes had begun to shut. She opened them again and looked at her grandson.

"The red horse, Grandma. He has returned. And this time, he has won his race."

ABOUT THE AUTHOR

Lori Windows grew up enamoured of the writings of Grey, Brand, Terhune, London, Burroughs, and Farley. Her father set her on a horse when she was two years old, and she has now ridden horses on six continents.

In 1982, she discovered the sport of distance racing. She and her variety of horses and mules have amassed multiple national titles and more than 63,000 sanctioned race miles.

A veterinary technician by profession, she has worked with all animals, domestic and wild. She has volunteered several times at the Iditarod and gives retired race dogs a good home mushing on her beloved Hennepin Canal in Central Illinois, a place she affectionately calls "God's Country."

An avid scuba diver, hiker, and animal enthusiast, she also leads safari groups to Tanzania yearly.

ABOUT ENDLESS SKY BOOKS

Founded by award-winning author Edward Willett, Endless Sky Books assists authors with publishing all kinds of books, from children's books to poetry to novels to nonfiction. Select titles, like this one, are released under the Endless Sky Books imprint.

Find out more about Endless Sky Books on our website, endless-sky-books.com, and visit our sister publisher, Shadowpaw Press, at shadowpawpress.com.

www.ingramcontent.com/pod-product-compliance
Lightning Source LLC
Chambersburg PA
CBHW071413200726
48294CB00002B/383

* 9 7 8 1 9 8 9 3 9 8 7 6 0 *